The Palace of Vengeance

FRENCH CLASSIC FANTASY

Barbot de Villeneuve. *The Naiads* * *Beauty and The Beast*
Chevalier de Béthune. *The World of Mercury*
Jean Carrère. *The End of Atlantis*
Charlotte-Rose Caumont de La Force. *The Land of Delights*
Félicien Champsaur. *Pharaoh's Wife*
Jacques Collin de Plancy. *Voyage to the Center of the Earth*
Gaston Danville. *The Perfume of Lust*
Paul Féval. *Anne of the Isles*
Charles de Fieux. *Lamékis*
Judith Gautier. *Isoline and the Serpent-Flower*
Gustave Kahn. *The Tale of Gold and Silence*
Marie-Jeanne L'Héritier de Villandon. *The Robe of Sincerity*
André Lichtenberger. *The Centaurs; The Children of the Crab*
J-M. & Randy Lofficier. *The French Fantasy Treasury 1-3*
Charles Lomon & P.-B. Gheuzi. *The Last Days of Atlantis*
Maurice Magre. *The Marvelous Story of Claire d'Amour; The Call of the Beast; Priscilla of Alexandria; The Angel of Lust; The Mystery of the Tiger; The Poison of Goa; Lucifer; The Blood of Toulouse; The Albigensian Treasure; Jean de Fodoas; Melusine; The Brothers of the Virgin Gold*
Camille Mauclair. *The Virgin Orient*
Hippolyte Mettais. *Paris Before the Deluge*
Charles Nodier. *Trilby* * *The Crumb Fairy*
Edgar Quinet. *The Enchanter Merlin*
Henri de Régnier. *A Surfeit of Mirrors*
Restif de la Bretonne. *The Fay Ouroucoucou* (2 vols.)
J.-H. Rosny Aîné. *Pan's Flute*
Marie-Anne de Roumier-Robert. *The Voyage of Lord Seaton to the Seven Planets*
Nicolas Ségur. *Penelope's Secret*
C.-F. Tiphaigne de La Roche. *Amilec* * *Giphantia*
Simon Tyssot de Patot. *The Strange Voyages of Jacques Massé and Pierre de Mésange*

The Palace of Vengance
and Other Tales
of Enchantment

by
Henriette-Julie de Murat

Translated, annotated and introduced by
Brian Stableford

A Black Coat Press Book

The Palace of Vengance
and Other Tales
of Enchantment

by
Henriette-Julie de Murat

Translated, annotated and introduced by
Brian Stableford

A Black Coat Press Book

ISBN 978-1-61227-774-5. First Printing. August 2018. Published by Black Coat Press, an imprint of Hollywood Comics.com, LLC, P.O. Box 17270, Encino, CA 91416. All rights reserved. Except for review purposes, no part of this book may be reproduced or transmitted in any form or by any means, electronic or mechanical, including photocopying, recording, or by any information storage and retrieval system, without permission in writing from the publisher. The stories and characters depicted in this novel are entirely fictional. Printed in the United States of America.

TABLE OF CONTENTS

Introduction

This is the fourth collection in a series translating the *contes de fées* [tales of enchantment] written by some of the writers who participated in the literary salons peripheral to the court of Louis XIV in the 1690s. The earlier volumes were *The Naiads * Beauty and The Beast* by Gabrielle-Suzanne Barbot de Villeneuve, *The Robe of Sincerity and Other Stories* by Marie-Jeanne L'Héritier de Villandon, and *The Land of Delights: Tales of Enchantment* by Charlotte-Rose Caumont de La Force. The other principal contributors to the subgenre in that period were Catherine Bernard, and, most famously and most prolifically, Marie-Catherine Le Jumel de Barneville, Baronne d'Aulnoy. Some of Bernard's contributions reached print slightly in advance of the others because she secreted them in a historical novel, *Inès de Cordoue* (1697), in which some of the characters participate in a story-telling competition. Some stories by Mademoiselle L'Héritier—the prime mover in the institution of the production of such stories for the relevant salons—had also reached print in a large miscellany of her work published in 1696, along with poetry, essays and fiction of other kinds.

The possibility of such stories reaching print, however, was suddenly and drastically transformed in 1697 when Charles Perrault released a small collection of them—some of them plagiarized from female authors—packaged as moral tales for children, initially attributed to his young son: *Contes de ma mere l'Oye* (tr. as "Tales of Mother Goose"), which became an unexpected best-seller, resulting in sudden rush on the part of printers and authors of such work to apply for the royal licenses still necessary at the time to allow legal publication. Because a considerable amount material already existed, at least in rough draft, it was possible to release a veritable flood of such works within the next three years.

Because Perrault's collection and its subsequent expansions obtained the lion's share of the publicity, and Madame d'Aulnoy's stories were also consequently marketed as works to be read to children, it is sometimes assumed today that all *contes de fées* were originally designed with that purpose in mind, but that is far from the truth. Nor is it true that they were based on "folktales," almost all of them being adapted from or modeled on literary originals. They were composed by aristocrats whose primary audience—many at a time when they had no strong reason to think that they might acquire another—was a population of courtiers. They were employed as an amusing means of passing time for people who, in essence had nothing to do but gossip and seek various amusements in order to stave off tedium. They were a form of adult play, the context, rationale and ambitions of which are nowhere better illustrated than in the works of the Comtesse de Murat. Second in abundance only to the works of Madame d'Aulnoy, Murat's stories show a much more marked evolutionary development, which maps out in advance some of the key ways in which *contes de fées* were ultimately to give birth to a large sector of modern fantasy fiction. Her career, too, mapped out more clearly than any other the problematic circumstances in which the stories were produced and published, and the problematic lives that their female authors led.

The initial nucleus of the vogue for producing *contes de fées* was one of the longest-lasting and most prestigious of the literary salons of Louis XIV's court, hosted by Madeleine de Scudéry (1607-1701), which had become the model for a number of imitations. Mademoiselle de Scudéry was very old by the time the vogue burst into print, and her salon was by then supervised by her protégée. Mademoiselle L'Héritier, who inherited it and continued it during the early decades of the eighteenth century. Scudéry was carrying forward a tradition herself, originated in the famous salon hosted at the Hôtel de Rambouillet by Catherine de Vivonne, Marquise de Rambouillet (1588-1665) from 1608 until her death, but Scudéry became the principal "theorist" of that salon, defining its rules of procedure and esthetic objectives, aided in that personal crusade by the fact that she became by far the best-selling author of her era, and the effective pioneer of the commercial publication of fiction. Much of what we now think of as "popular fiction" owes its ultimate origin to her work, just as modern "writers' workshops" owe their ultimate origin to her salon. Among other achievements, it was Scudéry who made it feasible for women to publish at all—her books were initially issued under the name of her brother, Georges, but her publishers eventually realized that the pretence was not only unnecessary but absurd.

From the very beginning, the Marquise de Rambouillet had set out to oppose the institutional sexism that required Mademoiselle de Scudéry to hide behind her brother's name in order to achieve publication, and Scudéry's own salon became the standard-bearer for that primitive and very moderate feminism—which was, of course treated with merciless and contemptuous mockery by the males whose cultural hegemony it was attempting to erode. Molière followed up his brief farce "Les Précieuses ridicules" [The Ridiculous Precious Women] (1659)—as a result of which the key salon members became known as the *précieuses*—with the long comedy "Les Femmes savantes" [The Savant Women] (1672); their parody set the tone for the backlash against the pride and impetus that the salon writers derived from the enormous and unprecedented popularity of Scudéry's works, which reached their peak of achievement and celebrity in *Artamène, ou le Grand Cyrus* (ten volumes, 1649-1653) and *Clélie, histoire romaine* (ten volumes, 1654-1660).

Those works were widely described at the time as *romans*, and that is why *roman* is now the conventional French term for works of prose fiction; it is often translated into contemporary English as "novel," although English literary commentary attempted for a long time to maintain a distinction between "novels" and "romances," and Scudéry's works arguably have more common with the latter category, their label having been chosen in order to assert a kinship with the prose romances of the twelfth and thirteenth centuries. In fact, they were serials of a sort, each volume being released separately, and they are ancestral in many of their narrative techniques and concerns to modern TV soap operas. Their central theme is the vicissitudes of *amour*, and, in particular, the conflicts of interest that often arose between daughters wanting to marry for love and parents wanting to barter them for social advantage.

Scudéry also pioneered the literary strategy of the *roman à clef*, in which contemporary individuals were disguised as fictional characters, in Scudéry's examples—though not those of many of her imitators—in the context of a Classical pseudohistory. The *précieuses* not only did that in their literary works but in their conversation too, frequently referring to their contemporaries by pseudonyms borrowed from her novels, partly to mask salacious gossip and mockery. It is now impossible to judge the extent to which the characters featured in the more fanciful tales improvised in the salons might be parodies of actual individuals at Louis XIV's court, but what is certain is that the fictitious world of fays, princes and princesses featured in the stories, and its social conventions and mores, is a carefully-distorted image of Parisian high society in the age of Louis XIV.

Because *contes de fées* have acquired the image of genteel moralistic tales written for children it is sometimes also assumed that their original authors must have been of the same ilk, and, in a way, they were, or at least pretended to be. In the context of the court, however, they were a perennial subject of scurrilous gossip and extravagant scandal. The most scandalous of the lot was perhaps Baronne d'Aulnoy, who led a hectic and colorful life before settling in Paris—long estranged by then from her husband—in 1690, where she hosted a salon in the Faubourg Saint-Germain attended by Mademoiselle L'Héritier, the Comtesse de Murat and Mademoiselle de La Force. Banished from the Court for a while, she was readmitted for unspecified "services to the crown," but some of her friends were not so lucky. Mademoiselle de La Force was ban-

ished to a convent in 1697, a few months before her collection of *contes de fées* was published. Her cousin, the Comtesse de Murat, was under surveillance by then by the Lieutenant-General of Police, who issued several reports on her conduct, and the fact that she left Paris in 1700 did not prevent her from further investigation and persecution.

It is impossible now to determine whether here was any truth at all in the scandalous gossip that circulated regard in writers of *contes de fées*, or what can be read into the circumstances that Mademoiselle de Scudéry always liked to call herself by the nickname Sapho, that neither Mademoiselle L'Héritier nor Mademoiselle de La Force ever married, and that Baronne d'Aulnoy and the Comtesse de Murat were long estranged from the husbands they had acquired early in life as a result of arranged marriages. In reading their works, however, it has to be remembered that they were writing under conditions of extreme censorship because the acquisition of the licenses required to reach print was difficult, and that all the work that acquired such licenses was, of necessity, conscientiously buried in thick layers of diplomacy, flattery, hypocrisy and artificiality. In that context, the fashionability of *contes de fées*, before and after Perrault opened the loophole of publishing opportunity, needs to needs to be considered with a severely ironic eye and a deep suspicion of their superficial rhetoric. Because the Comtesse de Murat's work is the most varied and most sophisticated oeuvre within the first flourish of the genre, it is perhaps the most interesting in that regard, and is certainly the most adventurous.

Henriette-Julie de Castelnau, Comtesse de Murat (1670-1716) was the daughter of Marquis Michel de Castelnau, the son of a famous Maréchal de France; he followed his father into a military career, and died of wounds sustained in battle in 1672. She was married by arrangement in 1691, apparently against her will, to Nicolas de Murat, the colonel of an infantry regiment. She gave birth to a son a year later, but fled the marital home not long thereafter—a scandalous thing to do in those days—and went to live in Paris. There she is known to have frequented the salon of the Marquise de Lambert, to which she might have been introduced by her cousin, Mademoiselle de La Force, and where she certainly met Baronne d'Aulnoy and Catherine Bernard.

It was probably in Lambert's salon that Murat became involved in the current vogue for *contes de fées*, but she was received at Court, and undoubtedly participated in the salon hosted by Mesdemoiselles Scudéry and L'Héritier as well. At any rate, as soon as Perrault had opened the door, she must have had printers flocking around her, begging to put her contributions to the genre into print while the going was good. She responded with alacrity, swiftly adding to her initial assembly of tales, published in two separate volumes in 1698, a third and markedly different collection issued in 1699. The latter almost certainly consisted of work done after Perrault's success, and written with the certainty of publication very much in mind. In spite of troubled circumstances, she produced a further two stories in a similar vein toward the end of her career; the present collection contains translations of all the prose works from the first three volumes and all the other tales in the same genre published during her lifetime.

Her first collection of *contes de fées* was not Murat's first publication; in 1697 she had published a two volume work whose first title-page bears the title *Mémoires de Madame la Comtesse de M****, although there is a second that relegates that to the subtitle, after the title *La Défense des dames*. Many people, perhaps not surprisingly, seem to have assumed that the book really consisted of memoirs and read it as if it were autobiographical. Indeed, many subsequent accounts of the author's biography borrowed from it freely, even in the knowledge of considerable contradictions between the narrative of the text and actual documentation of the author's life. For instance, the author of the French *Wikipedia* article on Murat points out numerous "inaccuracies" in the narrative but still appropriates other sections of the story as if they were accounts of Murat's own life. In fact, *Mémoires de Madame la*

*Comtesse de M**** is a work of fiction, pure and simple, and although its fundamental argument—that it is sometimes entirely justified for wives to leave their husbands—was evidently one that Murat had good reason to take an intense interest on her own account, the details of the life of the narrator of the story are entirely different from the details of Murat's life, so far as they can be independently ascertained. The narrator is married at sixteen (Murat did not marry until she was 21) at the insistence of her tyrannical father (Murat's father died while she was a child) and eventually flees the domestic abuse of her unnamed husband with her daughter (Murat fled her marital home with her son), etc, etc.

It is worth noting in this context that most of the authors involved in the boom in *contes de fées*, including Aulnoy, Bernard and La Force, had previously published other works, including other prose fiction, all of it historical fiction and much of it belonging to the curious genre of "secret memoirs," in which first-person narratives were attributed to real (but safely dead) individuals, supposedly relating incidents in their lives that they had been obliged to dissimulate at the time, usually because they were of a scandalous nature. Murat was obviously very familiar with that genre of work, and her own "memoir" has a great deal in common with it—but in setting it in the recent past rather than the remote past she was breaking new ground, in a slightly risky fashion.

We are now, of course, entirely familiar with the literary strategy of cultivating verisimilitude by passing works of fiction off as "true" memoirs, and few people, even at the time of publication, were likely to mistake the adventures of Robinson Crusoe as a factual memoir, let alone those of Moll Flanders or Lemuel Gulliver, but that was a generation later than the publication of *Mémoires de Madame la Comtesse de M****, when almost all works published as memoirs were, indeed, actual memoirs—which is to say, deliberate self-justificatory lies and obfuscations pretending to actuality rather than works of fiction in search of an essentially ironic verisimilitude. Did Murat realize that her work of fiction would be mistaken by some readers as an account of her own life? Probably. Did she come to regret it? Perhaps. One thing that is certain, however, is that it made some contribution to the scandal that followed her around for the rest of her brief life at court and long thereafter. Colorful as it is, though, it is considerably less so than the Lieutenant-General's reports, which accused her of persistent libertinage and lesbianism, and the accounts of her life compiled by other speculative biographers.

It appears that Murat was forced to leave the court in 1700 by the financial ruination of her family rather than the scandal surrounding her; the Marquisat de Castelnau had been sold in 1699. She appears to have resided in Limousin thereafter with an aunt on her mother's side of the family. She was, however, discreetly arrested following the last of the Lieutenant-General's reports in 1702 and imprisoned in the Château de Loches, then one of the largest of France's state prisons. Although the conditions of her imprisonment appear to have been moderately lenient, she nevertheless attempted to escape more than once, and was transferred twice in 1706 before returning to Loches under conditions that seems to have allowed more social interaction. She was eventually allowed to return to Limousin in 1709 in order to live with her aunt, albeit under a kind of house arrest. She resumed writing during her second sojourn in Loches, and published three works of fiction in 1708, 1709 and 1710, the last of which, *Les Lutins du château de Kernosy* (tr. herein as "The Goblins of Kernosy Castle"), contained the last two of her *contes de fées* to be published in her lifetime. She was, however, in poor health by then, and published nothing more before her death in 1716.

The first volume of Murat's first collection of stories was issued by Claude Barbin, the same printer/bookseller who had pushed the *Mémoires*, as *Contes de fées, dédiez à Son Altesse Sérénissime Madame la Princesse Douairière de Conty, par*

*Mad. la Comtesse de M****[1]—an attribution, probably added by the printer, that doubtless encouraged the confusion regarding the authenticity of the *Mémoires*. It contains three stories: "Le Parfait amour" (tr. as "Perfect Love"), "Anguillette" (tr. as "Anguillette") and "Jeune et belle" (tr. as "Young and Beautiful"). The version of the second volume, *Les Nouveaux contes des fées par Madame de M**** reproduced on *gallica* is an edition dated 1710, and there are several other undated editions of the collection in the Bibliothèque Nationale catalogue which are presumably also reprints, some of which have variant contents, but other bibliographies claim that its original publication was in 1698, which seems highly likely; it contains three stories, "Le Palais de la vengeance" (tr. as "The Palace of Vengeance), "Le Prince des feuilles" (tr. as "The Prince of Leaves") and "L'Heureuse peine" (tr. as "The Fortunate Penalty"), plus a brief narrative poem.

The first of the six stories establishes the theme of almost all of Murat's *contes*: the kind of amour held up by Mademoiselle de Scudéry as a supremely great ideal: emotionally and morally absolute, sentimentally all-consuming and utterly faithful. In that story and its many clones, however, the sentiment and the fidelity are subjected to enormous stress applied by relatives or jealous rivals intent in breaking the amorous bond between the noble and handsome hero and his inamorata, who is invariably the most beautiful woman who ever lived. The hero and heroine always end up at death's door, some-

---

[1] There were two Princesses de Conti at the Court in 1698, both the same age, but the one who had been married to the late Prince de Conti was known as the "dowager princess" to distinguish her from the one married to the present Prince, Francis-Louis de Bourbon, the younger brother of his predecessor, Louis-Armand de Bourbon. Both princesses appear to have been enthusiastic participants in literary salons, including Scudéry's and Madame de Lambert's, and feature extensively in dedications of works by the salon writers.

times several times over, frequently undergo mental and physical torture, but never waver in their commitment.

The convention of such fiction, then as now, is that the hero and heroine must be rewarded for their heroism; they must marry, and they must inherit a kingdom, and the entire literary purpose of fays [enchantresses] is to provide authors with a convenient *deus ex machina* with which to ensure that result. One of the most interesting features of Murat's early work is that it sometimes exhibits an overt skepticism regarding that convention, as is manifest in the tragic variant featured in the novella "Anguillette," the sourly perverse conclusion of "Le Palais de la vengeance," and the deliberately jarring note introduced out of the blue at the end of "L'Heureuse peine." Interestingly, it is only in her early work, probably written without the likelihood of publication in mind, that she actually violates the convention. She never forsook the subversive element in her work, but she refined its ironic rhetoric considerably as her career advanced.

In 1699 Murat published a portmanteau work, *Le Voyage de campagne* [An Excursion to the Country], in which a group of travelers tell one another stories in the course of a discussion of various matters of interest to them, mostly drawn from their personal histories, although they include one *conte*, "Le Père et ses quatre fils" (tr. as "A Father and His Four Sons") whose teller represents it as an experiment of sorts. Further interest is added to it by the comments surrounding it in the frame narrative, which include brief remarks on the appeal and literary propriety of tales of enchantment. The frame story is not as anodyne as the capsule description might make it seem; it is subtly subversive in both political and religious terms, and the characters have utopian aspirations; it is perhaps surprising that it was granted a license, but less surprising that it remained one of the author's most popular works, reprinted several times in the eighteenth century.

Literary experiments of a far more extravagant kind are featured in *Histoires sublimes et allégoriques par Madame la Comtesse D*** dédiées aux fées modernes*, published by

Florentin & Pierre Delaulne in 1699. It contains four stories: "The Roy porc" (tr. as "The Swine King"), "L'Isle de Magnificence (tr. as "The Isle of Magnificence"), "Le Sauvage" (tr. as "The Savage") and "Le Turbot" (tr. a "The Turbot". Although Mademoiselle L'Héritier used the terms *conte, histoire* and *nouvelle* interchangeably, Murat probably had a distinction in mind in choosing to label the stories in her 1699 collection *histoires* rather than *contes*, the label she invariably used elsewhere, and surely meant to imply more than the fact that the stories are, on average, longer than those in her 1698 collections, Whereas all the stories in the earlier collections are set in "the time of the fays," a remote mythical past, only the first of the four stories in the 1699 collection follows that convention; the other three all contain references establishing that they are set in 1697, and that the lands in which fays operate are only separated pseudogeographically from contemporary France.

The second and fourth stories in *Histoires sublimes et allégoriques* are peculiar novellas, portmanteau works of a less orthodox kind than *Le Voyage de campagne*, in which several narratives are intricately interwoven in a fashion that later became known as "the Galland method" because of its elaborate use in Antoine Galland's *Les Mille et une nuits* (12 volumes, 1704-1717). Portmanteau works had been common for a long time before 1699, and such packaging could even be regarded as the principal mode of presentation of prose fiction prior to 1700, but most previous examples of its use simply inserted stories into a frame, rarely overlapping and entangling them as Murat did in "L'Isle de Magnificence" and "Le Turbot." Both stories are also remarkable for the imaginative extravagance of some of their subplots; the depiction of the civilization contained in caves beneath the sea-bed in the former story, devoid of light and of women, is a superbly surreal invention, and the manner in which the fay queen of the Isle of Rocks contrives to counter the improbable conditions imposed by a rival for the liberation of re-transformation of a Prince metamorphosed into a butterfly in the latter is a *tour de force* of intricate absurdist plotting. It is notable that all the key motifs and narrative strategies subsequently employed by Madame Barbot de Villeneuve in the classic "La Belle et la Bête" (1740) clearly originate from *Histoires sublimes et allégoriques*.

We can only speculate as to how Murat's literary career might have developed if it had not been for the personal disasters that afflicted her severally after 1699, but in the event, her production was completely disrupted for several years, after the alleged publication of the exceedingly elusive *Un Dialogue des morts* (1700), which might be a phantom title. When she returned to literary work, it was a markedly different vein. *Histoire de la courtisane Rhodope* [The Story of the Courtesan Rhodope] (1708) and *Histoire galantes des habitants de Loches* [The Story of the Gallant Inhabitants of Loches] (1709) presumably having much more in common with the salacious secret memoir genre than her earlier works, to judge by their titles. The latter is reported by J.-M. Quérard in *La France Littéraire* (1829) to be a satire inspired and imitative of Alain-René Lesage's *Le Diable boîteux* (1707), while he simply annotates the former as "unfinished."[2]

Les Lutins du château de Kernosy is, by contrast, a fascinating portmanteau novel which provides a more interesting context for its two interpolated *contes de fées* and a third fantastic story of a different kind than *Le Voyage de campagne* had done for its much slighter inclusion. The juxtaposition of the second story, "Étoilette" (tr. as "Starlet") with its supposed author's account of his own experiences offers an interesting comparison between narratives that contain and exemplify elements of common sentiment, and the embedding of both those exemplary tales in the more elaborate frame adds a third layer to the comparative dimension, making up a unique and

---

[2] The conscientious Quérard also observes in his annotations that *Mémoires de Madame la Comtesse de M**** is a work of fiction, not an autobiography, but many of Murat's biographers ignored his judgment.

intriguing whole that tacitly raises many questions regarding the functions and the appeal of storytelling. It is a surprisingly sophisticated work for its time and remarkably modern in its lightly humorous tone and ingenious intricacy.

The last story in the present collection was only belatedly added to Murat's canon, having first been published in an unsigned 1718 collection entitled *Nouveaux contes de fées*, under the title "Le Buisson d'épines fleuries [The Flowery Thorn-Bush]; none of the other stories in the collection appear to be hers, but a manuscript version of that particular story appears to have been found among Murat's papers, where it bore the title "La Fée Princesse" [i.e. a fay named Princess] (tr. as "The Fay Princess"). The attribution is undoubtedly correct; appearances suggest that the story belongs to the earlier phase of Murat's writing of *contes de fées* rather than the more self-conscious phase of the *Histoires sublimes*, and it is possible that it was not included in any of her collections because the portrayal of the King in the story might have seemed a trifle risky to the author and printer alike, in terms of the granting of a license. (Murat's death was preceded by that of Louis XIV, reducing that risk.) It is typical of her work in many ways, featuring her characteristic imaginative extravagance, the extreme stress to which she routinely subjects her heroes and heroines, and its deliberately atypical conclusion—for which reason it makes an entirely appropriate terminus for the present collection, even though it was probably written long before "Peau d'ourse" (tr. as "Bearskin") and the flamboyantly quirky "Étoilette."

All the translations in this collection were made from the versions of the texts contained on the Bibliothèque Nationale's *gallica* website, with the exception of four pages that are missing from the copy of *Histoires sublimes et allégoriques* reproduced on the site, and which were filled in from the copy reproduced on Google Books. The copy of *Contes de fées* on the site is dated 1698 on the title page, and the royal license was issued in January 1698, so the date of 1697 given for the collection is some sources appears to be mistaken. The version of *Les Lutins du château de Kernosy* on *gallica* is a reprint contained in volume 35 (1789) of Charles Garnier's *Voyages imaginaires, songes, visions et roman cabalistiques*, where it is a somewhat surprising inclusion under the heading of "romans cabalistiques." The version of the posthumously-published story is the one contained in volume XXXI (1786) of Charles Mayer's *Cabinet des Fées*, where it retains the title "Le Buisson d'épines fleuries" in a reprint of the contents of the 1718 collection, and is unattributed.

Brian Stableford

PERFECT LOVE

The redoubtable Danamo reigned in one of the pleasant lands dependent on the Empire of the Fays. She was knowledgeable in her art, cruel in her actions and glorious in the honor of being descended from the celebrated Calypso, whose charms had glory and power in stopping the famous Ulysses and triumphing over the prudence of the vanquisher of Troy. She was tall, and grim of face, and her pride had only submitted with great difficulty to the harsh laws of marriage, amour never having been able to reach as far as her heart, but the design of uniting a flourishing kingdom with the one of which she was the Queen and another that she had usurped had caused her to espouse an old King, one of her neighbors.

The King died a few years after the marriage and he left to the fay a daughter named Azire, who was extraordinarily ugly, but did not appear so in the eyes of Danamo; she found her charming, perhaps because she resembled her perfectly. She was to be Queen of three realms, a circumstance that compensates for many faults, and she was requested by all the most powerful Princes of neighboring lands. That urgency, combined with the blind amity of Danamo, ended up rendering her vanity insupportable; she was desired with ardor, therefore she must be worthy of it. Thus the fay and the Princess reasoned between themselves, and enjoyed the pleasure of the deception.

Danamo only thought about rendering happiness to the Princess so perfect that she thought her deserving of it, and she brought up in her palace a young Prince, the son of her brother. His name was Parcin Parcinet. Everything he wanted to do he did well; he danced perfectly, he sang likewise and he won all the prizes in any Tourney that he took the trouble of disputing. The young Prince was the delight of the Court, and

Danamo, who had her designs, did not oppose the respect and admiration that everyone had for him.

The King who was Parcin Parcinet's father being the fay's brother, she had declared war on him without even seeking a reason. The King fought valiantly at the head of his army, but what could an army do against the power of a fay as knowledgeable as Danamo? She only allowed the victory to remain in the balance for as long as was necessary for her unfortunate brother to perish on that occasion. As soon as he was dead, killed by a thrust of a wand, she dispersed her enemies and rendered herself mistress of the kingdom. Parcin Parcinet was still in the cradle; he was brought to Danamo; it would have been vain to try to hide him from a fay. He already had the seductive graces that win hearts; Danamo caressed him, and a few days later she took him with her to her own realm.

The Prince was eighteen years old when the fay, wanting to carry out the designs formed so many years before, resolved to unite Parcin Parcinet with the Princess, her daughter. She did not doubt for a moment the infinite joy that the young prince would experience, having been born ambitious but destined by his misfortunes to live as a subject, in one day becoming the sovereign of three empires. She sent for the Princess, and finally revealed to her the choice that she had made for her.

The princess listened to that speech with an emotion that caused the fay to judge that the resolution in favor of Prince Parcinet did not please her daughter.

"I can see," she said, on remarking her disturbance increasing further, "that you want to take your ambition higher and combine with your empire that of one of the many Kings who have asked for you. But what King can Parcin Parcinet not defeat? His courage is above all; the subjects of a Prince so perfect might well become rebels one day in his favor; by giving you to him I am assuring you of the possession of his kingdom. For his person there is no need to speak; you know that the proudest beauties cannot resist his charms."

The Princess, suddenly throwing herself at the fay's feet, interrupted her speech and admitted to her that her heart had not been able to resist the young victor, famous for so many conquests, but she added, blushing: "I have given a thousand marks of my tenderness to the insensible Parcin Parcinet, but he has received them with a coldness that makes me despair."

"That is because he dared not raise his thoughts as far as you," replied the proud fay. "He doubtless fears displeasing, and I am grateful for his respect."

That flattering opinion was too convenient for the inclination and vanity of the Princess for her not to allow herself to be convinced by it.

Finally, the fay sent for Parcin Parcinet. He came to find her in a magnificent cabinet, where she was waiting with the Princess, her daughter.

"Summoning all you courage to your aid," she said to him as soon as he appeared, "not to sustain your woes, but that you should not succumb under your good fortune. You are to reign, Parcin Parcinet, and to complete your happiness, you are to reign by marrying my daughter."

"Me, Madame!" cried the young Prince, with an astonishment in which it was easy to remark that joy had no part. "I am going to marry the Princess?" he continued, recoiling several steps. "What god has come to meddle with my destiny, to whose care alone I can ask for aid?"

These words were pronounced by the Prince with a haste in which his heart played too great a part for them to be arrested soon enough by reason.

The fay thought that Prince Parcinet's unexpected happiness had overwhelmed him, but the Princess loved him, and love sometimes renders lovers more perspicacious than intelligence. "Whatever god it is whose aid you are imploring so tenderly, Parcin Parcinet," she said to him, emotionally, "I know only too well that I have no part in the prayers you have made to him."

The young Prince, who had had time to recover from his initial astonishment, and had understood the imprudence of what he had just done, summoned his intelligence to the aid of his heart. He replied more gallantly to the Princess than she had hoped and thanked the fay with an air of grandeur, which showed clearly enough that he was not only worthy of the empires that she was offering him, but that of the whole world.

Danamo and her proud daughter were satisfied by his speech; they arranged everything before emerging from the cabinet, and the fay only deferred the day of the wedding for some time in order to give the entire Court the leisure to prepare for that great celebration.

On their emergence from the Queen's cabinet, the news of the marriage of Parcin Parcinet and Azire spread throughout the palace instantly; a crowd gathered to rejoice with the Prince. Although the Princess was scarcely likeable, it was a great fortune to which she was about to enable him to climb.

Parcin Parcinet received all those honors with a cold expression that surprised his new subjects all the more because it seemed to be mingled with a chagrin and an extreme anxiety. It was necessary throughout the day for him to receive the congratulations of the entire court and sustain the testimonies of amour that Azire incessantly gave him. What a situation for a young Prince occupied with a vivid dolor!

Night appeared to him to have delayed its return a thousand times longer than usual. The impatient Parcin Parcinet pressed it with his wishes; it finally came. He emerged precipitately from the place where he had suffered so much and went back to his apartment. After having sent everyone away, he opened a door to the palace gardens and traversed then, only accompanied by a young slave.

A beautiful but not very extensive river flowed at the end of the gardens and separated from the fay's magnificent palace a small castle flanked by four towers and surrounded by a deep moat filled by the same stream. It was to that place that the prayers and desires of Parcin Parcinet incessantly went. What a marvel was contained therein! Danamo had that treasure guarded carefully; it was a young Princess, the daughter of her sister, who had confided her on her deathbed to the fay's care. Her beauty, worthy of the admiration of the whole world, appeared too dangerous to Danamo to allow Azire to be seen beside her. Sometimes, the charming Irolite—that was her name—was permitted to come to the palace to see the fay and the princess, her daughter, but she was never allowed to appear in public. Her charms were unknown—but not unknown to everyone.

They had appeared in Princess Azire's apartment to the eyes of Parcin Parcinet and he had adored them as soon as he had seen them. The proximity of the blood relationship gave no privileges to the young Prince with regard to Irolite; since the young Princess was no longer a child, the pitiless Danamo did not permit anyone to see her.

However, Parcin Parcinet burned with a flame as ardent as the charms of Irolite were bound to ignite; she was fourteen years old, her beauty was perfect; her hair was a charming color, without being entirely black or blonde; her complexion had all the freshness of spring; her mouth was beautiful, her teeth admirable and her smile gracious; she had large brown eyes, bright and touching, and her gaze appeared to say a thousand things of which her young heart was unaware.

She had been brought up in great solitude; although the castle where she lived was close to the fay's palace, she saw no more people there than she would have done in the middle of a desert. Danamo had that order followed exactly; the beautiful Irolite spent her life with the women destined to accompany her. Their number was small, but however little fortune could be expected in a Court so solitary and limited, renown, which did not fear Danamo, published so many marvels regarding the young Princess that the noblest young women of the Court offered to be imprisoned with the young Irolite. Her presence did not belie the expectations raised by renown, and they always found much to admire in her.

A governess of extreme intelligence and sagacity, formerly attached to Irolite's mother, had remained with her, and often bemoaned the rigors of Danamo for the charming Irolite. Her name as Mana; the desire to render the Princess the liberty she ought to enjoy and the rank she ought to have had caused her to tolerate the love of Parcin Parcinet. It was three years since, having been introduced into the castle one evening, dressed as a slave, he had found Irolite in the garden, and he had spoken to her tenderly. She was then only a child, but an admirable child; she loved Parcin Parcinet as if he were her brother, and could not yet understand that one could love differently.

Mana, who was rarely far away from Irolite, had surprised the young Prince in the gardens; he had told her about his love for the Princess and the design he had formed either to render her liberty one day or to die trying, and to go thereafter to show the people of his realm a glorious means of avenging themselves on Danamo and placing Irolite on the throne. The nascent merit of Parcin Parcinet was able to render the most difficult projects credible, and it was the only aid that was offered to the liberation of Irolite, so Mana permitted him to come to the castle sometimes when night had fallen. He only saw Irolite in her presence, but he spoke to her about his love and incessantly tried, by means of tender speeches and constant cares, to inspire an ardor in her as keen as his own.

For three years, Parcin Parcinet had only been occupied by his tenderness; almost every night he went to the Princess's castle, and every day he did nothing but think about her.

We left him traversing Danamo's gardens accompanied by a slave, penetrated by the dolor to which the fay's resolutions had reduced him. He arrived at the edge of the stream; a small gilded boat moored to the bank, in which Azire sometimes went out on the water, served to take the amorous Prince across. The slave rowed, and as soon as Parcin Parcinet had climbed a silken ladder that was thrown down to him from a small terrace that overlooked the façade of the castle, the faithful slave rowed the boat back to where it ought to be. He only approached the castle again in response to a signal that Parcin Parcinet made, by showing a lighted torch on the terrace momentarily.

This evening, the Prince followed his ordinary route; the silken ladder was thrown down to him and he entered without obstacle all the way to young Irolite's bedroom; he found her there, lying on a bed of repose, in tears. She was so beautiful in that dolorous state that her charms had never seemed so touching to the young Prince.

"What's wrong, my Princess," he said to her, throwing himself to his knees beside the bed on which she was lying. "Who can have made those precious tears flow? Alas," he continued, sighing, "I have even more bad news to tell you."

The tears and sighs of the young lovers were confounded, and it was necessary that they let them run their course before he could tell her the cause of that sharp dolor. Finally, the young Prince begged Irolite to tell him what new rigor the fay had imposed upon her.

"She wants to make you marry Azire," the beautiful Irolite replied, blushing. "Could these cruelties ever be so dolorous?"

"Oh, my dear Princess," cried the Prince, "you dread that I am marrying Azire! My fate is a thousand times sweeter than if I had not thought so."

"Can you praise destiny," said young Irolite, languidly, "when it is in haste to separate us? I cannot express the pain that fear is making me feel. Oh, you are right, Parcin Parcinet, one loves a lover differently from a brother."

The amorous Prince thought that he should thank fortune for his woes. Never had Irolite's young heart appeared to him to know amour, but finally, he could no longer doubt the happiness of having inspired the Princess to tender sentiments. That felicity, which he had not expected, raised all his hopes.

"No," he cried, transported. "I no longer despair of vanquishing our misfortunes, since I am assured of your tenderness. Let us flee, my Princess; let us flee the fury of Danamo and her odious daughter; let us go confide to a less dreary abode the ardent amour that alone can render us happy.

"If I depart with you," the young Princess said, with astonishment, "what will the entire kingdom say about my flight?"

"Forget such vain considerations, beautiful Irolite," Parcin Parcinet interjected, impatiently. "Everything presses us to quit this place; let's go...."

"But where will you go?" asked the prudent Mana, who had been present all along, and who, being less preoccupied than the young lovers, foresaw all the difficulties if their flight.

"I have designs that I shall explain to you," said Parcin Parcinet, "but how have you learned the news of the fay's Court so soon here?"

"One of my relatives," said Mana, "wrote to me as soon as the rumor spread through the palace, and I thought I ought to inform the Princess."

"How I have suffered since that moment," said the lovable Irolite. "No, Parcin Parcinet, I could not live without you."

The young Prince, transported by amour and charmed by those words, gave Irolite's beautiful hand an ardent and tender kiss, which had all the grace of a precious favor, and of a first favor.

The daylight, which was beginning to appear, warned Parcin Parcinet too soon that it was time to withdrew. He assured the Princess that he would come back the following night in order to make her party to his plans.

He went back to the boat and the faithful slave, and retired to his apartment. He was transported by the pleasure of being loved by the beautiful Irolite, and agitated by the difficulties that he foresaw clearly that he would encounter in his flight; sleep could not calm that anxiety, nor make him forget his happiness for a moment.

Scarcely had the morning entered his apartment than a dwarf presented him with a beautiful sash on the part of Princess Azire, who, in a note more tender than Parcin Parcinet would have liked, begged him insistently to wear the sash from that day forward. He sent a reply that embarrassed him greatly, but it was necessary to liberate Irolite, and to what constraint would he not have exposed himself in order to free her?

He had just sent the dwarf back to Azire when a giant came on the part of Danamo to present him with a saber of extraordinary beauty, the hilt of which was a single stone brighter than a diamond, which cast a light so dazzling that it illuminated the night. Engraved on the saber were the words: *For the hand of a Victor.*

That present pleased Parcin Parcinet; he went to thank the fay for it, and appeared before her wearing the marvelous saber that she had just sent him and Azire's beautiful sash. The tenderness that Irolite had for him suspended all his anxieties; it had spread in his heart the joy, so sweet and so perfect, that fortunate love makes felt. That air of contentment appeared in all his actions; Azire attributed it to her charms and the fay to Parcin Parcinet's satisfied ambition. The day was spent in pleasures that did not diminish in the slightest the insupportable impatience in which Parcin Parcinet found himself.

In the evening they went for a walk in the gardens and an excursion on the river that the Prince knew so well; his heart felt a keen emotion on entering the little boat; no matter how different from the pleasure to which it ordinarily led him was the mortal boredom he felt then, Parcin Parcinet could not help gazing several times at the dwelling of the charming Irolite. She did not appear on the terrace of the castle, for there was an express order that she should not emerge from her bedroom when the fay or Azire was out on the water.

The Princess, who was attentive to all the Prince's actions, noticed that his gaze often turned toward the castle.

"Why, Prince," she said, "in the midst of the honors that surround you, are you looking at Irolite's prison? Is it worthy of your attention?"

"Yes, Madame," said Parcin Parcinet, imprudently. "I am sensible to the suffering of those who have not attracted their misfortunes."

"You have too much pity," said Azire, disdainfully. "But to extract you from your trouble," she said, lowering her voice, "I will tell you that Irolite will not be a prisoner for long."

"And what will become of her?" asked the young Prince, brusquely.

"The Queen will marry her in a fortnight to Prince Ormond," Azire replied. "He is, as you know, of the same blood as us, and in accordance with the Queen's intentions, the day after his marriage, he will take Irolite to one of his fortresses, from which she will never return to the Court."

"What!" said the Prince, with a extraordinary emotion. "The Queen will give that beautiful Princess to such a frightful Prince, whose bad qualities even surpass his ugliness? What cruelty!"

The last word escaped him involuntarily, but he could not betray his courage and his heart any longer.

"It seems to me that it is not for you, Parcin Parcinet," replied Azire, proudly, "to complain of Danamo's cruelties."

That conversation would doubtless have been extended too far for a young Prince who had to pretend, but, fortunately for Parcin Parcinet, the young women of Azire's retinue approached her, and, the fay having appeared on the water's edge a moment later, Azire wanted to go and join her. On emerging from the boat, Parcin Parcinet feigned illness, in order at least to have the liberty to go and lament the unfortunate news without witnesses.

The fay, and Azire especially, testified a great anxiety regarding his illness. He retired to his apartment; there he criticized destiny a thousand times for the woes that threatened the charming Irolite, and he abandoned himself to all his dolor and all his tenderness. Finally beginning to remedy his woes, so dolorous for a faithful lover, he wrote, with the most touching expressions that his amour was able to dictate to him, to one of his aunts, who was a fay like Danamo, but who had as much joy in relieving the unfortunate as Danamo took in making them. Her name was Favorable. He explained to her, therefore, the cruel situation to which amour and fortune had reduced him, and, not daring to leave Danamo's Court himself for fear of betraying the designs that he had formed, he sent his faithful slave to Favorable.

When everyone had retired, he left his apartments, as usual, traversed the gardens and got into the little boat, taking an oar himself, without really knowing whether he would be able to make use of it properly. But what cannot amour teach? It achieves much more difficult things. It made Parcin Parcinet row with as much skill and diligence as the most expert in that métier, and he went into Irolite's castle. He was surprised only to find the sage Mana in the Princess's bedroom, in tears.

"What's wrong, Mana?" he Prince said to her, urgently. "And where is my dear Irolite?"

"Alas, Seigneur, she is no longer here," Mana said to him. "A troop of the Queen's guards, and a few women, to whom she is apparently confiding her, took her away from the castle three or four hours ago."

Parcin Parcinet did not hear the end of those sad words; he had fainted as soon as he learned of the Princess's departure. Mana brought him round with infinite trouble, and he only emerged from that torpid state to enter suddenly into fury. He drew a little dagger that he wore at his waist and would have pierced is heart with it if the sage Mana had not retained his arm as much as was possible for her.

Throwing herself to his knees, she said: "What, Seigneur! You want to abandon Irolite and life, to deliver her to Danamo's fury? Alas, without you, where will she find aid against the fay's cruelties?"

Those words immediately suspended the unfortunate Prince's despair. "Alas," he said, shedding tears that all his courage could not hold back, "where is my Princess? Yes, Mana, I shall live at least to have the sad satisfaction of dying for her and expiring while avenging her on her enemies."

After those words Mana implored him to leave that fatal abode, in order to avoid further misfortunes. "Go, Prince," she said to him. "We do not know whether the fay has someone here ready to give her an account of what is happening here; preserve a life so dear to the Princess you adore; I will let you know whatever I can learn about her."

The Prince left after that promise and returned to his apartment with all the dolor that a very tender and very unfortunate amour can inspire. He spent the night in a chair, on to which he had thrown himself on entering; daylight surprised him there, and it was already some hours after its commencement that he heard a noise at his bedroom door. He ran to it with the impatience one experiences when one is expecting news in which one's heart is keenly interested. He found his servants there, bringing him a man he wanted to speak to him without delay. He recognized him as one of Mana's relatives, who put a letter in Parcin Parcinet's hands. He went into his cabinet to hide the emotion that the letter caused him; he opened it precipitately, having recognized Mana's handwriting, and found these words therein:

Mana,
to the greatest Prince in the world.

Be reassured, Seigneur, our Princess is safe, if that word is permissible so long as she is in her enemy's power. She has asked Danamo for me, who has permitted me to rejoin her. She is being kept in the palace. Yesterday evening, the Queen had her come to her cabinet, and ordered her to look proudly at Prince Ormond, who would become her husband in a few days; and she introduced her to that Prince, so unworthy of being your rival. The Princess was so afflicted that she only replied to the Queen with tears. They have not dried up. It is up to you, Seigneur, to discover whether aid is possible against such pressing woes.

At the bottom of the letter, written in a tremulous hand, were these words, which seemed to be effaced in several places:

How sorry I am, my dear Prince; your woes are even more dolorous to me than mine; I will spare your tenderness the recitation of what I have suffered since yesterday; why should I trouble the repose of your life without, alas, my being able to make you happy?

What movement of joy and dolor did the heart of the young Prince not feel? What kisses did he not bestow on that precious evidence to the divine Irolite's love? He was so beside himself that he had all the difficulty in the world forming a reply that would have some consequence. He thanked the sage Mana, he informed the Princess of the aid that he anticipated from the fay Favorable, what did he not say about his dolor and his amour? Finally, he brought the letter to Mana's relative and gave him a clasp of precious stones of inestimable price and beauty, in order to begin to recompense him for the pleasure that he had just given him.

Mana's relative had only just left when the Queen and Princess Azire sent someone to enquire as to how the Prince has spent the night; it was easy for them to judge by his face that he was not in good health, and he was urged to go to bed. He understood that there would be less constraint than if he went to see the fay, and he consented to do that.

In the afternoon the Queen came to see him, and she talked to him about the marriage of Irolite and Prince Ormond as a matter that she had decided. Parcin Parcinet, who had made the resolution to constrain himself in order not to render his design futile, appeared to approve of the fay's intentions, and only begged her to wait until his health was fully restored, because he wanted to attend the celebration of that great marriage. The fay and Azire, who were in despair at his illness, promised him whatever he wanted, and at least Parcin Parcinet had delayed Irolite's sad wedding for a few days.

The conversation he had had with Azire on the water had bought forward the misfortune of the beautiful Princess he loved so tenderly. Azire had told the Queen what Parcin Parcinet had said, and about his pity for Irolite. The Queen, who never delayed in the execution of her will, had sent for Irolite that same evening, and resolved with Azire to complete the Princess's marriage and hasten her departure before Parcin Parcinet had a more established authority.

After ten days, however, the Prince's faithful slave arrived. What a joy it was for him to find, in the letter that Favorable had written to him, marks of her compassion and amity for him and for Irolite. She sent him a little ring forged from four different metals: gold, silver, bronze and iron; the ring could protect him four times from the persecutions of the cruel Danamo, and Favorable assured the Prince that the evil fay would only be able command that he be pursued as many times as the ring had the power to save him. That good news rendered health to the young Prince, and he sent someone to search for Mana's relative urgently. He gave him a letter that informed Irolite of the fortunate success that they had achieved.

There was no time to lose; the Queen wanted to complete Irolite's marriage in three days; the same evening there was to be a ball in Azire's apartment; Irolite was to be there. Parcin Parcinet could not resolve to appear neglected; he put on magnificent attire and appeared a thousand times ore brilliant than during the day. At first, he dared not speak to the divine Isolite, but what did they not say when their eyes sometimes dared to meet?

Isolite had the most beautiful costume in the world; the fay had given her marvelous jewels, and, only having to have her in the Palace for four more days, had resolved to treated her as she ought to be treated. Her beauty, which was not accustomed to be accompanied by so much ornamentation, seemed marvelous to everyone, and even more so to the amorous Parcin Parcinet; he even judged by some movement of joy that he saw shining in her beautiful eyes that she had received the letter.

Prince Ormond often spoke to Irolite, but he appeared so ugly of face beneath the gold and precious stones with which he was decked that he was not a rival worthy of the jealousy of the young Prince. The ball was nearly at an end when Parcin Parcinet, carried away by his amour, wished with an extreme ardor to be able to speak to his Princess.

Cruel Queen, and you, odious Azire, he said to himself, *will you take away from me any longer the charming pleasure of saying a thousand times to the beautiful Isolite that I adore her? Will you not quit this place, jealous witnesses of my amour? Amour can only triumph in your absence.*

Scarcely had Parcin Parcinet formulated than wish than the fay felt a slight indisposition, and summoned Azire, who went with her into the next room, where Ormond followed them. Parcin Parcinet had on his finger the ring that the fay Favorable had sent him, which could deliver him four times from Danamo's persecutions. He should have kept that assured help for more urgent occasions, but can a violent amour accord with prudence?

The young Prince had no doubt, given the departure of the fay and Azire, that the ring was beginning to serve his amour. He flew to the beautiful Irolite and spoke to her about his tenderness, with expressions more insistent than eloquent. He knew that he had perhaps employed Favorable's charm lightly, but he could not repent of an imprudence that had secured him the sweet pleasure of speaking to his dear Irolite.

Together they decided the place and time when they would finally free themselves from their painful slavery.

The fay and Azire returned after some time. Parcin Parcinet drew away from Irolite with regret. He looked at the fatal ring and perceived that the iron was confounded with the other metals and was no longer visible at all, so he could see all too clearly that he only had three wishes still to make, and resolved to employ them more usefully than the first for the benefit of his Princess. He only made the confidence of his departure to his faithful slave, and spent the rest of the night disposing all the things necessary for his flight.

The next day he seemed tranquil in the Queen's apartment, and even in a livelier humor than usual. He exchanged pleasantries with Prince Ormond regarding his marriage, and acted, in sum, in a manner capable of calming any suspicions that anyone might have regarding his amour.

At two hours after midnight he went into the fay's park; he found his faithful slave there, who, on his master's orders, had brought four of his horses. The Prince did not have long to wait for the beautiful Irolite to appear, walking unsteadily and leaning on Mana. The young Princess was taking the step with difficulty; it had required all of Danamo's cruelties and all Ormond's bad qualities to determine her to do it; amour alone might not have been sufficient.

It was summer, the night was fine and the Moon, which was illuminating the sky with the brilliant stars, provided a light more pleasant that daylight. The Prince advanced hastily; they had no time for long speeches. Parcin Parcinet kissed Irolite's hand tenderly and helped her to mount a horse; fortunately she had a marvelous seat, riding being one of the pleasures that had amused her during her imprisonment. She sometimes rode with her companions in a little wood a short distance from the castle, where the fay had permitted her to go.

After speaking for a few more moments to the Princess, Parcin Parcinet mounted his own horse; the other two were for Mana and the faithful slave. Then the young Prince drew the shiny saber that the fay had given him, swore to the beautiful Irolite to adore her as long as he lived and to die, if necessary, to defend her from her enemies. After those words, they set forth, and it seemed that the Zephyrs were on their side, or that they mistook Irolite for Flora, for they always accompanied them.

Daylight, however, revealed the unexpected news to Danamo.

The ladies who were with Irolite were astonished that she was sleeping later than usual. But, following the order that the sage Mana had given them the previous evening, they dared not go into the Princess's room without being summoned. Mana slept in Irolite's bedroom, and they had left by a little door that opened to a courtyard of the palace where few people went; that door was in Irolite's cabinet; it had been locked, but with a little difficulty, in two or three evenings, they had found a means of opening it.

Finally, the Queen sent someone to Irolite's apparent to summon her to her presence; everyone obeyed the fay's orders; they knocked on the door of the Princess's bedroom; there was no reply. Prince Ormond arrived, having come to take Irolite to the Queen; he was very astonished to see them knocking in vain. He had the door broken down; they went in and, seeing that the little door in the cabinet had been forced, no longer doubted that the Princess had fled the palace.

That news was taken to the Queen; she quivered with anger on hearing it. She ordered that people should search everywhere for Irolite, but it was in vain that they sought information out her flight; no one had been informed of it. Prince Ormond set forth by himself to search for Irolite, and the fay's guards were sent in all diligence along the roads that it was judged that they might have taken.

Meanwhile, Azire perceived that in the general turmoil, Parcin Parcinet had not appeared; she sent people to his apartment immediately, and jealousy finally opened Azire's eyes, causing her to think that the Prince had abducted Irolite.

As she had not yet suspected him of being in love with her, the fay could not believe it, but she went to consult her books, and found that Azire's suspicion was a verity. Meanwhile, the Queen having learned that Parcin Parcinet was not in his apartment, nor anywhere in the palace, she sent men to the castle where Irolite had lived for such a long time, to see whether anything could be found there that might justify or condemn the Prince.

The sage Mana had taken care not to leave anything there that might betray the intelligence of Irolite with Parcin Parcinet, but near the chair on which the young Prince had fainted for such a long time, they found the sash that Azire had given him, which she had detached during his faint, and which neither the Prince nor Mana, occupied with their dolor, had perceived.

What did the vainglorious Azire not feel at the sight of that sash? Her amour and her vanity made her suffer equally; she was excessively afflicted, and had everyone who had been in Irolite's service and that of the Prince put in the fay's prisons. The ingratitude that the Queen believed that Parcin Parcinet had shown to her pushed natural fury to the extreme, and she would willingly have given one of her realms to be able to avenge herself on the two lovers.

Meanwhile, they were pursued in all directions. Ormond and his troop found fresh horses everywhere, by order of the fay; Parcin Parcinet's were weary and no longer responded with their ardor to their master's impatience. Ormond caught up with them as they emerged from a forest.

The first impulse of the young Prince was to go to combat that unworthy rival. He was already running toward him, carrying his saber in his hand, when Irolite shouted to him: "Don't seek unnecessary danger, Prince; obey Favorable's orders."

Those words arrested Parcin Parcinet's anger and, in order to obey the Princess and the fay, he wished that the beautiful Irolite would be in security from the persecutions of the cruel Queen.

Scarcely was that wish formed than the earth opened up between him and Ormond; before his eyes a somewhat deformed little man appeared, magnificently dressed, who made him a sign to follow him. The slope was gentle and very smooth; he descended on horseback with the beautiful Irolite, Mana and the faithful slave, and the earth closed up again.

Ormond, surprised by such an extraordinary event, ran diligently to tell the story to Danamo.

Meanwhile, our young lovers followed the little man along a very obscure route, at the end of which they found a vast palace, which was only illuminated by a large quantity of torches and lamps. They were invited to dismount, and they went into a hall of prodigious grandeur. It was sustained by columns of shiny earth covered with golden ornaments; the walls were of the same material.

A little man covered with jewels was sitting on a golden throne at the back of the hall, surrounded by a large number of people of similar build to the one who had guided the Prince to the place. As soon as he appeared with the charming Irolite, the little man stood up from his throne and said to him: "Come, Prince; the great fay Favorable, who has been my friend for a long time, has asked me to save you from the cruelties of Danamo. I am the King of the Gnomes; be welcome in my palace, with the beautiful Princess who accompanies you."[3]

Parcin Parcinet thanked him for the aid he had just given him. The King and all his subjects were delighted by Irolite's beauty; they took her for a star that had come to illuminate their abode. A magnificent meal was served to Parcin Parcinet and the Princess. The King of the Gnomes honored them; a very harmonious but slightly barbaric music was the evening's entertainment; the charms of Irolite were sung to it, and these lines were repeated several times:

What Star descends beneath the earth
To embellish this tenebrous domain?
Let us not look too long at that bright light,
Which seduces and charms the eyes;

---

[3] The salon writers routinely included in the imaginary world of fays the four categories of "elemental spirits" defined by the sixteenth-century alchemical tract *Liber de Nymphs, sylphis, pygmaeis et salandriis et de ceatris spiriibus*, attributed—probably apocryphally—to Paracelsus: gnomes, sylphs, undines (sometimes called naiads) and salamanders. Their usage served to fill a conspicuous and crucial gap left by the strategic elimination from that imaginary world of all trace of the Christian religion. Where plots required gods as well as subsidiary spirits those evoked were usually those of the Graeco-Roman Pantheon, especially Amour, the Roman equivalent of the Greek Eros, but the supreme power of Destiny is also frequently cited.

The bright star that illuminates us
Is very dangerous to the heart.

After the music, the Prince and Princess were each conducted to a magnificent chamber. Mana and the faithful slave
served them. The next day they were shown the King's palace;
he disposed of all the treasures contained in the earth; it was
impossible to add anything to those riches; there was a confused mass of beautiful things, but art was lacking there in
everything.

The Prince and the Princess remained in that subterranean place for eight days, Favorable having given that order to
the King of the Gnomes. In the meantime, the Prince and Princess were given feasts every day, which were not very elegant,
but magnificent. On the eve of their departure, in order to immortalize the memory of their sojourn in his empire, the King
had their statues erected to either side of his throne. They were
made of gold, and the pedestals were white marble. These
words were written with letters formed of diamonds on the
pedestal of the statue of the Prince:

We no long desire the sight of the sun;
We have seen this Prince;
He is more handsome and brilliant.

And on the pedestal of the statue of the Princess were
these words, written in the same manner:

To the immortal glory
Of the goddess of beauty;
She has descended down here
Under the features and the name of Irolite.

On the ninth day the Prince was given the most beautiful
horses in the world; their harness was gold, covered in diamonds. They emerged from the somber abode of the Gnomes
with the little troop, after having expressed their gratitude to

the King. They found themselves in the same terrain where Ormond had attacked them. The Prince looked at the ring, and only found the silver and the bronze in evidence.

He continued his route with the charming Irolite, and they were hastening to arrive at Favorable's dwelling, where they would finally be safe, when all of a sudden, on emerging from a valley, they encountered a troop of Danamo's guards, who were still searching for them. The guards were preparing to fall upon them when the Prince promptly made his wish, and immediately, a large area appeared between Parcin Parcinet's party and the Fay's, covered with water.

A beautiful semi-naked nymph appeared in the middle of the water in a little boat of woven reeds. She drew nearer to the bank, and begged the Prince and his beautiful mistress to enter the little boat. Mana and the faithful slave followed them; their horses remained on land, and the little boat suddenly sank beneath the water, which made the fay's guards believe that they had perished in wanting to save themselves with their sailors.

Meanwhile, they found themselves in a palace, the walls of which were nothing but large sheets of water, which fell incessantly, forming, halls, rooms and cabinets, and surrounded by gardens, in which a thousand water jets of bizarre shape formed the design of flower beds. There were only Naiads in the empire where they were, who were able to live in that palace, as beautiful as it was singular. In order, therefore, to give a more solid dwelling to the Prince and the beautiful Irolite, the Naiad who was conducting them took them into grottoes of shells in which coral and pearls shone, and all the other riches of the sea. The beds were made of foam; a hundred dolphins guarded Irolite's grotto and twenty whales Parcin Parcinet's.

The naiads admired Irolite's beauty in their turn, and more than one triton was jealous of the gazes and cares that the young Prince attracted. As soon as they were in the Princess's grotto they were served a superb collation of all sorts of glazed fruits; twelve sirens came to charm the anxieties of the young Prince and the beautiful Irolite with their sweet and gracious songs. They finished their concert with these words:

In whatever places Amour leads us.
That God is able to render us happy.
Perfect lovers, charmed by your chain,
In the water's depths make your fire shine.
In whatever place Amour leads us,
That God is able to render us happy.

In the evening there was a feast in which only fish were served, but of a extraordinary size and an exquisite taste; after the meal the Naiads danced a ballet with garments of fish-scales of different colors, which had the most beautiful effect in the world; the horns of tritons, and other instruments unknown to mortals, composed the symphony; it was bizarre but new and very pleasant.

Parcin Parcinet and the beautiful Irolite were in that empire for four days, Favorable having thus ordered; on the fifth day, the Naiads came in a host to escort the Prince and Princess. The two lovers were in a boat made of a single shell, and the naiads, half out of the water, accompanied them as far as the bank of a little river, where Parcin Parcinet found his horses again. He set forth with all the more diligence because he perceived, on looking at his ring, that the silver had disappeared, and nothing remained but the bronze; but they were not far from Favorable's dwelling, so much desired.

They traveled for another three days, but on the fourth, the sun, which had just risen, glinted on distant weapons, an when the men carrying them came a little closer, they recognized them as Prince Ormond and his troop. Danamo had sent them back to pursue them, with orders not to quit them of they found them, not to leave any place where something extraordinary might happen and above all, to try to engage Parcin Parcinet in combat.

Danamo has realized, after Ormond had told his story, that a fay was protecting the Prince and the Princess, but she was so knowledgeable that she did not despair of vanquishing her by means of charms more powerful than hers.

Ormond was delighted to see the Prince and Irolite again, for whom he had been searching with so much difficulty and care. He ran at Parcin Parcinet, sword in hand, in order to try to fight him, following the orders he had received from Danamo. The young Prince also drew his saber, in such a proud manner that Ormod repented of his enterprise more than once; but Parcin Parcinet, who perceived Irolite all in tears and softened by that sight, made his fourth wish.

Immediately, a great fire that rose up almost to the clouds separated Parcin Parcinet and his enemy. That fire made Ormond and his troop retreat. The young Prince and Irolite, still followed by the faithful slave and the sage Mana, found themselves in a palace the sight of which initially caused young Irolite a great deal of fear. It was entirely composed of fire, but she was entirely reassured when she perceived that that she did not feel any heat more ardent than that of the sun, and that the fire only had the brilliance and the flame of the one she feared without having all the other qualities that rendered it insupportable.

A large number of young and beautiful persons clad in garments that appeared to be undulating flames came to receive the Princess and her lover. One of them, whom they judged to be the Queen of the realm by virtue of the respect that was rendered to her, said to them:

"Come, charming Princess, and you, handsome Parcin Parcinet; you are in the realm of the Salamanders; I am its Queen, and it is with pleasure that I am charged with hiding you in my palace for seven days in accordance with the orders of Favorable; I only wish that your sojourn here could be of longer duration."

After these words they were taken into a huge apartment, made of fire like the rest of the palace, and which shone with a brighter light than that of the sun. That evening, in the Queen's abode, there was a great delicate and well-prepared supper; after the meal they went on to a terrace, in order to watch a firework display of marvelous beauty and very singular design, which was held in a large courtyard of the Salamanders' palace. Twelve amours were on as many columns of differently colored marble; six of them appeared to be ready to fire arrows, and the other six were sustaining a large cartouche, on which these words were written in letters of fire:

The beautiful Irolite in this place
Has victory for her share,
However ardent our fires might be,
The one that shines in her eyes
Burns better, and pleases more.

Young Irolite blushed at her own glory, and Parcin Parcinet was delighted that they found her to be as beautiful as she appeared in his own eyes. Meanwhile, the amours fired arrows of fire, which crossed paths in the air, forming in a thousand places the monogram and the beautiful name of Irolite, and raising it as high as the sky.

The seven days that they remained in the palace were spent in pleasures. Parcin Parcinet remarked that all the Salamanders had intelligence and a charming vivacity, and that they were all gallant and amorous; even the Queen did not seem exempt from that passion for a young Salamander of marvelous beauty.

On the eighth day they emerged with regret from an abode in such conformity with their tenderness. They found themselves in a beautiful country. Parcin Parcinet looked at his ring and found that on the four metals, mixed together, these words were engraved:

You have wished too soon.

Those words afflicted the Prince and the young Princess, but they were so close to Favorable's dwelling that they hoped to be able to arrive there that very day. That thought suspended their dolor; they went on, invoking Fortune and Amour, but those are often infidel guides.

Parcin Parcinet was finally close to entering Favorable's lands, but Ormond, following the fay's orders, was not far from the place where the fire had separated them; he had camped behind a wood and sentinels that he had placed on perpetual guard came to warn him that the Prince and the Princess had just reappeared in the plain. Had his men mount up, and caught up with the unfortunate Prince and the divine Irolite that evening.

Parcin Parcinet was not frightened by the large number of those who were attacking him all at the same time. He ran at them with a valor that frightened them.

"I am keeping my promise, beautiful Irolite," he said, drawing his saber. "I shall die for you, or deliver you from your enemies."

After those words he struck the first who presented himself before him and laid him at his feet; but—an unexpected dolor—the marvelous saber that he had obtained from the fay shattered into a thousand pieces. That was what Danamo had anticipated of the young Prince's combat when she gave him weapons; she had charmed them in a particular manner, so that they could not be used against her; the first blow they struck caused them to break into smithereens.

Disarmed, Parcin Parcinet could not resist for long; numbers overwhelmed him; he was captured and laden with chains, and young Irolite had the same destiny.

"Oh, Fay Favorable," cried the Prince, sadly, "abandon me to all Danamo's rigors, but save the beautiful Irolite."

"You have disobeyed the fay," replied a young man of surprising beauty who appeared in the air. "It is necessary for you to bear the penalty; if you had not been prodigal with the aid of Favorable today, we would have saved you forever from the cruelties of Danamo. The entire empire of the Sylphs is afflicted by not having the glory of rendering such a charming Prince and such a beautiful Princess happy."

After those words, he disappeared, and Parcin Parcinet groaned then at his imprudence; he seemed insensible to his own misfortunes, but he resented those of Irolite keenly; the regret of having contributed to them would have made him die of dolor if Destiny had not resolved to make him suffer the most cruel punishments.

Young Irolite gave evidence of a courage worthy of the illustrious blood from which she was descended, and the pitiless Ormond, far from being softened by a spectacle so touching, tried to redouble the misfortune that he was causing her. He caused them to be conducted separately, and took away from them by that means the sad sweet sadness of lamenting together a misfortune without remedy.

After a journey so cruel, they arrived at the Court of the evil fay; she felt a malign joy on seeing the Prince and the young Princess in a state so worthy of giving birth to pity in any other soul than hers. Azire felt some for Parcin Parcinet but she dared not express it in front of the fay.

"I shall, therefore," said the cruel Queen, addressing the young Prince, "have the pleasure of avenging myself for your ingratitude. Instead of mounting the throne that my generosity had destined for you, go into the Prison of the Sea, where I shall end your unhappy life in frightful tortures."

"I prefer the most frightful prison," said the Prince, looking at her proudly, "to the favors of a Queen as unjust as you."

Those words irritated the fay further. She had expected to see him humiliated at her feet. She had him taken to the prison she had destined for him.

Irolite wept on seeing him leave; Azire could not retain her sighs; and the entire Court groaned in secret at an order so pitiless.

As for the beautiful Irolite, the Queen had her taken back to the castle where she had lived for such a long time, had her guarded with care, and treated her with all the inhumanity of which she was capable.

The prison to which the Prince was taken was a frightful tower in the middle of the sea, built on a little desert island,

and he was locked up there, charged with irons, and treated with all the harshness imaginable. What an abode for a Prince worthy of ruling the entire world! The memory of Irolite was his sole occupation; he only appealed to Favorable to help his dear Princess, and he wished a thousand times a day to die in order to expiate alone the fault that he had committed.

His faithful slave was locked in the same prison, but he did not have the satisfaction of serving his illustrious master; Parcin Parcinet only had with him grim soldiers devoted to the fay, who, while obeying her, nevertheless could not help respecting the unfortunate Parcin Parcinet. His youth, his beauty and, above all, his courage, touched them with admiration, which made them regard the Prince as a strong man, above others.

The sage Mana was treated in Irolite's castle like the Prince's slave in the Prison of the Sea. Only Danamo's women approached the Princess, and on the fay's orders they heaped her continuously with further dolor by relating the sufferings of Parcin Parcinet. The Prince's woes made Irolite forget the memory of her own, and everything renewed her tears in a place where she had so often seen the charming Prince swearing an eternal fidelity to her.

Alas, she said to herself, *had you only been less constant, my dear Prince, your infidelity would have cost me my life; but what would it matter? You would be living happily, after three months of suffering.*

One morning, Danamo, who had spent the time making a charm of extraordinary power, sent Irolite two lamps, one of gold and the other of crystal; the one of gold was lighted, and Danamo had her given an order always to keep one of the two lamps lit, but she was told that she could light them in accordance with her choice. Irolite replied with her natural meekness that she would obey, without even seeking to comprehend what the fay's command signified. She carried the two lamps carefully into a cabinet; the one of gold was lit and did not go out all that day, and the next day she lit the other; she continued thus to obey the fay.

She had kept the lamps for fifteen days when her health began to deteriorate; she did not doubt for a moment that her dolor was the cause, and she was told, in order to redouble her distress, that Parcin Parcinet was very ill. What news for Irolite! Her intense dolor and dejection softened all the women who were with her. One evening, when they were all asleep, one of them approached the Princess quietly and, seeing her light the crystal lamp, she said: "What are you doing, great Princess? Extinguish that fatal light; your days are attached to it; save such a beautiful life from the cruelties of Danamo."

"Alas," said the sad Isolite, in a languid fashion, "she has rendered my life so unhappy that it is a kind of favor on the part of the fay to give me the means of ending it." A moment later, however, she continued, with an emotion that brought beautiful colors to her face: "But what life is the golden lamp menacing, the light of which I take the same care to maintain?"

"The days of Parcin Parcinet," replied Danamo's confidante, for she was speaking to the Princess by her order; the evil fay wished to torment her by informing her what her cruel destiny was.

At that news, the dolor of having to take care of herself by terminating the days of Parcin Parcinet caused her to fall unconscious for a long time. She came to, and, in recovering her senses, she also recovered all her despair.

"Odious fay," she said, when she had the strength to speak, "barbaric fay, my death is not sufficient for your fury, you also want to make a Prince who is so dear to me, and is so worthy of the most perfect and the most mutual love, perish by my hand. But death, a thousand times gentler than you, will soon deliver me from all the woes that your rage can invent against a passion so violent and so faithful."

The young Princess wept incessantly over the fatal lamp that was attached to the days of Parcin Parcinet, and only lit her own henceforth; she watched it burn joyfully, as a sacrifice that she was making to her amour and to her lover.

Meanwhile, the Prince was tormented by tortures that all his courage could not resist. The fay had had one of the soldiers guarding him in his prison, and who pretended be sensible to the dolors of the illustrious Prince, tell him that Irolite had consented to marry Prince Ormond a few days after he had been taken to the frightful prison in which he was still groaning, that the Princess seemed content after her marriage, that she had been present at all the fêtes that had been held to celebrate it, and finally, and that she had departed with her husband.

That was the only dolor that the Prince had not expected, and it was also the only one that could possibly be stronger than his constancy.

"What, my dear Irolite," said the sad Prince, "you are Ormond's? You have not even lamented my misfortunes? You have only thought of ending those that my tenderness caused you? Live happily, ingrate Irolite. I still adore you, inconstant as you are, and I want to die for my amour, since you have not wanted me to have the glory of dying for my Princess."

While the unfortunate Parcin Parcinet was afflicting himself thus, and the tender Isolite was giving her life to prolong her lover's, Danamo was touched by Azire's despair. She was dying of dolor for the woes of Parcin Parcinet. Finally, the cruel fay, who saw clearly that, in order to save her daughter's life, it was necessary to pardon the Prince, allowed her to see him, and to promise him all the wealth for which he had once hoped, provided that he would marry her; and the fay resolved to kill Irolite as soon as the Prince had accepted those propositions.

The hope of seeing Parcin Parcinet again rendered life to the sad Azire, and the Queen permitted her to send to Irolite's castle for the golden lamp, which she wanted to keep herself in order to be more assured that it would not be lit. That order appeared more cruel than all the others that afflicted Irolite.

"What anxiety for the life of Parcin Parcinet!" said the women who were with her. "Don't worry so much; he's going to marry Princess Azire, and it's because she is careful of his

life that she has just sent for the lamp to which his life is attached."

The torment of jealousy had been lacking the woes of the
unfortunate Irolite. After those words she sensed it born within
her heart.

Meanwhile, Azire went to see the Prince, in order to offer him marriage and her kingdoms. Then, pretending to be
unaware that he had learned that Irolite had married Ormond,
she tried to convince him by means of that example that he
had pushed confidence too far.

Parcin Parcinet, to whom nothing was precious without
the charming Irolite, preferred prison and his woes to liberty
and empires. Azire was in despair at that refusal and her dolor
rendered her as unhappy as him.

In the meantime, the fay Favorable, who until then had
made a glory of the insensibility of her heart, had been unable
to resist the charms of a young Prince who was then shining in
her Court and was in love with her. At first Favorable could
not resolve to let him hear that the pride of her soul had allowed itself to be vanquished by his care. Finally, she yielded
to the desire no longer to leave him unaware of his triumph.
The pleasure of speaking to the person one loves then appeared to her to be so charming and so worthy of being desired that, approving of the fault that she had criticized so
much, she came diligently to the aid of Parcin Parcinet and the
beautiful Irolite.

A little later and she would no longer have had the time
to aid them; Irolite's fatal lamp was due to run out in ten days,
and Parcin Parcinet's dolor was near to ending his life.

Favorable arrived in Danamo's palace; her power was
well above her rival's, and she had herself obeyed in spite of
the anger of the wicked fay. The Prince was taken out of his
prison, but he only came out after being assured by Favorable
that the beautiful Irolite could still be his. In spite of his pallor
he appeared more handsome than the daylight that he had just
seen again. He went with the fay Favorable to the Princess's
castle. The lamp was now only giving off a feeble light, but

the dying Irolite did not want to consent to its being extinguished until she had been assured of the fidelity of her fortunate lover.

There is no expression vivid enough and tender enough to express the perfect joy they felt on seeing one another again. Favorable enabled them to recover all their charms in a moment, and endowed them with a long life and a constant happiness, but could find nothing to add to their tenderness.

Danamo, furious in seeing her authority overturned, killed herself. The fate of Azire and that of Ormond were placed by the Prince in Irolite's hands; she only wanted to avenge herself by marrying them to one another forever. Parcin Parcinet, as generous as he was faithful, only wanted to recover his father's kingdom, and allowed Azire to reign in Danamo's.

The marriage of the Prince and the divine Irolite was made with an infinite magnificence, and after having expressed their gratitude to Favorable and heaping the slave and the sage Mana with benefits, they departed for their kingdom, where the Prince and the lovable Irolite enjoyed the rare happiness of always burning with a amour that was as tender and as constant in tranquil good fortune as it had been ardent and faithful during their misfortunes.

ANGUILLETTE

To whatever grandeur Destiny elevates those that it favors, there is no felicity exempt from veritable chagrins; one cannot know the fays and be unaware that, however knowledgeable they might be, they have not been able to find the secret of protecting themselves from the misfortune of changing form for a few days every month and taking that of an animal, terrestrial, celestial or one of those that live in water. During those days, so dangerous, when they find themselves prey to the cruelty of humans, they often have difficulty avoiding the perils to which that harsh necessity exposes them.

One of them, who was transformed into an eel, was unfortunately caught by fishermen; she was immediately taken to a little pool of water in the middle of a beautiful meadow, where the fish reserved for the table of the King of the land were kept.

Anguillette—that was the name of the fay—found in that new abode a large number of fine fish destined, like her, only to live for a few more hours; she had heard the fishermen saying to one another that the same evening, the King was to give a great feast, for which those large fish had been carefully chosen.

What news for the unfortunate fay! She cursed destiny a thousand times; she sighed dolorously, but, after hiding for some time in the depths of the water to deplore her particular misfortune, the desire to escape such an urgent danger caused her to look in all directions to see whether there might be any means of getting out of that reservoir and returning to the river that was a short distance away. But the fay looked in vain; the pool of water was too deep for there to be any hope of getting out of it without help, and her dolor increased further on seeing the fishermen who had caught her arrive.

They began casting their nets, and in avoiding them skill-fully, Anguillette was only postponing her death by a few moments.

The youngest of the King's daughters was walking in the meadow at that moment; she approached the pond in order to amuse herself watching the fishing. The sun, which was set-ting, caused radiance to shine in the water; Anguillette's skin, which was very shiny, appeared gilded by the sun in some places, and mingled with various colors. The young Princess noticed that, and, finding her very beautiful, ordered the fish-ermen to catch her and to give her to her; they obeyed, and the unfortunate fay was soon placed in the hands that were going to decide her life.

When the Princess had looked at Anguillette for a few moments, touched by compassion, she ran all the way to the river bank and put her back in the water. That unexpected ser-vice touched the heart of the fay with a keen gratitude. She reappeared on the river and said to the Princess: "I owe you my life, generous Plousine"—that was her name—"but it is great stroke of luck for you. Have no fear," she continued, on seeing the young Princess ready to flee; "I am a fay, and I will make you know the verity of my words by an infinite number of benefits."

As people were accustomed to seeing fays in those days, Plousine was reassured, and paid a great deal of attention to Anguillette's agreeable promises. She had even begun making some response, when the fay interrupted her and said:

"Wait until after you have received my benefits to assure me of your gratitude. Go, young Princess, and come back to-morrow morning to the place where you are. See what wish you want to make, and I shall grant it immediately. Choose a perfect and touching beauty, the greatest and most amiable intelligence, or infinite wealth."

After those words Anguillette hid in the depths of the water, and left Plousine very satisfied with her adventure. She resolved not to make the confidence to anyone of what had just happened to her, for she said to herself: *If Anguillette de-*

ceives me, my sisters will think that it's a fable that I've invented.

After that little reflection, she went to rejoin her retinue, which was only composed of a small number of women; she found them trying to catch up with her.

During the night that followed that day, young Plousine was only occupied with the choice that she ought to make; that of beauty almost tipped the balance, but as she had enough intelligence to want to have more of it, she resolved to ask the fairy for that grace.

She got up at the same time as the day, and ran to the meadow, saying that she was going to pick flowers, in order to make a garland of them that she wanted to present to her mother, the Queen, when she got up.

The women dispersed in the meadow in order to choose the most beautiful and brightest flowers; it was entirely covered with them. Meanwhile, the young Princess ran to the river bank and found a the place where she had seen the fay a perfectly beautiful column of white marble; a moment later the column opened, and the fay emerged, and allowed the Princess to see her. She was no longer a fish but a tall, beautiful woman with a majestic air, whose hair and garments were covered in precious stones.

"I am Anguillette," she said to the young Princess, who was gazing at her with great attention. "I have come to keep my promise; you have made the choice of intelligence; you have it from this very moment and you shall have enough to merit the envy of all those who have, until now, been able to flatter themselves with having it."

After these words, young Plousine felt very different from what she had been a moment before. She thanked the fay with an eloquence that she had never had before.

The fay smiled at the astonishment that the Princess showed in finding so much facility in her speech. "I approve so much of the choice you have made," the gracious Anguillette went on, "in preference to the beauty that flatters of your age, that in order to recompense you I shall give you the beauty that you have so sagely neglected today. Come back tomorrow at the same time; I will give you until then to choose how beautiful you desire to be."

The fay disappeared, and left young Plousine more touched by her good fortune than she had been before. The choice of intelligence was an effect of reason, but the promise of beauty flattered her heart, and what touches the heart is always the most sensible.

After quitting the water's edge, the young Princess went to take the flowers that her women presented to her; she made a very pleasant garland of them and took it to the Queen, but imagine the astonishment of the latter, that of the King and the entire Court on hearing young Plousine speak with a grace that raised hearts. The Princesses, her sisters, tried in vain to find her less intelligent than the others; they too were constrained to astonishment and admiration.

When night came the Princess, occupied by the hope of being beautiful, instead of going to bed, went into cabinet filled with portraits, where, in the guise of goddesses, several Queens and Princesses of the house were painted. All those portraits were beautiful; she hoped that they would aid her to choose a beauty worthy of being requested of the fay.

A Juno was offered to her gaze first of all; she was blonde and had the air appropriate to the representation of the queen of the gods. Pallas and Venus were next to her, that paining representing the judgment of Paris.

The noble pride of Pallas pleased the young Princess greatly, but she thought the beauty of Venus would fix her choice. However, she passed on to the next painting, in which Pomona was seen, semi-recumbent on a bed of grass beneath trees laden with the most beautiful fruits in the world; she seemed so charming that the Princess, who, since that morning, knew everything, was not astonished that a deity had to take on various faces in order to try to please her.

Diana appeared next, such as the poets represent her, with a quiver on her back and a bow in her hand; she was pursuing a deer, followed by a large troop of nymphs. Flora caught the eye a little further on; she appeared to be strolling in a flower bed, the blooms of which, although admirable, were much less brilliant than her complexion. The Graces were seen next; they appeared beautiful and touching.

That painting completed the tour of the cabinet. However, the Princess was struck by the attractiveness of one that was employed as an ornament above the fireplace; it was the goddess of youth; a divine air spread throughout her entire person; her hair was the most beautiful blonde in the world. Her face was agreeably formed, her mouth charming, her figure and breasts perfectly beautiful, and her eyes appeared even more redoubtable for troubling the reason than the nectar with which she seemed to be amusing herself by filling a cup.

"I want," cried the young Princess, after having admired that likeable portrait, "to be as beautiful as Hebe, and for a long time, if possible."

After that wish she returned to her bedroom, where the daylight for which she was waiting appeared to her to be too slow in seconding her impatience.

It finally came, and she returned to the river bank. The fay kept her word; she appeared, and threw a little water over Plousine's face; she became as beautiful as she had desired to be.

A few marine gods had accompanied the fay; their applause was the first effect of the charms of the fortunate Plousine. She looked at herself in the water and could not recognize herself; her silence and her astonishment were then the only marks for her gratitude.

"I have fulfilled all your wishes," the generous fay said to her. "You ought to be content, but I shall not be if I do not surpass all your desires with my benefits. I am giving you, with intelligence and beauty, all the treasures at my disposal; they cannot be exhausted; only wish, whenever you want, for infinite riches, and you will obtain them at that very moment, for you and for all those you think worthy of them."

The fay disappeared, and young Plousine, now as beautiful as Hebe, returned to the palace. Everyone who encountered her was charmed; her arrival was announced to the King, who admired her himself, and it was by her voice and her intelligence that the lovely Princess was recognized. She told the King that a fay had made her all those precious gifts, and no one any longer called her anything but Hebe, because of her perfect resemblance to the beautiful portrait of that goddess.

There were new subjects of hatred against her for her sisters; her intelligence had given then much less jealousy than her beauty. All the Princes who had been touched by their attractions did not hesitate to become infidel. Similarly, all the other beauties of the Court were abandoned. Tears and reproaches did not stop those lovers, and that procedure, which then appeared so surprising, has, it is said, since passed into custom. All of them burned in Hebe's presence, but her heart remained insensible.

In spite of the hatred of her sisters, she neglected nothing that might please them; she wished for so many treasures for the eldest—for wishing and giving were the same thing for her—that the greatest King of the region asked for that Princess in marriage and espoused her with incredible magnificence.

The King, Hebe's father, wanted to send an army on campaign; the wishes of the beautiful Princess enabled all those enterprises to succeed, and his kingdom was filled with immense riches, which rendered him the most redoubtable of all kings.

However, the divine Hebe, becoming bored by the tumult of the Court, wanted to go and spend a few months in an agreeable house a short distance away from the capital city. She had banished magnificence therefrom, but everything there was elegant, and of a charming simplicity. Nature alone took care of embellishing the promenades; art had not been employed.

A wood whose paths had something savage about them, intercut by streams and little torrents that made natural cascades, surrounded that beautiful retreat. Young Hebe often walked in that solitary wood.

One day when she sensed an ennui and a languor that scarcely ever quit her increasing in her heart, she wanted to seek the cause of it; she sat down on the grassy bank of a stream, the noise of which entertained her reverie.

What chagrin, she asked herself, *has come to trouble the excess of my felicity? What Princess in the entire world enjoys a happiness as perfect as mine? By virtue of the generosity of the fay, I have everything that I wished; I can heap with wealth everyone that surrounds me; everyone I see adores me, and my heart only knows tranquil sentiments. No, I cannot imagine whence comes the insupportable ennui that has opposed itself for some time to the happiness of my life.*

That reflection occupied the young Princess incessantly. In the end, she resolved to go to the bank of Anguillette's river, in order to try to see her

The fay, accustomed to flatter her wishes, appeared on the water. It was one of those days when she was metamorphosed into a fish. "I always see you again with pleasure, young Princess," she said to Hebe. "I know that you have just spent some time in a rather solitary dwelling, and you appear to me to be in a languor that does not befit your fortune. What's wrong, Hebe? Make me that confidence."

"Nothing's wrong," said the young Princess. "You've heaped me with too many benefits for anything to be lacking to a happiness that you have made your work."

"You're trying to deceive me," said the fay. "I can see that easily. You're no longer content. But what can you still desire? Merit my gifts by a sincere confession," the gracious fay added, "and I promise you to accomplish all your wishes."

"I don't know what I desire," replied the charming Hebe." Lowering her beautiful eyes, she continued: "I feel, however, that I lack something, and that what I lack is absolutely necessary to my happiness."

"Ah" cried the fay. "It's amour that you desire; that passion alone can make one think as strangely as you are doing." The prudent fay continued: "It's a dangerous disposition. You want amour, and you shall have it; hearts are only too disposed naturally to acquire it; but I warn you that you will invoke me in vain to make that fatal passion cease, which you believe to be so sweet a happiness; my power does not extend as far as that."

"It doesn't matter," said the young Princess, promptly, while smiling and blushing simultaneously. "What shall I do with all the good things that you have given me, if I don't make the felicity of another in my turn?"

The fay sighed at that speech, and hid in the depths of the water.

Hebe resumed the route to the solitude with a hope that was already beginning to calm her ennui; the fay's threats made her anxious but those sage reflections were soon chased away by others, more dangerous but much more pleasant.

When she arrived she found a courier from the King, who summoned her to return that same day in order to attend a fête that he was preparing for the following day. A few hours after receiving it, she set forth, in order to return to the Court. The King and Queen received her there with pleasure and told her that, a foreign Prince who was traveling having arrived a few days before, they wanted to put on a fête for him, in order that he could say in other lands how much magnificence shone in their kingdom.

By virtue of a presentiment that was unfamiliar to her, young Hebe first asked Princess Ilerie, her sister, whether the foreigner was likeable.

"Nothing similar has yet been offered to our eyes," the Princess replied.

"Describe him for me," said Hebe, emotionally.

"He is such as Heroes are painted," said Ilerie. "His figure is fine, his air is grand, his eyes are full of a fire of which more than one insensible person of this Court has already recognized the power. He has the most beautiful face in the world; his hair is closer to black than blonde, and he only has to show himself to be sure of attracting the attention of all those who see him."

"You have made a very advantageous portrait," said young Hebe. "Is it not a trifle flattering?"

"No, my sister," replied Princess Ilerie, with a sigh that she could not retain. "Perhaps you will find him only too worthy to please."

That evening the Prince appeared in the Queen's apartment and was introduced to the beautiful Hebe, whom he had not yet seen. Never had two hearts been so promptly or so sharply touched, and never that any had so much reason to be.

The conversation only concerned indifferent things, but it was brilliant and agreeable, sustained by the vivacity immediately inspired by the desire to please.

The Queen retired, and the beautiful Hebe, as soon as she had paid a few moments of attention to her sentiments, recognized that she had lost the tranquility of which she did not yet know the value.

"Oh, Anguillette," she cried, as soon as she was alone, "what object have you permitted to come to offer itself to my gaze? Your sage advice is destroyed by his presence. Can you not give me the strength to resist such touching charms? But perhaps their power even surpasses that of a fay."

Hebe slept little that night; she got up quite early, and the care of adorning herself for the evening's fête amused her all day with an attention she had not previously known, because, for the first time, she wanted to please.

The young foreigner, occupied by the same desire, neglected nothing to appear likeable in the eyes of the charming Hebe.

Princess Ilerie also forgot nothing that might please; she had a thousand beauties, and when people saw her without Hebe, they thought her the most beautiful person in the world; but the latter Princess effaced everyone.

There was a magnificent ball that evening in the Queen's apartments; a magnificent feast followed it, and the young foreigner would have noticed its prodigious magnificence if he had been able to look at anything other than the beautiful Hebe.

After the meal, a brilliant and singular illumination caused a new daylight to appear in the east in the gardens of the palace. People went out in order to enjoy the pleasure of a stroll; the amiable foreigner gave her hand to the Queen, but that honor did not compensate him for the chagrin of being distanced from his Princess for a few moments. The trees were covered with festoons of flowers, and the lamps that contained the illumination were disposed in a manner that everywhere, they represented bow, arrows and the other arms of Amour, and in a few places they formed lines of writing.

They entered a little wood, illuminated like the rest of the gardens; the Queen sat down on the edge of a pleasant fountain, around which grassy seats had been placed ornamented with garlands, carnations and roses. While the Queen chatted with the King and a large group of courtiers who surrounded them, the Princesses amused themselves looking at a few characters formed by the little lamps of the illumination. At that moment, the amiable foreigner was close to the beautiful Hebe; she turned her gaze toward a place where arrows were represented, and she read the words that were inscribed beneath them:

Some are invincible.

"They are the ones that depart from the eyes of the divine Hebe," said the stranger, promptly, looking at her tenderly.

The Princess heard him, and was embarrassed, but her embarrassment appeared to the Prince to be a fortunate presage for his amour, for he did not remark anger therein.

The fête was concluded by a thousand new pleasures. The charms of the stranger had touched Ilerie's heart too keenly for her to take a long time perceiving that he loved someone other than her. Before the arrival of Hebe at the Court, the Prince had paid some attention to her, but since then, he had only been occupied with his tenderness.

Meanwhile, the young stranger tried to touch the heart of the beautiful Princess by means of his amour. He was amorous and lovable; destiny forced her to love, and the fay had abandoned her to the penchant of her heart. With so many excuses for surrender, she could not struggle against herself for long.

The charming stranger told her that he was the son of a King and that his name was Atimir. That name was known to the Princess; the Prince had done marvelous things in a war between the two kingdoms, and as they had always been enemies, he had not wanted to appear at the Court of Hebe's father under his true name.

After a conversation in which the heart of the young Princess completed its capture by the poison, so sweet and so dangerous, of which the fay had spoken, she gave Atimir permission to reveal his rank and his amour to the King. The young Prince was transported by joy; he ran to the King's apartment and spoke to him with all the ardor that his tenderness inspired.

The King took him to the Queen's apartment; the marriage being liable to establishing a constant peace in the realm, the beautiful Hebe was promised to her happy lover as soon as he had received the consent of his father.

That news spread, and Princess Ilerie felt a dolor equal to her jealousy; she wept and groaned, but it was necessary to constrain herself and hide her futile regrets.

The beautiful Hebe and Atimir saw one another incessantly then; their tenderness was augmented every day, and in those happy times the Princess could not understand why the fays did not always employ their science to make mortals sense amour when they wanted to make their felicity.

An ambassador from Atimir's father arrived at the Court then; he was awaited with an extreme impatience. He brought the consent that had been requested, and everything was prepared for the great marriage. Thus, Atimir no longer had any subject for dread—a dangerous state for a lover whom one wants to conserve ever faithful.

As soon as the Prince was assured of his happiness he became less sensible to it. One day, when he was going to join the beautiful Hebe in the palace gardens, he heard the voices of women in a honeysuckle arbor. He heard his name, and that gave him the curiosity to learn more, so he approached the arbor quietly, and easily recognized the voice of Princess Ilerie.

"I shall die before that fatal day, my dear Cleonice," she was saying, to a young woman sitting next to her. "The gods will not permit that I see the ingrate I love united with the excessively fortunate Hebe; my torments are too painful to let me live for long."

"But Madame," replied the young woman who was with her, "Prince Atimir is not unfaithful; he did not make you any promises. It's Destiny alone that has caused your misfortunes, and among so many Princes who adore you, perhaps you would find one more lovable than him, if a deadly prejudice were not occupying your heart."

"Is there anyone in all the world as lovable as him?" Ilerie said, an added, with a sigh: "Of all the gifts with which you have heaped the fortunate Hebe, powerful fay, I am only jealous any longer of the tender amour that Atimir has conceived for her."

The Princess's speech was interrupted by her tears. How happy she would have been if she had known how they had touched Atimir's heart!

She got up to leave the arbor, and the Prince hid behind some trees in order not to be perceived. Ilerie's tears and passion had moved him, but he thought they were impulses of pity in favor of a Princess that he had rendered unhappy involuntarily. He went to find Hebe, and her charms then suspended any other movement in his heart.

While traversing the gardens to take the Princess back to the palace he encountered something under his feet. He picked it up, and saw that it was a magnificent notebook. He was not far from the arbor where he had overheard the conversation, and he feared that by showing her the notebook he might give Hebe some knowledge of that adventure. He hid it, and the Princess did not notice it, being occupied at that moment in making an adjustment to her hair.

That evening, Ilerie did not appear in the Queen's apartment; it was said that she had felt ill on returning from her walk. Atimir understood that she wanted to hide the disorder in which he had seen her in the arbor; that thought increased his pity for her.

As soon as he was in his apartment he opened the notebook he had found, and on the first leaf he saw a figure formed by a double A crowned with myrtle and sustained by two little amours, one of which appeared to be wiping his tears with his blindfold and the other breaking his arrows.

The sight of that figure caused an emotion to the young Prince; he knew that Ilerie drew perfectly, and he promptly turned the page in order to be enlightened further. On the reverse he found these words:

> *Redoubtable Amour has made me see your attractions,*
> *Of my placid heart they have troubled the peace,*
> *Oh, what injustice is yours;*
> *On me, cruelly, you have tried the features*
> *With which you want to lure another.*

The handwriting, which he recognized, proved only too well that the notebook belonged to Princess Ilerie. He was touched by such tender sentiments, which, far from being sustained by his amour and his attentions, had only been supported by hope. Those lines made him remember that before Hebe's arrival in the Court he had found Ilerie likeable. He began to regard himself as infidel to that Princess, and he became so, only too veritably, for the charming Hebe.

He fought his first impulses, but his heart was accustomed to being fickle, and such a dangerous habit can rarely be corrected.

He threw Ilerie's notebook on a table, resolved not to look at it any longer, but he picked it up again a moment later, involuntarily, and found a thousand things therein that completed rendering Ilerie triumphant over the divine Hebe.

A thousand confused sentiments occupied the Prince's heart all night. In the morning he was in the company of the King, who informed him of the day he had chosen for his marriage with Hebe. Atimir replied with an embarrassment that the King, knowing little of the hearts of men, mistook for a mark of his amour. It was an effect of his infidelity.

The King wanted to go to the Queen's apartments. The Prince was obliged to go with him. They had not been there long when Princess Ilerie appeared, with a languor of whose cause the fickle Atimir was no longer unaware, which made her appear more lovable in his eyes. He approached her and talked to her for a long time; he made her understand that he was no longer unaware of the sentiments that she had for him. He explained himself with tenderness; that was too much felicity for Ilerie. In fact, what means is there of receiving without disturbance a happiness so sensible and so unexpected?

The charming Hebe then came into the Queen's apartment. The sight of her made Princess Ilerie and the fickle Atimir blush.

"How beautiful she is," said Ilerie, looking at the Princess with an emotion that she could not hide. "Flee her, Seigneur, or finish taking away my life."

The Prince could not respond to her, Hebe having approached them with a grace and charms that made a thousand reproaches to the ingrate Atimir. He could not sustain them for long, and he quit the Princess, to whom he said that he had to dispatch a courier to his father the King. She was so prejudiced in Atimir's favor that she did not notice a few glances that escaped him in favor of Ilerie. While the latter was secretly triumphant, the beautiful Hebe learned from the King and the Queen that in three days she would be Atimir's wife. How unworthy he now was of the sentiment to which that news gave birth in the lovable Hebe's heart!

Although occupied with his infidel ardor, the Prince spent part of the day with Hebe. Ilerie was a witness to that, and thought she would die of jealousy a thousand times; her amour had been redoubled as soon as it had sensed hope.

When he went back to his apartment that evening, the Prince received a note from the hand of an unknown man; he opened it precipitately and found these words:

I am yielding to a passion a thousand times stronger than my reason, since there is no longer occasion to hide from you the sentiments that hazard has revealed to you; come, Prince, come to learn what resolution the tender amour that you have given me has determined. What happiness it will be for me, if it does not cost me my life.

The man who had brought the note to the Prince told him that he was destined to lead him to where Princes Ilerie was waiting for him. Atimir did not hesitate for a moment to follow him, and after various detours he was taken into a little pavilion that was at the end of a covered pathway. The pavilion was illuminated, and he found Ilerie there with one of her women; the others were walking in the garden; when she had retired to that cabinet they only entered by her order.

Ilerie was sitting on a pile of crimson velvet cushions embroidered with gold; her attire was elegant and magnificent; the fabric was yellow and silver. Her hair, which was black and perfectly beautiful, was raised by ribbons of the same color as her dress, with yellow diamond clasps. At the sight of her, Atimir could not persuade himself that it was shameful for him to become infidel, and he knelt down close to Ilerie, gazing at her with a tenderness that marked well enough the movements of his heart.

"Prince," she said to him, "it is not to persuade you to break your engagement that I have made you come here; I know only too well that it is decided, and that a few words with which you wanted to flatter my woe and my tenderness do not permit me to believe that you wanted to abandon Hebe for me." With tears that completed the seduction of Atimir's heart, she continued: "But I no longer want a life that you have rendered so dolorous, and I shall sacrifice it without regret to my amour."

She showed him a little golden bottle that she was holding in her hand, and added: "This poison will save me from the frightful torture of seeing you as Hebe's husband."

"No, beautiful Ilerie," cried the fickle Prince. "I shall not be her husband; I will quit everything in order to please you; I love you a thousand times more than I loved Hebe, and in spite of my duty and my solemnly promised faith, I am ready to take you to places where nothing will constrain our amour."

"Oh, Prince," said Ilerie, with a sigh. "I have confided myself to an infidel, then."

"He will never be for you," said Atimir, "and the King, your father, who gave me Hebe, will not refuse me the lovable Ilerie, when she is in my power."

"Let us go, then, Atimir," said the Princess, after a few moments of silence. "Let us go where my destiny and yours leads us; whatever dolor it might cost me, nothing can balance in my heart the sweet pleasure of being loved by the man I love."

After those words, they made a few arrangements together for their departure; there was no time to lose. It was decided for the following night. They separated with difficulty, and in spite of Atimir's oaths, Ilerie still feared Hebe's charms. For the rest of the night and throughout the following day she was always occupied with that dread.

Meanwhile, the Prince gave in a very short time all the orders necessary to render his departure secret. The next day, as soon as everyone in the palace had retired, the Prince went to met Ilerie in the pavilion in the garden, where she was waiting for him, alone with Cleonice.

They set forth, and put an incredible diligence into leaving the kingdom.

In the morning that news was declared by a letter that Ilerie had written to the Queen and one that Atimir had written to the King. They were touching, and it was easy to see that amour had dictated them.

The King and Queen were extremely angry, but no words can describe the sharp dolors of the unfortunate and charming Hebe. What despair! How many tears! How many pleas to the fay Anguillette to terminate the woes, so cruel, that she had once predicted. But the fay kept her word. In vain, Hebe returned to the river bank; Anguillette did not appear. She abandoned her entirely to the most frightful despair.

The Princes whom the good fortune of the ingrate Atimir had driven away sensed their hopes reborn then, but their attentions and their amour appeared to the faithful Hebe to be further tortures.

The King desired passionately that she choose a husband, and pressed her hard on several occasions, but that duty appeared too cruel to her tenderness, and she resolved to flee her father's kingdom. Before her departure, however, she returned once again to look for Anguillette.

This time, the fay could not resist the beautiful Hebe's tears. She appeared. At the sight of her, the Princess renewed her tears, and did not have the strength to speak to her.

"You finally know," the fay said to her, "what the fatal felicity is that I always wanted to refuse you, but Hebe, Atimir has punished you too much for not having wanted to follow my advice. Go, flee this place, where everything recalls the memory of your tenderness; you will find a ship on the sea that will take you to the only place in the world where you can be cured of this unfortunate amour that is driving you to despair. But remember," Anguillette added, raising her voice, "when your heart becomes tranquil again, never to seek the fatal presence of Atimir; it would cost you your life."

Hebe wanted to see the Prince again, no matter what price amour made her pay for that pleasure, but a residue of reason and concern for her glory made her resolve to accept the fay's propositions. She thanked her for that last benefit, and departed the following day for the shore of the sea, followed by those of her women that she trusted the most.

She found Anguillette's ship. It was gilded all over; the masts were marquetry of a marvelous design and the sails of a silver fabric tinted with rose; and on everything that could be seen, the word *Liberty* was inscribed. The sailors were dressed in clothes the same color as the sails; everything in that place seemed to respire the sweetness of liberty.

The Princess went into a magnificent chamber; the furniture was admirable and the paintings perfectly beautiful, but she was no less afflicted in that new abode than in her father's Court. People tried to amuse her with a thousand pleasures, but she was not yet in a state to pay attention to them.

One day, when she was passing the time looking at the pictures in her chamber, in one that represented a landscape, she noticed a young shepherdess who, with a cheerful expression, was cutting nets in order to render liberty to a large number of birds caught therein; a few of those little animals, having already escaped, seemed to be flying toward the heavens with a marvelous rapidity. All the other paintings represented similar subjects; nothing there spoke of amour, and everything praised the charms of liberty.

"What!" cried the Princess. "Will my heart always be insensible to a happiness so mild, and for which my reason makes so many wishes?"

The unhappy Hebe spent her life thus occupied with her tenderness and the desire to forget it.

The ship had been sailing for a month without stopping when, one morning when the Princess was on deck, she perceived in the distance a land that appeared to her to be very beautiful. The trees were of a surprising height and beauty, and when the ship came close enough, she noticed that they were all covered with birds, the plumage of which was vivid and brilliant; they were making charming concerts; their songs were soft, and they seemed to be fearful of making too much noise.

The ship moored on that beautiful shore; the Princess descended with her women, and as soon as she had respire the air of the island, by virtue of an unknown power, she sensed her heart becoming tranquil, and allowed herself to be surprised by an agreeable slumber that closed her lovely eyes for some time.

That agreeable land, which she did not know, was the Peaceful Isle. The fay Anguillette, a near relative of the Princes who reigned there, had attached to it two thousand years before the fortunate gift of curing unhappy passions; it is even said that the gift still endures there, but the difficulty is in being able to land on the island in question.

The Prince who was ruling then was descended in a direct line from the celebrated Princess Carpillon and her charming husband, of whose marvels a modern fay more knowledgeable and more polite than those of antiquity has told the story so elegantly.[4]

While the beautiful Hebe was enjoying a repose whose sweetness she had not savored for six months, the Prince of the Peaceful Island was riding in his chariot in the wood that bordered the sea shore. It was drawn by four young white elephants, and was surrounded by a part of his Court. The sleeping Princess struck his gaze; her beauty surprised him. He descended from his chariot precipitately, with a vivacity that he had never felt before. At that sight he was smitten with all the amour that Hebe's charms were worthy of inspiring.

The noise woke her up, and, on opening her lovely eyes, she caused the young Prince to remark a thousand new beauties. He was then nineteen, the same age as Hebe; his beauty was perfect; a thousand graces were distributed over his person. His height was above the average of men and his hair, which descended in thick curls all the way to his belt, was the same color as Hebe's. His costume was made of feathers of a thousand different colors; his overcoat was a kind of transparent trailing mantle made entirely of swan feathers, attached at the shoulders by the most beautiful gemstone in the world; his belt was studded with diamonds, and suspended therefrom by means of little golden chains was a small saber covered in rubies. A kind of helmet, made of feathers, like the rest of his attire, covered his beautiful head, and to one side of the hel-

---

[4] "La Princesse Carpillon" by Madame d'Aulnoy, published in *Contes nouveaux ou fées à la mode* (1698).

met, attached by a diamond of prodigious size, were heron plumes, which gave it a great deal of grace.

The Prince was the first object presented to the young Princess when she awoke; he appeared to her to be worthy of her gaze, and for the first time in her life she looked at someone other than Atimir with some attention.

"Everything assures me," said the Prince of the Peaceful Isle to the Princess, "that you can only be the divine Hebe. What other could have so many charms?"

"Who, Seigneur," replied the young Princess, getting up and blushing at the same time, "can have told you so soon that I had landed on this island?"

"A powerful fay," said the young King, "who wanted to make me the happiest Prince in the world, and this land the most fortunate, promised to bring you here, and has even permitted me more glorious hopes—but I sense," he added, sighing, "that my destiny will depend far more on your good will than hers."

After these words, to which she replied with a great deal of intelligence, the Prince invited her to climb into his chariot, in order to be conducted to the palace. Out of respect, he did not want to take the place next to her; but as she had understood by his speech and its consequence that he was the King of the island, she obliged him to sit beside her.

Never had anything so beautiful appeared together in the same chariot. The Prince's entire Court, at that sight, could not help giving them abundant applause. On the way, the young Prince entertained Hebe with a great deal of wit and tenderness, and the Princess, satisfied at having recovered her tranquil heart, matched all his vivacity.

They arrived at the palace, which was not far from the sea; long and beautiful avenues surrounded by freshwater canals led to it; it was built entirely of ivory and covered in agate.

The Prince's guards were arranged in rows in all the courtyards; in the first they were clad in yellow plumes; they had silver quivers, bows and arrows. In the second courtyard they were all clad in feathers the color of fire, with sabers garnished with gold and ornamented with turquoises. They passed into the third courtyard, where the guards were dressed in white plumes; in their hands they were holding painted and gilded half-pikes ornamented with garlands of flowers. There was never any war in that land, so no one carried very redoubtable weapons.

When he descended from his chariot the Prince conducted the lovable Hebe into a magnificent apartment. The Court was numerous; the ladies there were beautiful, the men elegant and well-made, and although all the inhabitants of the Peaceful Isle were only clad in feathers, the art of arranging the colors rendered them very agreeable.

That evening the Prince of the Peaceful Isle gave a superb feast for the beautiful Hebe, which was followed by a concert of soft flutes, lutes, theorbos and harpsichords. They did not like instrument that made loud noises in that palace; the symphony was very gracious. When it had been going on for some time, a very beautiful voice sang these words:

I swear to your attractions an immortal ardor;
What happiness can be sweeter
Than that of wearing such a beautiful chain?
I will love tenderly, my heart will be faithful,
And the prize will depend on you.

The Prince looked at Hebe while they were being sung with an expression tender enough to persuade her that he was thinking everything that the lines had just said to her.

When the music had finished, as it was late, the Prince of the Peaceful Isle conducted the Princess to the apartment that he had destined for her; it was the finest of all those in the palace. She found a large number of ladies there whom the Prince had nominated for the honor of being with her.

The Prince quit the beautiful Hebe the most amorous of all men. The Princess was put to bed; the ladies withdrew, and the only ones who remained in the bedroom were those she had brought with her.

"Who would believe it?" she said to them, as soon as she was at liberty. "My heart is peaceful! What god has calmed my torments? I no longer love Atimir; I can think, without dying of dolor, that perhaps he is Ilerie's husband. Is everything I can see not a dream?" A moment later, she went on: "No, even my dreams have not accustomed me to being so tranquil."

After that, she rendered a thousand thanks to Anguillette, and then went to sleep.

When she awoke the next day, as she opened a curtain of her bed, the fay became visible to her with a gracious expression that she had not seen on her face since the fatal day when she had asked for amour.

"Finally, I have guided you here fortunately," the amiable fay said to her. "Your heart is free, so it will become content. I have cured you of a cruel passion; but Hebe, can I count on the frightful torments to which you have been exposed to make you shun forever the places where you might see the ingrate Atimir again?"

What did the young Princess not promise the fay? How many oaths did she not swear against amour and her infidel lover?

"At least remember your promises," said Anguillette, with an expression imprinted with respect. "You will perish with Atimir if you ever seek to see him again; but everything ought to remove that fatal desire from your life. I can no longer hide from you what I have resolved in your favor; the Prince of the Peaceful Isle is my relative; I protect his person and his empire. He is young, he is lovable, and no Prince in the world is so worthy to be your husband. Reign, then, beautiful Hebe, in his heart and in his realm. Your father, the King, consents to it; I was in his palace yesterday; I informed him and the Queen of the present state of your fortune, and they have handed over the care of it to me, absolutely."

The Princess had a great desire to ask the fay what had been learned subsequent to her departure about Ilerie and Atimir, but she dared not risk displeasing her after so many benefits. She employed in order to thank her all the intelligence that she had given her.

People then came into the Princess's bedroom; the fay disappeared. As soon as Hebe had got up, twelve perfectly beautiful children dressed as amours brought her on behalf of the Prince twelve crystal baskets filled with the most beautiful and most agreeable flowers in the world. Those flowers were garnished with gemstones of all colors, of a marvelous beauty. In the first basket that was presented to her, she found this note:

To the divine Hebe

Yesterday, I swore to you a thousand times that I love you;
Of those oaths formed by my extreme tenderness,
I shall never lose the lovable memory;
Amour dictated them to me himself,
And your charms will make them kept.

After what the fay had ordered the Princess to do, she understood full well that she ought to receive the attentions of her new lover as those of a Prince who would soon be her husband.

She received the little Amours graciously, and scarcely had she sent them away than twenty-four dwarfs appeared, bizarrely but magnificently dressed, charged with further presents. They were garments entirely made of feathers, but the colors, the workmanship and the precious stones were so beautiful that the Princess confessed that she had never seen anything so elegant.

She chose a rose-colored one to put on that day. Her hair was ornamented with a bouquet of plums of the same color; she appeared so charming with that new ornament that the

Prince of the Peaceful Isle, who came to see her as soon as she was dressed, sensed the passion that he had for her redouble again. The whole Court hastened to come and admire the Princess.

In the evening, the Prince proposed to the beautiful Hebe that they go down into the gardens of the palace, which were admirable. During the walk, the Prince told Hebe that the fay had made him hope for her arrival on the Peaceful Isle four years ago.

"But some time after that," the Prince added, "when I asked her urgently about the effect of her promises, she seemed sad and said to me: 'Princess Hebe is destined by her father for someone other than you, but if my science does not deceive me, she will not belong to the Prince who has been chosen to be her husband. I will bring you news of her.'

"A few months later the fay came back to this island. 'Destiny favors you,' she said to me. 'The Prince who was to be Hebe's husband will not be, and in a short time you will see in this place the most beautiful Princess in the word.'"

"It's true," said Hebe, blushing, "that I was to marry the son of a King, a neighbor of my father's estates, but after various events, the amour that he had for the Princess my sister resolved him to abduct her from my father's kingdom."

The Prince of the Peaceful Isle said a thousand tender things to the beautiful Hebe about his fortunate destiny, which, in accord with the fay, had brought her to his island. She listened to him with all the more pleasure because that speech interrupted the story of her adventures; she feared not being able to talk about her infidel lover without allowing him to remark the tenderness that she had had for him.

The Prince of the Peaceful Isle took Hebe into a grotto that was extremely ornamented and embellished with marvelous water jets. The depths of the grotto were obscure. There were a large number of niches there filled with statues, which represented nymphs and shepherds, but they could barely be distinguished.

When the Princess had been in the grotto for a few moments he heard an agreeable sound of musical instruments. A brilliant illumination, which suddenly appeared, allowed the Princess to see that some of the statues formed that concert, and the others came to dance a very elegant and very well-interpreted ballet before her, mingled with tender and agreeable songs. All the actors of that diversion had been placed in the depths of the grotto, in order to surprise the Princess more agreeably.

After the ballet, savages came to serve a superb collation under a bower of jasmine and orange blossom.

The fête had just finished when the fay Anguillette suddenly appeared in mid-air, on a chariot harnessed to four swans. She got down and announced to the Prince of the Peaceful Isle a charming happiness, by telling him that he would become Hebe's husband, and that the beautiful Princess had promised to consent to it.

Transported by joy, the Prince hesitated at first as to whom he owed his first thanks, Hebe or Anguillette, and although joy does not say such touching things as dolor, he nevertheless acquitted himself with intelligence and grace.

The fay did not want to quit the Prince and the Princess again until the day destined for their marriage. That was to be three days hence. She gave superb presents to the beautiful Hebe and the Prince of the Peaceful Isle.

Finally, on the day that she had marked, they went to the Temple of Hymen, followed by all the Court and an infinite number of the island's inhabitants. The Temple was formed entirely of interlaced olive branches and palms, which never withered, thanks to the power of the fay.

Hymen was represented there by a white marble statue crowned with roses; it was erected on an altar solely ornamented with flowers and supported on a little Amour of charming beauty, who, with a laughing expression, was represented with a crown of myrtle.

Anguillette, who had built the Temple, wanted it to be very simple, in order to mark that Amour alone can render

Hymen happy. The only difficulty is to unite them; as that is a miracle worthy of a fay, she had joined them forever on the Peaceful Isle, and, contrary to the custom of other realms, one could be a spouse, amorous and constant there.

In that Temple of Hymen, the beautiful Hebe, conducted by Anguillette, pledged her faith to the Prince of the Peaceful Isle and received his with pleasure. She did not have for him the involuntary penchant that she had felt for Atimir, but her heart, exempt from passion for now, received that spouse by order of the fay, as a Prince worthy of her by virtue of his person, and even more so by virtue of his amour.

That marriage was celebrated by a thousand feasts, and Hebe found herself happy with a Prince who adored her.

Meanwhile, Hebe's father, the King, had received ambassadors on the part of Atimir, asking him for permission for him to marry Ilerie. Atimir's father was dead; he was the absolute master in his realm. The Princess he had abducted was granted to him joyfully.

After that marriage Queen Ilerie asked her father the King and her mother the Queen, via new ambassadors, for permission to come to the Court herself in order to beg them for pardon for a fault that amour had made her commit, and that Atimir's merit ought to excuse. The King agreed to that, and Atimir came with her; a thousand pleasures marked the day of their arrival.

Shortly afterwards, the beautiful Hebe and her charming spouse also sent ambassadors to the King and the Queen, to give them the news of their marriage; Anguillette had already informed them, but the ambassadors were received with no less pleasure and magnificence.

Atimir was with the King when they presented themselves for the first time. The lovable idea of Hebe could never be effaced absolutely from a heart where it had reigned with so much empire; Atimir sighed involuntarily at the account of the happiness of the Prince of the Peaceful Isle; he even accused Hebe of being inconstant, without thinking about how many reasons he had given her for becoming so.

The ambassadors from the Prince of the Peaceful Isle returned, heaped with honors and presents; they told their Prince and their Princess how the King and Queen had expressed their joy at their happy marriage. But—O story too sincere!—they told Princess Hebe that Princess Ilerie and Atimir were at the Court. Those names, so dangerous to her repose, renewed her anxiety. She was happy, but can mortals conserve a constant happiness?

She could not resist the impatience she felt to return to her father's Court; it was, she told herself, only to see the Queen her mother again; she even believed it, and how often, when one is in love, does one deceive oneself regarding one's own sentiments?

In spite of the fay's threats, made in order to oblige her to shun the places where she might see Atimir again, she proposed that voyage to the Prince of the Peaceful Isle. At first he refused; Anguillette had forbidden him to allow Hebe to leave his kingdom. She continued to beg him. He adored her; he was unaware of the passion that she had had for Atimir. Can one refuse anything to the person one loves? He thought he would please the beautiful Hebe by his blind obedience; he gave orders for her departure; and never had so much magnificence been seen as that which appeared in her equipage and her ships.

The sage Anguillette, indignant at the scant respect that Hebe and the Prince of the Peaceful Isle had for her orders, abandoned them to their destiny and did not appear in order to give them her sage advice, of which they had profited so little.

The Prince and the Princess embarked, and after a very fortunate navigation they arrived at the Court of Hebe's father.

The joy of seeing the beautiful Princess again was very sensible to the King and the Queen; they were charmed by the Prince of the Peaceful Isle; their arrival was celebrated by a thousand fêtes throughout the kingdom; but Ilerie shivered on learning of Hebe's return; it was settled that they would see one another again, and that no mention would be made of anything that had happened.

Atimir asked to see Hebe again; it even seemed to Ilerie that he desired it with a little too much urgency.

Princess Hebe blushed when he came into her room, and they were both in an embarrassment from which all their intelligence could not extract them. The King, who was present, noticed that. He mingled in their conversation, and in order to cut the visit short he proposed to the Princess that they go down into the palace gardens.

Atimir dared not give his hand to Hebe; he bowed to her respectfully, and withdrew. But what ideas and sentiments did not overwhelm his heart? All the passion, so vivid and so tender, that he had felt for Hebe was reignited in a moment; he hated Ilerie, and he hated himself; no infidelity was ever followed by so much repentance, nor so much dolor.

That evening he was in the Queen's apartment. Princess Hebe was there, he had no attention except for her. He sought with a great deal of care to talk to her; she still avoided him, but her gaze made him understand too much for his repose; he continued for some time to signify to her by his actions that her eyes had regained their initial empire over him.

Hebe's heart was alarmed; Atimir still appeared to her to be too lovable; she resolved to avoid him with as much care as he was taking to seek her out. She only ever spoke to him in the Queen's apartment, and then only when she absolutely could not dispense with it. She also resolved to counsel the Prince of the Peaceful Isle to return soon to his kingdom; but there are so many difficulties when it is necessary to quit someone that one loves.

One evening, when she was occupied by that thought, she shut herself in her cabinet in order to think there with more liberty; she found a note that someone had put in her pocket without her perceiving it. She opened it, and Atimir's handwriting, which she recognized, caused her to feel a disturbance that she could not express. She believed that she ought not to read it, but her heart prevailed over her reason. She read it, and found these words:

"Oh, cruel individual!" cried the Princess. "What have I done to you that you seek to reignite in my soul a tenderness that cost me so much dolor?"

Hebe's tears interrupted her speech.

Meanwhile, Ilerie was languishing in a jealousy that was only too well-founded. Atimir, carried away by his passion, could no longer constrain himself. The Prince of the Peaceful Isle was beginning to perceive his amour for Hebe, but he wanted to examine Atimir's conduct further before speaking to the Princess about it; he adored her constantly, and he feared that his discourse might itself cause her to perceive that Prince's passion.

A few days after Hebe had received the note there was a tourney. The Princes and all the fine youth of the Court were to break lances in honor of the ladies.

The King and the Queen honored that diversion with their presence. The beautiful Hebe and Princess Ilerie were to give the prizes themselves; one was a sword, the guard and hilt of which were covered in stones of an extraordinary beauty, the other a bracelet of exceedingly perfect brilliant diamonds.

All the knights entered for the competition were of a marvelous magnificence and mounted on the most beautiful horses in the world; they all wore the colors of their mistresses and had devices on their shields appropriate to the sentiments of their heart.

The Prince of the Peaceful Isle appeared, superbly dressed and mounted on a light bay horse with a mane of incomparable beauty. The color rose shone throughout his equipment; it was the one that Hebe loved. Over the light helmet that covered his head a bouquet of plumes floated of the same color. He attracted the applause of all the spectators, and he appeared so handsome in his brilliant armor that Hebe made herself a thousand secret reproaches for the sentiments that her misfortune inspired in her for another.

The retinue of the Prince of the Peaceful Isle was numerous; it was clad in the fashion of his realm, everything therein appeared elegant and magnificent. A squire carried his shield; everyone strained to see the device. It was a heart pierced by an arrow; a little Amour was launching a large number of them, in the attempt to inflict new wounds, but all of them save or the first appeared to have fired uselessly. These words were written underneath: *I fear no others*.

The colors and the device of the Prince of the Peaceful Isle were easy to decipher; it was as the knight of the beautiful Hebe that he had wanted to enter the lists.

People were occupied with his magnificence when Atimir appeared. He was mounted on an entirely black horse, which appeared to be ardent and superb. The color that the Prince wore was dead-leaf; he had not mingled any gold, silver or precious stones with it; he had on his helmet a bouquet of rose-colored plumes, and although he affected a great negligence in his adornment, he was so handsome, he was leading his horse with so much grace, and he had such a proud air, that everyone ceased looking at anything else as soon as he had entered.

On the shield that he was carrying, an Amour appeared who was trampling chains underfoot, and to which others were attached very heavily; around it were the words: *Only worthy of me*.

Atimir's troop were dressed in dead-leaf and silver, and gemstones had been lavished upon them; it was composed of the principal members of his court; they had few benefits, and it was easy to judge by Atimir's attitude that he was born to command them.

Words cannot express the various movements that the sight of Atimir produced in Hebe's heart and that of Ilerie, and the cruel jealousy that the Prince of the Peaceful Isle felt when he saw plumes the same color as his own floating over Atimir's helmet. The reading of the device completed inspiring him with a fury, of which he only suspended the effects then in order to choose a better time to make his rival feel it.

The King and the Queen easily remarked Atimir's impudence and felt an extreme anger, but they did not have time to express it.

The courses commenced to the sound of trumpets, which resounded in the air; they were very beautiful; all the young knights made their skill appear therein. The Prince of the Peaceful Isle, although occupied with a furious jealousy, signaled himself therein and remained victorious.

Atimir, who knew that the first prize for the courses was to be given by Ilerie, did not present himself to dispute the victory of the Prince of the Peaceful Isle. The judges of the camp declared him the winner, and to the sound of acclamations and the praise of all the spectators, he advanced with the best grace in the world to the place where the King and the Princesses were to receive the diamond bracelet. Princess Ilerie presented it to him; he received it respectfully; then, having saluted the King, the Queen and the Princesses, he returned to resume his place in the ranks

The sad Ilerie had remarked only to clearly the scorn that the fickle Atimir had shown for a prize that was to be given by her hand; she sighed dolorously, and the beautiful Hebe felt a secret joy at that, which all her reason could not forbid her heart.

New courses commenced; they had the same success as the first. The Prince of the Peaceful Isle, animated by the sight of Hebe, performed marvels there, and was the victor for the second time. But Atimir, tired of being a spectator of his rival's glory and flattered by the thought of receiving a prize from Hebe's hand, went to present himself at the end of the lists.

The rivals looked at one another proudly, and the course between two such great Princes was celebrated by the cries of the spectators and the further disturbance that it inspired in the princesses. The Princes ran at one another with an equal advantage; they broke their lances without being shaken. The applause redoubled, and the Princes, without giving their horses time to draw breath, turned at the end of the career. They took new lances and ran with the same fortune and skill as the first time.

The King, who feared having to decide a victor between the two rivals by fortune, in order not to discontent an illustrious combatant, promptly sent someone to the Princes on his behalf to bid them be content with the glory they had acquired and begged them to conclude the courses for that day with the last, which they had just made.

The man the King had sent having approached them, they listened to his commission with impatience, especially Atimir, who spoke first. "Go tell the King," he said, "That I would be unworthy of the honor he does me in taking part in my glory if I could suffer a victor."

"Let us see," said the Prince of the Peaceful Isle, pushing his horse ardently, "who merits the King's esteem and he favors of fortune more."

The man the King had sent had not yet returned to him when the two riders, animated by sentiments stronger than the desire to carry off the prize for the course, had already turned their career.

Fortune favored the audacious Atimir; he was victorious. The horse of the Prince of the Peaceful Isle, wearied by the many fine courses it had made, was tipped over, and caused its master to fall on the sand. What joy for Atimir and what rage for the Prince of the Peaceful Isle! He got up promptly, and approached his rival before anyone had reached them.

"You have vanquished me in the games, Atimir," he said to him, in a manner that marked his anger well enough, "But it's with the sword that I want to decide our differences."

"I consent to that," replied the proud Atimir. "I'll wait for you tomorrow at sunrise in the wood that terminates the palace gardens."

The camp judges joined them as they finished speaking, and they both dissimulated their anger, for fear that the King might oppose their design.

The Prince of the Peaceful Isle remounted his horse and pushed the bridle to draw away from the place where Atimir had just vanquished him. Meanwhile, the latter Prince went to collect the prize for the course from Hebe's hand, who presented it to him with an embarrassment that marked well enough the various movements of her soul. Atimir made in receiving it all the extravagances of a man in love.

The King and the Queen, whose eyes were attached to him, saw that, and returned to the palace discontented with the end of the day. Atimir, occupied by his passion, left the lists without wanting to be accompanied by any of his men, and Ilerie, overwhelmed by dolor and jealousy, returned to her apartment.

What were Hebe's sentiments then! *It's necessary to leave*, she said to herself. *What other remedy can be found for the ills that I feel and those I foresee?*

Meanwhile, the King and the Queen resolved to ask Atimir to return to his realm in order to avoid the further troubles that his amour might cause. They also resolved to make the same proposition to the Prince of the Peaceful Isle, in order not to show any preference between the two Princes. But their prudence was belated; while they were deliberating the departure of the two Princes, they were preparing for combat.

On returning from the courses, Hebe first asked where the Prince of the Peaceful Isle was. She was told that he was in the palace garden, that he wanted to remain alone there, and that he seemed very sad. The beautiful Hebe thought that it as her duty to go and console him for the small disgrace that had happened to him, so, without stopping in her apartment, she went down into the gardens, only followed by a few of her women.

She began to search for the Prince of the Peaceful Isle when, on going into a coved path, she perceived the amorous Atimir, who, no longer listening to anything but what she inspired in him, threw himself at the knees of the Princess and, drawing the sword that he had received from her hand that day, said: "Either listen to me, beautiful Hebe, or let me die to your feet."

Hebe's women, frightened by the action of the Prince, threw themselves upon him in order to try to take away his sword, which he was already turning against himself with much fury. The unfortunate Hebe wanted to flee, but how many reasons there are for stopping close to someone that one loves!

The desire to calm the noise that the adventure might make, the design of begging Atimir to try to calm a passion that was deadly to them, and the pity to which an object so touching gave birth, all combined to stop the Princess. She approached the Prince. Hebe's presence suspended his fury; he let his sword fall at the feet of the Princess. Never had so much trouble, so much amour and so much dolor appeared in a conversation of a quarter of an hour.

There are no terms tender enough to express what the unhappy lovers felt then. Hebe, anxious in seeing herself with Atimir and so close to the Prince of the Peaceful Isle, made a great effort upon herself to quit Atimir, and she quit him, ordering him never to see her again in his life. What an order for Atimir! Without the memory of the combat he had to undertake against the Prince of the Peaceful Isle, he would have turned his sword against himself a hundred times over, but he wanted to perish avenging himself on his rival.

Meanwhile, the beautiful Hebe retired to her apartment in order to avoid Atimir's presence more surely.

"Pitiless fay!" she cried, "you only predicted death for me of I saw that unfortunate Prince again, but the evils that I sense are crueler than the loss of life!"

Hebe sent people to look for the Prince of the Peaceful Isle in the gardens and throughout the palace, but he was not to be found; she was in an extreme anxiety; the search went on all night, but in vain, for he had hidden in a little rustic house in the middle of a wood in order to make sure that no one would prevent him for being at the place destined for the combat.

He went there at sunrise, and Atimir arrived a few moments later. The two rivals, impatient to avenge themselves and carry the victory, drew their swords. It was the first time that the Prince of the Peaceful Isle was making use of his, for there had never been a war on his island. He appeared to be no less redoubtable an enemy for that to Atimir; he had little experience, but a great deal of valor and a great deal of amour; he fought like a man scornful of his life, and Atimir sustained in that combat the high reputation that he had acquired.

The Princes were animated by too many different passions for the end of their combat not to be deadly. After having conserved an equal advantage for a long time, they delivered two thrusts so furious that they both fell on to the grass, which was soon red with their blood. The Prince of the Peaceful Isle fainted by virtue of the loss of his, and Atimir, mortally wounded, pronounced Hebe's name in dying for her.

Some of those searching for the Prince of the Peaceful Isle arrived in the place and were seized by fear at the sight of that cruel spectacle.

Princess Hebe, drawn by her anxiety, had just descended into the gardens; she ran to where she heard he cries of the men, who were pronouncing the names of the two Princes confusedly, and found those objects, so sinister and so touching. She believed that the Prince of the Peaceful Isle was dead, like Atimir, and at that moment, they did not appear to be any different from one another.

After having darted a few glances at the unfortunate Princes, Hebe cried, dolorously: "Precious lives that have just been sacrificed for me, I shall avenge you by the loss of mine."

After those words she threw herself upon the fatal sword that Atimir had received from her, and she pierced her breast before the men, who were astonished by that cruel adventure, were able to prevent her from doing it.

She expired, and the fay Anguillette, touched by so many misfortunes, to which she had opposed as many obstacles as her science would permit, appeared at the place where those beautiful lives had just terminated.

The fay cursed Destiny, and could not help shedding tears; then, thinking of helping the Prince of the Peaceful Isle, knowing that he was not dead, she cured his wound, and had him transported in an instant to his island, where, by virtue of the marvelous gift that she had attached to it, that Prince was consoled for the loss he had suffered, and forgot the passion that he had had for Hebe.

The King and the Queen, who had no similar assistance, delivered themselves entirely to their dolor, and time alone was able to console them. As for Ilerie, no words can express her despair; she was always faithful to her dolor and to the memory of the ingrate Atimir.

Meanwhile, Anguillette, having had the Prince of the Peaceful Isle transported to his kingdom, touched the unfortunate remains of the lovable Atimir and the beautiful Hebe with her wand; in the same instant they were changed into two trees of a perfect beauty. The fay named them charms,[5] in order to conserve forever the memory of those that had been seen to burn in those unfortunate lovers.

---

[5] The French *charme* [charm, originally as in a magic spell] is also the name of the tree known in English as a hornbeam.

YOUNG AND BEAUTIFUL

There was once a savant fay who wanted to resist Amour, but that little god was even more savant than her; he rendered her sensible, without even employing all his power. A handsome knight arrived in the Court of the fay in search of adventures; he was the likeable son of a King and famous for his many fine deeds. His valor was known to the fay; renown had carried rumor of it all the way to that realm.

The person of the young Prince responded so well to his high reputation that the fay, touched by so many charms, received in very little time the vows that the handsome knight offered to her. The fay was beautiful; he was veritably in love with her. She married him, and rendered him by his marriage the most powerful king in the world. They were happy for a long time, after being united forever.

The fay grew old and the King her spouse, although he was old, like her, ceased to love her as soon as she was no longer beautiful. He attached himself to the young beauties of the Court; the fay sensed a jealousy in consequence, which became deadly to several of her rivals.

She had only had one daughter from her marriage to the handsome knight; she became the object of all her tenderness, and she was worthy of the attachment that she had for her. The fays, her relatives, had endowed her at birth with the most charming intelligence, the most lovable beauty, and graces even more touching than her beauty. She danced better than anything that had ever been seen, and her voice stole all hearts.

Her figure was perfectly beautiful, without being very tall; her manner was noble; her hair was the most beautiful black in the world, her mouth small and gracious, her teeth surprisingly white; her beautiful eyes were dark, bright and touching, and never had gazes as piercing and so tender given birth to amour in hearts. The fay had named her Young and Beautiful; she had not yet given her any gifts; she had suspended that favor in order better to judge by what species of happiness she could ensure that of a child who was so dear to her.

The infidelities of the King afflicted the fay incessantly; the misfortune of no longer being loved made her imagine that the sweetest of possessions was always to be lovable. After a thousand reflections that was the felicity with which she endowed Young and Beautiful. She was then sixteen years old; the fay employed all her science to make her remain forever such as she was then.

What could she have given to Young and Beautiful more precious than the happiness of never being similar to herself?

The fay lost the King, her husband, and although he had been unfaithful for a long time, his death caused her to feel such a veritable dolor that she resolved to abandon her empire and retire to a castle that she had built in a very deserted region. It was surrounded by a forest so vast that only the fay could follow its paths.

That resolution afflicted Young and Beautiful; she did not want to quit the fay, but the latter ordered her absolutely to remain, and before retiring to her desert, recalling in the most beautiful place in the world, the pleasures and games from which she had been exiled for a long time, she composed Young and Beautiful's Court. In that agreeable company she was consoled some time after for the absence of the fay.

All the Princes and Kings who believed themselves worthy of pleasing—for people flattered themselves no less in those days—came in a crowd to Young and Beautiful's Court in order to try by means of their attentions and their amour to render such a lovable Princess sensible.

Never has anything equaled the magnificence and charms of Young and Beautiful's palace; every day was marked there with new festivities; everybody was happy there except for the lovers who adored her hopelessly, none having been looked upon favorably; but they saw her incessantly and

the most indifferent glances were worthy of arresting them
forever.

One day, Young and Beautiful, satisfied with her felicity
and the mildness of her reign, was walking in a wood, only
accompanied by a few of her nymphs, in order better to savor
the pleasure of solitude. A pleasant reverie was entertaining
her; what could she think that was not agreeable to her? Insensibly, she emerged from the wood and turned her steps toward
a meadow delightfully speckled with flowers.

Her beautiful eyes were occupied by a hundred different
and agreeable objects, when she perceived a flock grazing in
the meadow on the edge of a little stream, the waters of which,
flowing over pebbles, were making a soft murmur. It was
shaded by a clump of trees; a young shepherd was lying on the
grass, sleeping tranquilly, on the bank of the stream; his crook
was leaning against a tree and a pretty dog, which looked
more like its master's pet than the guardian of a flock, was
lying beside the shepherd.

Young and Beautiful approached the stream and cast her
gaze upon the shepherd. What a sight! Amour himself, sleeping in the arms of Psyche, did not shine with more charms.

The young fay stopped, and could not help feeling a few
movements of admiration, which were soon followed by more
tender sentiments. The young shepherd appeared be about
eighteen years old; he had an advantageous stature; his naturally curly brown hair accompanied the most lovable face in
the world perfectly. His eyes, which sleep held closed, hid
other fires from the fay, of which Amour wanted to make further use in order to redouble her tenderness for the shepherd.

Young and Beautiful sensed an unknown emotion in her
heart, and it was not possible for her to draw away from that
place. Fays have the same privileges as goddesses; they love a
shepherd, when he is lovable, as if he were the greatest King
in the world, for everyone is below them.

Young and Beautiful found too much pleasure in her sentiments to seek to combat them; she loved tenderly, no longer
thinking from that moment on of anything but the happiness of

being loved. She dared not wake the handsome shepherd, for fear of allowing him to notice her disturbance, and, making a pleasure out of revealing her love to him in a gallant and agreeable manner, she rendered herself invisible in order to enjoy the astonishment that she would cause him.

Immediately, a charming music became audible; that symphony went straight to the heart. The gracious sounds woke Alidor, that being the shepherd's name. He thought for a few moments that it was an agreeable dream, but imagine his surprise when, on raising himself up from the grass where he was lying, he found himself dressed in an elegant and magnificent attire. It was yellow, flax-gray and silver; his scrip was embroidered with Young and Beautiful's monogram, and attached with a sash of flowers; his crook was marvelously sculpted and ornamented with precious stones of different colors, which formed gallant devices; his hat was formed of jonquils and blue hyacinths woven with great artistry.

Content and surprised by his new adornment, he admired himself in the nearby stream, and Young and Beautiful feared greatly that at that moment he might have the destiny of the handsome Narcissus.

Alidor's surprise increased further on seeing his sheep charged with a silk whiter than snow instead of their ordinary fleece and covered with a thousand knots of variously colored ribbons.

His favorite ewe was also more decorated than the others; she came to him, bounding over the grass, seemingly proud of her attire.

The shepherd's pretty dog had a golden necklace, in which little mounted emeralds formed four lines:

When one wants to burn with immortal ardor,
Let a tender soul be alarmed!
To be charming is sufficient to be loved
But to be happy it is necessary to be faithful.

The handsome shepherd judged by those lines that it was to Amour that he owed his agreeable adventure. The sun was setting; Alidor, occupied by a pleasant reverie, resumed the path to his cabin. He did not notice any change outside, but scarcely had he gone in than a delightful odor announced something new. He found his little cabin lines with a tissue of jasmine and orange blossom; the curtains of his bed were similar, heightened by garlands of carnations and roses; an agreeable freshness maintained those flowers in all their beauty.

The floor was of porcelain, in which were depicted the stories of goddesses who had loved shepherds. Alidor noticed that; he was very intelligent; the shepherds of that country were not ordinary shepherds. Some of them were descended from kings or great princes, and Alidor took his origin from a sovereign who had reigned over those people for a long time before they had come under the domination of the fays.

Until then the handsome shepherd had been insensible, but he began to feel amorous, without yet having a determined object, which his young heart yearned to encounter. He was dying with impatience to know the goddess or the fay who was giving him such gallant and gracious marks of tenderness.

Alidor was possessed by a pleasant anxiety that he had never felt before. Night fell; an agreeable illumination appeared that made a new daylight in the cabin. Alidor's reverie was interrupted by a magnificent and delicate repast that was served before him.

"What!" said the shepherd smiling. "Always new pleasures, and no one to share them with me."

His pretty dog wanted to attract his attention, but Alidor was too occupied to respond to its caresses. The shepherd sat down at table; a little Amour presented him with a drink in a cup made of a single diamond. He supped as well as the hero of an adventure. He tried to ask questions of the little Amour, but instead of replying to him, the child fired arrows, and soon as they reached the shepherd they changed into marvelously scented water. Alidor understood by that badinage that the little Amour had been ordered not to explain the mystery to him. The table disappeared as soon as Alidor stopped eating, and the little Amour flew away.

A charming symphony became audible; it gave birth to a thousand tender sentiments in the heart of the handsome shepherd; his impatience to learn to whom he owed so many pleasures increased incessantly, and it was with a great deal of joy that he heard these words sung:

Under what form, Amour, will you launch your arrows
At the young shepherd that I love?
Satisfied by my heart, my extreme tenderness,
Will he also be by my feeble attractions?
He cannot doubt my sincere ardor.
But that is not enough to please;
Mighty Amour, take care to augment my beauty
I can only guarantee my fidelity.

"Appear, then, charming object!" cried the shepherd. "Complete my felicity with your presence: I believe you to be too lovable ever to cease to be faithful to your charms."

There was no response to those words; the symphony finished shortly afterwards; a profound silence reigned then in the cabin, and invited the shepherd to the mildness of slumber.

He threw himself down on his bed, and went to sleep with some difficulty, agitated by his impatience and by his nascent amour.

Birdsong woke him at daybreak. He emerged from his cabin and guided his flock to the same place where his good fortune had commenced the previous day.

Scarcely had he sat down on the edge of the stream than an awning of exceedingly bright fabric the color of fire, green and gold, was attached to the branches of the trees to protect Alidor from the sun's ardor. Young shepherds and beautiful shepherdesses from the surrounding area arrived in the place looking for Alidor; his awning, his flock and his attire threw them into great astonishment. They advanced diligently and asked him, with a great deal of urgency, the cause of so many marvels. Alidor smiled at their surprise and told them about everything that had happened to him. More than one shepherd felt jealousy and more than one shepherdess blushed with chagrin; there were few in that locale who had not formed designs on the heart of the young shepherd, and a goddess or a fay seemed to them to be too dangerous a rival.

Young and Beautiful, who scarcely lost sight of her shepherd, suffered the conversation of the shepherdesses impatiently; there were charming ones among them, and a lovable shepherdess might be a redoubtable rival even for a goddess. The indifference that Alidor manifested for them reassured the young fay.

The shepherdesses quit Alidor with reluctance and guided their flocks further into the pastureland. A few moments later, when there was only a group of shepherds with Alidor, a delicious feast appeared, served on a white marble table; seats of verdure rose up around it, and Alidor shared that meal with his friends, who had come to join him. They sat down at the table and all of them found that they were elegantly dressed, but less magnificently than Alidor, who seemed then to be sparkling with gemstones.

A rustic but gracious music caused the echoes of the vicinity to resound, and they heard these words sung:

Admire the supreme good fortune of Alidor;
Through him Amour has made me feel his arrows;
Shepherds, who know his charms,
Respect the choice of my heart.

The astonishment of the shepherds increased continually. A group of young shepherdesses arrived on the bank of the stream; the sound of the symphony attracted them to that place less than the desire to see Alidor; a very agreeable little ball commenced under the trees.

The young fay, who was invisible but still present, with six of her nymphs, instantly put on the prettiest shepherdess costumes that had ever been seen; they were only adorned with garlands of flowers; their crooks were ornamented; and Young and Beautiful, simply coiffed in jonquils, which made a charming effect in her beautiful black hair, appeared to be the most marvelous person in the world.

The arrival of those beautiful shepherdesses surprised the whole assembly; all the local beauties felt chagrin; there was not one shepherd who did not seek urgently to do them the honors of the fête.

Young and Beautiful, unknown as a fay among them, received no fewer honors and attracted no fewer devotions. It is beauty that receives the most sincere homages; Young and Beautiful was flattered by the effects of hers, in which her dignity played no part.

As for Alidor, as soon as she appeared in the assembly, forgetting that the amour that a goddess or a fay had for him obliged him to be careful not to displease her, flew toward Young and Beautiful, and, having approached her with the best grace in the world said to her: "Come and take a place more worthy of you; a marvelous person is too far above other beauties to be confounded with them."

He offered her his hand, and Young and Beautiful, charmed by the sentiments that the sight of her was beginning to inspire in her shepherd, allowed herself to be conducted. Alidor took her beneath the brilliant awning that he had found attached to the trees that morning as soon as he arrived in the place. On Alidor's orders, a troop of young shepherds brought bunches of flowers and verdure, and built a kind of little throne, on which Young and Beautiful sat. The handsome shepherd placed himself at her feet; her nymphs sat down beside her, and the rest of the assembly formed a large circle in which everyone arranged themselves in accordance with their inclination.

That location, ornamented by so many beauties, made the most agreeable spectacle in the world; the sound of the water mingled with the symphony, and it seemed that all the birds in the surrounding area assembled in the place in order to take part in the festivities.

An infinite number of shepherds came in troops to pay their court to Young and Beautiful. One of them, named Iphis, approached the young fay. "However beautiful the place is that Alidor has made you take," he said to Young and Beautiful, "it is perhaps very dangerous."

"I believe so," the fay said to him, with a smile capable of stealing all hearts. "The shepherdesses of this hamlet will doubtless have some difficulty forgiving me for the preference that Alidor seems to have given me over so many beauties who merit it more than me."

"No," Iphis said to her. "Our shepherdesses render themselves more justice; but a goddess loves Alidor."

Iphis then told Young and Beautiful the young shepherd's entire adventure. When he had finished his story the young fay turned to Alidor with a gracious expression. "I do not want such a redoubtable enemy," she told him, "as the goddess by whom you are loved. Apparently, she has not destined the place that I occupy for me; but I shall render it to her." As she finished speaking, she rose to her feet.

"Stay," Alidor said to her, looking at her tenderly, and stopping her. "Stay, beautiful shepherdess. There is no goddess whose tenderness I would not sacrifice for the pleasure of adoring you, and the one of whom Iphis has spoken to you is not very knowledgeable, at least in regard to amour, since she has permitted me to see you."

Young and Beautiful could not respond to Alidor; someone came to take her away at that moment in order to dance, and never has anyone acquitted herself in that with so much grace. She took the handsome shepherd, who surpassed himself. Never, in the most magnificent fêtes at Young and Beautiful's court, had she had as much pleasure as in that rustic assembly. Amour embellishes all the places where one can see the person one loves.

Alidor sensed his amour augmenting continually, and made a thousand oaths to sacrifice all the goddesses and fays in the universe to the tender amour that the shepherdess inspired in him. Young and Beautiful was charmed by the sentiments of the handsome shepherd, but she wanted to put his tenderness to the test for a few moments. Iphis was likeable, and if Alidor had not been present, he would doubtless have been admired. The young fay spoke to him two or three times in a rather gracious manner and danced with him several times.

Alidor felt a jealousy as sharp as his amour; Young and Beautiful noticed it, and, believing herself to be sure of her shepherd's heart, she ceased to cause him pain. She did not speak to Iphis again for the rest of the day, and Alidor had her most favorable gazes. And what gazes! They bore amour into the most insensible hearts.

The day ended; the beautiful troop separated with regret; a thousand sighs followed Young and Beautiful. She forbade all the shepherds to accompany her, but she promised Alidor in a few words that he would see her if he returned to the meadow the next day. Then she quit the beautiful troop and her nymphs went with her.

The shepherds let them go; they hoped that by following them at a distance they might learn, without being perceived, in which hamlet those divine individuals lived. As soon as Young and Beautiful had reached a little wood that hid her from the shepherds' view, however, she disappeared, with her nymphs. They amused themselves for a while watching the shepherds searching in vain for the route they had taken.

Young and Beautiful remarked with pleasure that Alidor appeared to be one of the most persistent. Iphis despaired of having delayed to long in following them, and many other shepherds of whom the nymphs had made the conquest spent a part of the night searching for them in the words and the surrounding area.

Several authors have assured us that the nymphs, authorized by the example of the young fay, found some of those shepherds more lovable than all the kings they had seen until then.

Young and Beautiful returned to her palace, and even though a fay, always occupied with a thousand different cares, can always absent herself without consequence, she found all her lovers very anxious at not having seen her all day. Not one made her any reproach, however; it was necessary to be a submissive and respectful lover in regard to Young and Beautiful, or receive an order to withdraw from her Court. They dared not even speak to her about their tenderness; it was only by means of their respect and their constancy that they hoped eventually to touch her heart.

Young and Beautiful appeared scarcely occupied with anything that was presented to her eyes; she ate little and was often pensive, and the Princes, her lovers, attentive to all her actions, believed that they had heard her sigh several times. She dismissed the entire Court early and retired to her apartment.

When one is going to see the person one loves again, everything that presents itself while awaiting that agreeable moment seems very cold and very tedious.

The young fay, in company with the nymphs who had followed her all day, hidden in a cloud, was in the handsome shepherd's cabin in an instant.

He had returned there, very sad at being unable to find the path that the divine shepherdess had taken. Everything in his cabin was as charming as when he had left it, but having lowered his eyes while dreaming to the floor of the small room, he perceived that it had changed. Instead of the stories of goddesses who had had the amour of shepherds, he saw in their place the terrible examples of lovers who had not rendered themselves worthy of the tenderness of those divinities.

"You're right!" exclaimed the handsome shepherd, on looking at those little paintings. "You're right, I merit your anger. But why have you permitted an excessively lovable shepherdess to be offered to my sight? What divinity could defend a heart against her charms?"

Young and Beautiful was already in the cabin when Alidor pronounced the words; she sensed all their sweetness, and her tenderness was further increased by them.

As on the previous day, a magnificent repast appeared; but Alidor did not make such good usage of it as he had the day before, being amorous, and also a little jealous, for he still remembered that the shepherdess had spoken with some attention to Iphis. However, the promise that she had made him, that he would see her again the next day in the meadow, alleviated his chagrin somewhat.

The little Amour served him during the repast, but Alidor, occupied with his next anxiety, did not say a single word to him. The table disappeared and the young child, approaching Alidor, presented him with two magnificent portrait-lockets, and then flew away

The handsome shepherd opened one of the lockets precipitately; it contained the portrait of a young woman of a beauty so perfect that the imagination can scarcely represent it. Underneath that marvelous portrait, these words were inscribed in golden letters:

Your happiness is attached to her tenderness.

"It is necessary to have seen the shepherdess," said Alidor, looking at that beautiful portrait, "not to be enchanted by such a charming individual." He closed the locket again and put it on a table negligently.

He opened the other locket that the little Amour had given him, and how astonished he was when he saw therein the portrait of his shepherdess, shining with all the charms that had made such a vivid impression on his heart!

She was painted as he had seen her that same day, coiffed with flowers, and the little that could be seen of her costume appeared to be that of a shepherdess. The handsome shepherd was so transported by his amour that it a long time passed before he perceived that these words were written underneath the portrait:

Forget her charms, or your amour will be fatal.

"Eh!" cried Alidor. "Without my shepherdess, is there any felicity?"

That transport charmed Young and Beautiful. The beautiful portrait that Alidor had scorned was only an imaginary portrait; the young fay had wanted to see whether her shepherd would prefer her to such a beautiful individual, who appeared to him to be a goddess or a fay. Satisfied with Alidor's amour, she returned to her palace, after having assembled her nymphs by means of a signal agreed between them. That was causing a few flashes of lightning to shine in the air, and that is the origin of those that are not followed by thunder.

The nymphs returned; they too had wanted to see what their lovers were doing. Some were quite content; they found them occupied with them and speaking about them with urgency. Others were less satisfied with the effects of their beauty; they found their shepherds profoundly asleep. People sometimes appear very amorous by day, without being sufficiently so to keep them awake at night.

The young fay went to bed on arriving in her palace, charmed by the amour of her shepherd; she was only agitated by a pleasant impatience to see him again.

As for Alidor, he hardly slept; without being troubled by the threats that he had read beneath the two little portraits, he was only thinking about returning to the meadow. He hoped to see his shepherdess there during the day; he did not think that it could arrive too soon.

He guided his lovable flock to the fortunate place where he had seen Young and Beautiful; his pretty dog had the care of guarding it; the handsome shepherd could not think of anything but his shepherdess.

Young and Beautiful was occupied reluctantly that day in receiving ambassadors and several kings of neighboring countries. Audiences were never so brief; nevertheless, a part of the day was spent in their tedious ceremonies. The young fay suffered as much as her shepherd, whom a keen impatience caused to feel a thousand torments.

The sun was setting; Alidor finally thought that he would not see his divine shepherdess that day. What dolor for him!

He lamented, and sighed a thousand times; he composed verses about her absence, and with the iron tip of his crook he engraved on a young elm tree:

You at whom Venus cannot gaze without envy,
Brilliant beauty followed by the Graces,
You on whom Amour lavishes so many attractions,
That the god who made you so charming and lovely
Is surer of wounding by means of you than his arrows;
Shepherdess, how cruel your absence is for me!
Destined to spend an entire day far from you,
To my sadness at least I want to be faithful;
It is engendered by my amour.

He had just finished engraving those lines when Young and Beautiful appeared in the distance in the plain with the nymphs, still dressed as shepherdesses. Alidor recognized them from far away; he ran, flying toward Young and Beautiful, who greeted him with a charming smile worthy of making the felicity of the gods themselves.

He spoke to her about her amour with an ardor capable of persuading a heart less touched than that of the young fay. She wanted to see what he had engraved on the tree, and she was charmed by her young shepherd's intelligence and tenderness. He told her everything that had happened to him the previous evening, and offered, a thousand times over, to follow her to the ends of the earth, in order to flee the amour that a goddess or a fay had unfortunately conceived for him.

"I would lose too much by it if you fled that fay," replied Young and Beautiful, graciously. "It is no longer time to hide my sentiments from you, since I am content with yours. It is me, Alidor," the charming fay continued, "who has given you marks of a tenderness that will last forever if you are faithful to your happiness and mine."

The young shepherd, transported by amour and joy, threw himself at her feet. His silence enabled the young fay to understand more than the most fluent speech. Young and Beautiful raised him to his feet, and he found himself dressed in a superb costume. Then, as the fay touched the ground with her crook, a magnificent chariot appeared drawn by twelve white horses of a surprising beauty; they were harnessed four abreast.

Young and Beautiful climbed into the chariot; she made the young shepherd sit beside her; the nymphs also found their places there, and as soon as they were seated, the handsome horses, which had no need of a conductor to follow the intentions of Young and Beautiful, took them with a great deal of diligence to a castle that the young fay loved. She had embellished it with everything that her art could furnish of the marvelous; it was named the Castle of Flowers; it was the most pleasing place on earth.

The young fay and her fortunate lover arrived with the nymphs in a large courtyard whose walls were only thick palisades of jasmines and lemon trees; they were only high enough to lean on; below them, a beautiful river could be seen flowing, which surrounded the courtyard; beyond it was a charming little wood, and on the other side, meadows as far as the eye could see, where the same river made a thousand meanders, as if it regretted quitting such a beautiful dwelling.

The castle was more admirable in its architecture than in its grandeur; there were twelve apartments there, each of which had a different beauty; they were vast, but there were not enough of them to lodge Young and Beautiful and all her Court, which was the most numerous and the most magnificent in the world. The young fay only retired to the castle in order to be in a kind of solitude; she was ordinarily only accompanied there by those of her nymphs that she loved the most and the officers of her household.

Young and Beautiful took her shepherd to the apartment of myrtles; all the furniture there was composed of myrtles still in flower, interlaced with an artistry that made the young fay's power and good taste appear even in the simplest things. All the apartments in the castle were solely furnished with flowers; one always respired a sweet and pure air there.

By means of her power, Young and Beautiful had banished forever the rigors of winter, and if she sometimes permitted the ardors of summer to make themselves felt in such a agreeable place it was in order to enjoy with more pleasure the beauty of the baths, which were delightful there. That apartment was in white and blue porphyry of marvelous workmanship; the basins were made in various singular and agreeable forms. The one in which young and Beautiful bathed was made of a single topaz raised on a porcelain platform four amethyst columns of perfect beauty sustained a magnificent awning of yellow and silver fabric embroidered with pearls.

Alidor, occupied with the happiness of seeing the charming fay and seeing that she was sensible to him, hardly noticed all those marvels.

An amiable and tender conversation enchanted the fortunate lovers for a long time in the myrtle apartment. A magnificent supper was served in the jonquil drawing room; a fête followed it; the nymphs represented therein the amours of Diana and Endymion. Young and Beautiful forgot to return to her palace, and spent the rest of the night in the narcissus apartment.

Alidor, transported by amour, spent a long time without savoring the sweetness of slumber in the myrtle apartment, to which the nymphs had conducted him after the fête.

Young and Beautiful, who did not want to make use of her power to calm such an agreeable disturbance, also did not fall asleep until daybreak.

Alidor, impatient to see the charming fay again, waited for that blissful moment for some time in the jonquil drawing room; he had neglected nothing in his adornment that might add to the graces of natural beauty. Young and Beautiful appeared a thousand times more charming than Venus; she spent a part of the day with Alidor and the nymphs in the garden of the castle, the beauties of which were beyond the most marvelous description.

There was an agreeable picnic in a delightful wood, in which Alidor, for a few favorable moments, had the sweet pleasure of speaking about his ardent amour to Young and Beautiful.

That evening she wanted to return to her palace; she promised Alidor to return the next day. No absence of a few hours has ever been celebrated by so many regrets. The handsome shepherd desired passionately to go with the young fay, but she ordered him to remain in the Castle of Flowers. She wanted to hide her tenderness from the eyes of the entire Court. No one went into that castle without her order, and she had no fear that the nymphs would reveal her secret. The secrets of a fay are always safe; no one ever divulges them; the punishment would follow the fault too swiftly.

Young and Beautiful asked Alidor for his pretty dog, which had always followed him, in order to take it with her. Everything that pleases the person we love is dear to us.

After the young fay's departure, more to maintain his anxiety than to dissipate it, the shepherd went into the wood in order to dream about his adorable fay. In a little clearing covered with flowers and watered by a pleasant spring, which was in the middle of the wood, he perceived his flock bounding over the grass; it was guarded by six young slaves of pleasant appearance, clad in gold and blue, with gold necklaces and chains. His favorite ewe recognized her master and came to him. Alidor caressed her and was deeply touched by the care of Young and Beautiful for everything related to him.

The young slaves showed Alidor their cabin; it was not far away, at the end of a covered path. The little dwelling was built of cedar wood; the overlapping monograms of Young and Beautiful and Alidor appeared there everywhere, formed with precious wood. Over the door, inscribed in golden letters on turquoise granite, was this inscription:

In this beautiful place will be seen forever
The flock of the shepherd who charms my heart,
The shepherd by whom I am beloved;
The fate of gods has fewer attractions.

The handsome shepherd returned to the Castle of Flowers charmed by the young fay's generosity; he did not want any fête that evening. Can one desire pleasures when the person one loves is absent?

Young and Beautiful came back the next day, as she had promised her fortunate lover. What a joy to see one another again! All the young fay's power had never enabled her to feel such a sweet felicity.

She spent almost every day at the Castle of Flowers and only showed herself rarely at the Court. The Princes, her lovers, felt a mortal dolor, in vain; everything was sacrificed to the fortunate Alidor.

But can such sweet happiness last for long without being troubled? Another fay than Young and Beautiful had seen the handsome shepherd; she too felt her heart touched by his charms.

One evening, when Young and Beautiful had gone to give her Court a few hours of her presence, Alidor, occupied with his amour, was daydreaming profoundly in the jonquil drawing room when he heard a small sound at one of the windows, and, looking in that direction, he perceived a very bright light. A moment later, he saw, on a table near the one at which he was seated, a very small woman about a cubit tall, very old, with hair whiter than snow, a high collar and an antique farthingale.

"I am the fay Mordicante," she said to the handsome shepherd. "I have come to announce to you a good fortune far greater than that of being loved by Young and Beautiful."

"What could that good fortune be?" said Alidor, disdainfully. "The gods have none more perfect themselves."

"It is that of pleasing me," retorted the old fay, proudly. "I love you, and my power is far above that of Young and Beautiful, almost equal to that of the gods. Quit that young fay for me; I will avenge you on all your enemies and all those you would like to harm."

"Your favors are no use to me," said the young shepherd, smiling. "I have no enemies and I don't want to harm anyone. I'm too satisfied with my destiny, and if the charming fay that I adore were only a shepherdess, I would be as happy with her in a cabin as I am in the most beautiful palace in the world."

After those words, the evil fay suddenly made herself as tall and as gross as she had initially seemed petite, and disappeared, making a frightful noise.

The next day, Young and Beautiful returned to the castle; Alidor told her about his adventure. They both knew the fay Mordicante; she was very old, had always been ugly, and was very sensible to amour. Young and Beautiful and her fortunate lover made a thousand jokes about that passion, and did not worry for an instant about the effects of her vengeance. Can one be a fortunate lover and think about the evils of the future?

A week later, Young and Beautiful and the handsome shepherd, having climbed into a gilded boat for an excursion on the beautiful river that made a tour of the Castle of Flowers, were followed by all of their little court in the prettiest boats in the world.

The one that was carrying Young and Beautiful was covered by an awning of light blue and silver cloth; the oarsmen were dressed in the same colors. Other small boats filled with excellent musicians accompanied the happy lovers and formed an agreeable symphony. Alidor, more amorous than ever, only had eyes for Young and Beautiful, whose beauty that day seemed more charming than words can describe.

They were continuing their excursion when they saw twelve sirens emerging from the water; a moment later, twelve tritons appeared and arranged themselves with the sirens around Young and Beautiful's boat. The tritons made extraordinary symphonies with their horns and the sirens sang gracious airs, which amused the young fay and the handsome shepherd for some time.

Young and Beautiful, who was accustomed to marvels, thought that it was a diversion prepared by those who were in charge of contributing to her pleasures by inventing new fêtes. Suddenly, however, the perfidious tritons and sirens, having placed their hands on the young fay's boat, sank it.

The only peril that Alidor feared was that which the young fay might be in. He tried to swim toward her, but the tritons took possession of him in spite of his struggles, and Young and Beautiful, abducted at the same time by the sirens, was returned to her palace.

A fay having no power against another, the jealous Mordicante limited her vengeance to making Young and Beautiful feel the most cruel and dolorous absence. Meanwhile, Alidor was taken by the tritons to a terrible castle guarded by winged dragons. It was there that Mordicante had resolved to make the young shepherd love her, or to avenge herself for his scorn.

Alidor was put into a very dark chamber. Mordicante, brilliant with the most beautiful gems in the world, came to see him and tried to talk to him about her tenderness. The shepherd, in despair at being separated from Young and Beautiful, treated the evil fay with all the scorn she merited.

What rage for Mordicante! But her amour was still too violent for her to want to kill the person who had given birth to it. She resolved, after several days, in which Alidor was retained in a frightful prison, to vanquish the faithful shepherd by new artifices. She suddenly transported him to a magnificent palace. He was served with a pomp that ceded nothing to what he had seen in the Castle of Flowers. She tried to dissipate his dolor by mans of agreeable fêtes, and the most beautiful nymphs in the world, which formed her Court, seemed to be competing with one another for the honor of pleasing him. No one spoke to Alidor any longer of anything but the love of the evil fay, but the faithful shepherd languished in the midst of pleasures, and was no less desperate at the absence of Young and Beautiful among the most splendid fêtes than he had been in the horror of his cruel prison.

However, Mordicante hoped that the absence of Young and Beautiful, the continual pleasures with which she tried to amuse Alidor, and the sight of so many charming individuals would eventually bear the shepherd's heart to become infidel, and she only caused so many beautiful nymphs to appear before his eyes in order to take on herself the face of the one by whom he seemed most touched. She was disguised among the nymphs; sometimes she appeared as the most charming brunette in the world, and sometimes as the most beautiful blonde in the universe.

Amour, which can have any effect on hearts, had suspended her natural cruelty, but the despair of not being able to shake Alidor's fidelity reignited her fury so forcefully that she resolved to make the charming shepherd perish and to render him the victim of the constant love he conserved for Young and Beautiful.

One day, when she was observing him, without being visible, in a beautiful gallery whose windows overlooked the sea, Alidor leaned on a balustrade and dreamed for a long time without pronouncing a single word. Finally, however, sighing dolorously, he uttered plaints so tender and so touching, which marked so vividly the passion that he felt for the young fay, that Mordicante, transported by rage, allowed Alidor to see her in her natural form, and after heaping him with reproaches, had him taken back to his prison, announcing to him that in three days' time he would be sacrificed to her hatred, and that the cruelest tortures would avenge her scorned amour.

Alidor did not regret the loss of his life; it was insupportable to him far from Young and Beautiful. Satisfied with having nothing to fear for her from Mordicante's wrath, because the young fay's power was equal to hers, he awaited constantly the death that had just been announced to him.

Meanwhile, Young and Beautiful, as faithful as her shepherd, was bemoaning the dolor of his loss. The sirens who had returned her to her palace had disappeared instantly, and the young fay had no doubt that it was the cruel Mordicante who had stolen Alidor from her. The excess of her dolor informed the entire Court simultaneously of her tenderness for the handsome shepherd and the loss that she had suffered.

How many kings were jealous even of the misfortunes into which the evil fay had precipitated Alidor! What rage for those amorous princes to learn that they had a beloved rival and to see Young and Beautiful no longer occupied with anything but shedding tears for that fortunate mortal! The loss of Alidor, however, revived their hopes. They finally knew that Young and Beautiful knew how to love as well as how to please. They redoubled their attentions and their please; each of them flattered himself with the pleasant hope of one day taking the place of the fortunate lover. But Young and Beautiful, still equally afflicted by Alidor's absence, and fatigued by his rival's amours, abandoned her Court and withdrew to the Castle of Flowers.

The sight of that charming place, where everything recalled the memory of the handsome shepherd to her heart, further augmented her languor and her tenderness. One day, when she was walking in the beautiful gardens, looking at the various ornaments with which they were embellished, she said: "Alas, you were once my pleasures, but I am too occupied by my dolors even to think of giving you new beauties."

As she finished speaking, an agreeable Zephyr, who was agitating the blooms of a beautiful flower-bed, arranged them in an instant in various ways. First they represented the monogram of Young and Beautiful, and then other figures that she did not know, and, a moment later, they formed letters distinctly. Young and Beautiful, surprised by that novelty, read these lines inscribed in such a singular fashion:

To embellish this place Zephyr orders
The nascent flowers when he sighs;
He lavishes cares for Flora very day,
Far more glorious for being under your empire,

Young and Beautiful was reading those lines when she saw the god who had just declared his amour for her appear in the air. He was in a little chariot of roses harnessed to a hundred canaries, attached ten by ten with strings of pearls. The chariot approached the ground and Zephyr descended near the young fay. He spoke to her with all the grace of a very amiable and very gallant god, but the young fay, without being flattered by such a brilliant conquest, replied to him as a faithful lover. Zephyr was not astonished by Young and Beautiful's rigor; he flattered himself that he would soften her by his attentions, and he paid assiduous court to her, omitting nothing to please her.

Nothing more was lacking to Alidor's glory; he had a god for a rival, and he was preferred by Young and Beautiful.

However, that fortunate mortal was near to perishing by virtue of Mordicante's fury. It was almost a year since the young fay and the handsome shepherd had been separated, when Zephyr, who no longer hoped to vanquish the constancy of Young and Beautiful, and touched by the tears that he saw her shedding incessantly for the loss of Alidor, said to her one day when he found her even sadder than usual: "Since it is no longer possible to flatter myself with the good fortune of pleasing you, I want at least to contribute to your felicity. What is it necessary to do to render you happy?"

"It is necessary for my happiness," Young and Beautiful replied, with a charming gaze intended to reawaken all Zephyr's amour, "that Alidor is returned to me. I can do nothing against the power of another fay, but you, Zephyr, are a god, and you can do anything against that cruel rival."

"I will also try," Zephyr replied, "to vanquish the render sentiments that you have inspired in me, in order finally to be able to ender you an agreeable service."

After those words he flew away, and left Young and Beautiful flattered by a sweet hope.

Zephyr had not deceived her; he did not love for long without being assured of pleasing, and the young fay had appeared too constant for him to be able to hope to make her forget Alidor.

Zephyr flew toward the prison where the handsome shepherd was no longer waiting for anything but the loss of his life. An impetuous wind formed by six Aquilons who had accompanied Zephyr suddenly opened the doors of the prison, and the handsome shepherd, enclosed in a brilliant cloud, was taken to the Castle of Flowers.

After having seen Alidor, Zephyr was less astonished by Young and Beautiful's fidelity; he did not want to show himself to the handsome shepherd until he had returned him to the charming fay.

Who could express the perfect joy that Alidor and Young and Beautiful felt on seeing one another again? How lovable they found one another, and how tenderly they loved one another! How many thanks were rendered by those happy lovers to the god who had just assured their felicity! He quit them shortly thereafter to return to Flora.

Young and Beautiful wanted the entire Court to share their happiness. It was celebrated by a thousand games throughout the extent of the Empire, in spite of the dolor of the princes, her lovers, who were spectators of the young shepherd's triumph.

However, in order to have nothing further to fear from Mordicante's anger against Alidor, Young and Beautiful taught him the Art of Enchantment, and made him a present of the gift of Youth. After having assured her fortunate lover of such a sweet possession, thinking of the care of his glory, she gave him the Castle of Flowers and had him recognized as the sovereign of that beautiful region, where his ancestors had once reigned.

Alidor was the greatest king in the world, in the same place where he had been the most charming shepherd in the world; he heaped all those who had been his friends with possessions. He conserved all his charms forever, like Young and

Beautiful, which ensured that they would love one another forever, because they were still lovable, and Hymen was not involved in completing a passion that was the felicity of their life.

THE PALACE OF VENGEANCE

There was once a King and Queen of Iceland who, after twenty years of marriage, had a daughter, whose birth gave them all the more joy because they had despaired for a long time of having children who would one day succeed to their kingdom. The young princess was named Imis; her nascent charms promised as soon as her infancy all the marvels that are seen to shine in a slightly more advanced age. No one in the world would have been worthy of her if Amour, who believed it to be his honor to be able to subject such a marvelous person to his empire one day, had not taken care to have born in the same Court a Prince as charming as Princess Imis was lovable.

That Prince was named Philax and he was the son of a brother of the King of Iceland; he was two years older than the Princess, and they were brought up together with all the liberties that infancy and the proximity of blood give. The first movements of their hearts were given to admiration and tenderness. They could not see anything as beautiful as one another, so they did not find anything elsewhere that could deflect them from the passion that they felt for one another, even without yet knowing what it was called.

The King and the Queen saw that love born with pleasure; they loved young Philax; he was a Prince of their blood and no child had ever given rise to such high hopes. Everything seemed to accord with Amour to render Philax the happiest of men one day.

The Princess was about twelve years-old when the Queen, who loved her with an infinite tenderness, wanted to consult a fay, whose prodigious science was then greatly renowned, regarding her destiny. She departed in order to go find her. She took Imis with her, who, in the dolor of quitting Philax, was astonished thousands of times over that anyone could think of the future when the present was so agreeable. Philax remained with the King, and all the pleasures of the Court could not console him for the absence of the princess.

The Queen arrived at the fay's castle; she was received magnificently, but the fay was not to be found there. She lived ordinarily on the summit of a mountain that was some distance from her castle, where she remind alone, occupied with the profound knowledge that rendered her so celebrated through-out the world. As soon as she knew of the Queen's arrival she came back; the Queen introduced the Princess to her and informed her of her name and the hour of her birth, which the fay knew as well as she did, even though she had not been there; the fay of the mountain knew everything. She promised the Queen to give her a response in two days, and then returned to the summit of the mountain.

At the commencement of the third day she came back again, invited the Queen to go down into a garden, and gave her a book of palm leaves, firmly closed, but ordered her only to open it in the presence of the King. In order to satisfy her curiosity at least to some degree, the Queen asked her various questions regarding her daughter's fortune.

"Great Queen," the fay of the mountain said to her, "I cannot tell you exactly the species of misfortune by which the Princess is menaced; I can only see that Amour will have a large part to play in the events of her life, and that no beauty has ever given birth to such violent passions as those that Imis will inspire."

It was not necessary to be a fay to promise lovers to that Princess. Her eyes already seemed to demand of all hearts the amour that the fay assured the Queen that they would have for her. Meanwhile, Imis, much less anxious about her destiny than the absence of Philax, was amusing herself picking flowers; but, occupied by her tenderness and her impatience to depart, she forgot the bouquet that she had begun to make and, while dreaming, threw away the flowers that she had initially amassed with pleasure. She went to rejoin the Queen, who said adieu to the fay of the mountain. The fay embraced Imis, and gazed at her with the admiration that she merited.

"Since it is not possible for me, beautiful Princess," she said, after a moment of silence that had something mysterious about it, "to change the order of Destiny in your favor, at least I will try to help you avoid the misfortunes that it is preparing for you."

After those words she picked a bunch of lilies of the valley herself, and addressed young Imis. "Always carry the flowers that I am giving you," she said to her. "They will never wither, and as long as you have them about your person, they will protect you from all the evils with which Destiny threatens you." Then she attached the bouquet to Imis' hair, and the flowers, obeying the fay's intentions, as soon as they were on the Princess's head, arranged themselves and formed a kind of spray, whose whiteness only seemed to make it manifest that nothing could efface that of the complexion of the beautiful Imis.

The Queen departed after having thanked the fay a thousand times and returned to Iceland, where the entire Court was awaiting the return of the Princess with impatience. Joy had never seemed more brilliant and more amiable than it was in the eyes of Imis and those of her lover. The mystery of the spray of lilies of the valley was only explained to the King; it had such an agreeable effect in the beautiful brown hair of the Princess that everyone merely took it for an ornament that she had chosen for herself in the fay's gardens.

The Princess said much more to Philax about the chagrin she had felt in not seeing him than about the misfortunes that destiny promised her. Philax was alarmed nevertheless, but the joy of finding one another was present, and the misfortunes were as yet uncertain; they forgot them, and abandoned themselves to the sweet pleasure of seeing one another again.

Meanwhile, the Queen rendered the King an account of her voyage, and gave him the fay's leaves. The King opened them, and found these words written there in golden letters.

The King and Queen were greatly afflicted by that oracle, and sought in vain to be able to explain it. They did not say anything about it to the Princess, in order not to give her an unnecessary dolor.

One day, when Philax had gone hunting, which happened quite often, Imis was walking alone in a labyrinth of myrtles. She was very sad, because she thought that Philax was too late in returning, and she reproached herself for an impatience that he did not share with her.

She was occupied with her reverie when she heard a voice that said to her: "Why are you afflicted, beautiful Princess? If Philax is not sensible enough to the good fortune of being loved by you, I have come to offer you a heart a thousand times more grateful, a heart vividly touched by your charms, and a fortune sufficiently brilliant to be desired by anyone other than you, of which the entire world would recognize the empire."

The Princess was very surprised to hear that voice; she had believed that she was alone in the labyrinth, and as she had not spoken, she was even more astonished that the voice had responded to her thought. She looked around, and saw a little man appear in the air, mounted on a cockchafer.

"Have no fear, beautiful Imis," he said to her, "you have no lover more submissive than me, and although today is the first time that I am appearing before you, I have loved you for a long time and I see you every day."

"How you astonish me," the Princess said to him. "What! You see me every day, and you know what I am thinking? If that is the case, you must have seen that it is futile to have amour for me. Philax, to whom I have given my heart, is too lovable ever to cease to be its master, and although I am not content with him, I have never loved him so much. But tell me who you are and where you have seen me."

"I am Pagan the Enchanter," he said to her, "and my power extends over the whole world, except for you. I saw you in the garden of the fay of the mountain. I was hidden in one of the tulips that you picked; at first I took for a fortunate presage the hazard that had made you choose the flower where I was. I flattered myself that you would take me away with you, but you were too occupied with the pleasure of thinking about Philax; you threw the flowers away after having picked them, and you left me in the garden, the most amorous of all men. Since that moment I have sensed that nothing could render me happy but the hope of being loved by you. Think of me, beautiful Imis, if it is possible for you, and permit me sometimes to remind you of my amour."

After those words he disappeared, and the Princess returned to the palace, where the sight of Philax, whom she found again, dissipated the fear she had had. She was in so much haste to hear him justify the long time he had spent hunting that she almost forgot to tell him about her adventure. Finally, however, she told him what had happened in the myrtle labyrinth.

In spite of his courage, the young Prince feared a winged rival, against whom he might dispute the Princess at the expense of his life. But the spray of lilies of the valley reassured him against enchantments, and the tenderness that Imis had for him did not permit him to fear that it might change.

When she woke up the day after the adventure in the labyrinth, the Princess saw twelve little nymphs flying in her chamber, mounted on honey-bees, who were carrying little golden baskets in their hands. They approached Imis's bed, saluted her, and then went to put the baskets on a white marble table that appeared in the middle of the room. As soon as they were set down, they became an ordinary size. After having quit their baskets, the nymphs saluted Imis again; one of them came nearer to her bed than the others, and dropped something on top of it. Then they flew away.

In spite of the astonishment that such a novel spectacle gave her, the Princess picked up what the nymph had dropped beside her; it was an emerald of a marvelous beauty. It opened as soon as the Princess touched it; she found that it contained a rose leaf, on which she read these lines:

Let the universe learn with astonishment
The incredible effect of your eyes;
Even the torments are desirable
That you render me in loving you.

The princess could not get over her surprise; finally, she called her ladies in waiting; they were as astonished as Imis at the sight of the table and the baskets. The King, the Queen and Philax came running at the rumor of that adventure; the Princess only suppressed from her story the letter from her lover. It was only to Philax that she thought she ought to render an account of it. The baskets were examined with care and they were all found to be full of precious stones of an extraordinary beauty and great value, which further increased the astonishment of the spectators.

The princess did not want to touch them, and, having found a moment when no one was listening, she approached Philax and gave him the emerald and the rose leaf. He read the letter from his rival with a great deal of pain. In order to console him, Imis tore up the rose leaf in front of him.

But how dearly that sacrifice cost them!

A few days passed without the Princess hearing any mention of Pagan. She believed that her scorn for him had extinguished his amour, and Philax flattered himself with the same hope. The Prince went back to hunting, as he was accustomed to do. He stopped on the edge of a spring to refresh himself.

He had the emerald on him, which the Princess had given him, and, remembering that sacrifice with pleasure, he took it out of his pocket in order to look at it; scarcely had he held it or a moment, however, that it escaped from his hands, and as soon as it touched the ground, it changed into a chariot. Two winged monsters emerged from the spring and harnessed themselves to it.

Philax looked at them without fear, because he was incapable of having any, but he could not help feeling some emotion when he found himself transported into the emerald chariot by an invisible force and immediately lifted into the air, where the winged monsters enabled the chariot to fly with a prodigious facility and rapidity.

Meanwhile, night fell, and the hunters, after having searched the entire wood for Philax in vain, returned to the palace, to which they thought he might have returned. They did not find him there, and no one had seen him since he had gone hunting with them. The King ordered them to go back to search for the Prince. Everyone in the court shared his anxiety. They returned to the wood and traveled the surrounding area; they only came back at daybreak, without having learned anything about the Prince.

Imis had spent the night in despair at the absence of her lover, the cause of which she could not understand. She went on to a terrace of the palace in order to see the people who had gone to search for Philax returning, and hoped to see him returning with them, but no words can express the excess of the dolor by which she was seized when she did not see Philax arrive and she was told that it was impossible to determine what had become of him.

She fainted, and was carried away, and one of the women who hastened to put her to bed detached from the head of the Princess the spray of lilies of the valley that protected her from enchantments. As soon as it was removed, a cloud obscured the room and Imis disappeared.

The King and Queen were in despair at that loss and could never be consoled for it.

On recovering from her faint, the Princess found herself in a chamber of coral of various colors, with a floor of mother-of-pearl, surrounded by nymphs, who served her with a profound respect. They were beautiful, clad in magnificent and elegant garments. To begin with, Imis asked where she was.

"You are in a place where you are adored," one of the nymphs said to her. "Have no fear, beautiful Princess, you will find here everything that you could desire."

"Philax is here, then," said the Princess, with a surge of joy that appeared in her eyes. "I only want the happiness of seeing him again."

"You have remembered an ingrate for too long," said Pagan then, making himself visible to the Princess, "and since that Prince has quit you, he is no longer worthy of the love you have for him; combine chagrin and concern for your glory with the passion I have for you. Reign forever in this palace, beautiful Princess; you will find immense riches here and all the pleasures imaginable will be attached to your steps."

Imis only replied to Pagan's speech with tears. He quit her, for fear of aggravating her dolor. The nymphs remained with her, and tried to console her by means of their cares. A magnificent meal was served to her, but she refused to eat.

The following day, however, the desire to see Philax again made her resolve to live; she ate, and in order to dissipate her dolor, the nymphs took her to various places in the palace. It was entirely constructed of gleaming seashells, mingled with precious stones of different colors, which had the most beautiful effect in the world. All the furniture was made of gold, and of a workmanship so marvelous that it was evident that it could only have come from the hands of fays.

After having shown Imis the palace, the nymphs took her into the gardens, the beauty of which was indescribable. She found a brilliant chariot there harnessed to ten red deer, conducted by a dwarf. Imis was asked to enter the chariot; she obeyed. The nymphs sat at her feet; they were taken to the sea shore, where a nymph informed the Princess that Pagan reigned on that island, of which he had made, by the power of his art, the most beautiful place in the world.

A sound of instruments interrupted the nymph's discourse; the sea seemed to be entirely covered by little coral boats the color of fire, filled with everything that could compose a very elegant maritime fête. In the middle of the little boats there was one much larger than the others, on which Imis's monogram appeared everywhere, formed by pearls. It was drawn by two dolphins.

It approached the shore. The Princess boarded it with the nymphs; as soon as she was there, a superb collation appeared before her, and she heard a marvelous concert, performed in the boats that surrounded her own. Her praises were sung therein, but Imis did not pay any attention to any of it. She went back to her chariot and returned to the palace, overwhelmed by sadness.

In the evening, Pagan present himself before her again. He found her even more insensible to his amour than she had so far appeared to be, but he was not put off and he put his faith of his constancy. He was unaware as yet that in amour, the most constant are not always the most fortunate. Every day he put on fêtes for the Princess, diversions worthy of attracting the admiration of everyone except the person for whom they were invented. Imis was only touched by the absence of her lover.

Meanwhile, that unfortunate Prince had been conducted by the winged monsters into a forest of which Pagan was the master. It was known as the Dismal Forest. As soon as Philax had arrived there, the emerald chariot and the monsters disappeared. Surprised by that adventure, the Prince summoned all his courage to his aid, and that was the only help on which he could count in that place.

To begin with, he followed a few of the forest paths. It was frightful, and the sunlight never penetrated its obscurity. He found no one there, not even an animal of any species; it seemed that even animals were filled with horror by such a dismal abode. Philax lived on the wild fruits that he found there. He spent his days in mortal dolor. The absence of the Princess put him in despair, and sometimes he amused himself engraving the name of Imis, with the sword that he still had, on trees that were not destined for such a tender usage; but when one is veritably in love one sometimes makes use in the service of amour of the worldly things that seem most contrary to it.

In the meantime, the Prince advanced further into the forest every day, and he had been living in it for about a year when, one night, he heard plaintive voices whose words he could not make out. Frightful as those plaints might have been during the night, in a place where the Prince had never seen anyone, the desire no longer to be alone and at least to find other people as unhappy as himself, with whom he could lament his misfortunes, caused him to await the daylight with impatience in order to search for those he had heard.

He marched toward the place in the forest from which he thought the voices might have come. He marched all day, fruitlessly, but finally, in the evening, he found, in a place from which the trees had been cleared, the ruins of a castle that appeared to have been very spacious and superb.

He went into a courtyard, the walls of which were green marble, and still seemed sufficiently intact. He found nothing there but trees of a prodigious height, planted without order in various parts of the courtyard. He went further on, toward a place where he saw something raised on a pedestal of black marble. They were arms, piled confusedly on top of one another—helmets, bucklers and antique swords—which formed a kind of poorly arranged trophy.

He looked to see whether there was any inscription that might inform him of the names of those to whom the arms had once belonged. He found one engraved at the foot of the pedestal, of which time had partly effaced the characters, and it was with great difficulty that he read the words.

TO THE IMMORTAL MEMORY
of the glory of the Fay Ceore
IT IS HERE
that, on the same day,
she triumphed over Amour
and punished her infidel lovers

That inscription did not inform Philax of anything he wanted to know, so he would have continued to walk through the forest had night not fallen. He sat down at the foot of a cypress, and he had only been there for a few moments when he heard the same voices that he had heard the previous night. He was less surprised by that than to perceive that it was the trees themselves that were lamenting, as humans might have done.

The Prince rose to his feet, drew his sword and struck the cypress that was nearest to him. He was about to redouble his blows when the tree cried: "Stop, stop! Do not abuse an unhappy Prince, who is not in a state to defend himself."

Philax stopped, and, becoming accustomed to the surprising adventure, asked the cypress by virtue of what marvels he was both a man and a tree.

"I would like to tell you," said the cypress. "And since this is the first opportunity that Destiny has given me in two thousand years to complain of my misfortunes, I don't want to lose it. All the trees that you see here were once Princes, considerable in their century by virtue of the rank they held in society and their valor. The fay Ceore reigned in this land. She was beautiful, but her knowledge rendered her even more renowned than her beauty. She also used other charms to subject us to her laws. She had fallen in love with the young Orizee, a Prince worthy of a better fortune by virtue of his admirable qualities. He was originally," the cypress added, "The oak that you see beside me."

Philax looked at the oak and heard him utter a deep sigh, doubtless drawn from him by the memory of his misfortune.

"In order to attract the Prince to her Court," the cypress went on, "the fay advertised a tourney. We all ran to that opportunity to acquire glory. Orizee was one of a number of Princes who disputed the prize; it consisted of enchanted arms that rendered one invulnerable. Unfortunately, I was victorious. Irritated by the fact that Destiny had not declared in accordance with her inclinations, resolved to avenge herself on us for fortune's crime, Ceore enchanted the mirrors that filled an entire gallery of her castle. Anyone who saw her represented in those mirrors, only once, could not help feeling a violent passion for her.

"It was in that place that we were received the day after the tourney; we all saw her in the mirrors, and found her so beautiful that those of us who had thus far been indifferent ceased to be in an instant, whereas those who were in love became infidel as easily. We no longer thought of quitting the fay's Court; we no longer thought about anything but pleasing her. The affairs of our Estates recalled us in vain to our kingdoms. Everything appeared unworthy to us except for the hope of being loved by Ceore. Orizee was the only one that she favored and the passion of other Princes only served the fay to make sacrifices to the lover who was so dear to her, and to spread throughout the world the rumor of her beauty.

"For a time, amour seemed to have tempered Ceore's cruel humor, but after four or five years she resumed her original ferocity; she avenged herself for slight displeasures on the kings who were her neighbors by frightful murders, and, abusing the power that her enchantments had given her over us, she made us the ministers of her cruelties. Orizee tried in vain to stop her injustices; she loved him but she did not obey him.

"One day, when I was returning from fighting and defeating, for her interests, a giant whom she had sent me to challenge to combat, I brought her the arms of the vanquished. She was alone in the gallery of mirrors. I laid the giant's arms at her feet and spoke to her of my amour with an incredible ardor, doubtless augmented by the enchantments of the place where I was. Far from testifying any gratitude to me for the success of my combat, however, and for the love that I had for her, Ceore treated me with insupportable scorn, and, retiring into a cabinet, she left me alone in the gallery, in an inexpressible despair and fury.

"I stayed there for a long time without knowing what resolution I wanted to make, for the fay's enchantments did not permit us to want to fight Orizee. Careful of her lover's life, the cruel Ceore rendered us jealous, but took away the natural desire of men to avenge themselves on a fortunate rival.

"Finally, after having marched back and forth in the gallery for some time, remembering that it was in that place that I had fallen in love with the fay, I cried: 'It is here that I was gripped by the deadly amour that has rendered me desperate, and it is you, fatal glasses, that have represented the unjust Ceore to me so many times, with the beauty that seduced my heart and my reason; I will punish you for the crime of having offered her to my gaze with too many charms.'

"With those words, taking the giant's club, which I had brought to present to the fay, I delivered several blows to the mirrors, and scarcely were they broken than I felt more full of hatred for Ceore than I had felt amour for her. The princes, my rivals, felt their chains broken at the same moment. Even Orizee was ashamed of the love that the fay had for him. Ceore tried in vain to stop her lover by means of her tears; he was insensible to her dolor, and, in spite of her cries, we were all setting forth together to flee this fatal abode when, as we were passing though this courtyard, the sky appeared to catch fire. Frightful thunder was heard, and it was impossible for us to change place.

"The fay appeared in the air, mounted on a great serpent, and, addressing us in a tone of voice that marked her fury, she said to us: 'Inconstant princes, I shall punish you with a penalty that will never end for the crime that you have committed in breaking my chains, which were too glorious for you to bear. As for you, ingrate Orizee, I have finally triumphed over the amour that you gave me. Content with that victory, I shall make you experience the same woes as your rivals.'

"And she added: '*I order, in memory of this adventure, that when the usage of mirrors is known throughout the world, the loss of one of those fatal glasses shall always be an assured presage of the infidelity of a lover.*'

"The fay disappeared into the air after having pronounced those words. We were changed into trees, and the cruel Ceore doubtless left us our reason in order for us to suffer more. Time has destroyed this superb castle, which was the witness to our disgrace, and you are the only person who has ever come into this frightful forest in the two thousand years that we have been here."

Philax was about to reply to the speech of the cypress when he was suddenly transported into a very agreeable garden; there he found a beautiful nymph, who approached him graciously. "If you wish, Philax," she said to him, "I will enable you to see Princess Imis in three days' time."

Transported by joy at such an unexpected proposition, the Prince threw himself at her feet to testify his gratitude to her.

At that moment, Pagan was in the air, hidden in a cloud with Princes Imis. He had told her a thousand times that Philax was infidel; she had always refused to believe the word of a jealous lover. He had taken her there to convince her, he said, of the fickleness of a Prince that she preferred to him so unjustly.

The Princess saw Philax, with a contented expression, at the feet of the nymph. She was in despair at no longer being able to deceive herself regarding the thing that she dreaded most in all the world. Pagan had not taken her close enough to the ground for it to be possible for her to hear what Philax and the nymph were saying; it was on his orders that she had presented herself to the Prince.

Pagan took Imis back to his island, where, after having convinced her of the infidelity of Philax, he found that he had only redoubled the dolor of the beautiful Princess, and that she was no more sensible to him in consequence. In despair at seeing that pretended infidelity, from which he had hoped for a sweeter success more useful to him, he resolved to avenge himself on the constancy of the two lovers.

He was not as cruel as his ancestor, the fay Ceore, so he imagined a different vengeance from the one with which she had punished her unfortunate lovers. He did not want to kill either the Princess whom he had loved so tenderly or even

Philax, whom he had made to suffer enough. Limiting his vengeance to destroying a passion that had been contrary to his own, he built a crystal palace on his island, and took care to put into it everything that might be agreeable to life, except for the means of getting out it. He enclosed nymphs and dwarfs within it in order to serve Imis and her lover, and when everything was disposed to receive them, he transported both of them there.

They thought at first that their happiness was complete, and rendered a thousand thanks to Pagan. However, he did not want to see them together so soon; he understood that from day to day the spectacle could become less cruel for him. He drew away from the crystal palace after having engraved this inscription on it with a stroke of his wand:

> *The torments, ennuis and woes of absence*
> *Of Imis and Philax troubled the fine days.*
> *Unable to vanquish their confidence*
> *Pagan was offended by their perseverance,*
> *And, finally to destroy such tender amours*
> *In this place, witness to his vengeance, he has*
> *Condemned them to see one another forever.*

It is said that after a few years, Pagan was as avenged as he had desired to be, and that the beautiful Imis and Philax, accomplishing the prediction of the fay of the mountain, wished to recover the spray of lilies of the valley, in order to destroy agreeable enchantments, with as much ardor as they had once conserved it carefully to ward off the misfortunes that had been predicted for them.

> *Before the fatal term, the too-fortunate lovers*
> *Still burned with the same fires,*
> *Nothing troubled the course of their extreme happiness.*
> *Pagan enabled them to find the woeful secret*
> *Of becoming bored with happiness itself.*

THE PRINCE OF LEAVES

In one of the parts of the world to which poets alone have the right to give names, commonly known as the land of the fays, a King once reigned who was so renowned by his fine qualities that he attracted the esteem and admiration of all the Princes of his times. He had lost his wife, the Queen, some years before, of whom he had not had a son; but he had no longer desired one since he had had a daughter of such marvelous beauty that he had given her, as soon as she was born, all his tenderness and all his attachment.

She was named Ravissante by a fay who was a close relative of the Queen, who predicted that the intelligence and the charms of the young Princess would surpass everything seen thus far, and similarly the hope that they ought to have of the beauty she would be; but she added to that agreeable prediction that the happiness of the Princess would be perfect, provided that her heart was always faithful to the first impressions that it received of amour.

With only that circumstance able to assure a happy destiny, the King, only wanting Ravissante to be happy, desired passionately that her happiness had been attached to any other fatality, but one does not make one's destiny at will. He begged the fay a thousand times to make young Ravissante the gift of constancy, as he had seen her make others the gifts of intelligence and beauty, but the fay, who was knowledgeable enough not to be mistaken regarding the various effects of her knowledge, told the King sincerely that the power of fays cannot extend over the qualities of the heart. She promised him, however, that she would apply all her cares to imprinting the young Princess with the sentiments to which her happiness was attached.

On the strength of that promise, the King confided Ravissante to her as soon as she reached the age of five years, preferring to deprive himself of the pleasure of seeing her rather than risking by that pleasure becoming contrary to her fortune. The fay took the little Princess away, whom the joy and novelty of traveling through the air in a brilliant little chariot consoled in a few moments for having quit her father's Court.

On the fourth day after her departure, the flying chariot stopped in the middle of the sea, on a rock of prodigious grandeur. It was made of a smooth and shiny stone, the color of which imitated that of the sky perfectly. The fay remarked with pleasure that young Ravissante found that color very beautiful, and drew from that a fortunate presage for the future, because it is the one that signifies fidelity.

Shortly after arriving, the fay touched the rock with the golden wand she was holding in her hand. The rock immediately opened, and Ravissante found herself, along with the fay, in the most beautiful palace in the world. The walls were of the same substance as the rock, and the same color was found in all the paintwork and all the furniture, but it was so ingeniously mingled there with gold and precious stones that, far from being tedious, it was equally pleasing everywhere.

Young Ravissante stayed in that beautiful palace, with beautiful young women that the fay had transported from various lands to serve and amuse the Princess; she spent her childhood there in all the pleasures appropriate to her age. When she had reached the age of fourteen years, the fay consulted the stars again in order to discover very precisely the time at which Ravissante's heart was due to be touched by a passion that pleases even more than it is redoubtable, redoubtable though it is, and she saw distinctly in the stars that the fatal term was approaching when the destiny of the young Princess was to be accomplished.

The fay had a nephew who was infinitely dear to her; he was the same age as Ravissante, born on the same day and at the same hour. She had also found, in consulting the stars on his behalf, that they promised him the same fate as the Princess—which is to say, a perfect happiness, provided that he had a fidelity that nothing could vanquish. It was, however, easier to ensure his constancy than his happiness.

In order to render him amorous and faithful, she only had to enable him to see Ravissante; no one could escape her eyes, and the fay hoped that the attentions of the young Prince might one day touch her heart. He was the son of a King who was the fay's brother; he was lovable, and not only had the young Princess not yet had a lover, she had not even seen a man since she had been on the rock. The fay flattered herself that the novelty of the pleasure of being loved tenderly might perhaps engage her to love in her turn.

She therefore transported the Prince, whose name was Ariston, into the rock that served the beautiful Ravissante simultaneously as a palace and a prison. He found that she was amusing herself making garlands of flowers with the young women of her Court in a forest of blue hyacinths, where she went for walks, for the fay, in giving the rock the ability to produce plants and trees, had enclosed that power in the very color of the rock.

Some time before, the fay had told the Princess that Prince Ariston would be coming to the island, and she had added, in favor of the Prince, everything that she thought capable of making him desired, but she was disappointed this time, and when Ariston arrived, she did not recognize in the beautiful eyes of the Princess the disturbance and surprise that ordinarily presages a tender passion.

As for the Prince, his sentiments were in accord with the fay's hopes; he fell passionately in love as soon as he had seen Ravissante. It was not possible to see her without adoring her; never had grace and beauty been so perfectly united as they appeared to be throughout the person of that lovable Princess. She had a complexion of marvelous beauty, and her brown hair further enhanced its paleness; her mouth had infinite charms, her teeth were more admirably white than pearls; her eyes, the most beautiful in the worlds, were blue-brown, and they seemed so simultaneously bright and touching that it was not possible to sustain their gleam and their vivacity without yielding one's heart forever to the fatal power that amour had attached to their gaze; her stature was not very tall, but she was perfectly beautiful and all her actions had a particular grace; everything that she did, and everything that she said, was equally pleasing, and a smile or a single word was often sufficient to prove that she had as many charms in her intelligence as in her person.

Such as I have just described her, and a thousand times more lovable, it would have been very difficult for Ariston not to fall madly in love, but the Princess received his cares without attention, and did not appear to be touched by them at all. The fay remarked that, and had a dolor in consequence that was only surpassed by the one that the Prince felt. She had seen in the stars that the individual who was destined to possess Ravissante would extend his power over the entire earth, and even as far as the seas, so it was as much by virtue of ambition that she wished that her nephew might be able touch the heart of the Princess as because Ariston desired it by virtue of amour.

She believed, however, that if the Prince were as knowledgeable as she was in her art, he might find some secret to render himself more lovable in Ravissante's eyes. The fay, who had never loved, did not know that the secret of pleasing is not always to be found, whatever the urgency and ardor with which one seeks it. She therefore taught Prince Ariston, in a short time, all the sciences that are only known to fays.

He had no pleasure in learning them, and only thought of employing them with regard to his tenderness. He began by making use of them to provide the Princess with new amusements every day; she admired the prodigies, and even deigned to praise what she found most elegant in what the Prince did for her, but she received his attentions and devotions as homages justly due to her beauty, and of which she believed herself to be worthy by virtue of the generosity she had in receiving them without anger.

Ariston despaired of the scant success of his passion, but he was constrained thereafter by further information to admit that the time of which he complained so justly, and during which he felt the misfortune of his amour so keenly, had nevertheless been the happiest of his life.

A year after his arrival on the island, the day, so remarkable for him, on which he had seen Ravissante for the first time, was celebrated by games; in the evening he gave her a fête in the forest of hyacinths; there was marvelous music, which was heard equally in all the parts of the forest, without it being possible to see where such agreeable sounds were coming from. Everything that was sung by the invisible musicians expressed Ariston's amour for the Princess tenderly; they finished their admirable concert with these words, which were repeated several times:

> *Neither reason nor my rigorous fate*
> *Would be able to end my cruel suffering*
> *Without the aid of sweet hope;*
> *I sense my heart burning with the same fires.*
> *Amour would not know the excess of his power*
> *If I had not felt the power of your eyes.*

After the music, a superb collation suddenly appeared under a tent of silver gauze, held up by strings of pearls. It was open on the side that faced the sea, which bordered the forest in that place, and it was illuminated by a large number of chandeliers of brilliant diamonds, which cast a light little different from that of the Sun. It was by that light that the nymphs of Ravissante's Court drew her attention to an inscription on the entrance to the tent, written in golden letters on a ruby of prodigious grandeur, sustained by twelve little Amours, who flew away as soon as the Princess had read the inscription, which contained these lines:

> *No matter to how many places in the world*
> *Your beautiful eyes will carry irons*
> *You will not find a heart as faithful*
> *As the one that burns for you in this desert;*

But to ensure you of an immortal glory
And to see the world entire at your feet,
Princess, we shall publish to mortals
How beautiful you are.

The fête continued, and Prince Ariston at least had the pleasure of occupying the Princess's leisure, if he could not occupy her heart. But he was deprived of that pleasure by a surprising spectacle that appeared in the distance over the sea, and which attracted the curiosity and the attention of Ravissante and the entire Court. What they saw drew closer, and they discerned that it was an arbor formed of myrtles and laurels mingled together, closed on all sides, which an infinite number of winged fish were pushing with great rapidity.

The spectacle was all the more novel for Ravissante because she had never seen the color of that arbor. The fay, having foreseen that the color in question was to cause some misfortune to her nephew, had banished it absolutely from her island.

With an impatience that appeared to Ariston to be an evil presage for his amour, the Princess desired that what she could see might come closer; she did not have long to wait, for the winged fish pushed the arbor in a matter of moments all the way to the foot of the rock, where they stopped, and the attention of the Princess and her entire Court was redoubled.

The arbor opened, and a young man of marvelous beauty emerged, who appeared to be sixteen or seventeen years old. He was only clad in a few myrtle branches interlaced with a sash of roses of different colors.

The handsome stranger experienced an astonishment similar to the one that he caused; Ravissante's beauty did not leave him the liberty to amuse himself by gazing at the rest of the spectacle, the glare of which had attracted him to the rock from far away. He approached the Princess with a grace that she had never seen, even in herself.

"I am so surprised," he said, "by what I find on these shores, that I have even lost the liberty of being able to express my astonishment. Is it possible," he continued, "that a goddess like you does not have temples all over the world? By virtue of what charms or what prodigies are you still unknown to mortals?"

"I'm not a goddess," said Ravissante, blushing. "I'm an unfortunate Princess, sent away from the Estates of my father, the King, in order to avoid I know not what misfortune, which I am assured was predicted for me at the moment of my birth."

"You appear to me," said the handsome stranger, "to be far more redoubtable than the stars that might have attached some fatal influence to your beautiful days. Over what ill fortune can a beauty so perfect not triumph? I sense that it can vanquish anything," he added, sighing, "since it has vanquished in a moment a heart that I flattered myself that I could conserve insensible forever."

Without giving her time to respond, he continued: "But Madame, it is necessary that I go away, reluctantly, from this charming place where I see you, and where I have just lost my repose. I shall return soon, if Amour is favorable to me."

After those words he went back into the arbor, and in a short time he was lost to sight.

Meanwhile, Prince Ariston remained so bewildered and so afflicted by that adventure that he did not have the strength to speak to begin with; a rival had arrived by virtue of an event as surprising as it was unexpected; that rival had appeared to be only too charming, and it seemed to him that he had remarked in the beautiful eyes of the Princess, while the stranger was speaking, a languor that he had always desired to see there, but had never seen thus far. Transported by a despair that a dared not allow to burst forth, he took Ravissante back to the palace, where she spent a part of the night occupied with her agreeable adventure, of which she had the circumstances repeated several times by the nymphs of her Court, as if she had not been there herself.

As for Prince Ariston, he went to consult the knowledge of the fay, in order to seek to oppose some secret to the violent dolor by which he was tormented, but she had none against jealousy, and it is even said that none has been found since.

The Prince and the fay then redoubled their enchantments in order to forbid entry to the rock to the redoubtable stranger, whom they assumed to be an enchanter. They surrounded the island with frightful monsters, which occupied a large area of the sea, and which, animated by their own fury and the force of charms, seemed to assure Ariston and the fay that it would be impossible to take away from them the beautiful Princess whom they were guarding with so much care.

Ravissante felt more keenly the power of the handsome stranger's charms by virtue of the dolor caused to her by the obstacles that had been placed around the island against his return. She resolved at least to avenge herself on Prince Ariston; she began to hate him, and that was quite enough to ensure her vengeance. Ariston could not console himself for having attracted Ravissante's hatred by virtue of a passion that, it seemed to him, ought to have produced exactly the opposite effect.

The Princess lamented in secret the neglect of the stranger; it seemed to her that amour ought already to have made him keep the promise that he had made to return, but sometimes, also, she ceased to desire that return in remembering the perils by means of which the fay and Ariston had forbidden the approach of the island.

One day, when she was occupied with these various reflections, she was walking on her own along the sea shore, for Ariston no longer dared follow her, as he had done before, and the Princess even refused to see the fêtes with which he was accustomed to divert her. She had just arrived at the same place that the adventure of the unknown had rendered so recognizable, when she saw a tree of extraordinary beauty on the sea, which was floating toward the rock. Its color, which was that of the stranger's myrtle arbor, immediately gave her joy.

The tree drew nearer to the rock, and the monsters tried to prevent its passage, but a little wind agitated the leaves of the tree, and having dispersed a few of them against the monsters, they yielded to arms so slight and so lacking in danger, and even arranged themselves in a circle with a kind of respect around the tree, which approached the rock without encountering any other obstacles. It opened, and the stranger appeared within, sitting on a little throne of verdure.

He stood up precipitately at the sight of Ravissante, and spoke to her with so much intelligence and amour that after she had told him in a few words what her fortune was, she could not hide from him that she was touched by his return and even by his tenderness.

"But," she said to him, "is it just that I should know the sentiments that you have inspired in me before I even know the name of the person who has given birth to them?"

"I had no intention of hiding my birth from you," the charming stranger replied, "but in your presence one can only talk about you. However, as you want it I shall obey you by telling you that my name is the Prince of Leaves. I am the son of Spring and a sea-nymph related to Amphitrite, and that is what enables me to extend my power even over the waters; my empire is in all the places of the world that recognize Spring, but I prefer to live, almost always, on a fortunate island where no season ever reigns except the pleasant season that my father is accustomed to provide. The air there is always pure, the fields there are always florid, the sun does not make its ardors felt, only approaching it in order to illuminate it; night is banished therefrom, and that is why it is called the Isle of Day. It is inhabited by a people as gallant as the climate is agreeable; it is there that I offer you a mild and tranquil empire, where you would reign with even more sovereignty over my heart than everything else.

"It would be necessary, however, beautiful Princess," he continued, "for you to consent to be taken away from this rock, where you are retained in a veritable slavery, with a few honors, which are rendered to you in order to disguise it."

Ravissante could not resolve to go with the Prince of Leaves to his empire. In spite of the fear she had of the power of the fay and the counsels of her amour, she flattered herself that her constancy in refusing Ariston's pleas would perhaps resolve him to cease loving her and that the fay would return her to her father, from whom the Prince of Leaves could obtain her.

"But I want at least," she said to him, "to be able to tell you what is happening on this island, and I don't know how that can be possible, for everyone is suspect to me here."

"I shall, therefore, leave you subjects of a Prince who is among my friends," said the Prince of Leaves, "who will always remain with you, and by means of whom you can often give me your news. Only remember, beautiful Princess, the impatience with which I shall await that news."

After those words, he approached the tree that had brought him, and touched several of its leaves; two butterflies emerged therefrom, the prettiest in the world, one the color of fire and white, the other yellow and flax gray. Ravissante was looking at them when the Prince of Leaves, smiling, said to her: "I see that you're surprised by the form of the confidants that I am giving you, but these butterflies are not only what they appear to you to be; that is a mystery that those I am leaving you will explain to you, when you permit them to converse with you."

After that, Ravissante noticed in the distance some of the nymphs, coming to search for her in her solitude; she begged the Prince of Leaves to embark again. He obeyed her, in spite of the infinite pain that he felt in quitting her; but he could not depart quickly enough not to be seen.

The fay and Ariston were informed of his return to the island, and from that moment on, in order to remove from the beautiful Ravissante the means, and even the hope, of seeing him again, they built on the summit of the rock a tower of the same stone, and in order to be absolutely sure, as the adventure of the monsters had surprised them, they rendered the tower and the rock invisible for all those who came in search of it, no longer wanting to trust ordinary enchantments.

Ravissante despaired of an imprisonment so cruel and so difficult to break; Prince Ariston had not hidden from her that he had rendered it invisible; he had even tried to represent that care as a certain sign of his tenderness; but Ravissante's hatred and scorn for him were increasing every day, and he hardly dared appear before her any longer.

Meanwhile, the butterflies had not quit her, and she often gazed at them with pleasure, because they had come from the Prince of Leaves. One day, when she was even sadder than usual, dreaming on a terrace that was at the top of the tower, the butterfly the color of fire flew over one of the vases filled with flowers that ornamented he balustrade.

"Why not send me to inform the Prince of Leaves," it said, suddenly, to the Princess. "He will come infallibly to your aid."

Ravissante was astonished at first to hear the butterfly speak, although her lover had prepared her for that novelty. For a few moments, she did not say anything, but the name of the Prince of Leaves enabled her to dissipate her astonishment.

"I was so surprised," she said to the butterfly, "to hear you talking like us that I took some time to reply to you. I see clearly that you can go to inform the Prince of Leaves of my misfortune, but what can he do except suffer a futile affliction? He will not be able to find me in a place that the cruelty of my enemies has taken care to render invisible."

"It is less so than you think," replied the yellow butterfly, flying close to the Princess in order to join the conversation. "I have soon observed our prison: I have flown, and even swum, around it; it disappears when one is in the water, but it ceases to be invisible when one is high in the air. Doubtless the fay did not believe that route easy enough for her to think of defending it like that of the sea. That is advice that I was going to give you," the butterfly continued, "When my bother broke the silence that we have maintained until now."

Such agreeable news had rendered some hope to the Princess. "Is it possible," she said, "that Ariston has neglected some precaution to satisfy his cruelty and his amour? Undoubtedly, his power and that of the fay, which can do anything over the sea and the land, does not extend as far as the air; that is the reason that has prevented the Prince and the fay from rendering the isle invisible from the direction of the sky."

After a few moments of reflection, Ravissante added: "But can the Prince of Leaves do anything in the air?"

"No, Madame," said the butterfly the color of fire, "he can do nothing there, and your prison will be as invisible to him, even though he is a demigod, as it would be for a human, but...."

"The Prince will, therefore, be as unfortunate as me," interjected the sad Ravissante, shedding tears that augmented her beauty, and which moved the two butterflies extremely, "and I sense that I will be even more unfortunate by virtue of the woes of the Prince of Leaves than my own." With a sigh, she continued: "What should I do, then?"

"Send me forth immediately," replied the butterfly the color of fire, brusquely. "I will go and inform the Prince of Leaves of your misfortunes, and he will come to your aid; although his power does not extend over the air, one of his friends is a Prince who can do anything there, and of whom he can dispose, as of himself; that is what my brother, who will remain with you, can explain to you during my voyage.

"Adieu, beautiful Princess," the butterfly continued, fluttering above the balustrade. "Cease being anxious and count on my diligence; I will fly with as much rapidity as you wish."

After those words the butterfly was lost in the air, and the Princess then felt the joy, so keen and so charming, that is given by the hope of soon seeing someone whom one loves. She returned to her room, and the yellow butterfly followed her there; she felt an extreme impatience to know from what Prince her lover could expect an aid so necessary to their happiness. In order not to be ignorant any longer, she begged the yellow butterfly to tell her everything that might contribute to augmenting and flattering her hope. She put it in a little basket of flowers, which she brought to a table next to her, and the butterfly, which made it an honor to please her, commenced its story.

Near the Isle of Day, where the Prince of Leaves reigns, there is another isle, smaller but just as agreeable. The ground there is always covered with flowers, and we are sure that that is a grace that Flora has granted to our land in order to immortalize the memory of happy days when she came to find Zephyr there; for it is said that it was to our isle that they came when their love was still secret and new. It is called the Isle of Butterflies. Its inhabitants do not have the form in which you see me; they are little winged humans, very pretty, very gallant, very amorous and so fickle that they scarcely love the same thing for longer than a day.

When the Golden Age was still reigning on earth, Amour, who flattered himself then that all hearts would always be tender and faithful, feared that, by virtue of the facility that we had of flying all over the world, we might go to teach mortals the agreeable science of changing in loving, which that god called an error capable of destroying the happiness of his empire forever. In order to forbid us any commerce with the rest of the world, he came to our island, touched the ground there with one of his arrows, and then rose up again on the brilliant cloud that had brought him.

"If you wish," he said to the inhabitants of the island, "to continue to go through the air like the gods, I have just ensured my vengeance; you can no longer trouble the felicity of my empire without dangerous commerce." After those words he disappeared.

Amour's threats did not take away from the butterflies the desire for change, nor that of flying through the air, in order at least to have the pleasure of sometimes quitting he earth. Some of them rose into the air and found that they had the same facility there as before the time when Amour had come to forbid it, but as soon as they emerged from the limits of our island, they were changed into little animals such as you see me, all of different colors. Vengeful Amour had wanted to mark by that diversity how inclined to inconstancy they were.

Surprised by their metamorphosis, they returned to our island, and as soon as they had touched the ground they resumed their original form. Since that fatal time, Amour's vengeance has always continued among us; when we quit our homeland, nothing human remains to us except intelligence and the liberty of speech; but we never make use of the latter faculty outside our island, in order not to render that vengeance celebrated by publishing it ourselves throughout the world, and in order not to frighten those who, like us, have a penchant for inconstancy; but we have the pleasure of seeing and traveling the world.

Destiny has avenged us on Amour, without our having to interfere; inconstancy reigns with as much power as him throughout the extent of his empire. Some centuries after that change had occurred in the Empire of the Butterflies, the Sun, who seems to take pleasure in enabling the birth of flowers, applauded himself so well for his own work that he fell in love with a rose of extraordinary beauty. He was loved tenderly in return, and she sacrificed for him all the cares that the Zephyrs took of her; after a time, the rose became somewhat different in form from others; the Sun immediately enabled the birth of others similar to her, in order that she would be more easily confounded in that quantity of flowers, which then appeared to be specimens of a new plant. It is the one that has subsequently been called the rose with a hundred leaves.[6]

Eventually, a demigod was born of the Sun and that flower, whom the Sun destined to rule over our island. Until then we had not had a sovereign, but the son of a god who favored our land so constantly was received as its King with an extreme joy; he was named the Prince of Butterflies. It is that Prince, beautiful Princess, who will be able to help you by way of the route of the air, and whom the adventure I shall relate to you has rendered the friend of the Prince of Leaves forever, and so perfectly.

---

[6] i.e. *Rosa centifola*, sometimes known in English as the Provence rose or the cabbage rose.

In a land far away from that of the butterflies, a fay reigns who makes her dwelling in a very obscure cavern; she is known as the Fay of the Grotto; she is extraordinarily tall, an her face is a mixture of green, aurora and blue; her form renders her almost as redoubtable as her power, and she is so feared by mortals, that none of them has been bold enough to dare to approach the land she inhabits.

One day, the Prince of Butterflies, who was traveling for his diversion in the vicinity of her empire, perceived the fay, and, surprised by that encounter, he followed her for a long time in order to see what would become of such a frightful monster. She did not notice that she was observed, for the Prince, although a son of the Sun, has not been able to obtain from destiny the liberty to travel in any other form than the one we all take on when we leave our realm, because he was born on our island after the time when Amour made us feel his vengeance. However, he was not inconstant, as all his subjects are, and Amour, in order to grant him at least a small mercy, had permitted that when he changed form he would only be a single color, and that that color would be the one that signifies fidelity.

In that form, he followed the Fay for as long as he wished; he saw her enter her somber dwelling; urged by an impulse of curiosity, he flew after her, but what a spectacle awaited him in the depths of that cavern! He saw there a young woman more beautiful and more brilliant than the daylight, who was lying on a bed of grass, and who seemed to be extremely sad. From time to time, she shed tears, which fell from her beautiful eyes; her dejection and languor only served to make her seem more lovable.

The Prince of Butterflies remained so touched by that sight that he almost forgot a thousand times over the form that he had, only to remember that he was madly in love and burning to say so. He was extracted from such a sweet reverie by the terrible voice of the fay, who spoke to the young woman with a frightful harshness. He sensed dolor and anger in consequence, and was in despair at being unable to express either one.

The fay, who, by virtue of a natural restlessness, could not remain long in the same place, soon went out of the cavern; then the Prince approached the young woman by whom he was so charmed; he fluttered round her, and, wanting to enjoy the only liberty that his form permitted him, he alighted on her hair, which was the most beautiful blonde in the world, and then on her face.

He was dying of the desire to tell her how touched he was by her beauty and her dolor, but what means did he have of making her believe that he was a son of the Sun, without being able to appear before her in his own form? And how could he tell her about the vengeance of Amour and the inconstancy so natural to the inhabitants of his isle, while wanting to persuade her that he would never cease to love her?

He remained for several days in the cavern or in the forest that surrounded it; he could not resolve to quit that beauty, whom he adored, and although he dared not speak to her, he wanted to, and that was enough to make him prefer that frightful abode to the agreeable place where he had the pleasure of reigning, and that of being the most handsome Prince in the world.

During the time in which he did not quit that young person, he always saw the fay treat her with an incredible inhumanity, and he learned from their speech that the unfortunate beauty was the Princess of Linnets; that the fay, who was one of her relatives, had kidnapped her in her most tender youth in order more easily to usurp her realm, which was a little island situated not far from that of the butterflies. The Prince had been there many times; he had even heard mention that its Princess had been kidnapped and that no one had ever been able to discover what had become of her. That land was called the Isle of Linnets because of the large quantity of little birds of the species bearing that name to be found there.

The Prince of Butterflies pitied the misfortune of that lovable Princess, and in order finally to discover whether it was possible to liberate her, he resolved to go away. He flew to the Isle of Day without a moment's repose; he found the Prince of Leaves there, with whom he had been linked for some time in tender amity, and who had just spent a spent of a year in the Isle of Butterflies. He related his adventure to that Prince, and, after having examined all the means they might employ to set the young Princess free, the Prince of Leaves resolved to go himself to the fay's forest in order to inform the Princes of Linnets of the violent amour that that the Prince of Butterflies had for her, and of the reasons that still prevented the unfortunate Prince from appearing before her in his veritable form, if she would not consent to allow herself to be taken to the Isle of Butterflies.

However, the Prince of Leaves appeared to his friend to be too redoubtable a confidant; he feared, with reason, that the Princess might be more touched by the charms of such a perfect Prince than by the story of the amour of another Prince of whom she had never heard mention. He bemoaned the cruelty of his destiny, and searched for some other means of declaring his amour to the Princess, but in vain; no one other than a demigod could approach the fay's dwelling without immediately feeling the deadly effects of her vengeance.

He therefore embarked with the Prince of Leaves, agitated by a jealous dread; it seemed to him that the Prince would not be able to conserve for a single minute, at the sight of the beautiful Princess, the insensibility in which he had always gloried. Amour, touched by the awful state to which he had reduced him, wanted at least to reassure him against that just dread, and at the same time to triumph himself over the insensible heart of the Prince of Leaves.

It is by means of you, beautiful Princess (the butterfly continued) that the god expected the victory, and you alone were worthy of obtaining it. It was on the same day as the embarkation of the two Princes that they saw from afar, on a rock, an illumination so brilliant that the Prince of Leaves, pushed by his destiny, ordered the winged fish that were conducting the arbor of myrtles in which he was traveling to approach the place from which the bright light was coming.

You know the rest of that adventure. The Prince of Leaves found you in the forest of hyacinths and left at your feet a liberty that was so dear to him, and which, until that moment, he had always conserved. Pressed by the impatience of the Prince of Butterflies, who had only suffered with regret the pause on that shore, he tore himself away with an infinite difficulty from a place where his heart and his desires would have liked to arrest him forever. They continued their voyage, and the Prince of Butterflies was so satisfied to see the Prince of Leaves veritably amorous and so far from becoming his rival, that he did not doubt that it was a sufficiently favorable presage to promise him perfect good fortune in the remainder of his enterprise.

They arrived in the forest of the Fay of the Grotto; they went into the sad dwelling, and Amour, who had resolved to favor them, enabled them to find the Princess of Linnets alone and asleep.

There was no time to lose; the Prince of Leaves bore her away to the arbor of verdure, to which the Prince of Butterflies followed him. The fay returned at that moment. She uttered horrible cries at the sight of that abduction. She believed that she could prevent it by the power of her art and avenge herself on the person who had just taken the Princess of Linnets away, but her enchantments were useless against the Prince of Leaves, who drew away from that dismal shore in very little time.

Meanwhile, the young Princess woke up, and was equally surprised by the place where she found herself and the presence of the Prince of Leaves. It was, however, an agreeable astonishment, which was augmented by the discourse of the Prince, who informed her of the effects of her beauty, that she was liberated from the tyranny of the fay, that she could reign henceforth in her empire, and in a realm even more beautiful than her own.

The Prince of the Butterflies spoke to her about his amour with so much vivacity and tenderness that the Princess felt an infinite curiosity to see him in his veritable form, of which she had formed from that moment on the finest idea in the world. They continued their journey, and in a few days they arrived at the Isle of Butterflies, the ground of which the Prince hastened to touch, in order finally to appear to the eyes of the Princess as he was. The sight of him did not belie the idea that she had formed of him; he was fortunate enough to please her, and he loved her all the more tenderly for that.

The Princes of Linnets sent word to her own island to inform her subjects about her adventure; they came to find her in a crowd, and it was in their presence that she accepted the heart and the Empire of the fortunate Prince of Butterflies. Meanwhile, the Prince of Leaves had quit him as soon as he had conducted him to his island in order to return to you, Princess, where his impatience and ardent amour pressed him incessantly to render.

Ravissante was listening to the butterfly with an extreme attention when she saw Prince Ariston enter her room with a fury in his expression whose effects she feared.

"Destiny is threatening me," he cried as he came in, "and it promises me a great misfortune; it is doubtless that of losing you, there is no other that my heart can find sensible enough to merit being predicted to me! Look, Madame," he continued, addressing Ravissante, "look what color the walls of the tower are becoming: it is a certain sign for me of imminent misfortune."

As Ariston's woes were a source of pleasure for Ravissante, she looked at what the Prince was pointing out to her, and perceived that the blue stone had lost its original color and was beginning to turn green; she felt joy, because she had no doubt that it was a sure presage of the arrival of the Prince of Leaves. That joy, which the unhappy Ariston remarked, increased his despair. What did he not say to Ravissante? Rendered sincere by the excess of his dolor, he told her that he loved her enough not to cease adoring her, although he was assured of being unhappy all his life.

"I cannot doubt my misfortune," he said to the Princess. "Destiny has promised me, as it has you, that I will always be miserable if I were not faithful to the first impression amour made in my heart, and what means is there of accomplishing that cruel order? When one sees you, after having already become sensible, one forgets everything, even the care of one's happiness, only to think of loving you and only to seek to please you. A young Princess of my father's Court had appeared worthy of my vows; I believed that I would only think about returning to her when I had spent some time here, but a moment of seeing you overturned all my projects; my reason and my heart were equally in accord in my change, and I believed that nothing was impossible for the tender amour that you had inspired in me. I even flattered myself that it could change destiny, but your ever-constant rigors taught me that I was mistaken, and that no hope any longer remains to me but that of soon dying for you."

Prince Ariston had just finished that speech, which made him seem to Ravissante at least worthy of some pity, when they saw a throne of foliage in the air sustained by an infinite number of butterflies. One of them was entirely blue, and that color enabled Ravissante to recognize the son of the Sun; he flew toward her and said: "Come, beautiful Princess; it is to-day that you will recover your liberty and render the most amiable Prince in the word happy."

The butterflies set the throne down next to Ravissante. She sat on it, and they lifted it up.

Ariston, in despair at having lost the Princess, only consulted the excess of his dolor, and hurled himself into the sea. The fay immediately abandoned the rock, which that death had just rendered to disastrous for her, and in order to mark her fury she shattered it, along with the tower, by means of a thunderbolt, into an infinite number of pieces, which were transported by the waves and winds into various parts of the sea.

That is the species of stone from which rings have since been made that are named turquoises; those which are still named turquoise de la vieille roche[7] are all made from residues of that dispersed rock, and the others are only stones that resemble them. The memory of the misfortune predicted to Prince Ariston by the change in the color of the walls of the tower has been passed down to us; it is still said that if those rings turn green, some misfortune will occur to this who wear them, and it is even asserted that it is ordinarily amorous misfortunes that are thus predicted.

While the fay expressed her dolor by the destruction of her island, the Prince of Butterflies, satisfied to have rendered the Prince of Leaves a service similar to the one that he had received from him, conducted Ravissante through the air as far as a ship of rushes ornamented with garlands of flowers, where the Prince of Leaves was waiting with all the impatience that a violent amour can cause. Words cannot express the pleasure he felt on seeing the Princess arrive; joy and amour had never appeared more vividly than in the heart and in the speech of that Prince. He set sail diligently for the Isle of Day.

The Prince of Butterflies flew away to rejoin the lovable Princess of Linnets instead. Ravissante sent two butterflies to her father, the King, in order to inform him as to what her fortune had been; the good King praised Destiny and went as soon as possible to the Isle of Day, where the Prince of Leaves and the beautiful Ravissante reigned with all imaginable felicity and were always happy, because they never ceased to be amorous and faithful.

> *One ought to envy the fate of Ravissante;*
> *Because of a keen and constant ardor,*
> *Amour lavished his precious treasures upon her.*
> *To be able to enjoy them like her,*

---

[7] A variety that normally retains that designation in English, although it is also known as odontolite.

Alas, how happy one would be,
If it were sufficient to be faithful.

THE FORTUNATE PENALTY

There was once a great King who fell madly in love with a beautiful Princess of his Court. As soon as he loved her he spoke to her about his tenderness; Kings have other privileges than vulgar lovers. The Princess was not offended by an amour that might place her on the throne, but she always appeared so sage to the King that he found her charming; he married her. The wedding was celebrated with an incredible magnificence, and what was even more incredible is that he was a husband without ceasing to be a lover.

The happiness of such a pleasant marriage was only troubled by having no children to succeed good fortune and their kingdom. In order at least to have the relief of hope, the King resolved to go and consult a fay whom he believed to be a firm friend; her name was Formidable, but she had not always been so for the King; it is even said that one can still find humorous poems in old collections of the land that say a great deal about her, so bold were poets in those days; for the fay was greatly respected and seemed so grim that it was almost impossible to imagine that she had ever felt the power of Amour—but where are the hearts that escape him?

The King, who had always been gallant, and who had a great deal of intelligence, was not unaware that appearances are often deceptive. He had found Formidable in a wood where he had gone hunting; she appeared to his eyes in a form so gracious and with a manner so charming that the King did not doubt for a moment that she wanted to please. Rarely are so many charms made to shine without intention. The King loved her. His fay found more pleasure in being loved than always inspiring terror.

That tenderness lasted several years, but one day, Formidable, who counted on her lover's heart as a possession that would never cease to be hers, allowed the King to see her in her true form. She was no longer young, she was scarcely a beauty; she repented, by virtue of the disturbance that she saw in the King's face, of having had too much self-confidence. She recognized shortly thereafter that sentiments of the heart, no matter how tender they might be, cannot touch and cannot render amour happy, if they are not sustained by a lovable face.

The King was ashamed of only having been in love with a beautiful idea. He ceased to love his fay and only conserved respect and deference for her. By virtue of a glory that was natural to her, she pretended so convincingly to be content with the King's amity that she persuaded him that she was his best friend; she even came to his wedding, like the other fays of the land who were invited to it, in order not to give him cause to think, by virtue of a stinging refusal, that she had any reason to be upset by that marriage.

The King, therefore, counting on the amity of his former mistress, went to find her in her dwelling; it was a marble palace the color of fire in the middle of a vast forest. One arrived there via an avenue of prodigious length, bordered on both sides by a hundred lions the color of fire. Formidable only liked that color, and she had tinted thus all the animals born in her forest. At the end of the avenue there was a large square in which a troop of Moors dressed in the color of fire and gold, magnificently armed, mounted guard perpetually.

The King traversed the forest alone, he knew the paths very well; he even traversed the avenue of lions without danger, for when he went into it he threw them buttercups that the fay had once given him in order to be able to pass that way without fear of the redoubtable lions; as soon as the King had thrown those beautiful flowers to them, they became gentle and placid. Finally, he reached the guard of Moors; at first they turned their arrows toward him but the King threw them pomegranate flowers, which the fay had given him along with the buttercups; the Moors fired their arrows in the air and arranged themselves in a hedge to let him pass.

He went into Formidable's palace; she was in a drawing room, sitting on a ruby throne, in the middle of twelve Mooresses clad in gauze the color of fire and gold; her costume was like theirs, and so covered with precious stones that she shone like the sun, although she was not as beautiful. The King gazed, and listened for a few moments before going into the drawing room. There were a number of books next to the fay on a red marble table; he saw her pick one up and continue to instruct the Mooresses in the secrets that render fays so redoubtable, but Formidable only taught them the ones that were contrary to the repose and happiness of men. She carefully refrained from teaching them the ones that might contribute to their felicity.

In consequence, the King felt hatred for the fay, and, entering the drawing room, he interrupted that fatal lesson. His arrival surprised Formidable, but she collected herself, dismissed the Mooresses and, looking at the King with an expression of pride and anger, she said: "What have you come to seek here, inconstant Prince? Why have you come to trouble again by your odious presence the repose that I am trying to enjoy here?"

The King was very surprised by a speech that he had not expected, and the fay opened one of her books. "I can see what you want," she continued. "Yes, you shall have a daughter by the Princess that you preferred so unjustly to me, but do not expect to be happy forever; it is time for me to avenge myself. The daughter you shall have will cause as much hatred to everyone as I once had love for you."

The King did everything he could to soften the fay's anger, but it was futile; hatred had succeeded amour and it was amour alone that could soften that fay, for pity and generosity were sentiments that she did not know. Proudly, she ordered the King to leave her palace. She opened a bird cage, and a parrot the color of fire emerged. "Follow this bird," she aid to the King, and give thanks to my bounty, which is not delivering you to the fury of my lions and my guards.

The bird flew away; the King followed it, and, by a road that was unknown to him, and much shorter than the one he knew, he was conducted to his realm. The Queen, whom he found on his return in an extreme sadness, questioned him so much on the subject that the King told her about the fay's cruel prediction, but without telling her what had once happened between them, in order not to cause the beautiful Queen further distress.

That Princess knew that a fay cannot prevent absolutely what one of her peers has predicted, but that she can soften the penalties that have been ordered. "I shall go to find Luminous, the sovereign of the Fortunate Empire" said the Queen. "She is a celebrated fay who takes pleasure in protecting the unfortunate. She is my relative; she has always favored me, and even predicted the good fortune to which Amour has enabled me to achieve."

The King approved strongly of the Queen's voyage, and he had high hopes of it. When her equipage was ready, she went to find Luminous, who bore that name because her beauty was so brilliant that one could scarcely sustain its splendor, and the grandeur of her soul responded perfectly to her beauty.

The Queen arrived in a vast country, and saw a high tower in the distance; although it could be seen from far away, however, there were many detours to make in order to reach it. It was made of white marble, and had no door; the windows, arranged in arcades, were crystal. A beautiful river, whose waters seemed to be made of silver, ran along the foot of the tower, circling around it several times. The Queen and her entire Court arrived at the water's edge, where the first circuit that it made around the fay's dwelling commenced.

The Queen passed over a bridge of white poppies, which the power of Luminous has rendered as sure and as durable as if it had been made of bronze, even though it was made of flowers. It was redoubtable nevertheless; it had the power to put anyone who passed over it against the fay's will to sleep for seven years. In the distance, beyond the bridge, the Queen perceived six young men, magnificently dressed, asleep on beds of grass, under awnings of foliage. They were Princes in love with the fay, and as she did not want to hear mention of amour, she had not permitted them to go any further.

After having passed over the bridge, the Queen found herself in the first space that the river left free; it was occupied by a charming labyrinth of jasmines and oleanders; there were only white ones, because that was the color that Luminous loved. After having admired that beautiful promenade, and having easily negotiated the turnings, which were only embarrassing for those that the amiable Luminous did not want to be able to enter her agreeable dwelling, the Queen passed over the river again on a bridge of white anemones; it made its second tour there, and the space that it left free before making its third circuit was occupied by a forest of acacias always in flower. The paths therein were charming, but so dark that the sun could not penetrate them; tender doves were seen there, the plumage of which put snow to shame; all the trees were covered with an infinite number of white canaries that made agreeable concerts; with a stroke of her wand, Luminous had taught them the most beautiful and pleasant songs in the world.

One emerged from that beautiful forest by a bridge of tuberoses and entered a beautiful terrain covered in trees charged with such beautiful and delicious fruits that the least of the trees there put to shame the famous gardens of the Hesperides. Every evening, however, the Queen found the most beautiful tents in the world, and magnificent meals were served as soon as she arrived, without any of the diligent and skillful servants being visible. The fay, who had learned from her books of the arrival of the Queen, was taking care of the needs of her voyage; she did not want her to be fatigued for a moment.

In order to leave that marvelous region, the Queen passed over the river on a bridge of white carnations and entered into the fay's park. It was as beautiful as everything else; the Fay sometimes went hunting there, and it was filled with an infinite number of white stags and hinds, and other animals of the same color. A pack of white greyhounds was dispersed in the park, lying on the grass with hinds and white rabbits, and other animals that are ordinarily wild, but were not in that place, the fay's art having domesticated them; when the dogs chased some beast in order to amuse Luminous, it seemed that they understood that it was only a game, for that they did everything they could do to catch it, except that they never did it any harm.

In that place the river made its fifth circuit around the fay's dwelling. In order to leave the park, the Queen passed over a bridge of small jasmines, and found herself in a charming hamlet. All the little cabins there were built in alabaster. The inhabitants of the pleasant place were the fay's subjects; they guarded her flocks; their clothes were made of silver gauze, they were crowned with garlands of flowers and their crooks sparkled with precious stones. All the sheep were surprisingly white; all the shepherdesses were young and beautiful, and Luminous liked the color white too much to have forgotten to give them a complexion so fine that it seemed that the sun itself aided it to be more brilliant. All the shepherds were handsome, and the only fault that one could find with that agreeable country was that there was not a single brunette beauty.

The shepherdesses welcomed the Queen and presented her with porcelain vases filed with the most beautiful flowers in the world. The Queen and all her Court were charmed by such a pleasant voyage, and that Princess took it as a fortunate presage for what the desired of the fay.

As they set forth to leave the hamlet, a young shepherdess advanced toward the Queen, and brought her a little greyhound bitch on a cushion of white velvet embroidered with silver and pearls. The greyhound could scarcely be made out on the cushion, so similar was their color. "The fay Luminous, sovereign of the Fortunate Empire," the young shepherdess said to the Queen, "has ordered me to present White White to you on her behalf. That is the name of the little bitch; she has the honor of being loved by Luminous, whose art has made her a marvel. She has ordered her to conduct you to the tower; you have only to let her go and follow her."

The Queen received the greyhound bitch with pleasure, charmed by the concern that the fay was showing for her. She caressed White White, who, after having returned her caresses with a great deal of intelligence and grace, leapt lightly to the ground and started walking in front of the Queen, who followed her, with all her Court.

They arrived at the edge of the river, which made its sixth circuit there; they were astonished to find no bridge there to pass over. The fay did not want the shepherds to come and trouble her in her retreat, and there was never a bridge in that place, except when she wanted to cross over, or to receive her friends. The Queen was thinking profoundly about the adventure when she heard White White bark three times; immediately, a Zephyr agitated the trees on the other side of the river and caused a great quantity of orange blossom to fall into the water, which formed a bridge, and the Queen passed over the river thereon.

She thanked White White with caresses, and found herself in an avenue of myrtles and delightful orange trees. After having traversed it without any tedium, even though it was extremely long, she found the bank of the river, which was making its seventh circuit there. She could not see any bridge, but the morning's adventure reassured her. White White tapped the ground three times with her little paw, and at the same moment, a bridge of white hyacinths appeared. The Queen passed over it and entered into a meadow covered in flowers. The beautiful tents were set up there; she rested for a while and then continued her route and found herself on the water's edge again.

There was no bridge over it, but White White advanced, drank from the beautiful river, and a bridge of white roses appeared immediately, which enabled the Queen to enter the fay's garden. It was filled with marvelous flowers, extraordinary fountains and statues of a surprising beauty, of which it is not possible to make an exact description. If the Queen had

not felt an extreme impatience to prevent the evils with which
the cruel Formidable had threatened her, she would have
stayed longer in that beautiful place; her entire court left it
regretfully, but it was necessary to follow White White, who
guided the Queen to where the river made its final circuit
around Luminous's dwelling.

The Queen finally found herself close to the fays tower;
there was only the river between them. She gazed at it with
pleasure, as the goal of her voyage, and she read this inscription, which was written on the tower in golden letters:

This is the charming abode
Of perfect felicity.
Luminous has built this lovely retreat;
She receives laugher there, but has banished amour
For her, although she seems well made.

That inscription had been made to her glory by the most
renowned fays of her time; they had wanted to leave to posterity that testimony of their amity and their esteem.

While the Queen was amusing herself thus on the water's
edge, White White made the short journey swimming, and
having dived, brought out a mother-of-pearl shell that she allowed to fall back into the river; at that sound, six beautiful
nymphs clad in brilliant garments opened a huge crystal window, and a stairway of pearls emerged from it, which gradually approached the Queen. White White promptly climbed up
all the way to the fay's window and went into the tower. The
Queen took the same route, but as she climbed the pretty
stairway the steps over which she had passed disappeared, and
thus prevented anyone from following her. She went into Luminous's tower, and the window closed again.

All the members of the Queen's retinue were in despair
at no longer seeing her and being unable to follow her, for she
was extremely beloved; their cries were audible all the way to
the place where Luminous was conversing with the Queen,
and in order to reassure the unfortunates, the fay sent one of

the nymphs to conduct them to the hamlet, where they were to await the Queen's return. The stairway of pearls reappeared, and rendered them hope. The nymph descended, and the Queen appeared at the window to order them to go with her and obey her.

The Princess remained with the fay, who received her with a prodigious magnificence and a divine manner that won hearts. The Queen stayed there for three days, which were not sufficient to see all the marvels of the tower; it would have required entire centuries to admire everything, and the beauties of the fay as well.

On the fourth day, after giving the Queen presents as elegant as they were magnificent, Luminous said to her: "Beautiful Princess, I am sorry not to be able to repair the misfortune with which Formidable has threatened you, but it is the fault of Destiny. It permits us to spread benefits over those we favor, but forbids us to protect them from, and put an end to, evils ordered by another fay. Thus, to console you for the misfortune that is in preparation for you, I promise you that within a year you will have a daughter so beautiful that everyone who sees her will be charmed by her; and I will take care," the fay added, "to ensure the birth of a Prince worthy of her."

Such a favorable prediction enabled the Queen to forget the hatred of Formidable for some time and the misfortunes she expected of her. Luminous did not tell the Queen what had rendered Formidable her enemy. Even the fays who are not in accord with one another keep strictly between themselves the secrets that might render them despicable to humans, and it is certain that they are the only women who have the intelligence not to speak ill of one another.

After infinite thanks of the part of the Queen, Luminous ordered twelve of her nymphs to charge themselves with presents and conduct the Queen as far as the hamlet, and she escorted her personally as far as the ladder of pearls that appeared as soon as the window was opened. When the Queen and the nymphs reached the bottom step, they saw a silver chariot harnessed to six white hinds; their harness was covered with diamonds; a child as beautiful as daylight conducted the chariot, and the nymphs followed it, mounted on white horses that could compete in beauty with those of the Sun.

The Queen arrived in the hamlet in that elegant conveyance; she found her entire Court there, whose members were delighted to see her again. The nymphs took their leave of the Queen and presented her with twelve fine horses enchanted so as never to tire; they told her that Luminous begged her to present them to the King on her behalf.

Heaped with the fay's bounty, the Queen returned to her realm, The King came as far as the frontier to meet her, and was so delighted by her return and the agreeable news that she announced on the part of Luminous that he ordered public rejoicing, the noise of which reached as far as Formidable, further increasing her hatred and anger against the King.

A short time after the Queen's return, she became pregnant, and did not doubt that it was with the beautiful princess who was to charm all hearts, for Luminous had promised her birth within a year. Formidable had not prescribed the time over which her vengeance would be accomplished, but did not have the design of delaying it. The Queen gave birth to two Princesses, and did not doubt for a moment which of them had been promised by Luminous, by virtue of the urgency with which she sensed herself embraced by the one who saw the light of day first.

She found her worthy of the fay's promises; nothing in the world was as beautiful; the King and all those who were present hastened to admire the little Princess, and the other was absolutely forgotten; whereupon the princess, who judged by that general negligence that Formidable's predictions were also being accomplished, ordered several times that she be given the same care as her elder sister.

The maidservants obeyed her with a repugnance that they could not vanquish, and which the King and Queen dared not criticize, because they felt it themselves. Luminous arrived swiftly on a cloud, and named the beautiful Princess Beloved, in order to give her a name appropriate to the destiny she had

promised her. The King rendered to Luminous al the respects
that she merited; she promised the Queen that she would always protect Beloved; she did not make her a gift then because she had already given her everything.

As for the other Princess, it was in vain that the King
gave her the name of one of his provinces. People gradually
became accustomed to calling her Unloved, by virtue of an
opposition that was very cruel for her.

When the two Princesses reached the age of twelve
years, Formidable wanted them to be removed from the Court,
in order, she said, to diminish the hatred and love that they
divided between them. Luminous allowed Formidable to order
that; she was sure that nothing could prevent the beautiful Beloved from reigning in her father's realm and in all hearts; she
had caused her to be born with so much charm that it was only
necessary to see her to have no doubt of it. In order to try to
appease the hatred that Formidable spread over his household,
the King resolved to obey her. He therefore sent the two Princesses, with a young and amiable Court, to a marvelous castle
he owned at the extremity of his kingdom; it was known as the
Castle of Portraits, and was a place worthy of the savant fay
who had built it four thousand years before.

The gardens and all the surrounding promenades were
admirable, but its most beautiful feature was a gallery that
stretched as far as the eye could see, where the portraits could
be seen of all the Princes and Princesses of the royal blood of
the realm and those of neighboring lands. As soon as they
were fifteen years old, their portraits were painted there, with
an artistry that could only be feebly imitated by anyone except
a fay. That gift was to last until the time when the most beautiful princess in the world entered the castle.

That gallery separated two vast and magnificent apartments. The two Princesses occupied them; they had the same
masters and the same education; nothing was taught to the
charming Beloved that was not taught to her sister; but Formidable came to give her lessons that spoiled all the others, and

Luminous came for her part to render Beloved worthy of the admiration of the whole world by means of her conversation.

The Princesses had been in that castle, distant from the Court, for three years when they heard an unfamiliar noise one day, which was followed by charming music. They were looking in all directions to see where the noise and the agreeable concert were coming from, when they perceived three portraits that filled three places that had been empty a moment before.

There was one that was crowned with flowers by two Amours, one of whom was gazing at the beautiful portrait with all the attention it merited, and seemed to have forgotten the care of firing an arrow that was ready to depart from his bow. The other was holding a little streamer bearing these lines:

Beloved had at birth, from sage nature,
The solid beauties that never die;
The graces will take care to embellish her attractions,
And Venus has given her girdle to her forever.

They were not necessary to make the portrait of the beautiful Beloved known; all her features and the charming grace that attracted hearts were evident there. She had a complexion of surprising whiteness, the most beautiful colors in the world, a round face, admirably blonde hair, and blue eyes, which shone with a gleam so vivid that all eyes that had the pleasure of seeing them judged that it was unnecessary for Luminous to have made a present to Beloved of a gift she had in herself; her mouth was charming, her teeth as white as her complexion, and Venus seemed to have given her the ability to smile like her. It was that divine portrait that occupied one of the ends of the gallery.

The second was that of Unloved; she was blonde, and did not lack beauty, but the portrait was like her; it did not please. These words were written beneath it in golden letters:

Unloved with her features, which form beauty
Cannot find a place in any heart;

Those two portraits were occupying all the attention of the two Princesses and all of their young Court, when Beloved, who was not vain in regard to her own charms, leaving everyone else the care of admiring them, cast her eyes upon the third portrait, which had appeared at the same time as her own. She found the wherewithal there to attract her gaze; it was that of a young Prince a thousand times more handsome than Amour. He resembled a god rather than a man; his hair was black and fell over his shoulders in thick curls, and his eyes promised as much intelligence as his person gave evidence of charm. These words were written beneath the portrait: *The Prince of the Gallant Isle.*

His beauty surprised everyone, but how it touched the beautiful Beloved! Her young heart felt an unknown emotion. Unloved, similarly, at the sight of the handsome portrait, was not exempt from a passion by which one could be touched for her. That adventure did not surprise anyone, for people were accustomed to seeing such marvels in that place.

The King and the Queen came to the castle to see the Princesses; they had a large number of copies made of their portraits, and sent them to all the neighboring kingdoms. Meanwhile, Beloved, as soon as she was alone, drawn by an involuntary impulsion, went to the gallery of portraits. That of the Prince of the Gallant Isle occupied all her attention and attracted all her gazes; he appeared to be worthy of both.

Unloved, who had nothing in common with her sister except the same attraction to the portrait of the Prince, spent almost every day in the gallery. That nascent passion augmented Unloved's hatred of the beautiful Princess to such an extent that, not being able to find the secret of hurting her, she begged Formidable incessantly to avenge her on her sister's charms. The cruel fay never refused such opportunities to do harm, so, following her own inclination and Unloved's pleas, she went to find the charming Princess, who was strolling along the bank of a river that passed the foot of the Castle of Portraits.

"Go," Formidable said to her, touching her with an ebony wand she was holding in her hand. "Go along the bank of this river until you find a person who hates you as much as I do, and until that time you shall not remain long in any place on earth."

At that terrible order, the Princess began to weep, and what tears! In all the world there was only Formidable's heart that was incapable of being moved by them.

Luminous hastened to the aid of the beautiful and unfortunate Beloved. "Console yourself," she said, "the voyage to which Formidable has just condemned you will end with an agreeable adventure, and until that day you will find nothing but pleasures."

After those favorable words, Beloved departed, with the sole regret of no longer seeing the beautiful portrait of the Prince of the Gallant Isle; but she dared not express her dolor in that regard to the fay. She therefore set forth, and everyone on her route seemed sensible to her charms. Zephyr alone reigned in the places through which she passed. Everywhere, she found nymphs ready to serve her with an extreme respect; the meadows were covered with flowers as she approached, and when the sun was too ardent, the woods increased their shade.

While the beautiful Princess made such a charming voyage, Luminous did not limit her vengeance to rendering Formidable's design futile. She went to find Unloved and struck her with an ivory wand. "Go," she said, "depart in your turn from the river bank; you shall never rest until you have found someone who loves you as much as you merit being loved."

Unloved departed, and was not missed. Even Formidable, to whom everything appeared to be her taste as long, as she did not have to suffer any pain, no longer thought about Unloved, and did not deign to protect her any longer.

The two Princesses, therefore, continued their voyage; Unloved had all the fatigues imaginable; the most beautiful flowers turned into thorns as she passed by; but the beautiful Princess had all the pleasures for which Luminous had enabled her to hope, and she found them even more sensible than those she had been promised.

At the end of a fine day, as the sun was about to repose in the arms of Thetis, Beloved sat down on the edge of a river; immediately, an infinite number of flowers born around her formed a kind of bed of repose, the charm of which she would have admired for a long time if she had had not perceived another object on the river, which prevented her from thinking about anything else. It was a little amethyst boat, ornamented with a thousand streamers of the same color, charged with monograms and gallant devices.

Twelve young men dressed in light garments, flax-gray and silver, crowned with garlands of immortelles, were rowing with so much diligence that the boat was soon close enough to the bank to allow the beautiful Beloved to remark all of that various beauty. It was with an astonishment and an agreeable surprise that she perceived her name and his monogram everywhere, and a moment later the Princess recognized her portrait on a little topaz altar erected in the middle of the boat; below her portrait she read the words: *If this is not Amour, what is it?*

After her first movements of admiration, she feared seeing the strangers, who had initially seemed so elegant, descend from the boat.

Everything speaks to me of the amour of someone unknown, Beloved said to herself, *but I sense that the Prince of the Gallant Isle alone is worthy of inspiring in me the sentiments with which I see only too clearly that another has doubtless been touched for me. Fatal portrait*, she added, *why did Destiny offer it to my eyes at a time when, far from being able to defend myself, I did not even know whether it was possible to love anything more tenderly than flowers?*

That reflection was followed by a few sighs, and she would have remained in that sweet reverie for longer if an agreeable sound of various instruments had not extracted her from it. She gazed at the boat, from which the agreeable sounds were departing. A man whose face she could not see, clad in a magnificent costume of the same color that shone in all his crew, appeared to have no occupation but gazing at her portrait, while six beautiful nymphs formed a charming concert and accompanied these words, which were sung by the man who was still looking at the portrait of the Princess, to an air by Duboullay:[8]

Let everyone speak of my amour
And the charms of the one I love.
Beloved has more attractions than Amour himself
To flatter my extreme tenderness;
Nymphs, repeat in turn
That everything speaks of my amour
And the charms of the one I love.

The Graces abandon the heavens for her,
Quitting without regret the Queen of Cythera;
The pleasure of seeing her, the sweetness of pleasing her
Is worth more than the abode and pleasures of the gods.

Beloved has more attractions than Amour himself
To flatter my extreme tenderness;
Nymphs, repeat in turn
That everything speaks of my amour
And the charms of the one I love.

By one alone of her gazes a heart is inflamed;
Everyone yields to her, lays down their arms,
And until the glad times that her charms shine
One cannot have loved.

---

[8] The librettist, musician and poet Michel du Boullay, secretary to the Duc de Vendôme, wrote the words for Louis Lully's opera *Orphée* (1690).

Beloved has more attractions than Amour himself
To flatter my extreme tenderness;
Nymphs, repeat in turn
That everything speaks of my amour
And the charms of the one I love.

The sweetness of that concert stopped the beautiful Beloved on the river bank; when it was over, the unknown man turned his head in her direction and allowed her to remark, with as much disturbance as pleasure, the lovable features of the Prince of the Gallant Isle. What a surprise, and what a joy it was to see that charming prince, and to learn that he was only occupied with her. It would be necessary to be able to love as perfectly as in the time of the fays to understand fully all that the young princess felt then.

The Prince of the Gallant Isle experienced the same surprise; he hastened to descend on to the fortunate shore that offered the divine Beloved to his eyes. She did not have the strength to flee such a perfect Prince; she accused Destiny a thousand times for her weakness; on similar occasions, one rarely fails to hold it to account. It is impossible to express what the young lovers said to one another, and they often understood one another without speaking.

Luminous, who had guided the pretty boat and Beloved's footsteps to that place suddenly appeared, in order to reassure the timid Princess, who had finally made the decision to quit such a charming and dangerous Prince; she told them that they were destined to love one another and to be united forever. "However," added the fay, "before then it is necessary to finish the voyage ordered by Formidable."

One cannot disobey the fays; Beloved and the Prince were so satisfied by the pleasure of being together that everything that did not separate them appeared very pleasant to them. They therefore continued their journey, sometimes in the pretty boat, sometimes traversing a beautiful and vast solitude that the river irrigated with its waters. It was in that tranquil region that the Prince of the Gallant Isle completed losing the repose of his heart. He told the beautiful Princess everything that he had felt for her since the happy day that her divine portrait had been brought to the Court, and that one day, while walking by the water's edge dreaming about his amour, Luminous had appeared to him and, showing him the amethyst boat, had ordered him to embark thereon, promising a favorable success for his voyage an is amour.

While the Prince and Beloved continued obeying Formidable's order, and their ardors were augmented every day, they became so happy that they dreaded arriving, for fear of being occupied with something other than their tenderness.

For her part, Unloved also continued her difficult voyage.

The course of the river that the two Princesses were following led them gradually to the Gallant Isle, and they both arrived there at the same time. Luminous did not fail to go there. She told Beloved that Formidable's vengeance was accomplished, since, in encountering her sister, she had found the only person in the world who was able to hate her.

"And Unloved's voyage has also finished, then," said the beautiful Princess, "for nothing has been able to diminish the amity that I have for her"—and she begged the fay thereafter to ameliorate, if it were possible, the sad destiny of her sister. But it was futile to ask for that grace for Unloved; as soon as she saw the Prince of the Gallant Isle, whom she recognized easily as the man whose lovable portrait had touched her heart, and had heard Luminous say that the time of his marriage to young Beloved was approaching, she threw herself into the same river that she had been following for a year with so much difficulty without having had recourse to death. The misfortunes of Amour strike more sharply than those of fortune.

Luminous, who saw the Princess fall into the water, changed her into a little animal, which still marks by its manner of walking the humor of the unfortunate Unloved. Her destiny was accomplished even after her death; she was not regretted. It cost Beloved a few tears, but what misfortunes could not be consoled by the Prince of the Gallant Isle? She was so touched by his tenderness that she paid hardly any heed to the celebrations that were invented in order to receive her in his kingdom. The Prince also took little part in them. When one is very amorous, one no longer knows any true pleasure except that of being loved by the person one loves.

The King and the Queen, alerted by Luminous, came to find their lovable daughter. It was in their presence that the generous fay declared that the beautiful Beloved had had the glory of putting an end to the adventure of the Castle of Portraits, because nothing had yet appeared in the world as beautiful. The love of the Prince of the Gallant Isle was too violent to be able to wait any longer, and he begged the King and the Queen to consent to their happiness. Luminous honored with her presence a day so fine and so desired. The wedding was held with all the magnificence that one ought to expect of fays and Kings, but however happy that day must have been, I shall not make the description of it, for although Amour promises happiness, a wedding is almost always a sad occasion.

As long as Amour makes his dread torments felt,
And the sweet transports he inspires,
A hundred things remain to say,
For poets and lovers;
But for marriage one demands in vain
The god of verses and the nine docile sisters
It is the fate of lovers and of authors
To run aground on the epithalamium.

A FATHER AND HIS FOUR SONS

from *Voyage de Campagne*

This tale is narrated in the course of a portmanteau work of fiction in which a group of courtiers, on an excursion in the country, are delayed for two days in the company of a group of local people, and engage in a long conversation, in which various topics are discussed, in the course of which various members of the party relate their personal histories, mostly focusing on troubled marriages and amorous adventures. At one point the discussion surrounding the personal histories veers in the direction of the merits of different kinds of reading, and the merit of otherwise of "the new contes des fées." One of the participants dismisses such things as "bagatelles" and claims that her greatest delights come from "serious reading." The issue immediately becomes controversial, leading the narrator of the portmanteau—who considers herself "destined to calm storms" to suggest that she might narrate a story that "was once told in a famous house at a time when wit was a little more fashionable than it is at present," provided that she is permitted "not to follow my text scrupulously and can put what embellishments therein that I believe to be necessary." Everyone agrees, and she tells the following story.

In one of the continents of the world lived a great lord fatigued by the noise and tumult of the Court; he had shown his value and his magnificence until a very advanced age. The desire to see the four sons that he had had by a woman he had loved very much, who had died soon after the birth of the last, caused him to return to the castle where his forefathers had lived before recompenses had rewarded him for his services.

He found his children of an age to think about their fortune; they were well made and they had intelligence, but living in the country had given them a certain constrained and timid manner, of which he could only imagine one means of ridding them. He summoned all four of them to his room; he told them that his income was not sufficient to render them happy; that he found much injustice in giving the eldest a larger share than the younger ones, since they were of the same blood; and that he was going to give each of them a share of his wealth, and provide each of them an equipage appropriate to his condition. He ordered his eldest son to go and seek his fortune in Asia, the second to go to Africa, the third to America and the fourth to Europe. His health was good enough to hope to see them all come back richer and even more honest men than they were. He gave them a rendezvous for seven years hence, and told them that if Heaven disposed of his life before then they would find everything in good order and would have reason to bless and love his memory.

The four sons assured such a good father of their respects and their obedience; they departed a short time thereafter and followed the orders that had been prescribed to hem; their adventures have remained unknown, but they did not fail to return to their father's castle at the end of seven years.

They found him in good health. It was a sensible joy for the five individuals to see one another again after such a long absence. The father, whose name was Mondor, asked his eldest son, whose name was Haraguan, to relate the story of his voyage and how he had improved himself. He admitted to him with some shame that his principal friend in Asia had been a great Necromancer, and that he had become very skilful in that art.

"Which is to say," said Mondor, "to call things by their name, that you're something of a sorcerer. And you, my son," he said to the second, "have you exercised a less somber science?"

"Seigneur," said Fascinety, "I have become the most excellent conjurer in the world."

"A player with goblets," added the father. "Let's not disguise things." Then, turning to the third, he said: "Speak in your turn, Tirandor."

"As for me, Seigneur, I can boast of launching an arrow more accurately than any man in the world."

"Again, that's a little more honorable." Turing to the youngest, he added: "And you?"

"Oh, Seigneur," he said, throwing himself at his feet, "I have to beg your pardon a thousand times; I have become an artisan, without any respect for my birth; but if perfection diminishes my fault, you will doubtless grant me forgiveness."

The sad father began thinking profoundly; his eyes had changed completely; it was evident that he had begun to repent of having made his children travel; but as he had courage, he collected himself promptly and looked at them with a more serene expression.

"You have doubtless chosen estates worthy of neither you nor me," he said, "but it is necessary to be able to take things as they are and try to make use of what you can do, to rectify that which is base in your choice. In the nearby forest" he added, "there is the wherewithal to enable me to see whether you do not believe yourselves to be more skillful than you are. In fact, a bird that only builds its nest once every hundred years has come to build it this year in one of those trees. It is unknown to everyone; no one has ever found it. If you can take me to it," he said to his eldest son, "you will not have wasted your time in Asia."

Haraguan immediately made a few circles with his magic wand, and, going out with Mondor, he led him to the very tree in which the nest was.

"That's not bad," said the father, "but Fascinety, it's necessary to make a trial of your métier; climb up into the branches and go take the egg from underneath the mother without her perceiving it."

Lighter than a falcon, Fascinety flew rather than climbed up, and, stealing the egg without the mother suspecting it, he held it in the air at the top of the tree in order to mark his victory.

"That's not enough," added the father. "It's necessary, Tirandor, that you launch an arrow so accurately that you break the egg without injuring your brother's hand."

Tirandor did not miss his target; the hope of the bird was destroyed and the egg fell in a thousand pieces.

"Artidas," Mondor continued, "Now is the time to prove the skill of your hands."

Artidas did not delay for a moment resembling the beautiful egg so perfectly that the most clear-sighted eyes would not have been able to remark the faults.

The father appeared content with the proofs that the sons had just given of their skill; he took them home, and, speaking to them with the authority befitting the head of a family, he said to them: "You have chosen terrible métiers, but it is also necessary to agree that you excel in them, and that another theater is required to witness them than a country manse.

"The King has lost his only daughter; she was more beautiful than the daylight, she had intelligence; she was desired by all the neighboring kings, but her heart did not seem to be determined for anyone. One day, when she was walking on the terrace of the palace, she perceived a flying dragon of a grandeur so prodigious that she wanted to run away into order to shelter in the apartments; but the dragon, which had good eyes, and was incredibly nimble in spite of its weight, had seized her in its horrible claws before she could reach safety. That was terrible news for the King, her father; he sent troops in all directions, and he equipped fleets to search all the isles of the sea. All his measures were futile. It was a year ago that the princess was lost, without anyone being able to obtain any news of her."

Addressing Haraguan, he added: "If you can discover where she is by the power of your arts, that service would add infinitely to those I rendered to the state in my best years, and I could see you collect its fruits with all the joy of a tender father."

Haraguan promised to carry out that fine enterprise to the best of his ability; an equipage was prepared in a matter of days.

Mondor took his family to the Court; he presented himself to the King, who received him as a worthy and faithful subject whom he wanted to recompense, and his four sons as young seigneurs of great hope.

"Sire," said Mondor to the King, "Your Majesty has not dried up his tears; their cause is only too well known to me."

"And what remedy," replied the King, "can you bring to my dolor? I have omitted nothing to find my daughter; I have not been able to succeed, and nothing can console me."

"It is not vain commiserations, Sire, that I have come to offer you," said Mondor. "You see in the eldest of my sons a subject capable of rendering a great service to his King; only order that a vessel be equipped, and I promise you the return of the princess within two months."

The sad King hunched his shoulders and looked at Mondor pityingly; but the old man was not deterred, and it was believed that, being a very sensate man, he could indeed do what he promised.

A ship was therefore equipped; the family embarked on it, and after a month of navigation, they discovered the island where Haraguan was sure that the princess was. They even perceived shortly afterwards the monstrous dragon, which was asleep on the sea shore, and the sad Isaline—that was the name of the princess—embarrassed within five coils of the tail, which was thirty aunes long. She appeared to be looking tenderly at a young fisherman who was sailing around the island, and seemed to have an urgent interest in landing there; but she pointed out the ship to him and put her hands together.

The young fisherman, whose garments were neat and elegant, obeyed her order regretfully. The eyes of the two young persons revealed their sentiments, but Mondor, not wanting to waste time, had Fascinety climb into the launch, ordered that it be put to sea, and told him to go and extract the princess from the dragon's tail while it was asleep, and to bring her to the ship.

That order, which would have frightened anyone other than that skilled prestidigitator, found in him a disposition prompt to make the effects of his art seen. He went to the island and extracted the princess so rapidly that a flash of lightning would only have lasted a little less time than that expedition. Content with bringing back such a beautiful prey, he placed her in the vessel without young Isaline appearing sensible to that service.

Meanwhile, the young fisherman uttered cries so piercing that the dragon awoke, and, flying directly over the ship, it frightened the entire crew with its horrible figure. The dragon had only one vulnerable spot, and that place was so small that an arrow could scarcely enter it; but Tirandor launched one so accurately that the monster was deprived of its sight. It is true that its death was nearly fatal to the voyagers; it fell head first upon the vessel, and, piercing it through completely, caused it to take on so much water that it was all that Artidas could do to caulk it promptly enough for it not to be submerged—but it is also true that it was done with so much skill that no one could ever tell where the dragon had passed through.

All these events happened in such a short time that Isaline, astonished and confused, did not know with what people she was dealing. Mondor introduced himself to her; he told her that it was with the permission of the King that she had received the services of his sons. The princess thanked him in a melancholy fashion, and, going up on deck, she turned her beautiful eyes toward the island, as if regretful to be quitting it. There was no doubt that the handsome fisherman had a part in her regrets; that appeared, however, to be out of place; the four sons could not understand the eccentricity of such a liking; they were unaware that no distance is too great when amour is between two people.

Haraguan, proud of his profound science, was the first who wanted to make the most of the service that he had rendered the princess; he asked for recompense in the tone of a man accustomed to making the dark realm tremble and more accustomed to talking to demons than a beautiful princess, so he was received with anger.

Fascinety adopted a more subtle fashion; he sought detours, and chose the moment that he thought most favorable, but if he was listened to with more patience, it was with no less insensibility.

Tirandor, accustomed to never missing his target, thought he only had to appear to be victorious; but discovered he difference there was between hitting a bull's-eye and trapping a proud and prejudiced heart.

As for Artidas, his hopes were no less, but he made his declaration by means of arithmetical declarations. Isaline laughed at him, but he was no more fortunate than his brothers.

They arrived shortly afterwards at the Court; the King was in the port, and he perceived his daughter from afar, standing on deck in order to be visible; her sadness did not diminish the King's sensible joy; she was no sooner beside him than he held her embraced for an hour without being able to say a word. Everyone shared in the joy of such a good father. He only separated from his beloved daughter in order to thank Mondor and his sons for the importance of such a service and to offer them anything that depended on him as a mark of his gratitude.

"Sire," said Mondor, boldly, "we are your subjects, but my house is illustrious and ancient; it would not be the first time that a great king had chosen a son-in-law from among the nobility of his kingdom. Decide, Sire, between my four sons; the roles that they have played for Your Majesty are equal enough, as is their merit, and my amity does not act for one more than another."

The King found audacity in those words, but they did not displease him; and, looking at Mondor with generosity, he replied: "I believe that recompenses shared between you and your children would be sufficient to prove my gratitude to you, but since you consent that one alone will be fortunate, I am in accord with that, although, as my daughter is to be the prize, it will be necessary to consult her before choosing. Go and rest, and savor at leisure the joy of being the father of such children."

A few days passed without her appearing to want to make a decision; she was sad and solitary.

The King, her father, asked her how she had spent the year of her sojourn with the dragon.

"Tranquilly, Seigneur," she replied. "All my dolor was in not seeing you, but I believed that in the end that you would forget me and that you would choose an amiable wife, who would give you successors. In any case, the dragon did not exercise any cruelty upon me; I had a little cabin of leaves; I collected the flowers making up my bed myself; it was never cold on the island that I inhabited; I walked on the sea shore in the evenings; I slept tranquilly by night and I occupied my days in dreaming."

"But what reverie," the King interjected, "could amuse you agreeably? You could not hope for an end to your misfortunes; you were in the power of a frightful dragon and you did not see anyone."

Isaline blushed at those words, lowered her eyes, and then raised them again to look her father in the face. "Seigneur," she said, "you know that hope is a gift of nature, which we have or our consolation, and which only dies with us. The dragon only demanded of me that I accompany him for a few hours on the edge of the sea when he wanted to go to sleep, and I had the complaisance not to refuse. I watched a fisherman during those times, and those moments were not the most disagreeable of my life."

"Oh, my daughter," cried the King, who saw her blushing extraordinarily at that point, "what am I hearing? You have spent a year on a desert island without ennui? The sight of a monster did not horrify you and your most pleasant moments were when you saw a fisherman! A miserable fisherman," he added, "whom you sell me dearly the pleasure of having relieved the tedium of an inconsiderate princess!"

The King sent his daughter to her apartment. He sent for Mondor and had him repeat what he had seen of the fisherman, which he had already reported all too faithfully. That was a thunderbolt for the unfortunate father. He had did doubt that his daughter had allowed her heart to be surprised by an unworthy amour, and he resolved to constrain Isaline to choose one of the four seigneurs.

On the other hand, the sad princess could not contain in her heart her dolor and tenderness; she made the confidence of it to one of her women, whom she like a great deal, "They're going to make into a crime," she told her, "sentiments that have prevented me from despairing. That King, that father, would no longer have a daughter if the young Delfirio had not been visible to me with all his charms. He has so many, my dear Cephise," she added, weeping, "what heart would have been able to resist him? He would shine in the midst of the most flourishing Court. Imagine the impressions he made on my mind on an uninhabited island. But perhaps he's no longer thinking about me! The fickle are deterred by difficulties."

Cephise, who was very glad to be able to divert the princess somewhat from her displeasures, asked her to tell the story of her adventures; she did so in these terms:

"You know, my dear Cephise, how I was carried off by that formidable dragon. I thought I would be devoured a moment later, and I was resigned to that, when it put me down gently on a very agreeable but absolutely deserted island. It was still daylight when I arrived there. The winged serpent resumed its flight and left me alone. I had no other thought that death. *What does it matter to me, I said to myself, how I perish? It's better to serve as fodder to a monster than to drag out a miserable life exposed to hunger and the insults of the atmosphere.*

"I was walking around, turning those frightful thoughts over in my mind when I perceived a simple but pretty little boat on the sea, and a young man fishing. Adonis, the beautiful Adonis, never had so many charms. He had long hair as black as jade, beautiful eyes, an agreeable mouth, marvelous teeth and a perfect figure. He threw the line with a grace that gave a desire to go fishing; and he was so fortunate that he did not throw uselessly. His clothes were made of a fine yellow fabric, garnished with lace.

"He perceived me as I was watching him in my desolation. The magnificence of my garments rather than my beauty doubtless attracted his eyes. 'Great princess,' he said, 'what fatal star has brought you to these shores?' I told him my adventure; he seemed touched by it. He leapt ashore lightly, in a gallant and adroit manner, but even more urgent. He went to cut tree branches; he fabricated a very neat cabin; he collected moss and grass, and made me a very comfortable little bed. He strewed it with a thousand flowers. He assured me that the dragon was only cruel to those from whom it believed that it had received some outrage, and asked me for permission to come to see me every day. I granted it to him without difficulty. The métier that he exercised did not give me any scorn for him. What Prince could have disputed the advantage of beauty, grace and intelligence with him?

"The dragon did not appear for the rest of the day. My handsome fisherman came back the next day to the door of my cabin, and listened to see whether I was awake. He entered respectfully as soon as I had indicated to him that he could. 'Have you slept well, adorable princess?' he said to me. 'Have your eyes, those dangerous eyes, which take away repose from all mortals, savored the charm of slumber?'

"'Yes, Delfirio,' I said to him, 'I slept, and I even think that I could not have done otherwise, I ought to tell you, after the care you took to make me a comfortable and agreeable bed.' He sighed, and made no reply, but he went a few steps from my cabin in order to take from the hands of a little fisherman a large wicker basket, very prettily woven. He opened it in my presence; I saw linen therein of a surprising cleanliness; simple and elegant garments more appropriate to my present estate than those I had on; and a toilette-bag with all that is necessary to a woman.

"His cares appeared to me to be worthy of being recompensed. I asked him to walk for a moment; in the meantime, I undressed and put on one of the dresses he had brought me. Recalling him soon after, I took off all my jewels and presented them to him in a very grateful fashion. He recoiled several steps. I thought at first it was in astonishment, but a nobler sentiment caused that movement; he was indignant at what would have transported another with joy.

"What can I tell you, my dear Cephis? He vanquished me in generosity, and I gave him in recompense a portrait of me that I wore on my arm. He received it like that of Venus. His transports were ardent, but the air of grandeur never abandoned him, and everything about him was gracious. I thought, the first day that I was only touched in order not to be ingrate, but I knew soon afterwards that Amour launches his arrows accurately everywhere, that there is no desert impenetrable to them, and that a difference in conditions is only a feeble obstacle when one loves veritably.

"In sum, I allowed him to speak to me as a passionate lover; I responded to him in almost the same way. He brought me little rustic meals every day, but proper and well-prepared; we ate together. The dragon often came to his island, and did not seem annoyed by our union; sometimes he took me gently in one of his claws, in order to take me with him to the sea shore; he slept there peacefully. Delfirio jumped into his boat then and sang tender songs in order to divert me, for he has an admirable voice.

"That life seemed to me so pleasant and so tranquil that, far from thinking about my return, I had no other view than that of establishing myself on the island. Delfirio's condition was all that was opposed to that, but in the end, trying to rid myself of prejudices, I concluded that I could certainly give my hand to the man to whom I had given my heart. Delfirio, for his part, had as much respect as amour; he wanted to lead me to his goal gradually, but one day, when he saw me more tender than usual, he took such good advantage of the moment that, no longer able to resist him, and fatigued by combating myself, I extended my hand to him, and allowed him to take it ardently.

"'Delfirio,' I said to him, 'You love me, and you know full well that I love you; I will never be found on this solitary island; the gods alone will be witness to our union and I do not fear their reproaches since they have never disdained mortals when they appeared to them to be beautiful. And after all, what does the judgment of men, when they know my choice, matter to me?' I added. 'In all the world, I only have you.'

"Delfirio, carried away by amour and joy, embraced my knees, and made all the actions of a man transported by a supreme felicity. We took Neptune, Thetis and all the gods and goddesses of the sea as witnesses to the faith that we were about to give one another; we turned with our gazes toward those who inhabit brilliant Olympus, and we had reason to believe that we had been heard, since, on the most beautiful evening in the world, we head a clap of thunder to our right, and we saw the sea agitate slightly, although it had been very tranquil previously.

"That, my dear Cephise, is how our wedding was celebrated. We could not doubt that the Amours were involved in it, for after that happy day our chains appeared to us to be stronger, although lighter, and every hour was marked with some new proof of ardor, until the fatal moment of our separation. Alas, the unfortunate Delfirio wanted to board the vessel on which I was taken away; he did not doubt for a moment, as soon as he perceived it, the cruel zeal that brought it, but what could he do, alone and unarmed? I die of dolor when I think of the sad life that he is leading at the moment, and I dread even more that he is savoring a repose fatal to my amour.

"Admire, Cephise, admire," the princess added, "the point to which that amour occupies me, since I have omitted one circumstance that can alone justify me, since my misfortune has conducted me to a place where I am submissive to the censure of men. The day after our marriage he told me that he was the son of a King; that predictions difficult to understand, but terrible, had obliged his father the King to send him away

and to make him take the tire and the occupations of a fisherman; that he had news of his father the King from time to
time, and enough money to live happily; that he only had one
more month to remain in that estate, after which he could see
his fatherland again; but that, since a tranquil life pleased me
as much as him, he would never return there."

"Well, Madame," said Cephise, after the princess had
stopped speaking, "can you doubt that your amiable spouse
has gone to the realm of his father and that he will come thereafter to ask our monarch for a possession that belongs to him
legitimately?"

Isaline certainly hoped so but dread nevertheless found a
place in her soul

She did not have to combat that sad passion for long. The
following day, the news spread that a Prince as handsome as
daylight, the son of King Papindara, had arrived at the Court
to develop great mysteries; that was the charming Delfirio. He
asked for a secret audience with the King; he informed him of
his birth, and his marriage with Isaline. His adventure was
believed and admired. The King, who was a very good father,
thought that he would die of joy; and Mondor, who was vainglorious, was ready to die of chagrin.

Haraguan consoled himself because he was recompensed
magnificently and had one of Isaline's father's pleasure houses in which to exercise his black science. Fascinety hoped to
conjure as many women as he wanted from the very arms of
jealous lovers. Tirandor, who preferred war and hunting to
amour, did not deign to lament. Artidas took his disgrace in
such good part that he even imagined games and machines to
surprise the most ingenious for the celebration of the princess's wedding, which was to be remade with magnificence. It
was even Artidas who invented lockets with double bottoms in
which to put portraits; he presented one to Isaline and told her
that nothing could avenge him so well on Delfirio than seeing
that locket filled with another portrait than his. The three
younger brothers received expressions of gratitude from the

King capable of compensating them for any other loss than that of the princess.

Mondor also had reason to be content, and I would like you, Mesdames, to take my word for that, after such a long story, into which I have put enough of my own invention not to be very sure of having succeeded.

[The narration of the tale within the portmanteau is directly followed by the following discussion:]

When I had finished my story, everyone hastened to give me praise that I had doubtless not merited, and everyone wanted to know what I had added to it.

"Firstly," I replied, "I have narrated it in my own manner; I have removed a simplicity from it that rendered it very short. The entire adventure of Isaline and Delfirio, their names, and those of the rest of the actors, all of that is mine, and I do not believe that I am praising myself much in admitting it; there is none of the marvelous that one sees in all the other tales of that species, but it is also much shorter. I wanted to remove the fays, to see whether I could render my lovers happy without the help of those good ladies, who are exactly the *deus ex machina* that the ancients condemned."

The Comte smiled when I had said that. "I assure you, he said, "that you place your erudition marvelously, and that you do not read in vain."

"Don't make fun of me," I retorted. "Perhaps I am as redoubtable by virtue of my own thoughts as the erudition for which you reproach me, and I can avenge myself for your mockery."

Selincourt asked for mercy; the conversation became general. The same countrywoman who had criticized *contes de fées* so much praised me for having put a dragon into that one. The Marquis said that it was something worthy of remark that the best and most solid minds, those people who censured all bagatelles, could not help finishing a reading of that species once they had put their eyes on it.

"That doubtless comes," said Madame Arcire, "from the marvelous that one encounters therein, which is often more agreeable than the truth."

"For myself," said Madame Orselis, "I believe that the imagination that shines on all sides in these kinds of works rejoices that of the reader, and that there is no severity that it cannot cheer up, so to speak."

"I make another judgment of it," I added, "And I am persuaded that the truth that one mingles into them, covered with an agreeable veil, is what pleases sensate people; verity is beautiful everywhere, but presented bare and without ornament, it has something too harsh, and if the Comte will permit, I will remind you of the ancient who, having uncomfortable truths to say, necessary to a famous republic, assembled the people in order to announce to them sadly things that were sad in themselves. He made all his listeners yawn or flee; and it was only by making use of a fable, the imagery of which had nothing sinister, although the meaning signified the same thing, that he reassembled the fugitive audience, and even rendered it more numerous."

"What Mademoiselle de Busansay says is true," said the Marquis, "But it is nevertheless necessary to admit that people naturally like supernatural things. Evidence of what I am advancing is that there is no one who does not listen to ghost stories, although they do not add faith to them. And personally," he added, in a mocking fashion, "I amuse myself with them a little more than others, although I believe in them a little less. Our country folk sustain that one cannot be absolutely incredulous regarding those sorts of things without denying the immortality of the soul."

[The discussion then broadens out to consider ghost stories and other supernatural folklore, and their possible revelations regarding the fate of souls after death, with a few anecdotal examples, before the stranded courtiers return to telling their own life stories.]

PREFATORY MATERIAL FROM *HISTOIRES SUBLIMES ET ALLÉGORIQUES*

TO MODERN FAYS

Mesdames,

The ancient fays, your predecessors, only seem playful nowadays, compared with you. Their occupations were base and puerile, only amusing maidservants and nurses. Their entire care consisted of sweeping the house well, putting the cooking-pot on the fire, doing the laundry, putting the children to bed, milking cows, churning butter and a thousand other poverties of that sort; and the most considerable of their effects terminated in enabling the weeping of pearls and diamonds, sneezing emeralds and spitting rubies. Their amusements consisted of dancing by moonlight, transforming themselves into old women, cats, monkeys or *moynes bourus*[9] in order to frighten children and the feeble-minded. That is why all that remains to us today of their deeds and actions is nothing but *Contes de ma Mere l'Oye*. They were almost all old, ugly, poorly dressed and poorly lodged; and except for Melusine and a few half-dozens of her peers, all the rest were nothing but vagabonds.

But you, Mesdames, have taken a different route; you only occupy yourselves with great things, the least of which are giving intelligence to those who have none, beauty to the

---

[9] This phrase, referring to a kind of scary apparition, of which an approximate literal translation would be "surly monk," is employed by numerous seventeenth-century fabulists, including Cyrano de Bergerac, but does not seem to have survived into the literary usage of the eighteenth century,

ugly, eloquence to the ignorant, riches to the poor and splendor to the most obscure things. You are all beautiful, young, well made, elegantly and richly dressed, and you only live in the Courts of Kings or in enchanted palaces. You fill all these places with so much grace, by means of the mild influences you distribute, that we hope that you might put into our deregulated seasons the natural order that they once had, and procure us a mild spring, a summer appropriate to the maturity of our crops, a fertile and abundant autumn in which the Empire of Bacchus will resume its rights, and a winter confined within its ordinary limits, without becoming the tyrant of those companions.

It is thus, Mesdames that you oblige everyone; and to anticipate all the marks of gratitude that everyone will strive to give you, I offer you a few tales in my fashion, which. feeble and scarcely correct as they are, will nevertheless persuade you that there is no one in the Empire of Faerie who is more veritably one of you than the Comtesse de ***.

I would like to inform the reader of two things. The first is that I took the idea for some of these *contes* from an ancient text entitled *Les Facétieuses nuits de Seigneur Straparole*,[10] printed for the sixteenth time in 1615. *Contes* were apparently much in vogue in the last century, since so many impressions of that book were made. The Ladies who have written in this genre thus far have drawn from the same source, at least to a large degree.

The second thing that I have to say is that my tales were composed as early as the month of April last year, and that if I am similar to one of those Ladies in treating some of the same subjects, I have not taken any other model than the original, which is easy to prove by the different routes that we have taken. However mediocre the works that one gives to the public might be, one always feels a paternal love for them that obliges one to justify their birth, and one would be very sorry to see them appear with some fault.

---

[10] The work cited in the French translation of *Le piacevoli notti* (Venice, 2 vols, 1550 & 1553) by Giovanni Francesco Straparola, a portmanteau collection of tales very familiar to the salon writers, providing the bases for stories by Madame d'Aulnoy and Perrault as well as Murat. The tale known in the French version of the collection as "Le Roi porc" was also the basis of Madame d'Aulnoy's "Le Prince Marcasin," having previously been adapted by Giambattista Basile in a collection similar to Straparola's usually known as *Il Pentamerone*, and also well-known to the salon writers. "Le Sauvage" also borrows from Straparola's "Constance/Constantin," but both of Murat's stories are considerably more elaborate than the tales from which they take their inspiration.

THE SWINE KING

There was once a King who reigned in a certain kingdom of which I do not know the name. He married the daughter of a neighboring King, who was as beautiful as anyone can be. They were together for some time without having any children, which caused some chagrin to the King, who would have been very glad to have a successor.

He often went with the Queen to a beautiful country house, where she was very glad, because she did not like high society. Her greatest pleasure, when she went into the park, was to leave her women somewhere and stroll on her own.

One day, when she was enjoying that diversion, she sat down on the edge of a beautiful fountain surrounded by an area of grass covered with flowers and shaded by beautiful trees. She amused herself there for some time making bouquets, with which she ornamented her hair, looking at her reflection in the liquid mirror of the fountain; but gradually, the murmur of the water and the soft twittering of birds lulled her to sleep.

Three fays who were coming from witnessing the birth of a beautiful Princess, at which they had been regaled magnificently, passed by that place in their flying chariot. The great beauty of the sleeping Queen obliged them to stop in order to look at her attentively.

"That is a charming person," said one of them. "She certainly merits that we make her some gift; for myself, I would like her to conceive tonight the most handsome of Princes and the most accomplished of all men."

"And I," said the second, "shall give that Price the gift of tenderness and gallantry, which he will possess perfectly."

"As for me," said the third, who was an old fay who had apparently drunk too much at the feast from which they were returning, "wish that the Prince will be born a pig, and that he remain so until he has married three women."

"It's quite ridiculous," said the first fay, "to spoil our work with so much malice. You've just done as much in the house of the Princess from which we've come, in subjugating her to the amour of a river."

"It's true," said the second, that you've played these tricks more than once, and if my sister wants to listen me, we won't be caught by them anymore and we won't go out in your company again."

The malicious fay mocked them and went away. The other two fays remained, and sat down next to the Queen, who woke up a moment later. She was agreeably surprised to find herself in such fine company, for the fays were beautiful and well adorned.

The fay named Benevolent said to the Queen: "Madame, although we don't have the honor of being known to you, we are your best friends." Afterwards, she told her who they were and what had just happened, and about the chagrin that the malice of the old fay Rancor caused them, in as much as they could not undo what she had done, although they would aid her to hide the child to whom she would give birth.

The fay Benevolent also told the Queen that she would transform herself into a matron, that she would act as her midwife, and would take charge of the nourishment of the Prince until his troublesome years had passed. The Queen thanked her, as well as her sister, Tranquil, and she received several further instructions from them regarding the affair, of which they ordered her to keep the secret.

The fays withdrew, and the Princess gave evidence that it is not always true that women are incapable of keeping quiet, for she never revealed anything of what had occurred between her and the fays.

The Queen fell pregnant, to the great contentment of the King, her husband. Although the fay had promised to help her, she was anxious nevertheless when she saw that she was in the final stages of her pregnancy and imagined that she was carrying in her womb a child in the form of a pig.

While the Queen was agitated by those troublesome thoughts, the King heard the news that a neighboring Prince had attacked one of his frontiers and had already carried out several acts of hostility. He gave orders immediately to repel the enemy, and prepared to go there in person.

At another time that news would have caused he Queen a mortal chagrin, but the conjuncture with her childbirth caused her to see the King's departure with a different eye, considering that in his absence she would be more the mistress of her actions. Finally, the King departed at the head of such troops as he was able to assemble. The Queen went to the country house in order to give birth. Before leaving she told the nobles of the Court that when the time came for them to be able to see her, she would inform them. She ordered a search for the most skilful matron to stay with her, and the fay Benevolent did not fail to be the one who was chosen.

On the advice of the fay, the Queen had confided her secret to one of her women, and they both slept in the same room; she felt ill in the evening, but she did not say anything about it and retired early with her two confidantes, with whose aid she brought it the world the prettiest piglet that had ever been seen; it was not without tears being shed, but the charitable fay wiped them away by giving her good hopes. As soon as he was born she took him away without anyone seeing him and put him in a place that she had prepared close to her palace, which was not far from the place where the Queen was, to whom she returned.

Early the next day, people were told that the Queen's pregnancy had concluded in a false birth. That was taken for the truth, and the news was sent to the King, who was very displeased by it, but as he returned victorious over his enemies, the rejoicing on his arrival caused his chagrin to pass.

Meanwhile, Benevolent had put the little Swine Prince in a beautiful, very clean stable, lined with smoothly-woven fabric and furnished proportionately, in which she nourished him with the finest milk, which she gave to him in a solid gold trough. She sometimes went to the Queen's cabinet without being seen by anyone but her, and rendered her an account of his nurture. She had given the little pig the use of speech, and when he was of a reasonable age she taught him everything that a Prince ought to know in order to combine intelligence and politeness with the grandeur of his birth, of which she informed him, only telling him that he had to remain in his present form for a time marked by destiny. Sometimes, the fay transported the Queen to the stable to see her son, who gave her a thousand caresses, and for that they took advantage of the time when she was in the country and the King was in the city.

Eventually, the Swine Prince reached his fifteenth year, and the fay Benevolent let him leave his porcine skin in the stable and gave him back his natural form, which was the most charming that a Prince could ever have. She took him by night to her palace, where it was daylight when it was dark everywhere else; then, shortly before sunrise he became a pig again; thus the good fay deceived the malicious Rancor. When the Prince was in the palace he was diverted marvelously, and what gave him the most pleasure was conversing with the beautiful Ladies who composed Benevolent's Court, with whom he often flirted.

In a village not far away there was a fay of the lowest order named Bourgillonne. She was infatuated with two grisettes, her neighbors, for whom she wanted to procure some good fortune, and to that effect she had found a means of getting them into Benevolent's palace in the capacity of chambermaids of her sister, the fay Tranquil, the one who had given the Prince the gift of gallantry. They were quite pretty; Bourgillonne gave them nice clothes and jewels that, although fake, nevertheless shone. All that, combined with many affectations, enabled them to attract the attention of the Prince, who often came to the apartment of their mistress, to whom he rendered assiduous visits.

Eventually, the Prince became madly infatuated with one of the grisettes. He thought, in accordance with appearances, that he would not have much difficulty in making her love him, but although she listened to him favorably enough, she always employed a great reserve. She was not informed of the quality of the Prince and took him, at the most, for a fop. Bourgillonne, to whom she made the confidence of her adventure, fortified her in the resolution she had made to engage her lover to marry her. She played her role so well that the poor Prince became so smitten that he promised her all that she wished; but she was not content with promises, she wanted effects.

The fay perceived that her pig had some chagrin, and although she had soon divined the cause of it, she wanted to learn it from him. He had a great deal of trouble in making her that confession, but when he had made it, Benevolent was very annoyed, telling him that the Queen would never consent to such an unequal marriage.

"But Madame," said the Prince, "the time that I must be in this frightful form is unknown to me; if I am like his all my life, what Princess would want me?"

The clever Fay, who had a goal in mind, pretended to yield to his bad reasons, and she permitted him to marry the grisette, unknown to the Queen. His joy was extreme; the very next night he gave the god news to his mistress. The day after, he married her, in the presence of the fays Benevolent and Tranquil; afterwards, they took the two spouses to a chamber in which they put the bride to bed, and when the Prince had undressed, they left. But imagine his surprise when, on going to bed, he only found there, instead of his new wife, a large cardboard doll! His chagrin and his shame obliged him to flee to his stable and resume his pig skin.

The fay who had played that rick, transporting the grisette to a safe place, asked the sad pig why he had quit his wife so promptly; he told her, with a dolor mingled with confusion, what had happened.

"Well," said the fay, "what are you complaining about? Doubtless some superior power that is watching over your conduct did not judge it appropriate that such an unequal marriage be accomplished."

The Prince was not compensated by that reasoning; for several days he did not want to go to the palace and remained sadly in his stable, but the fay obliged him to emerge therefrom. She took him to the palace, where the diversions were redoubled in order to dissipate his melancholy.

He employed a very pleasant means of consoling himself, which was to become as amorous of the second grisette as he had been of the first. She, believing herself to be more fortunate than her companion, whom she secretly accused of some essential fault, made use of the same means of regularity, and soon put the Prince in the same predicament as the first time. He dared not say anything to Benevolent; he wept, sighed and did not want to eat, which obliged her to command him absolutely to tell her what she pretended not to know.

When she was informed of it she made much more difficulties than she had done before, going as far as threatening to tell the Queen, who would inevitably be dissatisfied with his conduct and his bad taste. Gradually, however, she calmed down and allowed herself to be persuaded. The same ceremonies were observed, except that when he got no bed, instead of a doll, he found a huge cat, which fled through the window, breaking the panes.

That second adventure put him in despair; he resolved not to return to his pig skin, and, in consequence, to die, since he had been warned by the fay that if the sun surprised him in his natural form he could not avoid death.

Benevolent, who was on watch, and who did not see him come back, was afraid that her art might have let her down, and that the grisette might have remained with the Prince, or that the despair of having been deceived for a second time might have led him to do something reckless. She hastened to clarify the matter immediately and found him in bed, almost drowned in his tears. She took him away in spite of his resistance, and when he had resumed his porcine skin and form she made him drink the water of the River of Forgetfulness, which effaced completely from his memory everything that had happened. The next day he returned to the palace as tranquil as he had been before is amorous adventures, which the fay hid from his mother the Queen, to whom she showed him in his charming form and whom she thought might die of pleasure.

One day—or, rather, one night—when the Prince was walking alone n the palace gardens, one the edge of a broad canal, he saw a monstrous carp that stuck her head out of the water and said to him: "Prince, if you want to abandon yourself to my guidance, I'll enable you to see the most surprising and most agreeable thing that has ever fallen under mortal eyes."

"But how, and where will you take me?" asked the Prince.

"Don't worry about anything," replied the carp. "I'll keep my word, provided that you come here at the same time tomorrow."

The Prince promised her to do that. He said nothing to Benevolent about that adventure, and he following night, he did not fail to go to the rendezvous. His friend the carp immediately appeared, harnessed to a little tortoiseshell boat, which she invited him to board. He did so. The adroit carp conducted it marvelously, and when he had been in the vehicle for some time, it landed on a little island where there was a small wood.

The carp told him to go into the wood, that he would find a dwarf there dressed in eel-skin, who would take him to the place where he would see what she had promised him; that she would wait there; that his guide would be careful to warn him when it was time to come back; and that he should not worry about anything.

The Prince went into the little wood, where he found the dwarf dressed as the carp had said. The dwarf greeted him with respect and took him into a very dark grotto. There he walked for a long time, preceded by the dwarf, who illuminated the way with a little glass lamp, which did not put out a great deal of light. They stopped in a place where the dwarf, having made the Prince approach a rock, showed him a small opening that his two eyes ought to occupy and told him to look until he came to fetch him.

The Prince was as surprised as one can be to see a chamber of unparalleled beauty and construction. It was illuminated by several rock crystal lamps placed on amber and coral candlesticks of a marvelous workmanship. Sheets of water that were lost soundlessly in golden sand, of which the floor was composed, formed its paneling; mobile suspended water formed the ceiling. A large mirror of talc with a multicolored enamel border representing flowers, on which flies of all species, moths, caterpillars, glow-worms and spiders could be seen, all imitated in natural size, was elevated above a cornelian table; and three or four armchairs of cane wood garnished with marine rushes, artfully wrought and colored, composed the furniture, as well as an Oriental cabinet in agate garnished with vases of serpentine and sculpted clay. A marvelous bed completed the ornamentation of that uncommon apartment; the curtains were golden mesh decorated with flowers of an admirable design, embroidered with a mixture of pearls and coral. They were raised by golden cords, at the end of which hung large clusters of pearls and coral; the quilt and the lining of the bed-head were in the same fabric, and the sculpted feet of the bed in crystal.

A shapely young woman clad in a garment of striped muslin, garnished with rose-colored ribbons, was rearranging a dressing table whose underlay was English lace of the highest and most delicate kind, and the top an embroidery similar to the bed, lined with silver fabric. The bottles and jars of powders, beauty-spots and false eyelashes, with all the other necessary equipment, were each composed of a single large pearl garnished with gold.

While the Prince was occupied in studying these rare things, he saw a young woman enter the room through a door of talc painted with flowers of natural size. She appeared to be about sixteen or seventeen years old, but of a beauty so surprising that he was dazzled by it. Her slender figure, proportioned in the utmost perfection, was the least of her charms; it is impossible to express the beautiful colors of her complexion, the regularity of her features, the brilliance of her eyes and their touching languor, any more than the inexplicable attractions of her beautiful mouth; her fair, of the most beautiful blonde that has ever been seen, was banded by a green and gold ribbon, and the remainder fell in a thousand curls around her forehead and her cheeks, mingled with flowers and gems. Her dress was green crepe striped with gold, enriched with pearls; she was leaning negligently on a pretty young woman dressed like the one in the room.

As soon as she had come in, she sat down in an armchair and, leaning on the cornelian table, she supported her head in her hand, with a melancholy expression. She remained like that for some time without speaking, while the maids were standing next to the dressing-table awaiting her orders. In the end, the one that had come in with her said: "Would you like to go to bed, Madame? It's late."

"Alas, Miris, replied the charming young woman, sighing, "What's the use of seeking a repose that I'm sure of not finding?"

"Will you permit me, Madame," replied Miris, "to ask you the reason for such a sudden change, the effects of which you have made the god, your lover, feel? When the River Pactolus, smitten with your beauty, abducted you with us while we were strolling on his shores, I was not surprised by your despair; the dolor of being snatched from the arms of your father the King and your mother the Queen was pardonable; nor do I criticize you for having had difficulty accustoming yourself to a place so different in every respect from the one where you were born; the extraordinary form of the River authorized the difficulty you have had in seeing him and suffering the marks of his passion; but Madame, all that had become familiar to you; the tenderness of Pactolus, the quantity of beautiful nymphs and demigods that compose your elegant

Court, were beginning to please you, and you saw without anxiety the magnificent preparations that are being made in this vast empire to celebrate the fortunate day that is to render you immortal by uniting you with such a powerful divinity. What, then, Madame, can have changed the disposition of your heart so rapidly?"

"This," said the Princess, languidly taking from her pocket a portrait enclosed in a little locket covered in diamonds. "This is what has caused my trouble and my dolor. I found this locket on the table of a little cabinet in the River's apartment. I had gone in there alone; the brilliance of the stones having caught my eye, I picked it up, and I found within it what you see."

She handed the little locket to Miris. The maid took it, and because she had gone behind the light of one of the lamps on the table in order to see it more clearly, the Prince was easily able to see that it was his own portrait. He had seen himself often enough in the mirrors of Benevolent's palace to recognize it. If the beauty of the Princess had already caused him to pass from admiration to amour, he passed at that moment from admiration to joy on seeing his portrait produce in the heart of an incomparable Princess sentiments that gave him preference over a divinity.

While he abandoned himself to that pleasure, Miris and her companion were admiring the surprising beauty of the painting.

"Well, Miris," said the Princess, "don't you find a great difference between that charming mortal and the bizarre form of Pactolus, and am I at fault for giving him a preference in my heart that he merits so well?"

"It's true, Madame," Miris replied, "that there is a great difference between the god your lover and the mortal who served as the original for that copy, if it is true that there might be one; for myself, I believe that it's an effect of the imagination of a painter. But even supposing, Madame, that the portrait is a copy of a veritable original, you can't know whether he has all the qualities that ought to animate his beauty, whether he has birth, intelligence, and, above all, a heart capable of responding to your tenderness."

"Oh, Miris," said the Princess, taking back the portrait and looking at it tenderly, "it's impossible that the interior of an object so accomplished is not as perfect as the exterior is charming."

"Well, Madame," Miris went on, "even if all that is as you imagine, what good does it do you, since you don't know what corner of the world is inhabited by the beautiful phantom that is causing you to quit the certain for the uncertain?"

"Don't overwhelm me," said the Princess, weeping. "I have enough to lament; Pactolus has only given me another six days to render him happy. Let me rather hope that the genius of hazard that enabled me to find that painting might perhaps enable me to see the original."

The Prince was on the point of speaking, and he was wondering how he could make himself visible to the Princess when the dwarf came to tell him that there was no time to lose in returning to the palace, and, having closed the opening, he obliged him to follow him. He drew away with extreme difficulty from a place where he had left his heart, and where he had seen and heard such surprising things. Eventually, he rejoined the carp, who took him back to the palace.

On the way he interrogated her about the marvels that he had seen, thanks to her. She told him that the beautiful Princess was the only daughter of Authomasis, King of the Cabalistic Isles, inhabited by philosophers who made a profession of secret sciences, who had at their head a great captain named Gabalis,[11] that the said Gabalis, with the old fay Rancor, his

---

[11] Murat would have been familiar with the highly influential guide to occult initiation *Le Comte de Gabalis* (1670)—which waxes lyrical about the conjuration of *ondines* [undines] and other elemental spirits; it had been published by her own printer, Claude Barbin, and was undoubtedly one of his best-selling titles. Barbin would have been one of the few people

colleague, had named the Princess Ondine, with a view to making her marry their friend the River Pactolus in recompense for the secret of the philosopher's stone, which he had given to them; that, with their aid, the River had abducted the Princess and two of her chambermaids; and that since that time King Authomasis had not had any news of her.

The Prince then asked his conductress whether he might see that incomparable person again, and whether he might be seen by her.

"That I can't tell you," the carp replied, "but don't fail to come every night to the bank of the canal, and I'll tell you what I can do for you."

The Prince thanked her, and retired promptly to the ugly skin of the pig, which had never been so insupportable to him, and in which he made agreeable and cruel reflections.

He did not say anything to the fay about that adventure. She knew all about it—the carp and the dwarf were only acting on her orders—but she had her reasons for keeping silent.

As soon as the sun had set, the Prince went to the palace, where he made, with the aid of his valets de chambre—of whom there was no lack—all the adjustments capable of augmenting his charms, in the hope that he might be seen by the beautiful Ondine. He had need of artistry to repair the natural vivacity of his complexion, which stating up late and the anxieties of the night—or, rather, the previous day—had adulterated.

When he had finished adorning himself and had his broth—for he only ate in his human form now, porcine aliments being forbidden to him—he went diligently to the canal bank, where he walked for some time, or, rather, ran, with impatience. Moments are centuries for lovers, and as he was already one of the most impatient, he was desperate to see his dear and good friend the carp.

---

who knew who had written it, and who knew full well that it was a joke.

Finally, he saw the water seething, and she appeared, but he did not see the little boat, which made him very anxious; but he was even more so when the carp told him that there was nothing to be done that night; that the Princess had been ill all day and was resting; that perhaps she would be better the next day; and that in any case, she would bring him news of her.

After those words the carp disappeared, and left the poor Prince in mortal chagrin. He consoled himself, however, with the thought that he might have played some part in the indisposition of the Princess. Lovers are the most unjust people in the world, and the proofs of amour that they receive from their mistresses are all the more agreeable the more they cost them.

He spent the night and the day very sad and solitary, and when the moment to go to the palace arrived he went there and got dressed with promptitude. As he thought he had remarked that the Princes liked green, he put it on everywhere that it could be tolerated.

He went to the canal bank and his joy was extreme when he found the carp and the little boat there. He stepped into it lightly, and that obliging friend seconded his desires and his impatience by carrying him rapidly. When he was on land he went to the wood, where he found the dwarf, who conducted him as before with the little lamp all the way to the desired opening.

"My dear friend," the Prince said to him, "can you not give me the means to be seen by the Princess?"

"That I cannot tell you, Seigneur," replied the dwarf. "If some new order reaches me, I will carry it out with pleasure."

The Prince looked into the chamber promptly; he found it illuminated and ornamented in the same manner as before, but there was no one there. He was glad; the absence of the princess assured him of her health. He did not remain in that state of mind long; a surge of jealousy soon troubled his tranquility. He imagined that she was with his rival, and he sighed more than once; but the arrival of the Princess, conducted by the River and followed by her maids, augmented his chagrin rather than diminishing it. He thought that perhaps Pactolus had married her, and that he was about to be witness to his good fortune.

While his mind is agitated by those cruel thoughts, let us make a description of the River Pactolus. He was tall and well made, his features handsome, although a trifle marked, and it was visible in his eyes that he had intelligence. His complexion was pale, as well as his lips, which were almost covered by a great blue beard that came down to his belt. Hs long and straight hair was the same color. A kind of vest, which came down all the way to his knees, made of a light and changing fabric the color of water and gold, constituted his clothing. His brodequins, made of rushes sewn with specks of gold, were fastened with clasps of nacre and pearls. At his side he had a saber made from a huge fishbone garnished with precious stones and sustained by a sash of gladioli and wild lilies; a similar crown enclosed his coiffure. That attire and that bizarre face nevertheless had its beauty.

As for the Princess, she was as she had been the first time, except that she seemed sadder.

"Madame," said Pactolus, as soon as he had entered her room, "you are putting my passion to a rude proof, and I am extremely surprised, after having found you almost sensible to my amour in the time when I had only begun to render you my cares, to see you becoming so contrary at the moment when you had permitted me to hope that I might be fortunate."

"Seigneur," the Princess replied, "I have already told you that I had not expected to dispose of myself without the consent of my father the King, and I believed that, after having returned me to his arms, you would obtain me from him in the ordinary way; and in that case I would not be opposed to your legitimate desires."

"Madame," replied the River, "the gods do not have the same usages as men, and they have the right to satisfy themselves without the aid of their will. I have already told you Madame, and I repeat again, that you only have four days to resolve yourself."

As he finished those words he went out, saluting in a chagrined manner.

As soon as the Princess was alone with her maids she threw herself on to the bed, weeping and sighing violently. Her dear Miris knelt down beside her and begged her to console herself and to accept the inevitable.

"No, Miris," said the afflicted Princess, "No, I cannot consent to give myself to anyone other than the charming object of my passion...."

"Well, Madame," said Miris, interrupting her, "if you think about what you're saying, will not you convince yourself that the object to whom you have given your heart is not in your power, and, according to all appearances, never will be?"

As she reached that point, and the Prince was dying of impatience to make himself known to the Princess, the dwarf came to tell him that he had orders to enable him to enter the Princess's chamber.

"But Seigneur," he added, "when you are there do not forget that when you see one of the lamps that are on the table go out, leave promptly."

As he said that he struck the rock with a reed three times, and it immediately opened sufficiently to allow the Prince to pass through. He did not have to be asked to enter; he ran to throw himself at the feet of the beautiful Ondine, saying to her: "Here, Madame, is the happy mortal to whom you have wanted to give your heart in preference to a god. He has come to make you a homage of his heart and a throne that he will occupy one day."

You can imagine the agreeable surprise of the Princess, who recognized easily the original of a painting that had made such a deep impression on her heart. She was so transported with pleasure in seeing the object of her amour before her that she could not speak; she remained thus, on her bed, for several seconds, as if nonplussed.

"Charming Princess," the Prince continued, taking her hands respectfully, "recover from your astonishment; I am not a phantom; the moments are dear to me, my Princess, permit me to employ those that I can spend in your company in persuading you that I love you, that I adore you, and that nothing will ever be capable of making me change my sentiments. You're not replying to me, divine Ondine!"

"Oh, Seigneur," she said, looking at him with surprise, "Pardon me for my disturbance; it is just. I find your portrait in a place to which no mortal can have brought it and I see you at my feet by virtue of a supernatural effect; and what is even more surprising, I find you informed of the most secret sentiments of my heart."

Afterwards, they said the most tender things that can be imagined on such an occasion. The Prince also informed her of the powerful protection of the fay who had always taken care of him since birth, of whom he only spoke in good terms, and without revealing the secret of the pig skin; and he assured her that, by virtue of the power of the fay, he would extract her from the power of Pactolus, provided that she wanted to consent to it.

"Alas," said the princess, "I consent to it, and wish it more than I hope for it."

"At that point, the Prince perceived that one of the lamps was extinct; he was sensibly touched by that, and said, sighing: "It's necessary to quit you, my Princess, and I am so unfortunate that, if I do not quit you immediately, I shall put myself in a sate never to be able to see you again. The power that has introduced me to your presence is unknown to me, but I perceive that it is acting in concert with my amour."

Finally, he tore himself away from that charming object, after having given her all the assurances of an eternal passion, and having received all those that the decorum and the virtue of the princess would permit. She reminded her lover that she only had the four days that Pactolus had prescribed to her, that she was going to pretend, for fear of irritating him, some amour for him, and that he ought to take account of that violence.

The Prince promised her that she would surely have news of him the following night; then he approached Miris, to whom he said, presenting her with his pocket mirror garnished with diamonds: "Amiable Miris, I beg you no longer to take the part of the god against the mortal." She took the mirror, blushing, and her surprise was not mediocre on seeing an unknown man informed of her name and her most secret sentiments. He also gave her companion a jar of emerald beauty-spots.

When he had emerged the rock closed again; penetrated with gratitude, he embraced the dwarf, and as he prepared to make him a formal compliment the other warned him to hurry and to return to the palace, in as much as he had remained with the Princess longer than he thought. His good friend the carp said the same to him, and urged him to climb aboard, which he had no sooner done than he saw Benevolent, who said to him with a chagrined expression: "Oh, Prince, how much anxiety you give me, and to how cruel a proof you have put my art! There is only a moment to save your life. I am retaining the Sun in the abode of Thetis."

He wanted to reply, but she prevented him from doing so, by touching him with her wand, which instantly put him back in his stable in his pig skin. The Sun immediately emerged from the bosom of the waves, after having frightened a part of the earth by his delay, with had been perceived by the jealous and lovers, as those who had most anxieties and who, in consequence, got up early.

The fay returned to her dear pig, who rendered an account to her of everything that had happened to him. When he had finished, she said to him, smiling: "I could have saved you the trouble of that narration, since everything that has happened in that adventure has only done so by my orders, the carp and the dwarf being mine. It is me who sent your portrait to the beautiful Ondine by means of an assiduous diving bird. She is the same Princess at whose birth we were present, and to whom my sister and I made the gifts of intelligence and beauty, while the malevolent Rancor, who made you a pig, gave her that of being loved and abducted by a River. I have destined you for her since birth, and I hope, with the aid of my art, to extract her from the damp palace where you have seen her. In order not to lose any time, which is dear to us, I hope to bring the Princess to my palace as soon as tomorrow night, while Rancor in occupied in rendering a service to her colleague Gabalis, who has become amorous of a sylphide. You will wait for me in the palace; I do not want to expose you again to the peril that your amour has caused us to run."

She did not fail, as soon as night fell, to put into execution what she had promised the Prince, who went with her to the edge of the canal, where the carp was waiting with a larger boat. The precaution was not unnecessary, the number of persons who were to occupy it being greater than usual.

The Prince saw Benevolent depart with an envious eye, but the hope of soon seeing his beautiful Princess consoled him. He went to wait for her in his apartment, full of joy and anxiety; he stayed there for some time, but his impatience soon brought him back to the bank of the canal, on which he perceived the fay; but gods! what became of him when he only saw the Princess's maids with her, who dissolved in tears! He thought he was falling from a height, and he needed to seek the support of the pedestal of one of the jasper figures with which the canal bank was ornamented.

After the fay had emerged from the boat, she said to the Prince in a manner that expressed her dolor: "Oh, Prince, I am in despair! Follow me."

As she spoke she advanced toward the Palace; she went into her cabinet, where she shut herself in with the Prince, who could not proffer a single word.

"Oh!" she cried stamping her foot on the floor. "You triumph, cruel Rancor! You triumph, and your maleficent art triumphs over the justice of my intentions!"

"Oh, Madame," said the desolate Prince, "don't retain me any longer in the terrible uncertainty that I am in. What has become of my Princess? Is she lost to me? Does the River possess her?"

"No," said Benevolent, "Whatever accident has stolen her has robbed me of the knowledge of her fate; I am only

certain that she is not in the power of Pactolus; I do not despair of finding a remedy for your woes. Calm your dolor,
Prince, and learn what happened to me.

"I went into the Princess's chamber by the same means
by which you were introduced to it yesterday. I found her at
the dressing-table with her maids, who were undressing her;
her beautiful hair was undone, almost touching the ground.
She seemed surprised to see me, but, your visit having begun
to accustom her to prodigies, she collected herself promptly,
and on the basis of what you had told her about me, having
realized who I was, she received me with a great deal of civility, and even joy.

"'Madame,' I said to her, "I am the fay whose protection
the amiable Prince you adore has promised you. I have come
here to make sure of it myself, and it only depends on you to
render happy this very day the worthy object of your tenderness, by escaping your kidnapper; and for that, beautiful Princess, you only have to come with me."

"'But Madame,' she said to me, in a timid fashion, 'must
I abandon myself to your conduct with no other guarantee that
that of your word? My father the King....'

"'Your father the King,' I sad interrupting her, "was not
consulted by Pactolus when he stole you from his arms, and I
do not see that any more precaution is necessary in order to
return you to them, unless you prefer to render him happy.'

"'Oh, rather death,' she said, 'and since you promise me,
Madame, to return me to the hands of my father the King, I
have nothing more to desire,'

"'Let's go, then, Madame,' I said to her, again. 'Let's not
lose precious moments.'

"She stood up in order to follow me, but at that moment
the liquid ceiling of the chamber opened up, Rancor descended therefrom, and having wrapped the Princess's hair around
her arm, she lifted her up with so much promptitude that all
ways of helping her were forbidden to me. Her poor maids
were tearing out their hair, and I made them leave the place,
and, in the dread that the malevolent fay had the design of

advancing the wedding of the Princess with the River, I froze the waters all the way to their bed.

"It only remains for me now," the fay continued, "To discover the place where Rancor is keeping Princess Ondine. I shall undoubtedly get to the bottom of it, and if my art cannot instruct me, I shall have recourse to Destiny."

After this speech, the fay obliged the Prince to resume his hideous form and she locked herself in a secret cabinet in which the most occult secrets of the art of Enchantment were contained.

It is claimed that she was obliged to go and consult Destiny in his invisible palace, but in the end, she learned that Rancor had put the Princess in a tower of lodestone in the middle of an obscure forest more than two hundred leagues from Benevolent's palace. That distance did not astonish her and she had vehicles with which she was not embarrassed to make that journey in less than an hour. She also learned that here was no other entrance to that tower than a little hole only large enough to allow a bird to pass through.

The fay did not fail to give that good news to the Prince, whom she instructed to return to the palace after sunset. She also told him to wait in his apartment, and that he could be sure of seeing his lovable Princess before midnight. The Prince, charmed by the agreeable hope that she was giving him, agreed to the rendezvous. She departed immediately in a light chariot harnessed to two bats, and having reached the obscure forest in very little time, she discovered the lodestone tower, which was of an inaccessible height.

After having descended from her chariot, she rubbed her face with the liquid contained in a little bottle that she had attached to her neck with a golden chain, and she became the most beautiful little swallow that had ever been seen. In that form it was easy for her to enter the tower, in the base of which she found the Princess lying on a scarcely magnificent bed of repose, bathing with her tears the portrait of the Prince, which she could only see with difficulty, the place only being illuminated by a little lamp attached at the very top, which was incapable of sending its feeble light as far as the Princess.

"Alas, fatal painting," she said, "have I only seen your original in order to feel so cruelly the dolor of his loss and that of my liberty? What am I saying, of my liberty? Alas, I have only exchanged chains. Was I not the captive of the River Pactolus, and am I not presently that of the wretched Rancor? Unhappy Ondine, what is your destiny? Has the powerful fay from whom you were to receive such marvelous help only served to increase your woes? Why have you abandoned me in such a pitiful state? If only dolor could end my life."

"No, Princess no," said the swallow, coming to perch on her head. "You shall not die, and, far from abandoning you, as you accuse me of doing, I have come to your aid. I am the fay whose power you doubt, and it will be by means of that power that you will get out of this edifice built by your enemy and mine. Let us not waste time in superfluous discourse."

Immediately, she showed her the little bottle that she had around her neck, and when she had told the the manner of using it, the beautiful Princess became a swallow like her. They emerged from the tower and returned to the chariot, where they resumed their natural forms and returned promptly to the palace.

Benevolent took the Princess to her apartment; she found her maids there, who had as much joy in seeing her again as they had had dolor when they lost her. The fay had something to eat brought to them, while she went in search of the Prince, who thought he would die of joy when he saw his dear Princess.

For her part, she felt no less pleasure. They would have gone a long time without thinking about anything other than rendering one another an account of their troubles, if the fay had not warned them that it was necessary to think about more serious matters.

She told them that she had sent her sister, the fay Tranquil, to the King of the Cabalistic Isles, Ondine's father, to inform him of what had happened, and to bring him back with the Queen, in order to be present at their daughter's wedding, which would happen very soon. Immediately, Tranquil appeared, followed by the King and Queen, whose contentment was extreme in rediscovering their charming daughter. They were informed of everything, and when Benevolent had introduced them to the Prince, they were agreeably surprised by his beauty. They received him as befit a man who was going to become their daughter's husband.

The fay did not waste any time; she transported herself to the apartment of the Queen, the mother of the Prince, and having entered her room without needing the door to be opened, she woke her up. Having told her in a few words what it was about, she had her get up in order to go into the apartment of the King, who was very surprised to see her awake so early, and even more surprised to learn that he had a son and that he would very soon be attending his marriage to the daughter of King Authomasis. It required nothing less than the testimony of two fays—for Tranquil was also there—to make him believe something so unexpected.

The fays took Their Majesties to their palace without making a sound, where, without any compliments, the wedding ceremony took place of the Prince and the Princess, who was put to bed immediately. While the Kings and Queens were reposing in the magnificent apartments to which they had been taken, the fays ran to the stable where the pig skin was, tore it into pieces and burned it in a fire composed of vervain, ferns and herbs collected before sunrise during the summer solstice. Then, having amassed the ashes, they sent the dwarf to throw them over the frozen waters of Pactolus, which became a liquid as before.

After those great things had been done, the fays went to repose, because they had need of it. There was still an hour before sunrise, and in that manner there was nothing more to fear for the Prince, who, with the aid of Benevolent, had accomplished by means of his three marriages the conclusion of the ridiculous gift of rancor.

Everyone got up late in the palace because they had gone to bed in the morning. The order of the day and night, which had been interrupted in order to give pleasure to the young Prince, was reestablished there. The indefatigable fays were again the first to get up. They organized the magnificent fêtes that were to accompany the charming wedding. They were also the first to enter the apartment of the newlyweds, to whom they gave marvelous presents. The Kings and Queens came in thereafter; they were very content with one another.

The rumor of those marvelous events spread throughout the kingdom; the Prince was named Aimantin[12] by Benevolent, in memory of the lodestone tower from which she had removed the beautiful Ondine, his wife. After several days had been employed in various pleasures, the King, Prince Aimantin's father, took the whole of that beautiful and illustrious company to the capital city, to which the young spouses entered in triumph, to the acclamations of all the people, who were charmed by the Prince and Princess.

The celebrations lasted a long time in the King's palace, and Rancor had such a violent chagrin at the poor result of her malice that she retired with her good friend Gabalis to the Isle of Forgetfulness, where they still are. Bourgillonne came to beg Benevolent to recall her friends, the two poor grisettes, which she did willingly, having no reason to complain of them, since they had served for the disenchantment of the Prince; and in order to recompense them, the fay married them richly.

Some time after Aimantin's marriage, his father died, and he succeeded him, to the great pleasure of his subjects, who were never afraid to call him the Swine King. The beautiful Ondine had children, from whom a long line of Kings and Queens emerged.

As for the River Pactolus, he experienced so much dolor at the loss of the beautiful Ondine that he dried up almost en-

---

[12] i.e. "Magnetic," the French for magnet or lodestone being "aimant."

tirely, and became no more than a petty stream, which is no
more known to poets than it is to the map.

THE ISLE OF MAGNIFICENCE

In the century when the fays were in vogue, one of the most famous had her Court on an island surrounded for a league around by a deep and profound lake, over which one could never pass without the consent of Queen Pleasure—as the fay was named—even by supernatural means such as riding on the back of a monstrous fish, a flying chariot, or something similar.

The island was called the Isle of Magnificence. The Queen's palace was in the middle of it; the architecture was of a new order, and very agreeable, for the material was the most polished white ivory. The interior, even more superb, displayed wall-panels, ceilings and floors of Oriental agate, turquoise, onyx, cornelian and aventurine of all colors. Those rich materials served as frames for the most beautiful paintings in the world; the furniture was made of the same substances. Here one saw an aventurine sofa the color of fire, there an agate banquette, lapis armchairs, cornelian stools and amber settees, expertly carved. The wood of the beds was no less precious than the other furniture, and the fabrics sustained gold, silver, pearls and precious stones. The cabinets, desks, tables and sideboards were unequaled, they were inlaid with precious stones representing landscapes, flowers, fruits, birds and animals.

Only golden vessels were employed there, but not for cooking, none being done on the entire island; cooks and scullions were unknown there. A quarter of an hour before serving, all the dishes to be served were arranged on large cedar tables in the servants' parlor, and on the bottom of each one the name of the foodstuff that ought to fill it. The door was closed, and a quarter of an hour later, the meats and the fruits were done to perfection.

The gardens were no less marvelous than the palace was surprising. The water features, flowers and fruits were distributed with an order and artistry so out of the ordinary that it was not difficult to judge, on seeing them, that nature played no part in it.

The fay Pleasure combined a rare beauty with a flourishing youth that was not subject to time. Her mild and cheerful humor won the hearts of her subjects, who loved her passionately; she only liked to do good.

The entire island was filled with small, comfortable and magnificent buildings occupied by the inhabitants, who were all noble Lords and beautiful Ladies, the majority of whom had quit crowns in order to be subjects of Queen Pleasure. Some of those buildings were in marble of several different colors, others of jasper, porphyry and nacre. There were some of burnished silver and Corinthian copper; their design was various, but the symmetry and the arrangement of colors had an effect so regular that what was on one side was found on the other.

The beautiful fay's Court was one of the most charming and most numerous. There was nothing but amusing diversions, sumptuous meals, balls, operas, comedies and apartments. Although the Queen had no affair of the heart, she was not sorry that her subjects became happy by means of unions in which only amour played a part. She did not confine her cares to her realm alone; she had a secret commerce with elemental peoples who rendered her an account of everything that was happening in the world, and when some extraordinary accident happened to persons distinguished by their merit or quality, she did not refuse her help, and sometimes quit her charming empire in order to be useful to them.

One day, that beautiful Queen was informed by her usual couriers that one of the most powerful realms of the earth, governed by a valiant and sage King, had been attacked by several neighboring Kings who, jealous of his prosperity, had joined forces in order to crush him. He had already been opposing that torrent of enemies successfully for several years, but the fay, who knew that arms are transient, was concerned for the glory of that great King, and, without being requested, she departed from the Isle of Magnificence in a coral chariot pulled by two swans, and went to the Courts of the Kings and Princes in league, where she appeared in forms appropriate to her designs.

She insinuated in one a desire for repose, rendered another amorous and caused a few to run out of money, and even went as far as making use of maladies and tempests in order to stop others. Finally, she arrived at making them accept the advantageous offers of peace made by their generous enemy, and when she saw that they were all in accord, she resolved to spend some time in the Court of the great King.

She appeared there in her ordinary form and with her veritable name. For as long as she was in that Court she received homages of every kind, and when she departed, she left everyone amorous for Pleasure.

Although fays do not always make use of seven league boots, they nevertheless make their journeys with diligence; the beautiful Queen only employed for hers a single day and night, during which she heard a women crying very loudly as she passed through a hamlet. Her inclination, which always rendered her ready to help the unfortunate, obliged her to go down to the ground, and, approaching a small window in which she saw a light, she recognized that the cries were coming from there.

She lent an ear and heard the voice of one woman saying to another: "Courage, my child, you have just put into the world two beautiful boys; you still have the strength to deliver this one. You will be no less fortunate than your neighbor, who has just done as much. She has only had three girls, and to all appearances, you will have three boys; if they live, it might well be that they will make three marriages.

The fay understood by this discourse that there was a woman in labor. The novelty of the circumstance made her curious; she knocked on a small door that she perceived. A peasant came to open it, without a light, but a carbuncle that she had, of which she made such use occasionally, soon illuminated the little hamlet, whose inhabitants were no less frightened than delighted to see a Lady so beautiful and adorned.

"Don't be astonished, my children, I am only here for your relief."

At that moment, the woman gave birth to a third boy. Pleasure had them brought, and after having looked at them attentively she said to their mother: "What will you do with these children? You're poor, and I believe that it would give you pleasure if someone were to relieve you of the responsibility of their nourishment. If you want to give them to me, I will take care of them; they will be more fortunate than you; but as their happiness depends on your neighbor's three daughters, it's necessary to know whether she wants to do the same."

Those good folk were very surprised to see a Lady so savant and so charitable. The peasant woman, poor as she was, nevertheless had difficulty in resolving to lose her children, but her husband, to whom such a great fecundity gave no pleasure, said to the fay: "Take them, Madame, you won't do me so much good as long as I live; treat them like the cabbages in your garden. I believe that my friend will be no less glad to be rid of his three daughters than I am of my three sons, and I'll take him the good news right away."

So saying, he ran toward the door, but Pleasure said to him: "Wait, my friend, I'll go with you in order to let your friend know who it is that wants to have his daughters."

She followed the peasant, by the light of her carbuncle. As soon as he had gone in he told the husband and the wife what it was about, and after they had recovered somewhat from their astonishment they showed the fay the three most beautiful little creatures than had ever been seen. She made her intentions known to them, and they consented to it; then she made them presents capable of enriching them, and when she had returned to the first hut she did as much for the father and mother of the three boys, without forgetting the midwife, whom she told to take from a little trunk that she would find behind the door everything necessary to wrap the three children richly. Their astonishment increased continually. Finally, she put the babies with her in her chariot and having rubbed their lips with an essence that put them to sleep, she continued her route.

The Queen arrived before dawn at her palace, where she gave them nurses and put them in separate apartments, the girls on one side and the boys on the other. The six children were raised in the same fashion until the age of fifteen, without ever seeing one another.

The three boys were handsome and well made; they had good minds, but of different species; that is why the fay gave each of them a name appropriate to his capacity. She named one Intelligence, because he had a penetrating mind capable of all sciences and all arts; the second she called Memory because he remembered everything with a surprising facility; and the third, who had a great deal of solidity and who seemed capable of great things, she called Understanding. Nothing was lacking in their education.

The girls were raised with similar care and as persons of quality. Their beauty was different, as was their humor. One of them was blonde, white and silvery, with lively and cheerful eyes, took pleasure in everything, took no chagrin and gave none to anyone. Pleasure named her Felicity. One of the others was neither brunette nor blonde, but her beauty attracted everyone's respect; she spoke fluently and in good terms, reciting everything she knew with verity and charm, observing the smallest circumstances. Her name was History. The other spoke little, justly, and never without necessity, knowing perfectly how to discern what it was necessary to say or not to say, in accordance with the occasion. Her beauty was regular, her complexion pale and bright, and her hair black. She was named Prudence.

One day, the charming Queen of the Isle of Magnificence had those six agreeable young people dressed in very rich and well designed garments that suited them perfectly.

She had them come into her cabinet, where she was alone. They had never seen one another, and after having given them some time to consider one another she told the young men to give their hands to the beautiful young woman and to chose freely and without constraint the one that they liked the best. They did that, after having bowed to them politely. It happened, by a fortunate effect of sympathy, that Intelligence gave his hand to Felicity, that Memory took that of History and that Understanding offered his to Prudence. The six young people were quite content with their choice, and it was not long before they perceived a reciprocal passion for one another.

Queen Pleasure gave the three brothers the three principal responsibilities in her household. Intelligence had the conduct of her enchanted gardens and he was the Grand Bostangi.[13] Memory had the care of the stones of the crown and the fay's magnificent wardrobe and was the Guardian of the Royal Treasury. As for Understanding, he had the direction of the furniture, the vessels and golden vases, and organized all the feasts and amusements, with the quality of Treasurer of Small Pleasures. The three beautiful young women, their mistresses, were Ladies of the Palace.

Two years went by in that fashion; the six young people were the delight of the superb Court. Only one year remained until the time that Pleasure had destined to render them happy, when one of the great Lords of the Court married one of the Queens maids of honor, who was a very beautiful young woman. Magnificent celebrations were held, and Pleasure did not forget anything to solemnize the wedding.

On the night that followed the last of the diversions, as he traversed the gardens to return to the palace, Intelligence found all the fruits on the ground, and the fountains that were accustomed to play uninterruptedly had dried up. He was

---

[13] Bostangi is a Frenchification of the Turkish word for gardener, also used as a title for a member of the Imperial Guard of the Ottoman Empire.

frightened by such a surprising thing, and, having thought about how such an accident could have happened, he remembered that when Felicity had joined him in order to tell him about something pleasant that she had just seen, he had amused himself chatting with her for so long that he had forgotten to release the fatal crow to whose nocturnal liberty the beauty of the gardens was attached. A fault so terrible in the most essential point of his responsibility, the rest being nothing but ceremony, almost caused him to die of dolor.

He ran to the crow's cavern, but he refused to come out, telling him that Pleasure merited the chagrin that the disorder of her gardens would cause her, since she had entrusted their conduct so lightly to an amorous young man. That crow was something more than he appeared to be; he was a famous magician that the fay had transformed thus as a punishment for some disorders he had caused on the island.

The unfortunate Intelligence, fearing the anger of the Queen, decided to run away. His amour wanted to retain him. Lose his mistress and lose her forever! That was something he could not envisage without horror. But when he thought that the fay's anger might cause him to lose it forever by virtue of some change of form, as had happened to the magician, he preferred to follow his initial plan.

How could he get away from the island, though, since no one could traverse the lake without Pleasure's permission? That difficulty, which appeared insurmountable, did not stop Intelligence. He ran toward the lake without knowing what he was going to do; on the way he tripped over something; it was a coil of thick rope. When he got closer to the lake he heard a noise in the water, and perceived in the moonlight that it was a diving bird. All the animals of that land had reason, so he spoke to it in this fashion:

"Diver, dear friend, come to my aid, I implore you."

The diver immediately came to him, saying: "What do you want of me, Sire Intelligence? You have only to command me, and I will follow your orders to the extent that is possible for me."

"What I want of you," said Intelligence, "is for you to take the end of this rope in your beak, traverse the lake, and when you reach the other shore, attach the rope to the nearest tall tree, and then come back to find me here."

The adroit diver set about carrying out the order that he had been given. As he advanced, Intelligence let out the rope proportionately. The diver was diligent; he came back in a short time to find Intelligence, and assured him that the rope was firmly attached. Intelligence did the same for his part, thanked the obliging bird, and told him to add to the pleasure he had just had the one of telling the charming Felicity, as soon as he found the opportunity, what he knew about the adventure, and assuring her on his behalf that, no matter where he might be, he would love her eternally.

Having said that, he climbed up the tree to which the rope was attached, on which he walked, making use of his arms adroitly as a counterweight, and traversed the lake in that manner. He had previously practiced that kind of amusement, and it served him usefully on this occasion.

While these extraordinary things were happening to Intelligence, his two brothers were not experiencing any better luck. Memory had gone to shut the Queen's jewel-cases and close her wardrobe, which had five different locks. He had already closed four of them when he heard History laughing; she was defending herself from the pursuit of a young Lord who was in love with her. That laughter offended Memory; he thought he ought to forbid such liberties with the utmost seriousness. Jealousy seized him, and, no longer thinking about closing the last lock, which had to be done in uninterrupted sequence, he ran to his mistress, whom he had no sooner joined than the gallant who was following her fled, laughing.

"I believe, Madame," Memory said to her, with a chagrined expression, "that if it were not for my presence, you would not have been sorry if some favor had been stolen from you."

"That is very insulting," she replied, proudly, "and I would like to think, Sire, that you know me well enough not to accuse me so lightly. You have not seen History emerge from the gravity that is natural to her, either for you or any other; I have never allowed any indiscreet complaisance to escape me." As she quit him she continued: "Go away; you do not merit my tenderness."

Those words struck Memory like a thunderbolt; he saw the fault that his jealousy had caused him to commit, and he stopped the beautiful young woman by throwing himself at her feet and begging her pardon a thousand times. He obtained it without difficulty; the anger of lovers is never difficult to calm. He tried to repair his fault by means of a thousand protestations of love and respect, and as they saw the Queen, who was returning to her apartment, Memory escorted his mistress as far as the door of her room.

When he was alone he remembered that he had not closed all the locks. He knew the consequence of that and fear seized him; he ran to the wardrobe, which he opened. But gods, what became of him on finding it empty, and the jewel cabinet as well? He made almost the same reflections that Intelligence had made, and although it seemed to him that he could never separate from his dear mistress, he resolved, by virtue of the fear of punishment, to flee that charming place.

He ran to the edge of the lake and saw the impossibility of traversing it. Then, in the moonlight, he spotted a herb, about the virtue of which he had been informed by an old inhabitant of the island. It was such that by running the herb in question on the soles of the feet, one could walk on water as solidly as on firm ground. He made the experiment immediately, and, having found it veritable, he made use of it and traversed the lake.

For his part, Understanding had put away the vessels that had been employed in the feast, as well as a quantity of magnificent carpets and rich rugs; he had closed the door of the cupboard in which the moneyed gold was kept that served for gambling, and only had to rub the lock with the water of security that he obtained from a little spring at the most remote part of the island, of which he always kept a small bottle about his person, when he heard Prudence cry out.

He ran to her; she had tripped and fallen. He lifted her up; she had hurt her foot slightly, and as she had difficulty sustaining herself, he helped her to walk as far as her room. While her maids were taking off her shoe and stocking and applying a few remedies, Understanding expressed to her the chagrin he felt in not having been close enough to her to prevent the accident; and, as lovers make use of all sorts of opportunities to say pretty things to their mistress, Understanding did not fail to say very tender and obliging things to his. But the solidity of her mind, which put her above bagatelles, made her say to her lover:

"Sire, I wonder whether the urgency you felt in coming to my aid might have made you forget some circumstance of your duty. You know how important it is for you not to fail in it, and I'd be very sorry if the help that you have just rendered me were to cost you any of the repose of your life."

That reflection on the part of Prudence caused Understanding to tremble. He quit her without expressing any of his dread, and ran to the cupboard. But imagine his surprise when he opened it and no longer found any of the riches he had put away herein. He realized, too late, the fault he had just committed of forgetting the water of security.

All the cruel thoughts that had agitated the minds of his unfortunate brothers tormented him even more cruelly. His penetration enabled him to envisage his misfortune with terrible circumstances.

"Oh, Prudence, my dear Prudence," he cried. "How wise you are and how unwise I am!"

Afflicted and amorous as Understanding was, he concluded that it was necessary to think of his safety, which he did by seeking a means of traversing the lake. He had been unable to think of anything useful to him when, while leaning sadly against a tree that he recognized as one of those from which cinnamon is obtained, he took a small dagger from his belt, which was the only weapon of which people made use on the island, more for convenience than defense, and he employed it to slit the bark of the tree, which proved to be very thick. He removed it in its entirety, and then cut four small branches from the tree. He put two of them across the two ends to hold the bark open, and the other two served him as oars. He put the bark into the water and, making use of it as a boat, he traversed the lake without any danger.

The three charming sisters, who knew nothing of what had happened, felt an extreme dolor on learning the sad news of the departure of the three Princes. Nothing was capable of consoling them, and they accused themselves of being the cause of their lovers' misfortunes.

Meanwhile, the fay, who had been woken up in order to inform her of all the disorder and the flight of the Princes, was extremely angry, and if the three brothers had not been out of her lands, they would have felt its effects. It was not the impossibility of remedying the losses that afflicted her—her art was capable of anything—but the shame of having been mistaken in her choice. The Art of Enchantment has rules, like the others, and the prodigious power that it gives to those who possess it almost always depends on certain secret conditions that are its soul, and which must only be confided to people who are capable of observing them and who know their consequences. That is what Pleasure had thought she was doing in choosing those three young pupils, but what had deceived her is that, not knowing amour herself, she did not know how dangerous it is to give employments of that consequence to people attained by the passion in question, which has too much power over the heart and the mind.

She had seen in her prophetic mirror how it had all happened. She sent for the three sisters, who had not dared to appear before her. The loss of Understanding was afflicting Prudence with despair; History was half-dead at the loss of Memory; as for Felicity, she had never experienced dolor until the moment when she had been deprived of Intelligence. When they came into the Queen's chamber, Prudence took the lead in order to hide the disorder of her sisters; she threw herself at Pleasure's feet along with them and said to her, respectfully, in a touching manner:

"Madame, we alone are culpable; only punish us, and pardon those who have failed in what they owe you because of having too much urgency for us. Their passion is innocent, Madame, since you have given birth to it, but the effects are not."

Those words spoken by Prudence touched Pleasure. She shed a few tears over them, which were surely the first of her life. "Get up," she said to Prudence. "I alone am criminal; I have put the youth of your lovers to too delicate a proof; I'm not sorry that they have escaped my anger; perhaps I would not have been the mistress of it. Console yourselves, and continue to live as usual; the absence of the lovable fugitives will not be long, and I shall take care of their fortune."

The disorder of the palace was soon reestablished, and the three sisters no longer felt any chagrin except that of the absence of their lovers. Let us see now what had become of them.

When Intelligence had passed over the lake, he walked for several days through a deserted country without encountering any towns or villages, only finding water with difficulty, and only small quantities of a few wretched wild fruits for nourishment.

"Alas, dear Felicity," he said, "what has become of you? I don't regret the loss of so much magnificence, I only feel yours, and I would be even more unhappy if I lost your heart."

After many difficulties and fatigues, he arrived in a beautiful forest, the cover of which was proof against the most penetrating rays of sunlight. There were beautiful springs there, the waters of which were marvelous, and one could not take twenty steps without finding trees laden with all sorts of fruits. Millions of birds of every species made continuous concerts there, and little branches that one encountered from time to time formed cabinets appropriate for repose. Intelligence went into them by night, and if he had not been in love, he would have found them very tranquil.

The forest was so vast that although he marched almost all day, he did not find an issue. "I can see," he said, sometimes, "that I shall spend my life here, that the anger of the Queen of the Isle of Magnificence has limited itself to depriving me forever of the sight of the one I love, and that in order to avenge herself more fully, she is augmenting my passion." People of intelligence are always unhappier than others.

He applied himself so well in that solitude to studying the song of birds that he discovered mysteries therein hidden thus far from everyone but him. He found that some were mocking the stupidities of humans; that others were giving them advice they did not heed; and that a few of them were informed of a few surprising events of which they had been the only witnesses.

Above all, however, he studied the nightingales with so much care that he knew that they had invented music, and that they expressed all the sentiments of amour by means of their song. Intelligence understood when they were lamenting absence or infidelity, whether they were happy or unhappy, and, in sum, he knew that they entered perfectly into all the delicacies of that passion. He became so fond of that little masterpiece of a voice that he followed it everywhere.

One day, when he was listening to one of them that seemed to him to be more knowledgeable than all those he had heard, filled with admiration, he cried: "Oh, most charming of all the animals, if only you could be understood by the Queen of the Isle of Magnificence. I'm sure that she would make you the gift of speech in order to be understood all over the world."

He had no sooner uttered that exclamation than the bird replied to him: "I'm much obliged to you, charming mortal, for the wish that you have just made in my favor, and which has been granted so promptly; I shall only make use of it to give you pleasure."

Intelligence was agreeably surprised by that adventure, all the more so as it made him know that the Queen was no longer irritated against him.

"All that I ask of you," replied Intelligence, "is that you enable me to get out of this forest."

"I'll do that," the bird replied, "and even more, if it's possible for me." As she spoke she came to perch on Intelligence's shoulder, and, having been told to march, he soon emerged from the forest, on the edge of which he found a little cabin, the door of which was open.

He went in. It was rather neatly furnished. What surprised him was not seeing anyone in it, and finding a table there on which a well-prepared supper was set. As night was about to fall, he decided to spend it there; to that effect, he waited for the mistress of the house to appear, in order to ask her for permission to do so. However, seeing that it was already late, and not having seen anyone appear, he thought that it must be a favor of Queen Pleasure. They joy that he experienced put him in a good mood; he supped better than he had done for four months, and his little friend kept him company by entertaining him agreeably with the following story.

The Story of Princess Blanchette and Prince Verdelet

There is a land not far from here that is named the Realm of the Cabbage Lettuces. All its inhabitants are gardeners, and the great lords are florists. There are no great riches, but the land is very agreeable. The Queen of the Cabbage Lettuces was a good Princess, whom I often diverted in her garden, and it appeared that she took great pleasure in hearing me sing. She died some time ago, and she left a son who was the heir to her estates, who is one of the most gallant Princes one could ever see. His name is Verdelet, and he fell in love with a beautiful Princess named Blanchette, the daughter of the King of the Frivolities, his neighbor.

Those people are stupid; they only amuse themselves by making bad verses and songs to sing on street corners. Their speech is filled with nothing but proverbs, sayings, quips and insipid jokes that are not very funny. Some of them travel the world and become tightrope walkers, operators of marionettes, Tabarins, Marquis d'Embreville and d'Angely.[14] The wittiest are Italian comedians under the names of Arlequin, Mesetin, Scaramouche and Doctor Balouade.[15] There are also women, some are Leances, others Columbines, Diamantines, etc., and by that means they enrich themselves, for they are all vagabonds in their homeland.

There are also people of another species, whose are not the most maladroit, but are the least esteemed; they are jesters and fools who, in the homes of Kings and Princes, often counterfeit madmen, telling them truths that sages dare not think.

The King of those peoples is a Prince who has nothing of their manners; he is as sage as can be, and is named Peudacquets.[16] It is very annoying for a Prince who has such merit to command fools, but, in order to make use of a proverb

---

[14] Tabarin was the pseudonym of a famous street performer, Anthoine Girard (1584-1633), who engaged in comic dialogues with his brother, known as Mondor, while selling quack medicines. Any claims to fame or notoriety possessed by the other two names remain enigmatic although both marquisats do seem to have existed in the seventeenth century, the latter as St. Jean d'Angely.

[15] All stock characters in the French adaptation of the Italian commedia dell'arte. The original of the second, Mezzetnio, is a schemer and drunkard; the original of the last-named, Dottor Balanzone is a decadent scholar. The female characters, except for Columbine, are far less well-known, and the other two named were probably *ad hoc* improvisations.

[16] i.e. "few acquisitions."

of the country, where the goat is tethered it is necessary to browse.

Princess Blanchette, the daughter of the King of the Frivolities, with whom, as I have already said, Verdelet the King of the Cabbage Lettuces has fallen in love, is a small person with a good figure; her breasts, her arms, her hands and her face are in marvelous proportion, and nothing was ever whiter than her skin; an imperceptible incarnadine is mingled with it on her cheeks, and has the same effect as pomegranate juice mingled with milk curds. Her eyes are large, blue, nicely spaced, mild and intelligent; they are crowned by two eyebrows as black as ebony, and seem to be made with a brush. Her hair is the same color, and it is necessary to agree, on seeing her, that she is utterly charming.

Verdelet has had no difficulty in making himself loved, since he is entirely lovable. Because they were neighbors they saw one another often; he made her presents of salad vegetables garnished with flowers and admirable fruits in baskets so well wrought that their gallantry more than made up for the magnificence they lacked. The King of the Frivolities approved of his suit, and to all appearances, their happiness was imminent when a malevolent fay named Berlinguette, who dwelt in the hollow of a nearby mountain, took it into her head to fall in love with Verdelet.

She was ugly and old, as malevolent fays ordinarily are, the good ones always being young and beautiful. Berlinguette did what she could to hide her faults under ceruse, carmine and beauty spots; jewels, ribbons and decorations were not spared therein. She came to the Court of the King of the Cabbage Lettuces under rather poorly-inventive pretexts; she made him presents adroitly in the manner of Sapates;[17] sometimes he found a sword garnished with diamonds on his dressing-table; once, rummaging in his pocket, he pulled out a

---

[17] Sapate is a Frenchification of the Spanish *zapato*, a a kind of shoe put out at Christmas, as stockings were and sometimes still are put out in England to receive presents.

snuff-box of great value filled with projection powder instead of tobacco; another time, they found at his feet a locket garnished with gems, in which there was a portrait of Berlinguette painted by Larzilière, who has the gift of rendering an ugly woman beautiful without changing her features; on waking up he found magnificent rings, purses full of gold, or barbs and Turkish horses in his stables. He found superb collations in out of the way places, to which he was conducted without thinking about it, and where Berlinguette did not fail to explain her sentiments to him, making him know that if he wanted to marry her, he would be the happiest and the richest Prince on earth.

He was embarrassed, as an honest man would be, when he did not find himself in a humor to take advantage of the advances that were made to him, and, at the same time, did not want flatly to contradict a Lady. One day, after one of those collations during which it started to rain heavily, she sent him home in her sedan chair, because he had no carriage. It was very elegant; the porters were two huge monkeys dressed in scarlet with silver Brandenburgs. Instead of taking him to his own palace they took him to Berlinguette's, which one entered through an opening at the foot of the mountain. She tried to reconcile him to that deception by telling him that it was in order to let him see the treasures of which she wanted to make him the owner.

Nothing was finer or richer than that dwelling. It would take too long for me to describe it, as I could do, because I followed the King without being perceived. All the riches had no effect on him, and he got himself out of it as best he could.

Until then he had not said anything to Princess Blanchette about the fay's amour, but her portrait, which he dropped inadvertently, and which put a hammer in the Princess's head, obliged him to reveal the whole mystery, and in order to make her see that he did not intend any trickery he went to see her father the King, with whom her fixed a day for the marriage, which he wanted to be made in secret.

On the morning of the happy day Verdelet set forth at dawn; he did not have far to go and he arrived in good time at the palace of the King. It was not yet daylight there, so he went to stroll in the garden, where he spent his time, as speculative lovers do, gazing at the window of his mistress's apartment. I had followed him, because I wanted to be at the wedding, and I was amusing myself singing in a cherry tree, occasionally nibbling a few cherries for my breakfast, when I saw the malevolent Berlinguette descending from the sky. She was not adorned, because she was angry, and her little eyes were sparkling like two hot embers. Her carriage was a rusty iron chariot as poorly greased as a fiacre; two dirty griffins with mud all the way up to their backs were pulling the rig. It was very close to Verdelet before he saw it.

"I've got you, traitor," she said to him, catching him by the arm and striking him with her wand. "You're not yet where you think."

Immediately, he found himself in the chariot, which rose up, and was surrounded in an instant by a black cloud that hid it from sight.

I was in despair over his misfortune, but all that I could do for my own satisfaction was to follow him. He arrived in a short time in an old half-ruined castle a day away from here. Berlinguette set her carriage down in the courtyard and took the poor King into a low apartment, unfurnished and very dirty. After having made him traverse three rooms, she went into a chamber hung with black, entirely closed and only illuminated by four green candles.

Showing the Prince a kind of coffin, she said: "This is where you'll be until you decide to marry me."

"I'll be here a long time, then," he told her, his eyes full of wrath, "since I'd rather die than do that."

Scarcely had the Prince uttered those words than he found himself in the coffin, which Berlinguette enveloped in a black cloth. She closed all the doors with so much promptitude that I had difficulty getting out, and then she climbed back into her chariot and left; the drawbridge of the castle was immediately raised.

I am the only one who knows about that adventure; since that time, the King and the Princess of the Frivolities have believed the Prince to be lost. I have no doubt that the savant Queen who has made me the gift of speech has done so with the design of extracting the unfortunate Prince from the sad abode where he has been detained for a year, and that that adventure is reserved for you.

Intelligence was surprised by the story that the nightingale had just told him, and had no more doubt that there was something supernatural about the bird. He lay down with that thought in his mind.

As soon as day dawned he got up, and was astonished to see beside him a sword and magnificent clothes, in which he found a very rich locket containing a portrait of Felicity. He kissed it a thousand times, with delight, and no longer doubted his reconciliation with Queen Pleasure. He took off his clothes and put on those presented to him. The nightingale, who was present, rejoiced with him at his good fortune.

He ate what remained of the supper, and when he opened the door to leave he found a beautiful, well-harnessed horse there; he mounted it without further ado, with his little friend, and set forth into a large and beautiful pastureland, where he rode almost all day. Toward evening he saw an ancient castle, which, the nightingale told him, was the one in which Verdelet was imprisoned.

He drew closer, all the way to the edge of the ditch, which was filled with brambles and thorns. The drawbridge was raised and he was thinking about how he might overcome those obstacles when the confidence that he had in the fay Pleasure caused him to address these words to her: "Since I am sure, charming Queen, that you are no longer angry with me, enable me to know what you want me to do to help the unfortunate King of the Cabbage Lettuces."

He had no sooner finished speaking than the drawbridge was lowered. Promptly, he traversed the courtyard, where he left his horse. The nightingale showed him the first door of the apartment where he had seen Verdelet imprisoned. Intelligence had drawn his sword, and he knocked on the door. It opened, as well as the windows, through which, the light having entered, he saw that the place was occupied by thick spider-webs, filled with a prodigious quantity of those vile insects, of supernatural dimensions.

The nightingale was afraid, and went to hide beneath the Prince's hair. He brought down the spider-webs by cutting through them with his sword, and all the monstrous spiders were enveloped by them; after which, finding the path free, he knocked on the second door, which opened, like the first.

He found that room full of large wasps, which were making a frightful noise, by which he was not astonished. Whirling his powerful sword, he obliged all those insects to get out of the way and thus leave him free passage.

Promptly, he touched the third door, through the opening of which he perceived four huge snakes, which rose up on their tails, surrounding him. Without being astonished, however, he touched them with his enchanted blade, and immediately, they fled through the windows, uttering horrible cries.

Only one door remained, which was open, like its predecessors, and through which Intelligence went into the black room, which he found exactly as the nightingale had described it. He approached the coffin, and, touching it with his sword, he said: "Prince, a power greater than the one that retains you in this place has send me to aid you; emerge from that long sleep and return to the charming Blanchette."

Immediately, a long sigh was heard, and the black drape fell away of its own accord. The King of the Cabbage Lettuces appeared. The Prince gave him his hand in order to help him climbed out, which he did promptly. He was richly dressed, but his beautiful blond hair was rather unkempt.

"Oh! Who are you?" he said, embracing his liberator. "How obliged I am to you, and for the fact that you have just pronounced a name that gives me joy."

"Sire," said Intelligence, "It is not a time to amuse one another with compliments; it is necessary to get out of a place where your enemy is omnipotent." As he said that, he took him by the arm and drew him out of that sinister dwelling.

When Intelligence reached the courtyard, he found a second horse with his own; he presented it to the King, and they drew away promptly from such a deadly place.

Without perceiving it, they took the road to the forest, and in a short time they found themselves in the cabin where Intelligence had spent the night. It was well-illuminated, and a very adequate supper was set out there, as well as a second bed. The King of the Cabbage Lettuces was very hungry, and he ate with a hearty appetite. The nightingale, whose acquaintance he had made, told him everything he knew about his adventures. What pleased him the most was that she gave him news of Princess Blanchette, whom she had seen not long ago, and who had appeared very touched by his loss.

Verdelet and Intelligence made the resolution to go as promptly as possible to the home of the King of the Frivolities. The nightingale offered to guide them there, and they set forth early the following morning.

While they are traveling cheerfully, let us see what had become of Memory.

When he had crossed over the lake with dry feet, thanks to the aid of his miraculous herb, Memory found himself on a road that led to a very populous city. While traversing it he saw a number of people assembled in a large square, in the middle of whom were several magistrates in ceremonial garb, who were examining people occupied in weighing herbs, powders and various sacks. There were others who were lighting furnaces and adjusting alembics of various shapes.

After Memory had examined those things without being perceived he moved closer. His fair face and the richness of his attire soon caused people to make way for him, and he asked what the purpose of the apparatus was. One of the magistrates told him that they were men who claimed to know the composition of theriac.[18]

"They're mistaken," sad Memory. "I've seen reliable manuscripts of that composition, and they don't have what they need in order to succeed."

All the magistrates, informed by the one he had just told, asked Memory to take charge of the enterprise himself. He did so, and in a very short time he brought the operation to perfection, to the great contentment of all the people, whom he promised to teach the secret of the veritable tincture of the purple of the ancients, which was accepted with pleasure.

Memory was given magnificent lodgings, people to serve him, a good table and more money than he wanted. He carried out his experiments with so much success that the people found themselves in a position to furnish the whole world with purple dye and theriac.

If Memory had had no other design than enriching himself, he had found the means of doing so, but that was not his intention. He was still thinking about his dear mistress, as well as the anger of Queen Pleasure.

One night, when those cruel thoughts had prevented him from sleeping, he got up with the sun and, on opening a window, he saw a sword on his table, sparkling with gems, to the hilt of which a locket was attached by a golden chain. He opened, it and found that it contained a portrait of History. I leave you to imagine his joy and surprise.

---

[18] Theriac was a medicine invented by the Greeks in the first century A.D., the use of which spread throughout the world and which acquired a reputation as an omnipotent curative agent, for which reason the term as often used by alchemists as a synonym for the mythical panacea. The famous French apothecary, Moyse Charas (1619-1698), published an ostensible (very elaborate) formula in 1676, with which Murat would probably have been familiar.

He knew that the present came from the Queen, of whose anger he was so justly fearful, but who, to all appearances, was appeased. He also thought that the sword was destined for some use that he would discover in due course. He resolved, therefore to quit that place, and got dressed. He did not forget to arm himself with the miraculous sword, and mounted a horse. Without wanting anyone to go with him, he left the city, and in order to conceal his tracks, he went into a large forest that was a few leagues away.

After having ridden for part of the day, a storm blew up, mingling rain, hail and thunder, which obliged him to seek shelter in a cavern he perceived. The obscurity of the place, and that of the forest, augmented by the storm and the decline of the day, prevented him from examining the cavern, which might have been a den of thieves, or that of some wild beast; that obliged him to remain on his guard.

After having been in the place for some time, he heard movement close by; large yawns followed. Then, looking attentively, he saw a gleam, which he recognized as the eyes of a large lion that was waking up. His first thought was to flee, but an unknown impulse prevented him from doing so.

Meanwhile, the lion woke up, stretching its limbs and, striking the ground with its tail, it approached Memory quietly. Having gazed at him, it caressed him in the same fashion as a dog he had known. Those manners, not usual to those sorts of animals, reassured him to the extent of giving him the boldness to return the caresses by stroking the animal's back and head.

The animal quit Memory and walked toward the back of the cavern. Turning toward him from time to time, it seemed to be inviting him to follow it. That uncommon procedure obliged our adventurer to take the risk. And, ready for any eventuality, he followed it. His eyes adapted to the obscurity; at the back of the lair he saw an opening, from which a faint light emerged, by the favor of which he and the lion entered another cavern.

It was illuminated by a lamp wedged into the rock, and he saw by the light of the lamp that the place was very tidy. A little bed of moss occupied one side, on the other was a kind of table of the same substance, on which there were beautiful fruits in a rush basket, with soft white bread.

In order to do the honors of his home, the lion tugged Memory's coat gently, to oblige him to sit down on the bed. When he had obeyed, the lion set itself at his feet, and, looking at him with as much mildness as its face would permit, it sighed several times, while placing its head on his knees.

Memory, who suspected the mystery of the extraordinary things he was seeing, said to the lion, while striking it: "What do you want with me, poor animal? With what design are you asking me so many caresses? Can I render you some service? If I were still in the home of the Queen of the Isle of Magnificence, I would beg her to give you the means of explaining your troubles. I am sure that, being as powerful as she is, she would give you that relief.

He had no sooner finished speaking than the lion stretched itself, put its paws around his neck, and said to him, in a human voice: "Oh, dear stranger, whom the gods have doubtless sent me in order to put a end to my woes, or at least to ameliorate them by giving me the ability to express them, the unfortunate King of the Arsacides is greatly obliged to you."

Memory's surprise was extreme, and if the lion's embrace had frightened him, he was at least as alarmed to find a King under that terrible form. Seeing his astonishment, the Lion King continued, saying: "You're right to be surprised by an adventure so uncommon, but you will be even more so when I've told you the details of it."

"I only want to learn them, Sire," said Memory civilly, "in order to be useful to you, being persuaded that the prodigy that has just occurred is an effect of the power of Queen Pleasure, who wants to make use of me to liberate you from such a frightful condition, which can only be an effect of an unjust power."

"Alas," said the lion, "what you say is all too true, and you are going to be instructed by the story that I shall tell you. But before commencing, let us eat a few of these fruits, which are doubtless presents from your benevolent Queen, since, during the year in which they have been made to me daily, I have not known where they came from."

They ate together, and after the meal, they sat down on the little bed in the attitudes that were appropriate to them, and the lion spoke in these terms.

The Story of Grandimont, King of the Arsacides, and Princess Philomele

My name is Grandimont, King of the Arsacides. If the happiness of a King depends on commanding savant and bellicose peoples, I ought to be the happiest Prince on earth, and I would have been, in fact, if I had never fallen in love. For several centuries the crown of the Arsacides has been in my house; in the same family there was a princess named Philomele, who was, without exaggeration, the most beautiful, the most sage and the most charming person there ever was. I loved her with all the passion of which a heart can be capable, and I was fortunate enough to inspire a parallel one in her.

A few wars I had had to sustain against my neighbors delayed our union, but after they had been fortunately concluded, I saw myself in a state to be happy, when a famous magician named Cameleor arrived in my country. He chose for his abode a high mountain near my capital, and in a single night, a castle of burnished gold appeared there, which, when struck by the Sun's rays, was the most splendid object that has ever been seen.

That magician took on different forms every day; he was sometimes young and sometimes old. He sometimes appeared with a very ugly face, and in an instant he became the most handsome of all men. He often transformed himself into a ferocious or domesticated animal, a bird or a fish.

He saw Princess Philomele and he fell madly in love. He did not fail to adopt his most agreeable face in order to please her, but he could not achieve his goal. He employed promises and presents in vain. She told me, with chagrin, about Cameleor's amour, to which I could find no other remedy than begging her to conclude our marriage secretly; but the scrupulous virtue of the Princess prevented her from consenting to that, and she wanted to accomplish it formally, with the ordinary solemnities. I prepared myself for that as promptly and as secretly as possible, but I could not do so well enough for Cameleor not to be alerted. He no longer held back, he resolved to do by the power of his art what he had not been able to achieve by that of his amour.

One evening, when it was hot and the Princess's maids were undressing her in her chamber, the windows of which were open, Cameleor entered in the form of a great eagle and carried poor Philomele away. The cries of her maids put the entire palace into upheaval, and I learned the terrible news as I was about to go to bed. I spent the night in the most cruel dolor of which a lover who loses the person he loves can be capable. I only interrupted my cries and plaints to give the necessary orders and to go at the head of my officers to ruin the fantastic palace of the thief of my wealth and snatch her from his power: a design as futile as it was reckless, since, when I advanced at daybreak toward the palace, I did not see the slightest vestige of it.

It was then that despair took entire possession of my soul, the cruel dolor of which overwhelmed my body with so much violence that it would have required very little to succumb to it. I was put to bed because I no longer had the strength to sustain myself. When night fell, I wanted to be alone, in order to afflict myself with more liberty. As I was engaged in that cruel occupation, I saw a man of evil appearance enter my chamber through the window, with a yew branch in his hand. He approached me, and said to me, with a grim expression. "You have only to make appeal to your Philomele and you will never see her again as long as you live,"

"Oh, traitor!" I cried "So it's you who have stolen the charming Philomele from me; what have you done with her, execrable enchanter?"

"I have not done with her what I wanted to do," he replied, "but no matter; I am content, since you will never have her; she is a bird and you shall be a lion, and you shall not no change that form unless you have aided in the slaying of a horrible dragon, which must be the work of the scorned passion of an amorous and cruel fay."

As he finished speaking, he touched me with the yew branch. I became a lion at the same instant. My change did not astonish me, and I wanted to make use of it to devour him, but he escaped me and disappeared.

I remained in that state until my servants, coming into my chamber, gave me the means of getting out of it; their fear was extreme on seeing a lion in a place where they expected to find their King, and I promptly ran to the nearest forest, which is this one. My amour and my dolor had no part in my change, and the speech that was taken away from me rendered me even more unhappy. I counted for nothing the loss of my kingdom, only that of my dear Princess was sensible to me. I found this first cavern, which serves as my retreat by night, and I spend the day listening to the birds, always believing that I might find the object of my tenderness among them.

I only have the form of a lion, and I have never been able to nourish myself by carnage; men and beasts had nothing to fear from me but fear, my aliments being nothing other than herbs and a few wretched spoiled wild fruits, only being able to eat those that fell from trees. I sometimes made the resolution, in the most violent fits of my despair, to allow myself to die of starvation, but a certain natural penchant, mingled with a faint and confused hope, gradually diminished the resolutions that I made against my life.

One day, when I had found almost no nourishment and my weakness had made me return to my cavern earlier than usual, I was very surprised to see a new opening. I approached it and it led me into this cavern where we are. It was illuminated as it is at present; I found bread and fruits here. Since that time, the lamp has always burned, and for a year, as I have already told you, I have not lacked that nourishment. That, amiable stranger, is the story of the deplorable fortune of the unhappy Grandimont.

Memory thanked him, and assured him that his misfortunes would soon be over, since, to all appearances, they were known to the fay Pleasure. They had some further conversation, and then they reposed until daylight, at the commencement of which they emerged from the cavern, which immediately closed again.

Memory found his horse, over which it appeared that the fay had extended her cares, for it was still eating. He mounted it, and obliged Grandimont to take the rump. They emerged from the forest, and when they reached the high road, their frightening equipage caused everyone to flee. They took the most out-of-the way roads, where they found nourishment from time to time, and as for the night, they spent it under a few trees, where they had no fear of being attacked.

They had traveled thus for several days without knowing where they were going, or where they wanted to go, when one evening, they were surprised by such a heavy downpour that they were obliged to seek a shelter other than the wood in which they had resolved to spend the night.

Memory perceived a light, which did not appear to be far away; he followed it, and it led him to a little hermitage, where he knocked. The hermit came to open the door, but when he saw the lion he tried to close it again; Memory, who was on the alert, prevented him from doing so, assuring him that the lion was a domesticated animal, as gentle as a lamb. The hermit had difficulty believing it, but he was not the stronger, and they entered in spite of him. Memory asked him whether he had anything to eat; he gave them what he had, with which they made a very frugal meal.

The lion was still leaning on the knees of his friend, who was stroking him gently. Memory asked the hermit what country they were in, and he said that it was that of the Frivolities, and that he was not far from the capital, where everyone was in great desolation since a cruel fay named Berlinguette, who had a grudge against King Pedaquets and his daughter, Princess Blanchette, had sent a horrible dragon into the country, which had caused a frightful disorder, eating all the people it could catch and spoiling the crops. By virtue of a surprising prodigy, it had said that if people wanted it to leave the country in repose, they had only to give it a daughter of the city every day, and the magistrates had resolved to make that decision, for the public good, while awaiting some means by which the cruel fay could be appeased.

To that effect, they had taken the names of all the daughters, not even excepting the Princess, which they had put into an urn in order to draw them by lot, and the first name that had been drawn was that of the Princess, who was to be taken to the dragon the following day, in spite of the anger of the King. He had not been able to do anything other than have it cried throughout the city that if someone should be fortunate enough to kill the dragon, he would give them his daughter the Princess in marriage.

It was said that she was not alarmed by a death so cruel; the dolor that she had felt for a year since the loss of her lover, the King of the Cabbage Lettuces, who had been abducted by the malevolent Berlinguette, who was in love with him, had rendered her insensible to the point of scorning life."

Memory asked the hermit whether the dragon was far away. He said no, that it had withdrawn to a cavern at the extremity of the wood.

The good hermit ceded his cell to his guests, and, as the company of the lion did not give him pleasure, he retired into another place, where he shut himself in as best he could.

When Memory was alone with Grandimont he told him that he could see clearly that the magician Cameleor's prediction was about to be accomplished, and that he would surely kill the dragon, whose death would liberate the Princess and return him to his original form.

"Alas," aid the King of the Arsacides, "what good will it do me to emerge from this state if I cannot recover my lovable Philomele?"

"Worry not, Sire," Memory said to him. "Abandon yourself to the guidance of the powerful Queen."

As soon as daylight appeared they found a good breakfast. They summoned their host in order for him to share it: the good man was a little surprised by that fare, but he ate it nevertheless, after which Memory asked him to be kind enough to show them the route that led to the dragon's cave, because he had resolved to liberate the princess.

The hermit did what he could to dissuade him from that design, but his rhetoric was wasted. He therefore led him through the wood, the greater number of whose trees had perished by the dragon's breath. He left them, recommending them to the gods.

At the same time, Memory and the lion saw several people coming from the direction of the city; it was the Princess, escorted by her maids, who were in tears.

When they were closer, they were surprised to see Blanchette's beauty. It was not sustained by any adornment; her clothes were very simple and negligent, her attitude was modest and her stride firm. Her gaze was sad, but no fear was visible therein.

Memory approached her and after having bowed to her, he said: "Madame, it is not just that so many charms should be prey to a monster; your subjects must be very cowardly for all of them not to be armed for your defense. I hope, beautiful Princess, that I shall extract you from this peril."

"Sire," Blanchette replied, "I do not love life enough to suffer that you should risk your for my conservation. Furthermore, Sire, I would like to tell you that if the promise of the

King, my father is engaging you in this enterprise, I warn you that, whatever merit you appear to me to have, I will not be the prize of your victory. I owe myself entirely to the unfortunate Prince to whom I have pledged my faith, and who might have lost his life in order to conserve mine."

"Although that recompense," Memory replied, "would be capable of arming all the Princes in the world for your defense, amiable Princess, it is not the motive that animates me. My heart would be too unworthy a present to offer you, since it has no longer been mine for a long time; so you will be satisfied. It is solely the glory of rendering you a service that will engage me in this perilous enterprise." He showed her the lion, who was a few paces away, and of which the Princess's maids were very frightened, and continued: "I hope to share the glory with this generous animal."

As he finished speaking, the frightful howls of the monster were heard in the distance. It emerged from its lair and came at a rapid pace toward its beautiful prey. It was enormous; its body was covered in black scales sown with red patches; it had six horrible claws; three tongues—or, rather, three darts—emerged from its frightful mouth, which was armed with four rows of teeth; it had four horns like those of a bull, and two huge wings soiled with blood.

At that sight, the Princess's resolution abandoned her and she fell almost dead in the arms of her women, who were scarcely in a better state. A few of the King's guards and a few young lords, who had followed her, fled, but Memory and the lion, losing no time, advanced toward the dragon.

The lion leapt on to its back and, seizing one of its wings, rendered it unusable. While it was making efforts to disengage itself, Memory delivered a sword thrust to its throat. That fatal blow, greater in effect than in force, caused the monster to fall backwards, covering the ground with a black liquid that emerged from the wound in abundance, and a moment later it lay lifeless.

Immediately, the lion disappeared, and in its place was seen the handsome and valiant King of the Arsacides, in his natural form. He ran to embrace his liberator, to whom he said everything that gratitude can produce in a great heart. Memory defended himself with modesty, making him know that he had not had the best part.

They ran to the Princess, who had recovered somewhat from her fear, her women having told her that the dragon was dead.

"Madame, the deal of the cruel monster that threatened your days has not only delivered you; it has also broken the charm that has retained the illustrious King of the Arsacides in the form of a lion for two years. Here he is, Madame," Memory showed her Grandimont, who approached her, and said to her the most intelligent things in the world, to which the Princess replied as much as her surprise would permit.

As Grandimont offered his hand to Prince Blanchette in order to return to the city, and Memory asked her to accept his horse, they saw two riders coming through the wood at a gallop. When they were thirty paces away, they descended from their horses, and one of them, who ran toward the Princess with open arms, was recognized by her as Verdelet.

Joy had almost the same effect on her as fear had just done a moment before; she leaned on one of her women while the Prince threw himself at her feet. Embracing her knees, he said: "Oh, my dear Princess, how happy I am to see you delivered from the peril that I learned you were in; but at the same time, I am covered in confusion because it is not to my arm that you owe your deliverance."

The Princess gave him the response that tenderness and joy inspired in her; she introduced her liberators to him, although she did not know them herself, and Verdelet did not fail to express his gratitude.

While that scene had unfolded between the two lovers, another had unfolded full of amity between Intelligence and Memory; the two brothers, who had recognized one another, could not find terms to express their sentiments.

Meanwhile, renown had informed the King of the Frivolities of the news of the dragon's death. He promptly put his horses to his caleches and came to meet his daughter, whom he found in better company that he expected. After several compliments on one part and the other, they resumed the route to the city and entered it in triumph. The Frivolities had at least as much joy at the death of the dragon as the deliverance of the Princess. The King regaled his guests marvelously.

When Intelligence had recovered somewhat from the surprise that the unexpected encounter with his brother had given him, he thought about his dear nightingale, whom he had not seen since the death of the dragon. He did not know what to think about her absence, and it gave him a veritable anxiety. He retired early with his brother to the apartment that had been prepared for them. It was there that they rendered one another an exact account of their adventures

Intelligence had reached the chapter of the nightingale, whose loss he regretted, when he saw the bird enter through the window. His joy was extreme; he asked the reason for their separation, and she replied to him as follows:

"Since the happy day when you made that wish, so advantageous to me, since it enabled me to recover the use of speech...."

"What!" Intelligence interrupted. "You were recovering speech? Had you had it before?"

"Yes, of course I had had it before," said the nightingale, "since I am more than I appear to you, and my misfortunes have constrained me to hide for two years in this paltry form the unfortunate Princess of the Arsacides."

"What!" cried Memory. "You are the incomparable Philomele, mistress of the charming and unfortunate King Grandimont, who has just resumed his original form, by virtue of the death of a frightful dragon, and has quit that of a lion, in which he has been groaning for two years, by virtue of the malice of the same enchanter who reduced you to the form in which you still are?"

"What!" responded the illustrious bird. "Grandimont has been a lion?"

"Yes, certainly," said Memory. "If you wish, I will tell you what I know of the story."

"You would give me pleasure," said the sad Princess, bathing her little eyes with tears. She perched on a table while Memory told her what he knew about the Prince.

When he had finished, he said to the Princess: "But Madame, I am astonished that you hid from the eyes of a man whom you love with so much passion, and who is suffering cruel pains in his uncertainty regarding your fate."

"Alas," said Philomele, "I am more to be pitied than criticized, since the cruelty of my destiny has reduced me to refusing him that consolation, which would be, in my regard, the most sensible that I could have. In order to inform you both of that cruel circumstance of my misfortune, I will tell you what Grandimont was unable to tell you, because he does not know it.

"Know, then, amiable brothers, that when the cruel Cameleor, in the form of an eagle, abducted me from within the arms of my women, he took me to his brilliant castle, where he tried to shake my constancy by means of the sight of his treasures and the promise of all imaginable grandeurs and pleasures, but he gained nothing by it and I always remained firm in the resolution never to belong to anyone but the King of the Arsacides.

"My firmness irritated the magician so much that his amour was converted into fury. He lost the respect that he had so far had for me, and he resolved to make use of force in order to satisfy himself. That resolution, which he made known to me in a manner that gave me no room to doubt it, frightened me. 'Alas,' I cried, on seeing the terrible state to which I found myself reduced, 'is there no propitious power that can help me? A Princess that had my name was once changed into a nightingale in similar circumstances; oh, I would be glad if I could have such a favorable fate.'

"I had no sooner formed that wish than it was accomplished; my body was covered in feathers and my natural size was reduced to that if this small animal, of which I no sooner had the form than I had the lightness, in flying away through a window.

"As I cleaved through the air, drawing away from the deadly castle of the enchanter, I heard something flying after me. Alas, imagine my fear when I saw that I was being pursued by a falcon, that could not be anyone but Cameleor, who, to all appearances, had had recourse to that transformation in order to oppose my flight. My dread diminished, however, when I saw that cruel bird stopped by a sparrow-hawk, which, having battled it for some time, obliged it to flee.

"I recovered my courage and, seeing that I was being visibly protected against the power of the enchanter, I began to fear him less, and I no longer found myself afflicted by anything but the absence of my lover, whom I imagined be in despair at my loss. I retired to the hollow of a tree in order to spend the night, during which I made terrible reflections on my condition. I made the resolution to return to the palace and do enough by my behavior in Grandimont's presence for him to be able to suspect who I was.

Daylight appeared, and I was about to cry out my plan when I heard a voice, which said to me: 'Refrain, unfortunate Princess, from carrying out your resolution. If Grandimont sees you in this form, you will remain in it all your life. The magician, in despair at your transformation, was unable to do anything worse than attach that fatal circumstance to it. It is therefore necessary to avoid the sight of your lover, and allow the time prescribed by destiny to pass, after which you can recover your original form, but that can only happen on the Isle of Magnificence. Follow me, and I will take you to a place where you can await tranquilly the opportunity to be conducted to that fortunate abode.'

"Immediately, I saw the sparrow-hawk that had fought against the falcon. I followed it, and learned on the way that I had been correct when I thought that the falcon was Cameleor; but my guide told me that I need not fear his power any longer.

"We arrived in the forest in which you lived for such a long time," she said to Intelligence, "and where I found you. The obliging sparrow-hawk told me that it was the place of my exile, and permitted me to go as far as the Kingdom of the Frivolities, about which it told me what I said to you. It also told me to go to the home of the Queen of the Cabbage Lettuces, and that I would be able subsequently to be useful to the Prince, her son. After those instructions, it left me.

"I had been in that place for two years when I found you. As soon as I had heard you mention the Isle of Magnificence, I had no doubt that you were the person who would take me there, and I followed you constantly. When we arrived in this country and I found Grandimont here, I hid, for fear of being perceived, and I shall continue to do so until we are on that island, so much desired."

The two brothers promised Philomele to help her, and they remained in accord with her that she would remain hidden in that room, where she would not be at risk of being exposed to the sight of the King of the Arsacides, and that when they left that place she would hide in Intelligence's hair, as she had done before.

The King of the Frivolities made preparations for the marriage of his daughter with King Verdelet, and it was due to be celebrated in a few days when the people were suddenly struck by a malady so sudden that in less than three days the kingdom was deserted, with the exception of a few people who fled by sea and took refuge where they could—and it is those who are the Frivolities of today.

The King suddenly found himself devoid of servants, and the most annoying thing was that his treasures and his most precious furniture were stolen in a single night. He had no doubt that all that disorder was an effect of the rage of his detestable enemy. That was true, and if they had not all been under the protection of the fay Pleasure, she would have caused them to perish.

Intelligence and Memory advised them to embark with them for the Isle of Magnificence, to which they had no doubt that they would soon find the route.

As they were getting ready to leave, Princess Feverolle and her lover, Prince Petitpois arrived at the palace. They each had a small estate belonging to the Kingdom of the Cabbage Lettuces, They were coming to inform their King, Verdelet, of the destruction of his palace and theirs. The fay Berlinguette had sent a wind that had entirely dried up the gardens, killed the gardeners and toppled all the houses, not excepting the King's palace.

While everyone is regretting their losses, let us see how Understanding's affairs had progressed.

When he had passed over the lake with his cinnamon bark, he took the road to the sea, which was not very far away. He found a ship ready to set sail, and without knowing how or why, he embarked on it. The dolor that the loss of his dear Prudence caused him, and the indignation that Queen Pleasure must have against him, occupied him so forcefully that he did not even take the trouble to ask where the ship was going.

He had already been sailing for several days with the same indifference when, on emerging from his cabin one morning, he was very surprised to see that there was no longer anyone on the ship; the pilots, sailors and passengers had all disappeared. He searched the vessel all the way to the utmost depths of the hold, but he found the same solitude everywhere.

Although he was perfectly instructed in everything that it is necessary to know in order to sail a ship, being alone, he would not have been able to carry out the maneuvers. Understanding was not unaware of all those difficulties, and that is why he decided to perish whenever it pleased the fay Pleasure, whom he believed to be the cause of such an unnatural event.

He shut himself in his cabin to await his last moment. A storm blew up, which made him see a more certain death. Sometimes the vessel was borne up into the clouds, sometimes it was precipitated into abysses. The wind, the hail, the thunder and the lightning were making a terrible din, when a great calm suddenly succeeded then, and a silence so profound that even the sound of the waves was inaudible.

Understanding thought at first that the vessel had perished, but he changed his mind a moment later, seeing that it was impossible that it had done so, not being in the water and not even feeling that of the rain. He went up on deck in order to clarify what was happening, but all that he was able to determine was that the ship was motionless; not the slightest breath of wind could be felt, and a thick darkness did not allow the sight of either the sky or the water.

"Where am I?" he said. "And what is this prodigy? What ought I to expect of my destiny? Which of the elements will contribute to my doom? Has any mortal ever been in such cruel uncertainty? How frightful this profound silence is! Am I suspended in the air? Have I sunk to the center of the earth? Alas, I know nothing, and what appears to me to be most probable is that I am going to perish, in whatever manner it might be.

"Well," he continued, "let's perish, since we must."

Having made that resolution, he remained tranquilly on the deck, where he spent several hours, at the end of which he heard a rather pleasant, but very distant, sound. The sound was augmented, in such a fashion that he discerned that it consisted of voices accompanied by instruments, such as theorbos, viols and flutes.

"I'm doubtless dead," said Understanding, "and the vessel has passed in an instant from the waves of the agitated sea to the dormant waters of the Styx. What I can hear can only be coming from the Elysian Fields."

After that reflection he continued to listen for some time, after which a bright light struck his eyes, with all the more force because he had been in darkness for such a long time. At first it occupied very little space, and appeared to be coming from some profundity, but its clarity and extent were gradually extended. After an hour or so, it appeared close enough for him to determine that it was on land, but a land obscured by a dark night; nothing could be glimpsed by the means of that profound light but a great void in which the sight was not arrested by any object.

Finally, the light, which appeared to be occupying a hollow path, rose as far as the surface of the ground, on which he saw two men appear, each of whom was holding a large candle of white wax. He recognized by the light of those candles that the men were almost naked, except for a small sheath, which descended from the belt to the knees. It was made of a fabric decorated with several colors on a silver background. They each had a double bandolier of the same fabric, as broad as a hand, which crossed over the stomach. The skin of their bodies and faces was olive in color; their features were not disagreeable, but they had slightly crooked noses, fingers and toes. Their eyes resembled two grains of black jet, without any apparent whites. The little hair they had was black and curly, and only covered the top of the head, leaving their ears visible, which were very large.

Those two figures, marching abreast, slightly apart, had no sooner appeared than they were followed by two others, and then by two more, until they numbered twelve, after which a man appeared on his own. His stature was a little shorter than average, but noble and well formed. He was perfectly handsome, and seemed to be between twenty-six and thirty years old. His complexion was slightly brown, but nevertheless fine, smooth and polished. He had large black eyes, soft and intelligent; his hair, of the same color, fell in thick curls over his shoulders; his costume, almost Roman, was velvet, patterned with leaf-green on a bright gold background. Silk stockings the color of fire covered his legs and thighs; light shoes of a cloth similar to his coat, attached with diamond buckles, formed his footwear. His coiffure was a little toque of similar adornment, around which was a string of precious stones, from beneath which six or seven feathers the color of fire protruded negligently, the shafts of which were covered with pearls and diamonds mixed together.

After that charming object, twelve more attendants similar to the first were marching, in the same order. No spectacle had every appeared more beautiful than that brilliant march in that tenebrous place, and Understanding, who was accustomed to magnificence, was charmed by it. After having marched for a few strides, one of the attendants was detached on his master's order, and approached the vessel where Understanding was. When he was close, he struck the ground with his foot, and immediately appeared on deck near Understanding, to whom he said, in an unknown language, which was nevertheless understandable: "My master, the King, having learned of your arrival in this country, asks you to come to find him."

"And who is your master, the King?" asked Understanding.

"He is the person you see" replied the envoy. "His name is Antijour, and this land is the Realm of Lost Riches." He continued: "Give me your hand and stamp your foot like me."

He did so, and found himself on land outside the ship. He approached King Antijour with a great deal of respect and was received very civilly.

"Amiable stranger," the King said to him, "you must be something marvelous, and the prodigious manner in which you have arrived in my domain leaves me in no doubt of that."

Understanding, although slightly surprised, was about to reply to him, when the other said, offering him his hand: "This is not the place where I want to learn about your adventures; follow me."

Immediately, the King and his entire retinue returned whence they had come, resuming the hollow path, which descended gradually.

When they had marched for about an hour, always descending, they found themselves in a flat country where the same silence and the same obscurity reigned in which Understanding had seen something very bright shining from afar. When he was closer he discerned that there were seven great porticos built in varnished clay, so beautiful and so lustrous that they resembled mirrors: ornaments of architecture were marked there by an infinite number of small lamps, which had the same effect in that obscurity as the stars in a beautiful night.

Understanding noticed that those lamps and the candles that Antijour's attendants were carrying did not produce any smoke, and that although he had seen them burning for more than an hour, they had not diminished.

When the King had passed under the middle portico with Understanding and all of his magnificent retinue, they came into a large courtyard paved in squares of black and white marble, like a checkerboard, at the back of which seven more porticos corresponded to the first. They supported a large building on the same material, illuminated in the same way. The two sides of the courtyard were each limited by seven porticos similar to the others and filled with the same illuminations, but the greatest marvel was that the porticos at the back of the courtyard and those at the sides were as many theater decorations, composed and illuminated like those in the Opéra. Some represented gardens as far as the eye could see, ornamented by fountains, flowers and figures; others enabled the sight, in the distance, of seas, ships and marine monsters. Others were visible that represented magnificent palaces, forests, meadows, fields and, in sum, everything that the art of perspective has of the finest and most natural.

Antijour allowed his new guest to admire these marvels for a while; then, having entered a kind of vestibule, he went up a great staircase illuminated at intervals by crystal chandeliers filled with candles. From there he went into an apartment, the first room of which was a hall hung with beautiful haute-lisse tapestries, and furniture in proportion, as well wrought as in France. The second and third rooms were equally neat but with different adornments; admirable paintings and portraits were visible everywhere, and they only walked on the most exquisite Persian and Turkish carpets.

Finally, the King entered his bedroom, which could have passed for a masterpiece of magnificence, especially the bed, which was at least as beautiful and rich as the one that Aubelle once showed in Paris in the Hôtel de la Ferté. A quantity of lords followed His Majesty there. They were sufficiently well made and quite magnificent, but it would have needed a great deal for them to be as handsome as the King.

That Prince took Understanding into his cabinet, which was full of the rarest curiosities; he invited him to sit down beside him, and asked him to tell him who he was and how he had been brought to his realm.

Understanding gave him the satisfaction he desired, and gave him a description of the beauties and riches of the Isle of Magnificence, as well as the charms and the profound intelligence of Queen Pleasure, above all her power and her science. He did not say anything about himself except the circumstances that had been advantageous to him, carefully refraining from making him the confidence of his flight. Intelligent people always know how to be sparing when the occasion demands.

When he had finished his story, Antijour made known the pleasure that he had obtained from listening to him, and seemed charmed by the great things that he had just learned about the beautiful fay. He said to Understanding:

"I suspected strongly that you were an extraordinary man, since no one else has come to this land in the manner in which you were brought here, and we will see in due course what might have produced such an uncommon event. It is necessary that your art penetrates the entire depth of the sea, that it has traversed the realm of the undines and the earth that separates us, the routes of which are only known to those people. My kingdom as has much extent as the seas that are above us; all the riches that are swallowed up in their bosom are ours. The undines, whom I have just mentioned, and who live on the sea bed, receive them and send them to us, being my subjects and belonging to my empire. All the rich furnishings you have seen, and will see, come to us by that route.

"Ordinarily, we live entirely on fish and a few marvelously good vegetables that come from the sea bed; the undines furnish us with both. When vessels perish, those people, who know physiognomy perfectly, rescue and revive, in order to send them to us, the people who are useful to us, such as painters, set-designers, musicians, sculptors, architects, butlers, cooks, tailors, upholsterers and several sorts of artisans. They do not live long here, the air not being appropriate to them, but they teach our subjects what they know, and succeeded in that quite well.

"The music that you might have heard when you arrived here is made by persons of that sort. Two years ago, the undines of the Rhône, who have commerce with ours, sent us an entire Opera company, which had perished in the river. We also have knowledge off the sciences, by way of scholars who are also sent to us, and the books that fall into our hands. Our soil produces hardly anything because of the lack of air. We have worms that make wax, like your bees, and that wax has the property of not making any smoke and lasting ten times as long as yours. As for the oil of our lamps, it is the undines who furnish us with it, which they prepare in a manner so particular that it is almost inextinguishable, and our lamps which burn permanently, only have to be filled at intervals of several years.

"We have no women, we live or two hundred years, and we worship darkness; our generation is accomplished by taking an ounce of powder taken from a substance desiccated by fire, the composition of which was taught to us by the gnomes, who also have commerce with us; that desiccated substance is also what makes us stronger and more robust. We soak that powder in a precious liquid that flows from a unique tree that we have in this land; then we put it in a particular soil, and after nine revolutions, which are measured like your days, we find an egg there, which is placed in a box made of a whale's egg, filled with halcyon down. After nine more revolutions, a little embryo emerges from that egg, which is enclosed in a glass bottle a cubit high and sealed hermetically. When the embryo is as large as the bottle, which always happens after forty-nine revolutions, it breaks of its own accord and the child that emerges is clothed and nourished like us, and reaches adulthood within a year.

"There is never more than one Prince; his generation is made like those of others, from the body of a dead and desiccated Price, except that his formation requires double the number of revolutions."

When Antijour reached that point in his story, a little carillon was heard, composed of tiny bells of a marvelous softness and harmony. "Let's go to supper," said the King. "Those bells inform us of it; as we have no light to regulate our days, they mark our hours; there are some of them at the doors of all the rooms, which are rung by mechanisms like clocks. In the morning they tell us to get up; they do the same at the mid-day meal and supper, and when it is time to go to bed."

As he was speaking, they arrived in a hall, where the supper was served with an admirable abundance and neatness. The salvers, plates and all the garniture of the sideboards were silver. After having washed his hands the King sat down at table. He had Understanding placed facing him, and ten or twelve lords sat down in the adjacent places. All the dishes were very well prepared. Fine Mayence and Bayonne hams were served as entremets, as well as sausages of good quality; fat capons and other poultry were not forgotten.

"Hazard is giving us extraordinary fare today," the King told his guest. "A French vessel, which sank near here this morning, has furnished us with these meats. We are also drinking champagne, of which there was an abundant provision. Our undines are faithful; they send us even the slightest things."

The dessert was very tasty; there were solid and liquid marmalades, royal marzipans and all kinds of pastries and conserves, as well as an abundance of all sorts of fruits. They rank liqueurs, and wines from Spain, the Canaries, Muscat and Assiotat; distilled liquids and Ratafia were not lacking.

When the meal was over the King asked Understanding what opera he would like to see. He replied very respectfully that is desire would be regulated by his. "In that case, said the King, we'll see *Issé*,[19] which is the latest."

Immediately, the curtains of Gennes damask the color of fire, garnished with golden fringes, that closed the windows of the palace were opened. There were no other closures. The windows opened over one of the decorations I mentioned. The opera of *Issé* was performed there; the younger actors took the roles of women, who never entered that land. Everything was very well staged, and the music almost as good as in Paris, when Le Rochois and Dumensny were not singing.

After that diversion, coffee, tea and chocolate were brought, served in the rarest Chinese and Japanese cabinets, garnished with the finest porcelain. The little golden bells— for they were made of that metal—rang not long thereafter, and they were informed that it was time to retire. Understanding took his leave of the King, who had him conducted to a very beautiful apartment, where he lay down on a beautiful and good bed.

His mind was so full of the marvelous things that he had seen and heard that he had a great deal of difficulty going to sleep, although it was much easier to repose tranquilly in that world than in ours.

The next day he was woken up be the clockwork carillon, and a short time afterwards, one of the King's courtiers came into his room, followed by servants carrying magnificent clothes, in the fashion of the country; they presented them to Understanding on behalf of the King, who wanted him to wear them. He accepted the present politely, and had himself dressed in a blue and gold brocade coat with rose-colored silk

---

[19] *Issé*, a pastoral opera by André Destouches, with a libretto by Antoine Houdar de La Motte, had its official première at Versailles on 17 December 1697, as part of the celebrations of the Marriage of Princess Marie Adélaïde of Savoy to Louis, Duke of Burgundy, Louis XIV's grandson. The title role was played by Marthe Le Rochois and the role of Apollo, disguised as a shepherd, by Louis Gaulard Dumesny.

stockings. His toque was surrounded by a string of rubies and pearls, and feathers of the same color as the silk stockings. That outfit suited him perfectly, with his fine complexion and black hair.

As he finished dressing, he wanted to take a fine watch from the pockets of the coat he had been wearing the day before in order to carry it with him, but he was strangely surprised, when he took it out, that it was not the one that he had brought from the Isle of Magnificence, but another, far richer, on lid of which was a portrait of Queen Pleasure, surrounded by large diamonds of an infinite value. The courtier who was present, dazzled by the richness of the jewel, asked Understanding whose painting it was. Without making known his astonishment, he told him that it was the portrait of a beautiful Queen, of whom he had the honor of being the subject.

He understood that there was a mystery hidden beneath that adventure, and what gave him more pleasure was that he believed that, since he Queen had made him that present in such an impenetrable place, she had the design of making use of him, and that, in consequence, her anger must have relented in his regard.

While he was making those reflections, he was conducted to the King's apartment, where he found a large Court gathered for his rising. That Prince received him perfectly, and after he was dressed he went into his cabinet with him. He was no sooner there that the King asked him to tell him a few particularities about his homeland, principally concerning its beautiful Queen.

Understanding satisfied the King's desire, and after having left him with a very advantageous idea of his homeland and its princess, he continued: "Sire, I was so occupied with the extraordinary things that happened to me yesterday that I did not think of showing you the portrait of the Queen of the Isle of Magnificence."

So saying, he took it out of his pocket and presented it to Antijour, who was struck by an extreme surprise. He remained motionless for some time gazing attentively at the portrait, and then collected himself.

"Amiable stranger," he said, "Would you like to confide such a precious jewel to me?"

"It's yours, Sire," Understanding replied, bowing profoundly.

"Thank Heaven," replied the King, sighing. He left the cabinet without saying anything more, and when he had returned to his room he ordered one of his courtiers to show Understanding the rarest things that he had.

He was taken to the library, where he saw an infinite number of books and manuscripts containing marvelous secrets, secret negotiations and original histories that it has never been possible to recover. He saw all the riches and all the beauties of the palace, after which his conductor invited him to sit down in a chair carried by two men similar to the King's attendants. The courtier took one like it, and the men carried them so rapidly that no postillion would have been able to keep up with them.

In that vehicle Understanding was carried to the factories of foreigners and those of the country; then his conductor took him to see the productive land, which was of small extent. It was enclosed by a golden wall, as was the place where the powder of desiccated bodies was kept, of Kings well as their subjects. In another closed space he also saw the unique tree that the King had mentioned to him.

Afterwards he was taken to the Temple of Night, which was built in black marble. The goddess was represented there in the form of a golden bat, covered in black crepe; poppies were sacrificed to her—those being the only flowers that grew in that land, the leaves and stems being dead-leaf in color and their flowers brown violet—burned on a altar of black stone, washed with all the poppy-syrup that was found in sunken ships. No one ever spoke in loud voices in the Temple, nor for a league around; it was only illuminated by one lamp. The King only came to make his devotions there once a year, and that devotion consisted of sleeping in the Temple for one night, on an ebony bed set up for him, with a black velvet awning.

Understanding went for a walk on the bank of a river whose water seemed as black as ink, but when it was drawn therefrom, it was very clear and very good. The only animals seen in the land were the worms that made wax, their work being done in soft earth where they made holes similar to our hives.

After having shown him all the beauties of the land, the lord who had accompanied Understanding, took him to his house, where he regaled him. It was very clean and well-illuminated inside and out. What seemed most surprising to Understanding was the infinite number of lamps and candles that illuminated those somber dwellings continuously.

The entire revolution, to use the local term, passed in that manner, and they covered more territory in that space of time that one would have done in a fortnight in our world.

Understanding returned to have supper with the King, where everything happened as it had the day before, except that the King seemed pensive and ate very little, and there was no opera. When the meal was over, Antijour took Understanding to his cabinet, sat down in an armchair, made him a sign to do likewise, and then, leaning on a marble table and supporting his head in his hand, he remained silent for some time. Then he took the portrait of Pleasure out of his pocket.

He gazed at it tenderly, and, turning to Understanding, he sighed, and said: "You're right to say that the power of your Queen is great; it must be so, since her painting has put my heart into a state that it had not yet known. There are portraits in my palace of the most beautiful women in the world, but I have never felt anything in seeing them except the pleasure that a beautiful work of art gives. Alas, it is not the same with his one; the hours marked by this fatal watch, which it accompanies, have caused me to find the last of my repose, and although amour is a passion that is only known here by way of books, I sense that it has taken possession of my heart, and that I can no longer live happily without the possession of that incomparable person. I have sensed in the time of a single revolution the most delicate sentiments of amour; jealousy, absence and impatience have made themselves felt in my heart with all their force.

Understanding was very surprised to hear the King of Lost Riches speaking thus, but, making an instant's reflection on his adventure and the manner in which the portrait of Queen Pleasure had been sent to him, he had no doubt that she had played a large part in it. That is why he said to the King: "Sire, I am not astonished by the sentiments that you have for the Queen of the Isle of Magnificence. Her power is great enough to extend into these subterranean places, and it adds to her grandeur to receive the homage of a Prince whose merit and origin are so extraordinary. Abandon yourself, Sire to the sweetness of the passion that you are beginning to feel, and be sure that, provided that you can find a means to get out of this region, it will not be impossible for you to become happy."

Antijour was charmed by the beautiful hopes that his dear confidant gave him; he embraced him a thousand times and told him that he would send for a magician who had given talismans to several of his subjects that enabled them to accomplish impossible things. Understanding quit the King and retired to his apartment.

The next day, the magician came to find Antijour, to whom he promised everything that he wished. He told Understanding that, and expressed the joy that he felt. He also told him of his fear that his people might oppose his departure. He was going to think about the production of another Antijour, that name being annexed to all the Kings of the land. He did not lose any time, and after eighty-six revolutions, the new Prince was in a fit state to emerge from his bottle, that being the time at which he had the use of his reason.

In the meantime, Antijour became ever more amorous of the fay Pleasure. He talked about her continually with Understanding, for whom he provided all the diversions that were in his power. For himself, he no longer cared about them, finding no other pleasure than thinking about his passion. After he had put the young Antijour in the hands of those of his subjects he thought most capable of his education, he no longer thought about anything but leaving.

He had given orders to the undines to send him the crew of the first ship that fell into their hands; they had already de that, and he had put Understanding on the vessel, which was equipped with everything necessary, and on which immense riches were embarked, although Understanding had told him that it was quite unnecessary to carry treasures to a place that was the source of them.

Finally, when everything was ready, Antijour had the new King recognized, and then he departed, greatly regretted by his subjects, to whom that departure seemed all the more surprising because there was no precedent for it.

The King, who had not wanted anyone to accompany him, boarded the vessel alone with Understanding. As soon as he was there, the magician caused a wind so violent and im-petuous to emerge from the earth that it lifted the vessel up, with so much promptitude that it pierced the solid ground and was in the realm of the undines in an instant. Antijour stopped there for some time in order to give those people a few orders regarding their new monarch, and the utility of the kingdom that he was quitting.

Meanwhile, Understanding remarked the surprising situation of that place and the form of its people, who live on the sands of the sea, the suspended waters of which serve as the sky, from which a faint light emerges similar to that of dusk. The men there are tall and well-made, the women rather beau-tiful, but pale, as are the men. The women have long hair, al-most white; the men have blue hair. Both are semi-clad in a fabric made of green mesh, so beautiful and so delicately worked that it resembled velvet.

Their retreats are hollowed-out rocks, which compose very neat and very comfortable habitations. The points of those rocks, rising above the waves of the sea, are the reefs that cause so many vessels to perish. One also sees large well-cultivated market gardens, where there are quantities of vegetables. Understanding remarked amphibious animals there, strolling in large numbers over the sand, strewn with shells of all kinds.

As soon as Antijour had finished his conversation, the magician, who had followed him, raised another wind, with lifted the ship again, caused it to pierce the waves and immediately set it afloat. Understanding saw the light again with great pleasure. The King was greatly inconvenienced by it for several days, during which he was obliged to keep to his cabin. He gradually accustomed himself to it, his amour and the sight of the portrait of the charming fay completing his cure.

After three or four days of navigation, the pilot notified them that he could see land, and that the wind was impelling them toward a very comfortable port. Understanding advised the King to drop anchor there, which they did in very little time, Antijour and Understanding went ashore in order to discover what land they were in, for the pilot, who did not seem to be very experienced, or had lost his memory during his resurrection, did not know.

After they had gone a short distance, Understanding, who had better eyesight than Antijour, who was not yet accustomed to seeing so far, perceived several people coming toward them. They went forward, and when they were closer, it appeared from the richness of their clothing that they were not common people. There were men and women, but how surprised Understanding was to recognize his two brothers, who were among them. It was, in fact, them, who had come in search of a vessel in order to escape with King Peudacquets of the deplorable kingdom of the Frivolities. He was accompanied by Princesse Blanchette, Grandimont, Feverolle and Petitpois.

If Understanding had recognized his brothers, they had done likewise in his regard; they all came together and embraced with a great deal of joy and astonishment. Intelligence introduced his brother to the illustrious persons he was accompanying, and Understanding did as much for Antijour, whose beauty and fine manners won the admiration of the beautiful troop. The merit of the latter had the property that it was only necessary to see him to hold him in esteem. All those distinguished individuals exchanged reciprocal civilities, and when Antijour had learned the design that they had of embarking for the Isle of Magnificence his joy was extreme. He offered them his vessel, which was accepted with pleasure.

They embarked immediately, and, the wind being favorable, they set sail promptly. The conversation was agreeable, and everyone recounted his adventures. For the three brothers, they could not quit one another, and could not find enough time to tell one another everything that had happened to them. Understanding was chagrined when he learned from his brothers that they had portraits of their mistresses, while he did not have one of his.

"You have no grounds for complaint," Intelligence said to him, "since you have that of the Queen in exchange."

"That's true," he said, "but that portrait is not a favor for me, since, to all appearances, it was only sent to me in order to surrender it to the King of Lost Riches." As he finished speaking, without thinking about it, he put his hand in his pocket, and was agreeably surprised to take out a painting of the beautiful and sage Prudence.

There was only poor Philomele who had no part in the conversation; she was still hiding in Intelligence's hair; but when he was with his two brothers he told Understanding that, to whom he related his adventure in a very low voice, for fear of being overheard by the King of the Arsacides.

Their navigation was short and fortunate, and they landed to the great contentment of everyone. Antijour wondered where he could find a means of conveying his riches, but he was soon relieved of the embarrassment, because scarcely had they all disembarked than the ship disappeared.

"I told you, Sire," Understanding said to Antijour, "that that apparatus would not be to the liking of Queen Pleasure; she is doubtless sending your treasures back whence they came."

That Prince had too great a soul to be touched by that loss; it could only have been sensible to him in relation to his amour, but what Understanding said to him made him know that it had no part to play therein, and he did not think about it any longer.

The agreeable troop had not taken a hundred paces over the strand than they found themselves at the entrance of a long avenue of myrtles as large as oaks. One walked there over short grass dotted with flowers, and thousands of birds were singing marvelously there.

"These trees," said Memory, "have been the symbol of amour in all times, and as there is no one here who does not feel that passion, I believe that we would do well to make crowns of it to ornament our heads triumphantly."

Everyone applauded that speech, and as they prepared to break the lowest branches in order to employ them for that purpose, fourteen doves as white as snow, each of which was carrying a crown of myrtle enriched with gems, came to flutter over the heads of the lovers, whom they crowned. Antijour, Grandimont and the three brothers each received two. They deciphered that mystery clearly, and understood that the double crowns were for their mistresses.

There was only the King of the Arsacides who sighed dolorously, saying: "Alas, unfortunate Prince and even more unfortunate lover, what will you do with that crown, and where will you find the one who would like to receive it from your hand?"

"Don't be afflicted, great King," Intelligence said to him. "You are not far from the end of your troubles, and the charming Queen that we are going to see will not fail to bring a conclusion to them."

With those agreeable adventures, they found themselves at the end of the avenue of myrtles, which terminated at the shore of the lake that served as the limit of the isle so much desired. Three launches, shining with gold and gems, appeared on the lake, advancing propelled by oars. One was furnished in green, another the color of rose and the third in blue, all fringed and braided with silver. The oarsmen were dressed in the same livery.

When the launches were within range, the three brothers recognized their mistresses in the middle one. They were as beautiful as stars and ornamented like goddesses. The other two launches were empty. As soon as they had touched he shore, Understanding, Intelligence and Memory ran to give their hands to the charming sisters; they were so transported that they could only speak with their gazes; the responses were in the same language.

Prudence advanced first and made her compliments on the Queen's behalf to the illustrious individuals, whom she then obliged to enter the launches. When they were all aboard, the oarsmen did their duty, and reached the other shore in very little time. While those magnificent vessels were making the waters of the lake seethe, which seemed to be proud of such a beautiful charge, the lovers were at the feet of their mistresses, full of joy and hope.

Finally, they touched that beneficent soul. Intelligence had no sooner set foot on it that Philomele appeared as she had been before Cameleor had abducted her. Although everyone was touched with admiration for such perfect beauty, Grandimont thought he would die of pleasure; he threw himself at her feet, saying: "Is it you, charming Princess? Is it you, my lovable Philomele? Alas, where have you spent so much time, and how have you escaped the hands of the cruel Cameleor?"

"Sire," she said, raising him up and looking at him tenderly, "I cannot tell you those things now; I'll inform you of them at a more convenient time. It's sufficient that we can see one another, that our misfortunes have not diminished our tenderness, and that we no longer have anything to fear from our enemies." She indicated Intelligence. "This is the man to whom I have the obligation for my transformation."

Without knowing any more, Grandimont testified his gratitude to him.

As they advanced into the island, the beauties that they discovered at every moment augmented their pleasure and admiration, but it was another matter entirely when they approached the palace. All the lords composing the magnificent Court advanced to meet the Princes and Princesses and conducted them to the Audience Hall, which was the most beautiful, the most grandiose and the richest room imaginable. But nothing could compare to the beautiful Queen who presided in that place. She was seated on a throne elevated by several steps, which was filled with carbuncles whose glare was unsustainable, considerably augmented by a sun of diamonds by which the architecture was terminated.

The Queen was wearing a costume so covered in gems that its color could not be distinguished. She was holding a golden wand garnished with emeralds, at the end of which there was one that represented a cock. Her necklace was composed of thirteen pearls, each of such great value that the great Queen Cleopatra's were only fit for making a stew for her lover. She had no crown, because she was awaiting one from the hands of Amour. All the ladies of the Court, dressed in various colors and brilliant with gold and gems, were sitting on the steps of the throne, which were covered in blue velvet sown with golden stars. All the officers were lined up on the two sides of the hall

The first who entered was King Antijour; he stopped at the first step; the sight of the beautiful Queen surprised him so much that he was immobilized. For her part, Queen Pleasure was not exempt from agitation; her hour had come, and her heart, which had never been sensible, became so at the sight of the man who was to vanquish it.

The initial surprise of the King of Lost Riches having diminished slightly, he advanced and threw himself at the feet of the beautiful fay, where he placed his two myrtle crowns. He said to her: "Incomparable Queen, I have no other crowns to offer you but these; the one I possess at the center of the Earth is not worthy of you, so I have quit it forever, and I have reserved nothing but my heart, of which I make you a sincere homage, and although it was formed in an extraordinary manner, it was nevertheless sensible solely to the features of your painting. If you care to accept it, charming Queen, I will doubtless be the happiest of all men, but if I am unfortunate enough to displease you, I shall die at your feet of amour and dolor."

He said the last words in such a touching fashion that Pleasure was moved by them. "Get up, Prince," she said to him, holding out her hand, which he kissed. "I am not unjust, and although my heart has never been sensible, I cannot respond for the future. Love, hope and repose on your merit."

She blushed as she spoke those words, which appeared to have escaped her against her will. Antijour perceived that, and he thought he would die at the feet of Pleasure, who made him a sign to get up in order to make way for the King of the Frivolities, who was followed by his daughter, Princess Blanchette and the King of the Cabbage Lettuces.

The King explained all his misfortunes to the Queen. She knew them at least as well as he did; she commiserated with him and promised him her protection. She was charmed by the beauty of Blanchette, on whom she lavished a thousand praises. It can be said that no one ever merited them more than that admirable Princess. The Queen congratulated Verdelet on his good fortune.

The King of the Arsacides came in his turn with the beautiful and intelligent Princess Philomele. The Queen made them know that all the help they had received in their transformations had come from her, and that it was her who had changed Philomele into a nightingale, in order to extract her from the hands of Cameleor.

Petitpois and Feverolle had their turn, and although that young Princess only had a mediocre beauty, she nevertheless had a certain air of freshness, as had her lover, who also had his merit.

Finally, the audience was terminated by the three brothers, whose pardon was duly signed.

The Queen descended from her throne and was conducted by Antijour to her apartment, where she was followed by the most beautiful and most numerous Court imaginable. It was already late, and a supper was soon served, the description of which would require an entire volume.

After that meal, there was a ball of great magnificence; the newly arrived Princes and Princesses shone therein, the liberalities of the Queen having augmented their adornments with jewels of consequence, of which she made them a present. Antijour danced there perfectly well; no one was astonished by that, for he had learned from a master of the Opéra. Above all, however, Petitpois and Feverolle carried off the prize. When they danced together nothing was more agreeable; no one had ever seen such a disposition until then, and it seemed that they were not touching the floor.

After the ball, all the Kings, Princes and Princesses were conducted to apartments proportionate to their quality and the Queen's wealth, but principally Antijour, who advanced his affairs so far in such a short time that everyone perceived by the manner in which he was served and respected that he would soon become the King of that Magnificent Isle, in possession of its charming Queen.

In a quarter of an hour, she gave orders for the next day's fête, in which so many lovers were to become spouses. Everything there was grandiose, superb and beyond all description. Antijour married Queen Pleasure. Grandimont became happy by virtue of the possession of a person for whom he had suffered so many woes, and who had suffered no fewer for her part. As for Blanchette and Verdelet, they completed the wedding so often interrupted by the malicious and cruel Berlinguette. Feverolle and Petitpois were united forever, and that agreeable union is still seen today, perpetuated over the centuries. The three brothers and the three sisters were to enjoy a perfect happiness together; Intelligence would never be separated from Felicity; History would always shine with Memory; and Understanding was so charmed with Prudence that he never did anything without her advice.

The pleasures and the diversions that followed the sumptuous weddings lasted for a long time. Afterwards, Queen Pleasure summoned the King of the Frivolities, his son-in-law Verdelet, the King of the Arsacides and Petitpois to her cabinet one day, and asked them what they wanted to do. She said that if Peudacquets wanted to return to his homeland she would send him more intelligent and more laborious people; and that she would reestablish the Kingdom of the Cabbage Lettuces, with the Principality of Petitpois and Feverolle, and assured them that they no longer had anything to fear from Berlinguette, since she had imprisoned her in the Fearful Castle with the griffins, the spiders the wasps and the snakes, who were nothing but four magicians, one of whom was Cameleor.

The Princes thanked the fay very much for her advantageous offers, but told her that they would rather remain on the Isle of Magnificence and become subjects of such a powerful Queen than command peoples, whoever they might be. Petitpois made the same decision, and there was only Grandimont who wanted to return to his kingdom. He loved glory, and he could not see any to acquire among the pleasures of the Court. He departed some time after, with the charming Queen of the Arsacides. The fay heaped them with presents and gave them an equipage worthy of their rank.

Pleasure went a long time without having any children, and it was believed that she might never have any, because of the difference of origin between King Antijour and herself, but she finally became pregnant, to the great contentment of her husband, for it is usually husbands who love their wives who want them to have their children. She gave birth to a Prince who was a marvel of intelligence and beauty. He was named Antinuit, and after two or three centuries he inherited his mother's realm, and had a long posterity, who still bear his name.

THE SAVAGE

The Tercere Isles were once governed by a King named Richardin.[20] He had married a beautiful Princess, the daughter of King of the Cataracts of the Nile; her name was Corianthe. Richardin had been passionately in love with her, and as her father had not wanted to give her to him, because he had promised her to the King of the Bitter Springs, whom she did not love, he made him sustain rude wars before he became here possessor. Finally, he did so, to the great contentment of both, for if Corianthe was beautiful, Richardin was the best made Prince in the world.

A year after their marriage, Corianthe gave birth to a Princess as ugly as a beast. That did not give her any pleasure, nor the King either, for he was convinced that a beautiful daughter costs less to marry than an ugly one. She was named Disgrace.

A year after that, the Queen gave birth to another daughter at least as ugly as the first, causing further chagrin to the King and the Queen, but it was necessary to be patient; they named her Dolor.

A few months later, Corianthe became pregnant again, and her King, who feared that she might eventually have some monster, took care only to put beautiful people in her company, and had portraits of the most beautiful women he could find in her apartment; he even had some painted from imagination for want of originals. Finally, in spite of all those precautions, the Queen gave birth to a Princess even more horrible than the others. In the violence of his chagrin, the King named her Despair.

There he was, the father of the three most frightful she-apes in his kingdom. He told the Queen that it was necessary

---

[20] Tercere is the French name for Terceira, one of the Azores.

to stop there, and that he had no desire to populate the world with monsters. So it was said, and so it was done. The Princesses lived, and reached puberty. They had as little intelligence as beauty. What could be done with such merchandise? Poor Richardin was very embarrassed; he decided to have it proclaimed to the sound of trumpets throughout the kingdom that if any princes, knights, barons or gentlemen wanted to marry his daughters that he would give each of them as a dowry one of his islands, with the title of King.

Some time passed before anyone appeared; in the end, three knights arrived at the Court as disgraceful by nature as the three Princesses. One was hunchbacked and named Magorin; one was one-eyed and lame, named Gamille; as for the third, he only had one arm and one leg, and as known as Trottemal. Those disfigured individuals augmented the chagrin of the poor father, but he could do no better; the three knights were intelligent and they had done good deeds.

"Alas," said the Queen to her husband, "you were afraid of populating the world with monsters; it will be even worse when these six individuals are united."

"It's not inevitable, Madame," replied the King. "One sees every day well made persons with children that turn out very badly, as has happened to us; on the contrary, one sees ugly parents producing very agreeable ones."

"So much the better," said the Queen.

In sum, Richardin married his three daughters, without any great ceremony, and, after having rid himself of his three islands in their favor, he retired to a country house with a mediocre income and a similar retinue. He was living in repose and without ambition while he forgot that he no longer wanted to have any children and, I know not how, Corianthe found herself pregnant again.

When she was certain of it, she felt a cruel affliction. "Alas," she said to the King, "what will become of the unfortunate child whose mother I am going to be. What will we do if it's another girl as ugly as the others, having nothing more to give? If it's a Prince, what disorder will occur when, as is only just, he wants to possess his father's Estates and expels his brothers-in-law?"

Richardin could see that she was right, and did not know what to oppose to a speech so full of plausibility. He only said that the gods would sort it out, and that it was unnecessary to create woes in advance,

Finally, the afflicted Corianthe gave birth to a Princess who had never had a peer for beauty. She consoled herself, after a fashion, hoping that it might take the place of riches. She was right to think like that, for no one was ever so perfect. The older the child grew, the more her charms were augmented, but her mind was even finer; all her inclinations were great and noble; she rode a horse perfectly, used a bow and handled a sword with marvelous skill. She loved the sciences, and, what was even more admirable is that those heroic occupations did not prevent her from excelling in all the qualities of her sex. She embroidered, she drew and she cut out, all to perfection. No one had ever sung better, played instruments better or danced better. In sum, the divine Constantine—that was what they named her—was a prodigy of perfection.

Richardin and Corianthe would have liked to be able to do it, but they could not find anyone to ask for her. She was already eighteen years old, and their anxieties increased. The King, who always had fine expedients, took it into his head to make the charming Constantine marry one of his officers, who was a man without wealth, without charm and without intelligence, and to whom he could not give any other advantage than leaving him the little wealth he still possessed after his death.

He spoke to the Queen about it, who did everything possible to make him change his mind, saying that it was better to leave her alone with that small wealth than to share it with a family who could not help but be poor with so few resources; and that she was not yet beyond the age of making some encounter in accordance with her merit. But she gained nothing; the obstinacy of the King prevailed over her reasoning.

He made his will known to Constantine, who told him respectfully that she would rather remain a spinster than make a misalliance of that sort, but he was inexorable. He named a day for the accomplishment of such an ill-assorted union. The poor Princess dissolved n tears, and begged her mother to give her the means of avoiding an evil that seemed to her to be the most frightful thing of all. The Queen, who thought that there was nothing she could do to help her, mingled her own tears with hers.

Finally, after much weeping, Constantine said to the Queen: "Madame, permit me to flee and abandon myself to the guidance of the gods. Give me a man's clothes, and in that disguise, I shall seek an honorable death in a distant country, which I shall always prefer to a shameful life."

Corianthe had a great deal of difficulty making use of that expedient, but seeing no other way open, she consented to it. The following night, she ascertained that there was a merchant vessel due to set sail the next day. The Queen had Constantine put on one of the King's outfits, and, giving her what she could, which was not very much, she embraced her tenderly and enabled her to get out under cover of darkness. The poor Princess embarked and set sail for Sicily with the merchant ship.

When Richardin could no longer find his daughter, he hurled fire and flames at the Queen, suspecting strongly that she knew what had become of her, but she did not admit anything. Meanwhile, Constantine, under the name of Constantin, arrived in Sicily. When she left the ship she did not know which way to turn; what the Queen had given her was so very little that it was incapable of putting together any equipage, however mediocre.

While she was in that difficulty she went to sleep in a wood through which she was passing. She was woken up by something pushing her, and when she opened her eyes she saw a beautiful Lady next to her, dressed as Diana is depicted; she had in a loose green and gold garment, and morocco leather brodequins the color of fire, embroidered with gold and attached with diamond buckles. Her blonde hair was knotted behind with a poppy-red and gold ribbon. An ebony quiver garnished with gold and filled with arrows was dangling over her hip, sustained by a magnificent sash, and she was holding a bow of the same assortment. A small Greek morion with plumes the color of fire shaded her coiffure.

The Princess was agreeably surprised, but she was much more so when the charming person said to her, cheerfully: "Beautiful Princess, I've come here to offer you my help; you have need of it and it won't be lacking. Here's a horse," she continued, showing her one of the most beautiful attached to a tree, "you only have to mount it and let it guide you; it will take you to a place where you'll find a refuge."

"Madame," said the Princess, surprised, "permit me to ask you who can have told you that I am fleeing, in a land where I cannot be known?"

"Don't make difficulties for yourself, lovable Constantine. I know as much about your affairs as you do; I can't say any more." As she said that, she embraced her tenderly, and, having touched it under the neck, she said: "Embletin, do your duty."

The Princess leapt on to it with a marvelous disposition, and after having taken her leave of her benefactress with all possible civility, she departed.

Embletin progressed at such a gentle pace, and yet so rapidly, that in less than no time she emerged from the wood and, having traversed a great plain, she found herself at the gates of a city, which she thought she about to enter, but Embletin, having turned to the right, took her to the bank of a beautiful river, where she found a quantity of cavaliers and ladies, some of whom were on foot and others on horseback, in the middle of whom was a lord of admirable appearance and dressed magnificently, who was holding the hand of a richly ornamented young lady of singular beauty.

Constantine—or, rather, Constantin, since we shall name him thus henceforth—asked a page who the lord and lady were. The page told him that it was the King of Sicily and his sister, the Princess. Constantin advanced a little beyond the guards on horseback, in such a way as to be able to see the King. It did not take long for him to be perceived; his beauty, his fine figure and his foreign clothing gave the King the curiosity to know who he was; he commanded one of his officers to have him come forward.

As soon as the officer told him what the King wanted, he descended from his hose very gracefully and presented himself before His Majesty in a manner so noble that the latter was charmed.

"Who are you, amiable stranger?" the Prince asked him, "And what brings you to this country?"

"Sire," Constantin said, "I am a gentleman from the Tercere Isles, who, having no wealth to sustain my quality, by virtue of the large number of my brothers, has been obliged to seek among foreigners the fortune refused to me in my homeland."

"That fortune is very unjust," replied the King, "to refuse its favors to so many merits. What is your name?"

"My name is Constantin," he replied.

"Well, Constantin," the Prince said, "if you would like to remain with me, you will find all the protection you merit."

"You do me much honor, great Prince," replied the false Constantin. "I accept with pleasure the opportunity you are offering me, and I will try by my zeal and my attachment to merit a part of the grace with which you honor me."

The King put him in the hands of the first officer of his chamber and ordered him to equip him with everything necessary to put him in the number of his gentlemen of honor, which was done, and that very evening he appeared before the Prince in that quality. The magnificent clothes in which he was dressed further heightened his beauty and fine bearing.

The King was charmed with the beautiful manners of the new gentleman, but Princess Fleurianne, his sister, could not weary of admiring him. Constantin did not fail to pay his court in the entourage of that Princess; he made more than one conquest, but the most considerable was that of the Princess herself, who felt for the handsome stranger something that surpassed ordinary esteem; but as she was sage, she hid her sentiments.

The King of Canaria had sent a magnificent ambassador to the Court of the King of Sicily a little while before in order to ask for his sister for Prince Carabut, his only son. That Prince was hunchbacked and very disagreeable, and the Princess had no reason to be content with him. He had sent her magnificent presents; among others there were two hundred canaries of all colors in gold filigree cages, garnished with precious stones. Those birds sang and whistled divinely. And what was most marvelous of all was that they spoke all sorts of languages, and said the prettiest things in the world to the Princess on behalf of their master, who had a great deal of wit and gallantry, although that did not diminish his ugliness.

Prince Carabut arrived at the Court, and the sight of his faults, compared with the charms of the handsome Constantin, put the Princess into a cruel irresolution. She became very melancholy, and the King, who perceived it, and did not doubt that the unpleasantness of the Prince was its cause, did not want to say anything about it. He repented of having listened to the propositions for the marriage, finding it too disproportionate. However, the intelligence of the Prince spoke in his favor; he pressed for the accomplishment of his happiness, because he was very much in love with Fleurianne, but the King was always evasive, and gave birth to a thousand difficulties.

Meanwhile, there were great diversions at the Court; there were tourneys, in which Constantin always won the prize. If there was a hunt, he had all the honor of it; if he danced at a ball he effaced the best dancers. There were sometimes concerts in the Princess's apartment; his beautiful voice and the grace with which he played instruments made everyone admire him.

The Princess made her maidservants work on embroideries for her clothes and furniture; Constantin always gave them new inventions and worked with them—which surprised everyone, but only augmented Princes Fleurianne's passion. She said so much about him to the King on several occasions that he said to her one day: "My sister, I see that you have so much esteem for Constantin that, although I have a great pleasure in having him with me, I would rather deprive myself of him by making you a present of him. You need a squire, I give him to you in that quality."

The Princess blushed by virtue of a surge of pleasure of which she was not the mistress; she collected herself promptly and thanked the King, in a fashion that let him know that she was giving him a great pleasure.

Constantin was introduced to the Princess's retinue in a quality that rendered him almost inseparable. He was very content with that, and his sex was less subject to suspicions in the Princess's entourage than the Prince's, but he did not take long to perceive that she had sentiments for him that prepared difficulties of another species for him. He always dissimulated with great skill.

Meanwhile, the King ran out of reasons for delay, and Prince Carabut pressed him so forcefully to conclude his marriage with the Princess that he was obliged to say to him that his natural faults caused Fleurianne repugnance, and that, it not being in his character to force her inclination, he advised him to defer for some time, while he redoubled his efforts to please her by means of everything he could see that gave her the most pleasure. The Prince accepted that decision, albeit reluctantly. He had perceived the esteem of the Princess for Constantin, and in order to recruit him to his interests, he gave him magnificent presents.

One day, when the Princess was walking in the gardens of the palace apart from her maids, she saw a diamond of admirable beauty of Constantin's finger. "You have a fine jewel there," she said. "Where did you get it?"

"From Prince Carabut, Madame," he replied.

"He's very liberal," said the Princess, "and if nature had given him a body similar to his soul, one could say that he would be an accomplished Prince."

"Madame," Constantin said to her, "the beauty of the soul is always preferable to that of the body; the one often passes very quickly, but the other lasts eternally."

"That is quite true," said Fleurianne, "but when one is obliged to spend one's life with a monster, whatever other good qualities he has, one has much to lament. I could like Carabut as a friend, but I feel that I will never love him as my husband. How unjust Nature is," she continued, darting a languid gaze at Constantin, "since a Prince would have been happy to have received from her a beauty that becomes useless in a subject to whom she has provided it in such profusion!" She fell silent, lowering her eyes.

Constantin understood her clearly and he replied: "Madame. I wish it were in my power to communicate to Prince Carabut that which could render him agreeable in your eyes."

"Oh," said the Princess, "it would be much easier to combine with so many charms the quality that they lack; the choice of a Princess can make a Prince of a man who lacks that quality in order to be worthy of her, but she cannot give what Nature refuses to someone who is deprived of her favors." Blushing, she continued: "I have said too much; it is no longer in my power to dissimulate the sentiments that I have just brought to light involuntarily. Yes, dear Constantin, you have all my tenderness, and if I were the mistress of my fate, I would not hesitate for a moment to take you for my husband, but since I cannot do that without failing in what I owe, I am resolute never to have another."

As she finished speaking and Constantin was about to reply to her, they heard a noise behind a nearby palisade. The Princess thought that it was her maidservants, but when she turned round she saw them a few paces away. At that moment, the ladies joined them, and the conversation became general but very languid on her part. Carabut joined her too, and seemed rather disconcerted.

They returned to the palace and the Princess retired to her apartment. The Prince did not stay there very long. Constantin was in the antechamber when he came out. He approached him and said in a low voice: "Constantin, I have something to say to you. Follow me."

He obeyed him; they traversed a gallery together, at the end of which there was a staircase that led to one of the extremities of the gardens, where there was a door that opened on to a deserted area. Carabut opened it, and when he had passed through it with Constantin, he closed it again. Seeing that they were alone, he said: "It's necessary that you give me a reckoning for the sentiments that the Princess has for you, of which you are unworthy. I heard the conversation that you just had with her in the garden."

"Sire," replied Constantin, "If you heard the whole conversation you must know my innocence. I am not culpable if...."

"It is futile," said the Prince, interrupting him, "to justify yourself; I heard enough to be convinced that you occupy in Fleurianne's heart a place that she refuses to me. It is necessary that your blood avenge me for that preference." As he said that, he drew his sword.

He was short, and Constantin's stature gave the latter a great advantage over him. Whatever Constantin might have done to avoid the combat, it was impossible for him to do so, but it became deadly for poor Carabut, for in no time at all he was pierced by two sword thrusts and fell dead.

Constantin found himself in a cruel predicament, but, seeing that the safest course was or him to flee, he went back into the palace by another route and ran to the stables, saddled Embletin, mounted up and emerged from the city with promptitude.

While Constantin fled, Princess Fleurianne had people search for him everywhere, but it was in vain; his absence and the death of the Prince seemed to create the belief that he was culpable. The King, who loved Constantin passionately, would have liked to overlook it, and was not sorry that he could not be found. He sent men to look for him, but they had secret orders to let him escape if he was found. As for Fleurianne,

she was in despair, and to hide her dolor she pretended to be
ill and went to bed.

The King sent ambassadors to the King of Canaria in order to take him the body of his son and to try to appease him,
which appeared to be quite difficult.

Meanwhile, Constantine was still fleeing with Embletin,
without knowing where she wanted to go. She had been traveling day and night for some time, almost without eating or
sleeping, when she entered a dense forest. The further she
went, the darker the forest became; night overtook her there.
She went on for some time in the dark, saying: "Alas, unfortunate Princess, it is your destiny to be reduced to allowing
yourself to be conducted by an animal."

With that reflection and similar ones she found herself in
a place that was a little less dense, in the vicinity of a magnificent castle. The door opened of its own accord, and Embletin
went in, traversed a large courtyard and stopped at the foot of
a perron.

Constantine dismounted, and Embletin, who evidently
knew the place, promptly went to the stables. The Princess
went up the perron, and traversed a vestibule, which seemed to
her to be beautiful, to the extent that the obscurity allowed her
to judge it. Then she went up a broad staircase, and when she
had taken a few steps she saw a young man who was holding a
candle in a silver candlestick. He was handsome, and very
elegantly dressed.

"Princess," he said, bowing to her, "The fay Obliging,
lady of this castle. Having been alerted to your arrival, has
sent me to meet you, in order to take you to her apartment."

Although surprised to find that she was known in that
place, the Princess expressed her gratitude to him. She was led
through an enfilade of several rooms, which appeared to her to
be of surprising magnificence. Her guide opened a door for
her, through which he allowed her to enter alone a well-
illuminated and magnificent room filled with large mirrors,
whose frames were covered in gems. The parquet was strewn
with carnations, jasmines and tuberoses. A lady of great beau-

ty, richly adorned, was in a bed of silver and green fabric, strewn with flowers.

As soon as the lady saw the Princess she held out her arms, saying: "Approach, charming Princess; come and savor in my company the repose that you merit, and which Destiny has refused you thus far."

The Princess approached her, and was agreeably surprised to see that the lady was the same one who had made her a present of Embletin. "Oh, Madame," said Constantine, as she received her caresses, "I can see that it is to you alone that I owe all the good fortune of my life."

Obliging told her that she knew everything that had happened to her in the home of the King of Sicily, and told her that she could expect in the castle the end of all her troubles. "Go and rest," the fay said to her. "We'll talk tomorrow entirely at leisure." She showed her a door, which she told her to open. She did so, and went into an elegantly furnished room; two very beautiful and very well-dressed young women received her there politely; they offered her fruits and preserves, and she ate them; then they undressed her and put her to bed.

When she woke up, the same two maids came to dress her in rich and elegant clothing of her own sex. When she was fully adorned she went into Obliging's room, and found her at her dressing-table; she welcomed her with a great deal of amity. After a meal, several fays of the first order came to visit her; she introduced them to the Princess, to whom she showed all the beauties of the castle and its marvelous gardens.

The next day, Obliging told her that she wanted to show her everything that the art of Enchantment had of the most marvelous, and to that effect she took her into a gallery full of cabinets, mirrors, tables, side-tables, girandoles and chandeliers of infinite richness, at the end of which she opened a door of sculpted bronze, which let them into a large cabinet, in which the floor on which they walked, the vaults and the wall-panels were composed of clouds, the color of those that accompany the setting sun on a fine day.

"This is the Cabinet of Destiny," said Obliging to the Princess, "and you are going to see things that will give you astonishment and pleasure." She touched one of the sides with a bronze wand and continued: "This is where one can see everything that is happening in the realm of the King that the entire would knows as Louis le Grand. On this other side is contained the general destiny of the entire earth, and this one here is for what regards the destiny of a particular individual."

After that she touched the side of the destiny of humans in general three times, and immediately, the clouds formed distinct shapes, which represented the most extraordinary events: battles, sieges, the massacre of kings, others dying naturally, others dethroned, happy and unhappy marriages, burning cities, edifices toppled by earthquakes and struck by lightning, the flooding of rivers, naval combats and shipwrecks, the changing of the seasons, and the end of the present century,[21] in which the weakness of stars and planets cause a general deregulation of time, and the horoscope of the future century.

After having particularity of all these things, she struck the wand on the Destiny of France, and the figures that formed there represented all the marvels of the reign of Louis le Grand: his numerous conquests; his armies on land and at sea; the portraits of all the great captains who commanded them and their individual actions; his immense and inexhaustible wealth; his palaces, the beauties of which held enchantment the magnificence of his Court; his beautiful and numerous family, of which he saw almost three generations; the civility

---

[21] The word *siècle* [century] can also mean age or era in a much broader sense, so, although the author is setting this scene in the year 1697, she might not be anticipating the effective end of the world within three yearsGiven the precariousness of her personal situation, however, perhaps she is. The naked flattery of the next paragraphs notwithstanding, Louis XIV was very old, and one of his official mistresses had famously remarked: "*Après nous, la déluge….*"

of his subjects; the sublimity of the sciences and arts they possessed; the grandeur of his cities; the beauty and abundance of his provinces; the flourishing commerce he maintained with all the nations of the Earth; and above all, his unparalleled generosity, which rendered him the protector of oppressed innocence.

But that was nothing by comparison with an agreeable spectacle that appeared: that of a young and beautiful Princess, who emerged from the milieu of an accumulation of sheer mountains. She was brilliant with gems, and bore a crown of myrtles on her head and an olive branch in her hand. A lady whose attitude and bearing seemed divine was holding her with one hand and presenting her with the other to the King of France, who received her with open arms and introduced her in his turn to a young prince almost her age, as handsome as Amour, the grandson of the great monarch, whom was destined to be her husband, and whose union ended a cruel war and brought peace to a large number of Powers allied by jealousy against that flourishing Empire.[22]

"Behold," said the Fay to the Princess, "the greatest event of our days."

After she had said that she touched the third side. "This is what concerns you, Princess," she said to her.

Immediately, she saw the Tercere Isles appear, her father the King and her mother the Queen, afflicted by her loss, her three sisters and their husbands overwhelmed by civil wars and domestic chagrins. Constantine, who was good, was touched by that and shed a few tears. Then the fay enabled her to see the Kingdom of Sicily, and in the King's palace, Prin-

---

[22] The marriage of Marie-Adélaïde of Savoy and the Duke of Burgundy, mentioned in the previous story, came about as a result of the Treaty of Turin, signed in 1696 between her father, Victor Amadeus II of Savoy, and Louis XIV, which pledged the former's support for the latter in the Nine Years War, against the Alliance of which he had previously been a part; the war came to an end in 1697, before the marriage.

cess Fleurette, to whom he wanted to give a frightful satyr as a husband.

"Alas!" exclaimed the Princess, "I have delivered her from one monster by killing Carabut, but now there is another, even more terrible. Oh, Madame, is there no means of helping that lovable Princess?"

"It will be you," replied the fay, laughing, "who will extract her from that predicament again, but the time has not yet cone."

The last figure that was presented to Constantine was her own. She was sitting on an elevated throne, and the King of Sicily was placing a crown at her feet.

"What does this mean, Madame?" said the Princess.

"You will know that in due course," replied the Fay, after which everything returned to its original state and they emerged from the cabinet, which was closed again.

A few days later, the fay told Constantine that she wanted to enable her to see all the Courts on Earth, and that she would commence with that of France, where the most superb celebration was about to be held that had ever taken place among mortals. To that effect, Obliging prepared a chariot composed of the skull of a giant, who had been found in her domain, and whom she had exterminated by the force of her at. The giant had been ninety-six feet tall; she had the skull worked in such an admirable fashion that everything necessary was found there, including the undercarriage and wheels, and as she only wanted to travel by night she had it coated with black varnish. She harnessed two huge mastiffs to it, to which she attached the wings of Indian bats, which are as large as cows in that land.

She also dressed the Princess in black crepe lined with cloth of gold, and, having put into their mouths a herb that rendered them invisible, of which they took a good provision, they departed with their equipage and arrived in a short time in Versailles, on the eve of the marriage of the Princess of Savoy. They were present at the ceremony without being seen, as well as the meal, and they ate the fruits and preserves that were served there. The fay pushed the servants who were carrying the baskets of the dessert, and when they turned round to see who had committed that impudence, they took what they pleased without them noticing. They saw the Prince and the Princess dressed, undressed and put to bed; they visited her dressing-table and all her jewelry.

As they were emerging from the bedroom the King emerged too, and as Constantine ran to say something to Obliging, she pushed the King without meaning to. He was all the more surprised because he could see no one nearby; after having looked around with some anxiety he continued on his way.

Afterwards they were at the ball and the opera of *Issé*, which they found very beautiful, as well as the apartments, and, in sum, everything that happened during those celebrations. The fay confessed that only the Art of Enchantment could surpass the magnificence of that Court.

Every evening they retired to the abode of the fay Marline, who lived in an invisible palace near the Château de Marly.

After having seen the French Court they went to Spain, where they saw nothing worthy of their curiosity, any more than in Germany and the residences of the Princes of the North, but they were quite satisfied with the magnificence of the Great Sultan and the beauties and riches of the Seraglio, of which they disentangled the intrigues and penetrated all the secrets. They went to Siam, to China, to the abode of the Mogul, to Persia, and finally returned to England to see King William, of whom renown published such different things

They were curious to see a sitting of Parliament, but the confusion of laws, bills, taxes on tea, chocolate, coffee, tonnage and poundage, as well as their fashion of counting in sterling, frightened them so much that they emerged very rapidly, and in order to relax they went to Paris, where the Tuileries, the Opéra and the Comédie amused them for a few moments. They realized that they had not yet been to Venice, and went there, spending a good part of the Carnival there, after which they returned to the fay's castle.

Although they had been diligent, they had spent nearly two months in their travels; the beauties of the castle enabled them to recover from their fatigues; in that beautiful abode, pleasures succeeded one another.

While Constantine was leading such a pleasant and tranquil life, it was not the same in the home of the King of Sicily. He had endured a rude war against the King of Canaria, irritated by the death of his son; his troops were joined by so many canaries that the subjects of the King of Sicily thought they would be stifled by them, but fortunately, he thought of making use of hot embers from Mount Vesuvius, and by that means he roasted them all like pigs. What gave him even more difficulty were the two hundred talking canaries of which Prince Carabut had made a present to Princess Fleurianne; they had escaped from their cages and spread throughout the kingdom; they had given such bad advice there that they had ignited a civil war that had been difficult to stifle.

The King had hardly begun to breathe again when someone came to tell him that a species of men—or, rather, hideous and cruel monsters, half-human and half-goat—had emerged from mountains not far from the capital city, who were doing frightful damage in neighboring places, carrying off the children, eating the livestock and spoiling the crops, after which they retired to inaccessible places.

The King resolved to go in person to exterminate that foul breed. He took his guards with him, mounted and on foot, his gentlemen, and anyone else who wanted to follow him. The mountains to which the monsters had retired were at the extremity of a great forest; the King sent men to scout the routes, and in order to attract them dispersed a few flocks and jars full of milk and wine, which they liked very much. Then, hiding in the trees with his men, he waited for them to come down from the mountains, which they did a short time later.

When they were occupied with their meal, his forces hurled themselves upon them, and, taking them surprise, killed many of them; but, having rallied, they fell upon the King's men with such fury and rapidity that they killed several; they threw themselves on to the rumps of horses and killed them with their claws or put out their eyes. That frightened them so much that they fled without thinking of the King, who found himself abandoned by his men and surrounded by a troop of the monsters.

Fortunately, they did not throw themselves on to the rump of his horse, as they had done to the others; they cried around him in a frightful manner, and tried to trap him with the branches of trees that they had broken; but the King, who was extremely skillful, and rode a horse marvelously, killed a large number of them, and the rest fled into the mountains.

When saw that he was free, he thought about returning, and as night approached he sounded his horn in order to see whether he could be heard by his men; but there was no response. He had commenced walking when he saw one of the savage monsters emerge from behind a tree, which threw itself on to the rump of his horse, and, embracing him, prevented him from using his arms.

The King was doing what he could to get rid of him when he heard the monster say to him: "Have no fear, Prince, I shall not do you any harm, provided that you promise to do what I say."

The King, surprised to hear that species of animal talk replied: "If you do not ask the impossible of me, I promise to execute it."

"I only ask," the other said, "that you take me to your palace, that you put me in a place where I am only seen by you, and after I have been there for some time I will tell you things that will not be disagreeable to you."

"I would like that," said the King, "and I promise."

Immediately, the monster let go of him and sat on the rump of his horse, and the King set forth toward the city.

As it was night, they traversed it without being seen. His men had spread the news everywhere that he was dead; he found the palace unguarded, and when he was in the courtyard, a few of his servants, who saw him, fled in fear or dread. He made use of that solitude to reach his apartment without being seen; he entered with the savage, who held him by the arm, and having opened a little cabinet where he kept rare and precious jewels, he left the savage there, telling him that he would take care to give him what was necessary.

After that he went to his sister's apartment, where the nobles of the Court had assembled on the news of his death. He found her in tears; she uttered a cry of joy on seeing him come in.

"Don't be afraid," he said to her, "the news of my death is an effect of the cowardice of my officers; Heaven has preserved my life, and I forgive them for their scant affection."

The Princess embraced him tenderly and passed from great dolor to great joy. All the officers, very ashamed, came to beg his pardon, and he granted it to them. He did not say anything about the savage; he had food and drink brought to his room under pretexts, and when he was alone he took him what was necessary to live. He received a thousand caresses from the animal, and he thanked him in terms that gave him admiration.

The monster had already been in the palace for some time when one day, when the King brought him food, he said to him: "Sire, it is time for me to tell you what you need to do in order to become the most fortunate Prince in the world. It is necessary that you tell all your subjects that you wish to marry, and that you make all the preparations for a celebration of that nature. Everyone will be very surprised not to know whom you want to marry; the Princess, your sister, will urge you to tell her, but you will not open up to anyone, and when the day has come, you will close the apartment that you will have had prepared for your spouse, the Queen. You will take the key and you will come and collect me from here; I will enter it with you and the Princess, and you will see what Heaven destines for you."

The King was as surprised as one can be, and did not know what he ought to do, but the savage, who saw his uncertainty, reassured him by saying: "Have no fear, Prince; abandon yourself to the destiny that ordered all these things a long time ago."

The King promised him to execute scrupulously all that had been asked of him, and that same day he began to make the preparations for his marriage. The Princess was astonished by the secrecy that the King was maintaining with regard to the person he wanted to marry, but he told her that she would know when the time came.

Everyone in the Court and the city believed that the King had fallen in love with the daughter of one of his subjects, and did not want to say anything for fear that the nobles of the Court would not be content. There was no beautiful young woman who did not flatter herself in secret that she might be the fortunate person in whose favor the King would declare himself.

Finally, the time came; the day before, King took the key of the future Queen's apartment. The following day he dressed in his ceremonial garb and ordered his sister, the Princess, to don her most magnificent attire. All the Queen's servants and maids of honor had orders to be ready. After getting dressed, the King went into his cabinet, and from there into the one where the savage was, whom he took by the arm, and traversed his apartment thus, followed by the Princess.

She was very frightened to see the King holding that monster. Everyone maintained a profound silence, not knowing how such extraordinary conduct would end. The King opened the Queen's apartment and traversed it as far as the antechamber. The savage told him in a low voice to make everyone remain there except the Princess, which he did.

The three of them went into the bedroom, the door of which the savage closed behind them.

The King was very surprised to see the furniture of that room changed into others, of unusual magnificence. Among other things, there were twelve large golden baskets garnished with gems, filled with the most beautiful jewels and the most beautiful clothes that one can imagine.

They had been there for a few moments when the door of a cabinet opened and two ladies emerged of a beauty and adornment beyond imagination, but the King was much more surprised when he recognized in the more beautiful one the features of the handsome Constantin. He was not mistaken, for the Princess Constantine whom he saw and Constantin were one and the same person.

The fay Obliging was conducting her, and when she had bowed to the King of Sicily, she said "Sire, this is the beautiful Princess Constantine, the daughter of the King of the Tercere Isles, who has been in your Court under the name of Constantin, and for whom you conceived so much amity; it is her that the gods have destined for you to marry. But that is not the only prodigy that I must accomplish here; the savage that you see must be the husband of the charming Princess Fleurianne.

"Don't be frightened, Madame, she said then, "that form hides a Prince worthy of you; he is the King of the Aimantine Isles, whom the anger of an unjust fay, who wanted him to love her in spite of himself has kept in that form for several years, and who will only lose it by means of the marriage of Princess Constantine with the King of Sicily." To the King she said: "It only depends on your consent, Sire, to liberate that Prince from the terrible condition to which he has been reduced."

The King, who had had time to recover from his initial astonishment, as had the Princess, replied to the fay: "I consent to everything you wish, Madame, and provided that the beautiful Constantine wishes to render me happy, I have nothing more to desire."

The Princess gave marks of her submission with a great deal of decency and modesty, and, the fay having tapped the savage with a golden wand, he became the most handsome Prince that had ever been seen. He went to throw himself at the feet of the beautiful Fleurianne; they conceived for one another at that moment the most tender of all passions.

The King embraced Constantine, and the Princess, who had loved Constantin so much, loved him no less as Constantine. She testified her tenderness to her with some confusion; Obliging told the King in a few words the history of the beautiful Princess that he was about to marry, and when she had finished, she said: "It is necessary, Sire, that we go to receive King Richardin and Queen Corianthe, who will arrive presently in the palace to witness the marriage of their daughter, as well as the three Queens, her sisters, and the Kings, their husbands, who have been informed by my orders."

Princess Constantine blushed, and the deformity of her family put her in confusion. The fay, who was observing her, perceived that. "I have anticipated everything, beautiful Princess," she said to her. "I never oblige by halves, and although the Queens your sisters are not as beautiful as you, they are sufficiently so at present to serve as an ornament to this celebration, and Nature, aided by a powerful art, has rendered the Kings, her husbands, participants in their changes."

As she finished speaking, she led the way; the King followed her, holding Constantine's hand, and the King of the Aimantine Isles that of Fleurianne. They traversed the apartment, to the great astonishment of the entire Court, and arrived in the great hall of the palace, where all the nobles and ladies were assembled, to whom the King introduced the Princess as the person who was about to become their Queen.

Everyone was enchanted by her beauty, and remained surprised by the resemblance she had to the false Constantin. That enigma was explained, as well as that of the savage. Afterwards, the King and Queen of the Tercere Isles were seen to enter, with their three daughters and their husbands, who were as good looking and well made as they had been ugly and deformed, although their names remained the same. They could not weary of caressing one another and admiring one another.

The ceremony of the double wedding took place, to the great contentment of everyone. The good and obliging fay did the honors, and received the thanks of all those that she had obliged so liberally. She gave magnificent presents to Queen

Corianthe and her sisters; the festivities were marvelous, and the fay organized everything. It was she who put the spouses to bed, and as the King of the Aimantine Isles had no equipage, she made him one, which he found the next day when he got up.

The jousts and tourneys lasted several days, and Magotin, Gamille and Trottemal performed marvels there. The prizes were distributed by the fay, and were found to be priceless.

After all the diversions, which lasted for several months, the King of the Aimantine Isles took his charming wife to his kingdom, with a sumptuous equipage and immense riches; the three Kings of the Tercere Isles returned there, but King Richardin and his wife, the Queen, remained in Sicily with Queen Constantine, and ended their days here. The fay returned to her magnificent castle.

THE TURBOT

There was once a King named Lucidan, who reigned in peace on the isle of Caprare, in the Sigustic Sea. He had married a young woman who was of no great quality, but he had loved her very much; she was beautiful, and he was satisfied. He only had one daughter of that marriage, whose beauty far surpassed that of her mother. She was a most piquant beauty; she was blonde; all her features were regular and delicate; her figure was lovely, her complexion marvelous; in sum, she had everything necessary to make a perfect beauty, but above all, she had such a great penchant for joy that the slightest thing made her swoon with laughter.

If the maids that served her dropped their needles or heir thimbles, or they happened to say one word when they meant another, the laughter of the Princess was never-ending. One could say with good reason that she laughed more than anyone else in the kingdom. That perpetual laughter was the reason why her father called her Risette, and although she had a different name, that one stuck.

Several young Princes, the sons of the Kings of neighboring islands, asked for her hand in marriage; although she was not yet fifteen years of age, the renown of her beauty had made her desired passionately. King Lucidan looked around for the man to whom it might be most appropriate to marry her, but before declaring his choice, he spoke about it to his daughter. She begged him so insistently, however, not to marry her so soon, that he wanted to give her that satisfaction.

In the capital city where the King ordinarily resided, there was a poor widow named Isotte, who only had one son, who followed the profession of fisherman; his name was Mirou, and as he had an alienated mind, he was commonly called Mirou the Fool. His folly was supportable; he did no harm; he went to the sea shore every day carrying his nets and his fishhooks, but he was so unfortunate or so maladroit that he almost always came back without having caught anything, and while he traversed the city to return to his mother he shouted at the top of his voice: "Bring couches and couchettes, seches and sechelettes, mattelles and mattelettes,[23] for Mirou is bringing back many fish."

That gibberish meant that many vessels ought to be prepared in order to receive what he had caught, although he never caught anything, and the good Isotte, who was caught by that every day, always got everything ready that she could, for fear of annoying him. Ordinarily, he went past the palace, and when young Risette was in her apartment, which overlooked the square, and she heard Mirou shouting, she ran to the window and laughed with all her might. Mirou was very angry about that, for all his chagrin was in hearing himself mocked, and he had that in common with many people who do not like others to laugh at their stupidities. The laugher of the Princess annoyed him more than that of anyone else, and he hurled many insults and threats at her, as many by means of gestures as words; and the more irritated he became, the more pleasure Risette had.

One day, among others, he was fortunate enough to catch a turbot of extraordinary size; he rejoiced greatly in that, and expected to make a good meal of it, but he was very surprised when, as he pulled out his net, the fish spoke to him, saying: "Give me my life, I implore you, and as a recompose, I promise to grant all the requests you make of me, no matter how difficult they might be, and in addition, you'll catch more fish than you can carry."

Mirou was afraid; he dropped the net and the turbot leapt into the sea; and immediately, the net was full of large fish of every species, in such great quantity that Mirou had reason to be content. The turbot stuck its head out of the water and said

---

[23] These words are impossible to translate literally in context, but give the impression of referring to racks for drying fish as a preservative measure..

to him: "I'm much obliged to you, Mirou, and I won't be ingrate; when you have need of me you only have to come here
to call me, and you'll always find me ready to give you pleasure."

The turbot went back into the sea, and Mirou charged
himself with as many fish as he could, and repeated his jargon
with more justice than usual.

It seemed to him as he went past the palace that the Princess was laughing more than usual; his good fortune had in-
flated his courage, and he was all the more angered by it—
which is why, after having unloaded his fish, he ran to the sea
shore, where he called to the turbot, which appeared immediately. "I want you," he said, "in order to prevent Princess
Risette from mocking me, to act so that she becomes pregnant
without knowing how."

"I won't fail in that," said the turbot, "and you'll see the
effect shortly."

Mirou returned, very content, and went some time without going fishing, having an abundant provision. When he
returned to it, he no longer saw the Princess, at which he felt a
great joy, but he had not been able to see her because she was
very ill. Continual heart troubles were making her suffer a
great deal; nauseas followed, and then the desire to eat a thousand bad things.

The Princess's governess, who was a very experienced
woman, was very chagrined to see her in that condition. The
physicians said that it was "pale colors," and the Queen agreed
with them, but the governess, to whom the Princess's maids
complained every day that her clothes were becoming too
tight, was not taken in by that reasoning. The poor lady said to
herself: *I never quit the Princess, I'm with her night and day,
and yet to all appearances, she's pregnant.*

She interrogated all her maidservants adroitly, but she
could not obtain any enlightenment from them. Finally, she
resolved to make the Queen the confidence of her suspicions.
She found her in her cabinet, where she was plucking roses
with her maids of honor. The King liked rosy vinegar greatly,

and the good princess, who sought every means of pleasing her husband, gave herself the trouble of applying herself to it she could in order that it would be better. The governess told her that she would very much like to speak to her in private, and the Queen immediately dismissed her ladies. When they were alone she told her what it was about.

The Queen became angry with her and told her that if the misfortune she feared had occurred, she was the cause of it, since she had left the education of her daughter in her care. She got up so precipitately that she upset all the roses, and ran to Risette's apartment, where she treated her very badly, trying to make her say what she did not know. After having vented her spleen, she went to find the King, to whom she gave the bad news without precaution.

He thought he would die of dolor. He loved his daughter, but he loved his reputation even more. He fell into accord with the Queen that the governess was culpable, and without wanting to hear the poor lady. He had her put in an obscure prison, where she was made to suffer the cruelest privations, which did not make her say anything other than what she had already said.

Poor Risette had changed her laughter into tears. She was narrowly confined in her room, and all the maidservants she liked best were taken away.

Finally, the time for her to give birth arrived, and she brought into the world the most beautiful boy that had ever been seen. He had cheeks as white and pink as lady-apples, large blue eyes in which gaiety was painted, and a small vermilion mouth. He had curly blond hair, as long as if he were a year old; but what was most surprising of all was that he already smiled at everyone. The poor Princess, afflicted as she was, could not help caressing him, but the pleasure she obtained from it was soon taken away from her, and he was given to a nurse.

The King's intention had been to hide the accident, but the Queen was so little able to control her chagrin and her laments that everyone in the Court and the city was informed of it.

A year passed after the Princess gave birth without her emerging from her apartment, or the governess from her prison. The Princess had named her son Princillon; he had grown so big that it was a prodigy, and he seemed three times his age. One of the noblemen of the Court, who took pity on the unhappy state of the Princess, advised the King to assemble add the young men of quality in the Court, and even the city, in the great all where the Council was ordinarily held, to bring little Princillon there, and to make the person whom he caressed most the husband of the Princess.

The King had difficulty in making use of that expedient, but in the end he allowed himself to be persuaded. The day was fixed, and he found a large number of handsome youths who aspired to the happiness of possessing such a beautiful Princess, and also that of succeeding to a kingdom that would belong to her after the death of her father, the King—for the King had added that condition, in order to rid himself more easily of his daughter, whose accident, he had no doubt, would wound delicate consciences. But what faults cannot be repaired by a crown?

In order to avoid trickery, it had been expressly forbidden to allow little Princillon to see anything that might determine his choice, even smiling at him. The King was in a place where he could see everything without being seen. The nurse brought the little Prince, made him walk around the room, and then took him in her arms and paused before the young noblemen one after another, but he was not amused by any of them. In the end, however, they suddenly saw the handsome child extend his arms and lean toward the door of the hall, laughing. They were very surprised to see that his caresses were addressed to Mirou the Fool, who had slipped behind that door without being seen.

The King thought he would die of dolor at such an unexpected choice, but when his astonishment had given way to anger, he ordered that the unfortunate fellow be seized and throw into a dungeon. Immediately he sent to search the ports for the most wretched vessel that could be found, and had it brought to the place closest to the palace. When it was there, he had the unhappy Risette stripped of her ordinary clothes and gave her those of a poor girl who worked in a kitchen, and in that outfit he made her descend from her apartment, without being touched by her tears and the tenderness that she expressed toward him,

When she was in the courtyard of the palace, Mirou was taken out of his dungeon and he was dragged to the port with the Princess, in whose arms poor Princillon had been placed.

The Queen had fainted in her apartment; all the officers, noblemen, ladies and the people dissolved in tears. When those innocent criminals had arrived in the port they were put aboard the vessel, deprived of everything that was necessary to them. A few of the Princess's maidservants, who loved her tenderly, wanted to go with her, but she would not permit them to do it. "It is for me alone," said the desolate Princess, "to bear the punishment of a sin that I have not committed, and of which I am innocent."

The same maidservants had put a basket full of peaches, apricots, figs, wine, water and bread in the boat. On seeing those things, poor Risette said, weeping: "This nourishment is quite useless, alas, to people who will not be alive tomorrow."

Finally, the unfortunate vessel was pushed out to sea. Contrary to everyone's expectation, it headed straight for the open sea, in spite of its lack of masts and sails, and in a short time it was lost to sight.

The unhappy Princess was holding her son in her embrace, awaiting the moment of their death. As for Mirou, he ate and drank what was in the vessel without any concern for his destiny. Princillon cried, because he was hungry, and his mother gave him some figs in order to appease him.

When Mirou had eaten well, he said to the Princess, who was shedding a torrent of tears: "You aren't laughing now, are you? This is what my friend the Turbot promised me, because you mocked me too much."

"What do you mean," replied the Princess, "about your friend the turbot? Explain yourself, if you can, wretched fool."

"Oh, you're insulting me!" replied Mirou. "That's a fine way to get what you want!"

"Well" said the Princess, "I won't say any more about it. Tell me the reason for my misfortune before I die."

"Yes, indeed," said Mirou; then he told her what had happened to him with the turbot.

"Alas," said the Princess, sighing, "if that turbot has so much power, why don't you call him, to your rescue and mine, to get us out of the certain danger we're in?"

"I'd like to," said the insensate, "but what do you want me to ask him?"

"Only tell him," she said, "to do what I say."

Immediately, Mirou cried: "Friend Turbot, friend Turbot, come to the aid of your friend Mirou."

He had no sooner spoken than the turbot stuck its head out of the water and asked him what he wanted.

"I want you to do what this woman tells you," he said.

The Princess appeared, and addressed the turbot, saying: "Prodigious fish, who is the cause of the pitiful state in which I find myself, have pity on an innocent Princess who has not offended you. Content yourself with having rendered me the mother of a child whose father I don't know; the fault that you have punished so cruelly was very light, but no matter; I won't complain, provided that you grant me two things. The first is to allow this wretched vessel to reach land, and the second is that you render Mirou so handsome, wise and intelligent that I can marry him without shame, and by that means recover the honor that I have innocently lost, and to which I am sacrificing all legitimate hopes of a marriage proportionate to my birth."

"Beautiful Princess," replied the turbot, "Destiny has played a greater part in your misfortunes than I have; however, I grant your requests; you will be content, and I hope that I will procure you more advantages than I have caused you woes." After having spoken those words, he plunged into the sea.

It was a day and a night after the Princess had quit the shore of Caprare, and there had already been two hours of daylight when she spoke to the turbot, but about an hour later, she was agreeably surprised to see the vessel make landfall in a place so convenient that she disembarked very easily. Mirou leapt on to the shore joyfully; the lack of his reason not having taken away the love of life. The place was dry and arid; there did not appear to be any habitation, nor even a tree or a bush. That frightened the Princess, and, mistrusting the promises of the turbot even though a part of them had already been fulfilled, she said: "Alas, which is better, dying on land or at sea? I do not see myself any more sheltered here from the insults of fortune than I was on that retched boat."

Princillon was weeping; his needs augmented his mother's woes; she embraced and kissed him, saying the most tender things in the world to him. As for Mirou, he ran hither and yon, sometimes laughing or weeping, in accordance with his whim.

The Sun, which was almost in the middle of its course, was darting its rays over the arid sands, and greatly inconveniencing the Princess, who could not see anything that could shelter her from it. She advanced with difficulty toward rocks that she hoped might serve her, but she had not taken twenty paces when she saw a lady of surprising beauty and magnificence emerge therefrom. Her costume was sea green embroidered with silver fish scales; a quantity of diamonds and pearls made her shine like a sun; her black hair, which fell in thick curls over her beautiful cleavage, made an admirable effect, and heightened the brightness and vivacity of hr complexion. A little page a cubit tall, clad in green and gold gauze, was carrying the end of her long robe; her coiffure consisted of a small turtle shell garnished with gold.

Risette, whose rags rendered her confused, tried to hide, but the lady stopped her, saying in an agreeable tone: "Stay. Princess, stay; I have only come here to put an end to your troubles and render you the most fortunate person on earth; and to begin to give you evidence of it, I want to render you that of your quality." As she said that, she touched her with a crystal wand garnished with gold, and Risette's wretched garments were immediately transformed into magnificent attire. Her garments were the color of roses and silver, and her adornment of precious stones, emeralds and amethysts. Little Princillon was no less adorned than his mother, and Amour has never been painted more elegantly clad.

The gratitude of the Princess threw her at the feet of her benefactress, but the latter lifted her up again and embraced her. "It isn't time to thank me," she said. "I haven't done anything for you yet."

Mirou saw those metamorphoses from afar, and he was as surprised by them as he was capable of being. The fay—for she was one of the most powerful of them—called him by his name and commanded him to approach, which he did, trembling, and when he was close enough she touched him with her wand and ordered him to go and dive into the sea.

He ran there, but what a marvel! He had no sooner touched the first waves than he disappeared, and in his place there was the most handsome, the best made and the most magnificent man in the world. No Baron ever appeared in the theater to play the role of an Emperor and lover with more grace and bearing, with a finer wig and better-placed beauty spots.

"Beautiful Princess," the fay said to Risette, "there is the man that Destiny orders you to take for your husband, and who ought to be this very day." Then, turning toward that charming object, she said to him: "Come, Prince Fortunate, come and receive from my hand this amiable Princess for your wife, and repair by your tenderness the woes that you have innocently caused her."

Fortunate ran to the Princess, and, throwing himself at her feet, he said the most tender and gallant things in the world to her. She was charmed by that, and sensed the birth, along with pleasure, of a passion that she had not yet known. As for Fortunate, he was already the most amorous of all men. He said to the fay Turbodine—for that was her name—everything that gratitude can produce in a generous heart.

Immediately thereafter, two of the most handsome and best-dressed pages appeared. They were clad in green satin garnished with gold mesh folded into furbelows. A dozen young women, each more beautiful than the last, and elegantly adorned, came to arrange themselves around the Princess. One of them presented her with a beautiful fan, another opened a pocket mirror garnished with gems for her, while a third prevented her with a jar of beauty spots made of a single huge pearl. Three or four presented her with baskets full of fruits and preserves, garnished with flowers, and the others held crystal vases decorated with gold, on similar saucers, with carafes full of refreshing liquors.

After a light meal, of which Princillon and the Princess had great need, the fay said to them: Let's go; let's quit this uncomfortable place in order to render you to the palace destined for you. The Prince offered his hand to the fay, but she did not want to accept it, and told him to take that of the Princess, which he did, with pleasure.

In a moment they found themselves within view of five marvelous avenues composed of orange trees, rose bushes, pomegranates and jasmines of an extraordinary grandeur. Those flowers perfumed the air, and the ground was covered with them. They reached the far end in very little time, although they were very long; when one travels with fays, one covers a great deal of ground without tiring. The avenues were terminated by a large square paved with red and green marble, which served as the courtyard of a palace of unparalleled structure.

There was a huge main building of mother-of-pearl, the ornaments of which were coral or lapis. The entire edifice was sustained by a large number of spiral columns of rock crystal twelve feet high. Two beautiful rivulets that bordered the two sides of the avenues came to lose themselves under the building, their silvery waves flowing over golden sand, where an infinite number of extraordinary fish were visible, the scales of which were gems of different colors. The door of the palace was made of ebony enriched with golden inlay, of a marvelous design and workmanship. The perron climbing up to it was composed of fifteen crystal steps, through which beautiful waters could be seen, with the golden sand and the rich fish, all of which made a effect unknown to the eyes.

Turbodine went up first, and when she had touched the doors with her wand, they opened. Two doormen appeared clad in uniforms of green velvet and golden cloth; they were holding halberds, the shafts of which were of calemboux wood and the blades of gold.

They went into a large vestibule, the vault of which was brilliant with gold and crystal, and the floor composed of the same material, as transparent as the perron. They saw two great staircases, the ramps of which were made of crystal and the steps of porcelain. On each side, two large crystal doors, although they were closed, allowed the sight of infinite apartments.

Princess Risette and Prince Fortunate were overcome with admiration, but Turbodine told them that it was nothing compared with what they would see subsequently. They traversed the vestibule and descended into gardens by means of a perron like the one opposite. Four huge flower-beds were presented first, the box-hedge that composed the embroidery was gold enameled with green. They were surrounded by vases of the finest crystal and porcelain, filed with unknown flowers. In the middle of the flower-beds was a large round pool, the edges of which were porcelain and in the center of which was a crystal Venus sitting on a Triton of the same material; a jet of water was emerging from its mouth that seemed to lose itself in the air as soon as it had risen, and fell back over the goddess, who seemed to be vainly occupied in drying her hair.

Two other pools similar to the first, whose figures were different, occupied the extremities of the flower-beds, beyond which were several pathways composed of palisades covered with fruits of all seasons, including strawberries and redcurrants, which could be picked without bending down. The Princess's maidservants, who were taking turns to carry Princillon, gave him as many of them as he wanted.

All those beauties did not prevent the Prince from being touched by that of the Princess, and expressing to her everything that a lover on the point of being happy can think. A few ladies had joined the fay; she was amusing herself with them in order to give them time to converse.

They arrived at a large intersection, where eight paths converged, terminated by porticos and pyramids of crystal. Eight bowling greens were placed in the spaces that separated the pathways; they were covered with jasmines, oleanders, honeysuckle, pomegranates and myrtles. In the middle of each bowling green was a pool even larger than those of the flower-beds; the edges were crystal, enriched at intervals by marine monsters in enamel of all colors; the entire surface of the water was agitated by large bubbles, placed symmetrically, from the middle of each of which emerged a jet two feet high, which fell back in foam as white as snow, and the center of the pool was occupied by a spray of surprising width and elevation.

Turbodine went into one of the bowling greens, where a mixed collation was set out in crystal bowls garnished with gold; the plates were similar and the tablecloth of silver gauze with large tassels garnished with pearls. After they had eaten they passed along pathways ordered by fountains of crystal, enamel and porcelain, with jets of exquisitely scented water in a thousand shapes. The gardens were only bordered by rivulets similar to those of the avenues. Their edges were ornamented with florid lawns and trees laden with fruits and filled with birds, as rare in the beauty of their plumage as their marvelous songs.

They went back into the palace as night began to fall, and found the vestibule illuminated by a huge crystal chandelier that bore two hundred candles; then they went into a great hall, the floor of which was transparent, and the wall-panels of crystal, which served as the frames of mirrors of extreme size. The furniture was upholstered in gold and silver cloth, and the wood of the chairs, the tables, the side-tables and the cabinets was inlaid with amber and ivory; one saw all those riches by the light of an infinite number of candles in golden girandoles and chandeliers.

A large number of beautiful and magnificent ladies led by handsome cavaliers came to render their respects to the fay, who said to them, indicating the Prince and the Princess, that they were the ones who were to be their sovereigns. They passed into another hall, even more richly furnished, with different ornaments. All sorts of games were prepared there: ombre, beste, lansquenet, basset and berlan. The cards were painted with miniatures; double louis served as chips, and rubies, emeralds and topazes as markers. The candlesticks and chandeliers in that hall were precious stones. Some people were gambling, playing for high stakes.

Turbodine took the lovers, with the rest of the company, into a third hall, where there were all kinds of instruments, and the best musicians of the Opéra, who composed a most perfect concert, the words of which were in praise of the fay and for the happiness of the two lovers.

After the concert, they went into the hall where they were to have supper; the places were set at a table garnished and surrounded by festoons of flowers; four huge sideboards occupied the four sides, one garnished with vessels and vases of gold, another of the same material enriches with precious stones, another with crystal garnished with gold, and the last of amber and coral. The table had eighty place-settings; all the ladies and the cavaliers were placed there; the Prince and the Princess occupied the most eminent place, and the fay did the honors. What was marvelous was that as soon as they wanted to eat a foodstuff, the dish presented itself of its own accord, and although those impulses were frequently different, there was no confusion.

There was talk during the meal about affairs of State, music, poetry, good and bad authors; agreeable questions were agitated, and there were witty replies; enigmas were proposed, which were well or poorly explained, and, in sum, the good cheer was seasoned by everything that might render it agreeable to intelligent people whose greatest pleasure is not eating and drinking.

As for the Prince, he was only occupied with the beautiful Princess; he looked at her tenderly, he sighed appropriately, and whispered sweet things in gallant and well-chosen terms. In sum, he forgot nothing of all that might express his passion, and he had the pleasure of knowing that he was not wasting his time. He was not exempt from anxieties, however; the fay had promised that he would marry the Princess that sane day, but the length of the meal put his patience to a rude proof.

The meal finished, and the Prince thought that he would soon see the end of so much magnificence, which ought to be the commencement of his happiness, when, after passing into an enchanted drawing room, they found a ball prepared there, and twenty-four violins that were playing the *Descent of Apollo*.[24] It was, however, necessary to go through it, and on Turbodine's order, Fortunate and Risette commenced the ball.

While everyone was busy dancing, the fay took the Prince and Princess and went out with them through a secret door, which led them into a great vestibule; they traversed it, and went into the apartment that had been prepared for them, which they found even more superb than anything they had seen. Above all, the bedroom and the Princess's bed were beyond all expression; the pearls, the gold and the precious stones being the least estimable things there.

---

[24] A piece by the prolific baroque composer Jean-Baptiste Lully. This reference and such subsequent ones as mention of the Duchesse de Bourgogne (i.e., Marie-Adélaïde de Savoy) establish that this story, like the previous two, is set in 1697 rather than a mythical past, in spite of such apparent anachronisms as the officiation at the marriage of a "Druid." The fay's palace is an obvious transfiguration of Versailles, and the wedding celebrations held there

All three of them went into a large cabinet lined and furnished with pearls distributed in compartments, with enamels of every color. It was filled with vases and caskets of precious stones filled with flowers; an old Druid was waiting for them there; he had a robe of amaranth velvet with a fringe of pearls, a belt and clasps of diamonds; and a white beard covered his stomach. He had a crown of violets, and he was holding two of roses, which he put on the heads of the two spouses, to whom he presented two rings of great value, which they took and which they gave to one another reciprocally thereafter.

After that short ceremony, the Druid retired through a little door that Turbodine opened for him. They went back into the bedroom, where there was a dressing-table that could only be compared to that of Madame la Duchesse de Bourgogne; add to that some two or three millions in precious stones. The Princess's maids of honor put her to bed, and the Prince was put there by his officers. The fay embraced them, wishing them eternal happiness; then she retired to her apartment and everyone did the same, for there were as many in that palace as were necessary.

The next day, the newlyweds were allowed to stay in bed very late. Turbodine was the first to go into the bedroom, and she made them all the caresses that a mother can make her children on such an occasion. The new bride was dressed in clothes even more magnificent than those of the day before; she was coiffed with flowers and movable pins of an infinite richness and beauty, and the Prince similarly found all possible magnificence in his attire.

The morning meal was served with the same magnificence as the supper had been the previous day. The same company was there, with the costumes of all sorts of nations. After the meal they played cards, and then the *Amours of Psyche*[25] was performed by the troupe of the Théâtre de Guénégaud. Afterwards there was a stroll, during which a dif-

---

[25] Presumably an adaptation of Jean de La Fontaine's poem "Les Amours de Psyché et Cupidon" (1669).

ferent collation was served in each of the bowling greens. When the day came to an end, the gardens were suddenly illuminated; the porticos and crystal pyramids all appeared transparent with light; as was the façade of the palace; the avenues were filed with girandoles and chandeliers, and when everyone returned to the palace, the illuminated avenues allowed the sight of the most beautiful object imaginable.

Afterwards, there was a firework display beyond the flower-beds, over an amphitheater of crystal garnished with water jets, between which the fireworks emerged in a thousand different fashions. The twelve signs of the Zodiac were represented there by the fall of rockets, and the names of the Prince and the Princess; the Moon and the stars appeared there with a supernatural artistry.

Several days passed in various diversions. The courses in which knights aimed their lances at rings and heads were magnificent. Sometimes the ladies were dressed as nymphs and the men as fauns and sylvans; at other times they were dressed as shepherds and shepherdesses, and in several other agreeable fashions. The merchants and the tailors gained nothing from those disguises, and all of that was done with a single stroke of a magic wand, as well as the manner in which so many amiable persons were fund in that place. Some husbands believed that their wives were at the fair, at the Tuileries or the Opéra, who were actually in Turbodine's house, or that of some other fay of similar consequence.

There never was a better household than that of Prince Fortunate and Princess Risette, for they loved one another perfectly. The Princess became pregnant, and the fay felt a great pleasure in consequence.

One day, when she was strolling alone with Risette in a labyrinth of orange trees, the Princess confessed the desire she had to know the story of the marvelous fish that had been the cause of her troubles and her pleasures, and in the interests of which she seemed to be so powerfully involved.

"You're right, my daughter," said Turbodine, sighing, "when you believe that I am acting in the interests of that dear fish, since they are my own, being those of another self, and in order for you to learn his fortune, it is necessary that I also tell you mine, since they cannot be separated."

She sat down with the Princess on a seat of moss covered in flowers, and then she spoke as follows.

The Story of the Queen of the Isle of Rocks and the King of Coquerico

I possess, by virtue of a long line of succession, the realm of the Isles of Rocks, which are where coral, crystal, gems, amber and pearls are found. There are also very considerable gold and silver mines in that land. All those who think of themselves as the people work in sculpting stones and putting them in mounts, being excellent lapidaries, and the traffic they carry out in those precious items of merchandise renders the country immensely rich.

After the death of my parents, I became the sole heir of that flourishing realm; the art of Enchantment, which I received from my mother, further augmented my power. Several Princes wanted my alliance. The King of Coquerico was one of those who sought to please me; his Estate was very small, the only commerce of his people being flowers, but his person was utterly charming, and he was also my neighbor. He sent me ambassadors with his portrait; I was touched by it, and if he had amour for me, I was not long without having any for him. I accepted his suit, and he came to my court with an equipage that was not as rich as it was elegant. In sum, I married him with all possible pleasure and satisfaction.

Our days were spun like silk; our hearts had the same desires, and no union was ever more perfect. Not far from the realm of Coquerico there was a small province whose inhabitants called it Barbaux. It was governed by a young Princess named Bluette. She was beautiful—blonde, with a fine figure, brilliant eyes and a cheerful manner—but she had a light mind and a great deal of coquetry. She had wanted passionately to marry the King of Coquerico. The proximity of their Estates, and the good intelligence that had always existed between their subjects, seemed to authorize the pretentions of the Princess, combined with a personal esteem that she was not lacking. She was greatly chagrined by our marriage, but she dissimulated it, and even came to pay her court to me.

Some time after she had arrived I was solicited by a great Prince whose Estates were a long way from mine to go to help him after an unfortunate accident that had befallen him, which was of a nature that it could only be helped by my presence. The amity that he had always had with my mother, the Queen, obliged me not to refuse. I departed promptly in a light chariot composed of an ostrich egg and marine rushes, pulled by four halcyons. I separated from the King, my husband, with a great deal of dolor; his own was so violent that he thought he might expire of it.

I applied all possible diligence to bringing the great things that it was necessary for me to execute to an end. As soon as I had brought them to a conclusion, I returned swiftly to the Isle of Rocks. My amour gave me wings, and I was fully occupied in the pleasure of seeing again the object of my tender and legitimate passion.

I was already nearing the gardens of my palace, and I was looking for a suitable place to land my little chargers when I saw my spouse on the sea shore, engaged in gallantry with Bluette. That sight surprised me and touched me so sharply that I was immobilized, but anger seen returned the power of movement that I had lost. I leapt from my chariot and ran toward them, crying: "Ah, infidel Prince, is it thus that you respond to my tenderness? Go, traitor, go extinguish your criminal flames in the waves, which have all too much resemblance to your inconstancy; be a turbot for twenty years."

As I said that, I touched him with a yew wand. The unfortunate Prince was changed in an instant, and dived into the sea. I neglected to avenge myself on the flighty Bluette; I merely augmented her amour in order to render her loss more sensible. She did, indeed, sense it in a manner so violent that she would have hurled herself into the sea in order to follow her lover, if a surge of jealousy had not obliged me to prevent her from doing so by transforming her into a little plant that does not quit the edge of the sea and is known as rock samphire.

I returned to my palace, more afflicted than one might think. I still loved the perfidious Prince, and the vengeance I had taken fell back upon me with the utmost rigor. The dangers to which his transformation exposed him reawakened all my tenderness, and if I had been able to change what I had done I would not have hesitated for a moment to extract him from that state, but it was impossible for me; his transformation was conditional, the twenty years that I had fixed could not be revoked, Destiny, stronger than my art, rendered me impotent. All that I could do was to render him the usage of speech, and I sent a halcyon to assure him on my behalf that I would help him in all the dangers to which he might find himself exposed.

He sent me word by that little messenger that he still loved me, that he was not as criminal as I thought, and that he had been surprised by the artifices of Bluette.

The fay wept at that point in her story, and Risette mingled her own tears with hers. She asked whether the King, her husband, still had a long time to remain in that form, and the fay told her, weeping more forcefully, that he still had fifteen years.

"Madame," said the Princess, I beg your pardon for stopping you for so long on circumstances so distressing, but I have one more question to ask you, to which I beg you to reply."

The fay told her, while embracing her, that she only had to ask whatever she wished, and that she would always satisfy it with pleasure.

"I will ask you, then, Madame," said Risette, "how it came about that, being as good and tender as you appear to me to be, you rendered me so unhappy in order to grant the ridiculous wish of a madman?"

"Alas," replied Turbodine, "that was in spite of myself. Although anger had carried me away to the extent of putting the condition of twenty years on the transformation of my husband, I still had sufficiently scant precaution to engage myself to granting without exception anything that he might demand of me, provided that it was to save his life. But, my dear daughter, when you are instructed of the verity of that adventure, you will agree that you are more in my debt than you believe."

"Oh, Madame," said the Princess. "It is not necessary to add anything to your generosity in order to oblige me to be in your debt all my life."

"Let's not talk about that any longer, said the fay, getting to her feet and taking her by the hand. "When the time comes to tell you those things, you will change your sentiment."

A few days after that conversation, Turbodine departed to go to her Estates, where her presence was necessary. She told the Prince and the Princess what they ought to do in her absence, and that if anything happened to them that they wanted to bring to her attention, they only had to ring a golden bell that was in a small crystal tower at the top of the palace and she would send them one of her halcyons, to whom they could say everything.

She gave Fortunate a little wooden casket of campeachy wood garnished with gold, full of louis d'or. That casket would always be full, provided that he made sure always to leave one of the gold coins within it.

The fay then told the Princess that when she felt ill prior to giving birth she should ring the bell twice, and that she would immediately come to her. They embraced tenderly, and the fay left. Risette felt a great chagrin in consequence, but the caresses of her husband, the Prince, and all the pleasures that they savored in that charming place consoled her.

She did not fail to summon Turbodine to her labor, to which she came immediately. Risette gave birth to a beautiful princess, to whom the fay gave the most advantageous gifts.

When the Princess was out of bed again, she took her to her cabinet one day, and after shutting herself in with her, she talked to her in these terms:

"My dear daughter, it is time that I informed you of the denouement of all your adventures, and that I tell you things that I'm sure you do not expect. You have believed until now that your husband, Prince Fortunate, is none other than Mirou the Fool, transformed by the force of my art. Nothing, however, is further from the truth.

"When I touched Mirou with my wand and ordered him to dive into the sea, you saw him disappear as soon as he touched the waves, but instead of being transformed, he was transported to a very distant land, where he still is, and I caused to appear in his place Prince Fortunate, brother of the King of Coquerico, my husband."

"Oh, Madame," said Risette, interrupting, "is it possible that what I hear is true, and will I be fortunate enough to be liberated from the almost continual fears that give me the dread I have that my charming spouse might one day become the frightful Mirou again? The cruel necessity of my misfortunes had reduced me to wishing for his transformation, but alas, how many times have I repented of it, and how many times had that dread poisoned my pleasures?"

"You can savor them confidently, amiable Princess," replied Turbodine. "You had more real things to dread, but I have taken care to hide them from you; presently, the danger is past and you are going to learn the surprising things that remain for me to tell you.

"When I married the King of Coquerico, he had a brother a few years younger than him. As I was rich enough to do without his brother's Estates, I wanted to ensure his possession of them and enable him to marry Princess Bluette. If he had accepted that arrangement I would have avoided my misfortunes, but Destiny had doubtless ordered otherwise, and he was to be the husband of the beautiful Princess of Caprare. He did not accept my offers, and for his reasons he told me that he was too young to take an engagement, and that he had a desire to travel. He begged me to conserve my good will.

"It is true that he was only fifteen years old when I was married, and as soon as the diversions that followed my wedding were concluded, he departed. I wanted to give him an equipage proportionate to his quality, but he opposed it, and only took two of his servants with him. The King, his brother, insisted absolutely that he take his tutor with him, but he gave him the slip on the second day of his voyage, and eight or ten days later the two servants returned, without knowing what had become of him—which gave us a great deal of chagrin.

"After the double transformation of my husband, the dolor into which I was plunged rendered me insensible to all pleasures. I fled them with care; I even neglected to make use of my art, and it seemed to me that I would have been happier if I had never possessed it, since I accused it of my misfortunes. I was almost alone in my palace, and I spent entire days in my cabinet or in my gardens, and even there in the remotest and least agreeable places.

"One day, I plunged into the turnings of a labyrinth of cypresses, which seemed to touch the clouds. Their excessive height rendered the place obscure, and, in consequence, very appropriate to entertain the sadness of my thoughts. After having walked for some time, I sat down on a marble seat. The repose I was seeking only served to give more agitation to my mind; I lamented the infidelity of my spouse, and then I deplored his unhappiness and mine, all that with as much violence as if the things had only just happened, or as if I wanted to inform someone of them.

"I perceived my aberration, and I was weeping at the shame of it when I heard a noise nearby. I thought it was some bird, although there were hardly any in that place, but, having looked, I found that it was a butterfly of an extraordinary size and a surprising beauty. As soon as I had perceived it, it settled on the ground beside me; one might have thought that it was looking at me; it flapped its wings, raised itself up on its legs, and approached my feet as if it wanted to kiss them.

"Eventually, not understanding any of those things, I tried to stand up, but the butterfly seemed to want to retain me. It attached its feet to the hem of my robe, making a little cry that did not seem to me to be natural. I sat down again, and, beginning to suspect something, I spoke these words, which I accompanied with a secret virtue: 'If you wish to recover with my aid another form than this, I command you to resume it, provided that your transformation is not conditional.'

"I had no sooner spoken those words than the poor butterfly fell on its side, almost motionless. I knew that the dolor of not being able to obey me put it in that state, which as why I said to it: 'Don't be afflicted, poor creature, since I can do something else for your relief. I can at least give you the means of using speech, which will give you the means of explaining your misfortunes to me.'

"The afflicted butterfly recovered courage. It rose up slowly and alighted on the edge of the seat where I was sitting. Then it said to me: 'Madame, you will doubtless be surprised to learn that the unfortunate person on whom you have taken pity is the brother of the infidel Prince whom you are lamenting, with justice.'

"'What!' I cried. 'Is it possible that you are Prince Fortunate?'

"'Yes, Madame,' the butterfly said, 'I am he, or, rather, the most unfortunate of men.'

"'Tell me the story of your adventures,' I said to him, 'and I promise you that I will give you all the help that I can.'

"He thanked me, and then he spoke to me thus:

The Story of Merline and Prince Fortunate

Madame, some time before my brother, the King, married you, I had fallen madly in love with the young and charming Merline, the daughter of the fay Mandarine and, so it is claimed, of King Merlin. He had married her mother but for some discontentment that he claimed to have received, he had repudiated her.

It was, therefore, Madame, with that beautiful young woman that I had fallen in love. I had seen her waking on the sea shore. It was difficult to see her at her home, her mother seeing few people. She had promised her to the King of the Metheores, who was to marry her in a year, but as the fay was convinced that Merline did not love that Prince, she kept her on a tight rein, for fear that she might form some other inclination. I had learned all these details from a lady who was one of Mandarine's friends and mine; I had made her the confidence of my passion, and she had combated it by the scant appearance she saw of the success of my designs.

That lady gave a great ball at her home; Mandarine and her daughter were invited. I was at the fête, but although there were many people there, I could never talk to Merline in private, her mother always being with her. When anyone took me to dance, I did not fail to go to take her afterwards. We danced a rather long figured dance in which there as a moment when one held hands; I squeezed hers gently and said to her: "Divine Merline, I love you, and will love you eternally. How happy I would be if you wanted to have some in return for me."

My gaze said as much as my words. She blushed, but she did not have the time to reply to me. The next time that she danced, she had me take her; we danced the same dance again, and when I had taken her hands, she squeezed mine in her turn, and said to me, turning her eyes away for fear of encountering mine: "Prince. if what you have said is true, be faithful and know that you are not indifferent to me."

No joy was ever similar to mine on seeing my good fortune pass far beyond my hopes.

I did not say anything about those things to my confidante, but a few days later, I asked her to take me to Mandarine's abode under the pretext of showing me the beauties and riches of her palace, which was in a large wood a league from the capital city of the kingdom of Coquerico. As I feared not being able to converse with my beautiful mistress, I wrote a note that contained these words:

I cannot live without seeing you and without telling you of my passion, charming Merline, and in order to succeed in that, I am ready to attempt the impossible.

Things happened as I had foreseen, and it was impossible for me to speak to Merline other than with my eyes, and all that I could do was to give her my note surreptitiously.

The next day, as I was walking and dreaming in the gardens of the palace, I saw a piece of paper fall at my feet. I opened it promptly, and I read these words thereon:

If you are ready to attempt the impossible to see me, I am even more ready to do it, since I have the power. Only find yourself in this place at midnight; I will take care of the rest.

You can imagine, Madame, the transports of joy to which I abandoned myself on seeing myself, it seemed to me, at the highest point of felicity to which a lover can aspire. I went to the rendezvous in good time for the appointed hour. I saw an ebony chariot arrive pulled by two large cranes, one of which said to me: "Enter."

I did not have to be asked twice. I climbed into the chariot; the cranes immediately took flight, and soon rendered me to a large marble terrace that extended along the entire length of the apartments of Mandarine's palace. I went into Merline's apartment, which was indicated to me by one of the cranes.

I found her in her bedroom, sitting in a ruby armchair; her dress was blue taffeta garnished with the finest English lace; a diamond girdle marked her waist; her beautiful cleavage, which was only covered by negligently folded lace, was surrounded by a chain of diamonds similar to her belt; her beautiful ash-blonde hair was crowned with pearls and attached artlessly with three ruby and diamond pins.

That charming person appeared such to all the eyes in the world, but she was incomparably more so in mine. I threw myself at her feet and I said to her all that an amorous young man can say when he believes himself to be loved.

We saw one another several times in that manner, and the beautiful Merline made me understand that I was loved as much as the King of the Metheores was hated, and that there was nothing that she would not do to avoid marrying him; that she was determined to go and find King Merlin, her father, in order to inform him of the violence that her mother was doing to her.

I was frightened by that resolution, and the dread that I had of losing her caused me to propose to her that if she wanted to abandon herself to my guidance, I would put her in your hands; that the King, my brother, was about to marry you, and that your power was at least as great as Mandarine's. In sum, Madame, I was bold enough to make much of your protection, although I had not had any assurance of it, nor even the temerity to ask you for it.

The beautiful Merline had difficulty making that resolution, but finally, she promised me. Things were at that point, Madame, when you were married. That engagement caused me to refuse the advantageous propositions that you were kind enough to make to me. I pretended that I wanted to travel in order to have the liberty to carry out my plan. I therefore left, Madame, as you know, and I soon rid myself of the few people who had accompanied me.

Merline was uncertain for a long time; sometimes she wanted to go to the Isle of Rocks, at other times she wanted to seek refuge with King Merline. I was in despair with all her irresolution. One evening, however, I was so well able to persuade her that she resolved to allow herself to be taken to the Isle of Rocks. I took her by the hand in order to take her out of her apartment, and we were almost outside when we encountered Mandarine; she had been alerted by the perfidious cranes, who were Merline's chambermaids.

Gods! What became of us at that sight! Merline uttered a scream, saying: "Oh, Prince, we're doomed!" She fled I know not where, and I remained alone, exposed to Mandarine's anger.

She said to me: "It's a fine thing to do, you little fool, to come and abduct my daughter. You're very fortunate that I want to shield you from the vengeance of the King of the Metheores and to put you in a state only to be burned by a candle." As she said that she touched me with her wand, and immediately, I became a butterfly. She made me pass into a cabinet where there was a lapis desk, in which she opened a drawer lined with perfumed satin the color of fire; there she imprisoned me. No dolor was ever more cruel than the one I felt, and I would have preferred death to such an unfortunate state, which was further augmented by the anxiety I had for my mistress; the uncertainty of her fate made me suffer as much as the certainty of mine.

From time to time, the fay came to open my rich prison in order to throw a fortifying essence over me, which conserved my life, I spent a year thus without Mandarine saying a single word to me and without seeing daylight. At the end of that time I heard a great movement in the palace or two or three days in succession, and while I was in difficulty wondering what that might be, Mandarine came to open my prison.

She threw the essence over me, as usual, and then she put flowers and fruits in my drawer, saying to me: "It's only just that you perceive the celebration. Merline has married the King of Metheores today, and if you want to see her for the last time, you have only to look through the windows; you will see her pass by in a quarter of an hour with a superb equipage, and you will see that she is a greater lady than if she were Queen of Coquerico."

She seasoned that speech with a mocking tone that put me in despair, knowing full well that I could not reply to it, for I would certainly have said many insulting things, but I could not do anything to testify my chagrin to her than to draw away from her presence.

She went out and left me the liberty of the cabinet. I therefore went to attach myself to the window, with enough difficulty, in order to see that sad spectacle. By then I had less amour than anger, the long penance that I had done having deadened my flame.

It was not long before I saw the King of Metheores pass by. He was in a chariot of thick cloud, which seemed to be ablaze. His coat was the color of smoke, decorated with rainbow braid; his stature seemed gigantic, his face was half an aune long and four fingers broad, with small eyes, a large pointed nose, and a mouth extending all the way to the ears. The color of his complexion was very similar to that of his coat; his red hair and beard were very unkempt.

The sad Queen was beside him, and in spite of her beautiful garments and the jewels with which she was covered, I was unable to find her as beautiful as before. She was pale, and I think the thunder and lightning that were following and preceding the chariot were scaring her. Two very ugly comets clad in old tinsel, with long tangled tails, appeared to be her maids of honor, and occupied the front of the chariot, which was drawn by six horses the color of fire, as transparent as red glass struck by the Sun's rays. The coachman and the postillion were also transparent figures.

That chariot was rolling over huge black and red clouds, like those that enclose storms, and the wheels were scintillating like iron extracted from the forge. The satellites of Jupiter served as footmen, as well as several newly minted shooting stars. Armed men on foot and on horseback were escorting them; they were in several colors and as diaphanous as the rest of the equipage. Their faces were sometimes seen to elongate excessively; then, suddenly, they became no longer than a finger, and six times as broad; the heads of the horses did the same. An arm or a leg of one of the cavaliers often fell, and those figures did not remain in the same state for a minute; an infinity of those little leaping fires that one sees by night around waters and are knows as will-o'-the-wisps were sown all along the route, some of them serving as tips for the cavalier's lances, and the ensigns of the footmen, which were made of half-burned paper, were all sown with them.

I had time to notice all those things, because the chariot stopped for rather a long time, Merline having forgotten her mask and her gloves. Cured as I was of my passion, I could not help lamenting the fate of such a beautiful person, by whom I had been loved tenderly, and, to all appearances, still was. Alas, I was not in any state to take advantage of it. Mandarine came to imprison me again, with mockeries that continued to cause me chagrin.

A few days passed without me hearing mention of anything, and during which the fay left me the liberty of moving about the cabinet, where she brought me flowers overflowing with dew, which gave me great pleasure. I hoped that Mandarine, no longer having anything to fear for her daughter, might return me to my original condition, and that the good treatment she was giving me was intended to appease me, but alas, it had a different cause.

She came one morning to bring me flowers and fruits. She was in her finest adornment, brilliant with jewels. She sat down, and, assuming a tender expression, she said to me: "I'm convinced that you're weary of your estate and that you wish me ill for being the cause of it, but Prince, I have been forced to act thus. If I had not promised my daughter to the King of Metheores, it would have been a pleasure for me to give her to you, but if I had broken my word he would have doomed us all, and the slightest effects of his vengeance would have been plague and famine.

"To give you proof that I have no hatred for you, it only depends on you to quit this form, in order to resume our own, with the condition that you promise to marry me and that the ceremony will take place before leaving this place. I believe that I am an advantageous match for a younger brother: I'm rich, and although I have a daughter of sixteen, I can still pass for young; my beauty is not so mediocre that I'm not worth as much as another.

"Think about it, Prince, and think about it seriously; your transformation depends absolutely on the gift of your heart and your hand; but if you refuse my proposition, I'll attach conditions to your transformation so impossible that you'll have to settle for remaining a butterfly all your life. Don't put any reliance on the power of Turbodine; things have changed greatly in your regard; the King of Coquerico, her husband, has been unfaithful, and she has changed him into a turbot for twenty years.

"Let me know your sentiments," Mandarine continued, touching me with her wand. "Speak, now that you can."

I found myself in the most afflicting situation that one can imagine. The terrible state to which I saw myself reduced, and the apprehension of remaining in it, almost made me accept the bargain that was offered to me. *What does it matter if I marry her*, I said to myself. *When I'm at liberty, I'll leave her; I'll go to take refuge with the Queen of the Isle of Rocks; what I've been told about the King, my brother, was doubtless only to take away the hope of powerful protection.*

Suddenly, however, a surge of hatred that I felt for that woman, and even more so the shame with which I would have been covered all my life by a cowardice so unworthy of a Prince, made me resolve not to hide my sentiments no matter what might happen to me.

"Madame," I said to her, "I don't doubt that your wealth, your beauty and, if you wish, also your youth, are capable of limiting and satisfying the ambition of anyone but the unfortunate Prince that you have overwhelmed with your injustices, I cannot love you, Madame. Someone else in my place might not say so with as much sincerity, and might seek to deceive you, but I would rather be the most miserable of all men than reproach myself for such cowardice. It is not the passion that I had conceived for the charming Merline that prevents me from being sensible to yours; I no longer feel for her anything but the chagrin of having been deceived by her; but Madame, once again, it is that I cannot love you. You can now do whatever you please, and I am ready for anything, including the loss of my life, which is quite indifferent to me."

The firmness of my response put the fay in a terrible anger, which became a kind of fury, and, touching me rudely with her wand, in such a fashion that my frail form suffered a great deal in consequence, she said: "Well, traitor, unworthy of the generosity I have for you, lose once again the speech that you have employed to outrage me, be a butterfly since you do not want to be otherwise, but be one until you have married the same Princess twice, once in a dream and the second time in the most beautiful palace in the world, and from those two marriages two children have emerged, a Prince who will be suspected of being the son of a madman and a Princess who will render you your original form."

After those imprecations, she imprisoned me again, saying: "And to prevent some unknown power being able to give you an impossible aid, I shall render myself the mistress of your fate forever."

She left me in a state in which death would have been a great boon for me. I wished for it, as the sole remedy for my woes. I hoped that the violence of my dolor would soon give me that relief, but it was an error to think that it can make one die. I resolved not to make use of any aliment, but the cruel fay defeated my measures again, conserving my life by means of the virtue of the fatal liquid, with a view to making me feel her vengeance with more vigor.

I remained thus for another year, at the end of which, one night, I heard the voices of women crying "Fire!"

What ordinarily frightens everyone gave me joy, in the hope that the accident in question might give me the means to escape either from life or my prison. As I was in that uncertainty, I heard the door of the cabinet open and close again, and these words struck my ears:

"Our artifice has succeeded, and the fire we started in our apartment has given us the means to take the keys and he wherewithal to change form. We're going to be compensated for the avarice of our mistress, who gave us nothing at the wedding of her daughter."

Another voice replied: "I'm very sorry that we betrayed Prince Fortunate; he would have given us a much better recompense than that vile blacksmith, and we wouldn't have caused the woes that he's been suffering for two years, nor the death of poor Merline, who was unable to console herself for his loss. But in order to repair in some fashion the woes of which we're the cause, I'm going to set him free; he's here, and I'm the only one who knows that."

So saying, someone opened my drawer and said to me: "Come out, poor Prince. I'd like to be able to do something more for you."

The windows were opened, and I flew out. I paused for a moment to draw breath, and I saw that the people who had set me free were the same chambermaids that poor Merline had transformed into cranes to pull the chariot that brought me to see her. They opened the drawers of the lapis desk and took out a quantity of gold and precious stones, which they put into two bags that they suspended around their necks. They rubbed their hands and faces with a liquid that immediately changed them into cranes, after which they flew away with their booty.

I don't know whether the fire was extinguished or not, but I know that the fay came into the cabinet a moment after the cranes and I had emerged from it. I did not pause to see what she did or hear what she said; I only thought about getting away promptly; and all that I could do was to employ the rest of the night getting out of the wood. I still loved Merline more than I thought, and the news of her death, of which I had no doubt that I was the cause, reawakened all my tenderness. I shed as many tears for her as the dryness of my little body could furnish.

With those sad thoughts, I arrived here, Madame, and I saw you enter this labyrinth, into which I followed you. I heard from your mouth the verity of something that I had taken thus far for an artifice of Mandarine's. I hesitated for some time to put myself in a state to implore your aid, but the certainty of your good heart finally determined me. I was not mistaken, Madame, since I have already felt its sensible effects.

"Prince Fortunate finished his marvelous story thus," Turbodine said to Princess Risette, and continued in the following fashion: "I was surprised by the ridiculous conditions that Mandarine had attached to the transformation of the poor Prince. I consoled myself as best I could, and I gave him hopes that I did not have myself. I offered him my palace and my gardens, where he would find in abundance the refreshments appropriate to his estate, and I told him that when it was necessary for him to take shelter from the insults of the weather and the chill of the night, he would always find a retreat in my cabinet, to which I would be careful to leave him free entry. He accepted my offers, and thanked me with a great deal of gratitude.

"A year passed thus, during which I often conversed with him, and I found him infinitely intelligent, and firm enough to suffer his misfortune.

"One day, when I was walking alone in the labyrinth, I saw one of the halcyons coming toward me that I had set to mount guard on the edge of the sea, in order to bring me news of my husband. It told me about the accident that had befallen him off the shore of Caprare. I criticized him for having passed the limits that I had prescribed for him, which were not to quit our shores, but the halcyon told me that he had been forced to do so by a tempest. I was in despair at the misfortune that had caused him to fall into the hands of a madman, who had engaged him by his ridiculous demand to the execution of something impossible, there not being any example of the art of Enchantment, or even the blackest magic, ever being able to form a pregnancy. I foresaw all the consequences of such a cruel and uncommon adventure, and, by virtue of my oath, my life and that of my wretched husband were in danger; I could not violate it without all the superior Powers on which my art is dependent revolting against me.

"I could have used underhand ways to get out of that predicament, but they would have been prejudicial to you, Princess, and I would have died a thousand times, had that been possible, rather than do anything contrary to my honor and yours. Thos terrible uncertainties agitated me for the rest of the day; the night did not give me any more tranquility, and I spent almost all of it in my library, leafing through my books and the memoirs that my mother had left me, in which she had made observations about the most difficult and most extraordinary aspects of her art.

"I did not find anything sufficiently positive therein to get me out of the difficulty I was in completely, but I glimpsed things that gave me some hope, and after having brought some order to the confusion of my thoughts, I formed a design that appeared to me to be appropriate to extracting me from the intrigue. I became all the more certain because I found therein a means of ending the misfortunes of Prince Fortunate, and that adventure, which had seemed to me to be so strange a few hours before, then appeared to me as a effect of the conduct of destiny, which had taken that route in order to render possible the impossible conditions of Mandarine and enable me to keep my oaths.

"I threw myself on to my bed with the design of taking some repose there, but it was impossible. I therefore went into the cabinet where Prince Fortunate spent his nights. Daylight was beginning to appear, and I found him sleeping tranquilly on a piece of velvet. I called to him and he woke up. 'Where are you going this morning, Madame?" he asked me.

"'I've come,' I told him, 'to bring you good and bad news, and to share my anxieties with you. Since you've been here, I've found you very reasonable, and I believe you to be capable of keeping a secret. That's why I'm going to confide one to you, on which your happiness and mine depend, as well as that of your unfortunate brother.'

"He thanked me for the good opinion I had of him, and, after he had promised me to respond to it, I told him about the adventure of the King, my husband and what I had resolved to do for our common relief. He was charmed by the hopes that I was giving him, and in order to begin to work on them, I told him to go and wait for me in the labyrinth, where I would soon come to find him.

"I got dressed quickly and went to join the Prince, with whom I went to the most remote place in the labyrinth, and with a stroke of a wand I formed a porphyry cabinet with crystal windows, furnished with rich benches. After a few ceremonies necessary to my plan I touched him with my crystal baguette and he immediately resumed his original form. We both felt a sensible joy, and although that transformation would only last a few hours, there was still a great deal to gain.

"The Prince was then eighteen years old, and I admired him, so handsome and well made was he. I enabled him to have a meal more solid than any he had enjoyed for three years. He remained in that form for two hours, after which he resumed that of a butterfly.

"That fortunate commencement gave me good hope for the future. I began to prepare everything that very day. The following morning I experimented with the transformation of the Prince again; it succeeded and lasted for four hours, and the day after for six. I thought that was enough for the execution of my plan, and I did not waste any time. At the end of the day I departed in my flying chariot with the Prince in butterfly form, and although it is a long way from the Isle of Rocks to that of Caprare we arrived a few hours before midnight in the gardens of the palace of the King, your father. I formed a pavilion here that composed a fantastically furnished apartment, very poorly illuminated. I left the Prince there in butterfly form and surrounded the building with a cloud in order to hide it from curious eyes; then, climbing into my chariot, I went to touch the windows of your apartment silently, which opened, and I entered with the same silence.

"The first thing I did was go to the bed of your governess, whom I caused to inhale a soporific essence. I approached yours, and after having caused you to sniff the same essence, I took you in my arms and cared you to the pavilion, where I put you in an armchair, dressed and adorned in the same costume that I gave you two years later on the sea shore. Then I caused you to inhale something to wake you up, and I hid in order to have the pleasure of seeing your astonishment."

"Oh, Madame," interjected the Princess, "what are you saying to me, and what are you going to say? Is it possible that you have a part on things that I remember as a dream?"

"I have no doubt," the fay went on, "that this story is causing you an extreme surprise, but don't interrupt me, in order that you will be convinced that I am informed of all the circumstances of what I am telling you.

"You woke up, therefore, and after having yawned and rubbed your eyes several times, you looked around with surprise and anxiety. In the chamber where you were, the wall-hangings were blue and the seats flax-gray. There were only two candles, in glass candlesticks, were on a table with a red cloth, above which was a mirror composed of a large border and a small glass. You approached it in order to look at yourself, but it was futile; you only saw two cats that were playing together.

"The richness of your costume occupied you for some time; I thought I remarked that you were beginning to become anxious at finding yourself alone. You went into the next room, which was only hung with large illuminated prints representing monkeys, figures from Callot,[26] and marionettes. That chamber was a little better illuminated than the other; there were four candles in wooden martinets hanging from a grilled cupboard full of rats and mice, which were striking a thousand humorous poses. Two of your chambermaids were chatting together in that place. 'Where are we?' you asked them. 'What is this house, and how were we brought here?'

---

[26] The prints made in great abundance from etchings and engravings by Jacques Callot (c1592-1635) had multitudinous subjects, but he became and remained most famous for those depicting grotesque dwarfs, copied in a wide range of porcelains.

Instead of replying to you, however, they looked at you with astonishment, and then fled. Two dwarfs dressed as Polchinels emerge from another place, fencing with reeds and assuming grotesque postures.

"While you were occupied with these ridiculous encounters, I had gone into the cabinet where the butterfly was waiting for me, to whom I returned his natural form. He saw you without being seen, and was sensibly touched by your charms. I had instructed him in everything he had to do, and he executed it perfectly. I left him in the cabinet and appeared to you in the semblance of your mother, the Queen. You had already gone into a kind of hall sanded like a garden, with fruit trees to either side, illuminated by a large lamp with several sections, which was hanging in that place, and I accosted you.

"You ran toward me, saying: 'Oh, Madame, how glad I am to see you; tell me, if you please, how we come to be in such an extraordinary place.'

"'What do you find extraordinary about it?' I said to you. 'For myself, I only see what I'm accustomed to see here. Come on, let's go, the King, your father, is getting impatient.'

"'Oh, Madame,' you replied, 'what does he want with me?'

"'How can you not know what he wants?' I replied. 'Is he not waiting for you for the ceremony of your wedding to Prince Fortunate?'

"With those words, the Prince appeared; he took you by the hand and kissed it without saluting you.

"'Sire,' you said to him, blushing, 'does one act in that fashion the first time one sees a lady?'

'The first time?' said the Prince, laughing heartily. 'In truth, Madame, I find you admirable; I think you're making fun of me. Don't we see one another at every hour of the day?'

"You did not reply, and you seemed very embarrassed. Meanwhile, we went into another cabinet, which was furnished a little more appropriately than the others; the wall-hangings and a few squares were in yellow satin, and it was illuminated by a little glass chandelier bearing four candles.

The King, your father, whom you found there, said to you: 'You seem quite astonished.'

"'Sire, you replied. 'I believe that anyone would be, at the least.'

"'I do not see that you have any reason to be,' said the King. 'You have been preparing to marry the Prince for a long time.'

"'But Sire,' you replied to him, 'you'll permit me to tell you that I don't remember having seen this Prince anywhere but here, that that this is the first time that…'

"'Shut up,' said the King, interrupting you.' You're trying my patience. I believe that you're dreaming, and that, apparently, you haven't had enough sleep. Tomorrow morning, you'll be more reasonable.'

"As he finished speaking, your governess came in with a Druid; she approached you and said: 'Wait, Madame, while I adjust your hair slightly.'

'Good,' the King said to her, laughing. 'It's not worth the trouble. Leave it, leave it, Madame, it's fine.'

"Immediately, the Druid advanced and asked you whether you consented to take the Prince for your husband. You were as red as fire; you lowered your eyes, and then you raised them coyly to the face of the Prince, who had the most humorous expression in the world. You looked at me then, and then the King, but you only saw people who had a desire to laugh, which redoubled your embarrassment. Finally, the person to whom I had given the resemblance of King Lucidan, who was the husband of the fay that you mistook for your governess, said to you in an absolute tone: 'Princess, put an end these fashions, which are out of place, and respond promptly to what is asked of you.'

"That command determined you; you gave your consent, and the ceremony, finished, with the exception of the ring that is ordinarily given, and which would only be given to you at the second ceremony, held two years late in this palace, in the same cabinet where we are at present, and which, properly speaking, was only the continuation and completion of the first.

"We immediately left the cabinet, the Prince holding you by the hand and saying a thousand foolish things to you, at which you had a great deal of difficulty laughing. In traversing the first chamber you no longer found the lamps there, but four old spinners, each illuminating us with a lantern, while dancing and singing. In the second chamber we saw that the Callotesque figures, the monkeys and the marionettes had quit their places and were holding a ball, to the sound of several ridiculous instruments, which were making a fine racket. The rats and mice of the grilled cabinet were playing their part in it by singing in deep voices, while a large cat was beating time.

"The Prince made you dance in spite of yourself, and I also danced with King Lucidan. The governess and the two chambermaids laughed uproariously. For my part, I found the success of my art so pleasant that I forgot my chagrin for a few moments. Afterwards, a very disorganized collation of fruits and preserves was served to us; no one ate very much, except for the Prince, who officiated very well in no time.

"During the meal, people only made incoherent speeches and interrupted statements. As for the Prince, he played a thousand teasing tricks on you, untying your ribbons, detaching your ear-rings, embracing you from behind, and stealing some petty favor from you surreptitiously, which did not please you. That was not manifest in your actions, for you maintained a profound silence, and rubbed your eyes from time to time, like someone trying to wake up.

"Finally, the racket diminished slightly, and we entered the room where the bed was. Your chambermaids set about undressing you, but by touching you with the tip of my finger I had you in the bed in the blink of an eye. I did as much for the Prince, who lay down with as much promptitude. I closed the curtains and the door. Everyone retired and everything remained in great repose. It was only half past midnight, and everything that I have just described happened in less than half an hour.

"Four hours later I approached your bed quietly and made you inhale the essence of sleep; then I put you back in your own bed, after which I returned to collect the Prince, who had already become a butterfly again. I annihilated the ridiculous dwelling of dreams that had served me so usefully, and although my realm was very distant from that of Caprare, I returned there in two hours,

"The poor butterfly thought himself much more unfortunate than he had been before his marriage; he loved you madly and your absence caused him to suffer a great deal. I had left a large fly near you in order to render me an account of what happened, and by that means we often had news of you. It told me about your pregnancy and its consequences. The Prince was extremely joyful, which was further augmented when he knew of the birth of his son, the handsome Princillon.

"I was careful not to make him the confidence of all your troubles; he would have died of dolor; I could not exempt you from them, and I shared them with you without letting him know. In spite of all the Prince's impatience, he always obeyed me, and found it so easy to abandon himself to my guidance that he did nothing without my order. I procured him a conversation with his unfortunate brother. They spoke in their enchanted forms and rendered one another accounts of their fortunes.

"I then prepared everything to put an end to what I had begun so fortunately. To that effect I worked on the construction of this palace, and when it was ready, I brought the Prince here, who was only any longer a butterfly for two hours every night, and always has been until the birth of Princillette, which destroyed the terrible charm of the vindictive Mandarine entirely."

Turbodine finished her marvelous story thus, after which Risette said to her: "Oh, Madame, what surprising things you have just told me, and I was far from taking for a verity what had never seemed to me to be anything but a dream. I will tell you, Madame, in order to render you an account of what cannot have come to your acquaintance, that in the morning that followed that surprising night, I opened the curtains of my bed promptly, as soon as I was awake, to see where I was, and on seeing that I was in my bedroom, I was convinced that everything that had happened to me was nothing but a dream. I was dying to recount it to my governess, in whom I had great confidence, but there were circumstances by which my modesty was so very alarmed that I resolved never to say anything about it.

"When my indispositions had put me in a state no longer to be able to doubt my pregnancy, I said to myself: *Alas, might this strange state that I am in have something to do with the surprising dream that is still so present in my imagination? Why is it necessary for the handsome phantom of that imaginary husband to occupy me eternally?*

"When the Queen, my mother, and my governess asked my questions to which I had no response, I was sometimes on the point of telling them what had happened to me; then, considering that it could not lead to anything but making me pass for a lunatic or a liar, and that people would undoubtedly believe that I had invented that imposture to hide a veritable intrigue. I always strengthened my resolve to say nothing about it.

"I confess to you, Madame, that during all the persecutions that I have suffered, my entire consolation was in thinking about the agreeable image settled my heart by mans of movements that I could not disentangle. It seemed to me that my son resembled Prince Fortunate, and in that thought, I named him Princillon, which formed an enigma, or, rather, a diminutive, of the word Prince, although it did not leave me satisfied. But Madame, nothing equals the astonishment I felt on seeing the Prince. I believed him to be Mirou transformed, and hearing you name him, those clothes and mine being the same as in the dream, further augmented my surprise. But when I saw that the Prince behaved with me as if he had never seen me, and his seriousness had nothing in common with the excessive hilarity in which I had seen him, I concluded that the dream had only been a prediction of what was happening to me at that moment.

"In sum, Madame, all these prodigious events are the effects of the sublimity of your Art and the goodness of your heart, which enabled you to conclude the misfortunes of a Prince who renders me today the happiest person on earth."

The fay was charmed by the sage reflections and good sentiments of the beautiful and grateful Princess. She sent someone to fetch the Prince whom she informed that she had just told his charming wife everything. The three of them had a very agreeable conversation on the subject of the pretended dream. The Druid was also summoned, and certified to the Princess the authenticity of the ceremony of her first marriage, of which she was already quite convinced.

Turbodine departed a few days later in order to go to her realm, where she took little Princillette in order to be nourished in her palace. She divided her time in such a way that she spent a part of it on the Isle of Rocks and the other in Fortunate's beautiful palace, where he had a more delightful life than ever with Risette and Princillon.

It was not the same for the King and Queen of Caprare, who were in a mortal dolor at the loss of their dear daughter and the rigor they had employed with her. They mourned her death every day, which they believed to be quite certain. A neighboring King named Grimaut, with his wife, Queen Grimasse, decided to make war on Lucidan. They had held a grudge against him for a long time because they believed that he had not wanted Prince Trudon, their son, to marry Risette, for whom they had asked on his behalf, and that young Prince had died of the chagrin that the loss of the Princess had caused him. They therefore entered the isle of Caprare with a formidable army, and as Lucidan was not on his guard, he was soon reduced to the last extremity and was constrained to flee on a ship with the Queen, his wife, very few people and even less money.

When they were at sea, they thought about where they might retreat. They had heard mention that the King of France received all unfortunate Princes in his Court, which was why they decided to turn in that direction, but they were surprised by a tempest so furious that in a very short time their vessel was broken into a thousand pieces. The few people they had with them perished, but the King and Queen were carried to land by a little debris in a miraculous manner, all the more surprising because it was at the very spot that poor Risette had once landed.

They did not know anything about that, but their misfortune made them think of hers, and the justice of Heaven seemed to them to be reproaching them for their cruelty, which was punishing them less rigorously than they merited, since they were still alive and they believed her to be dead.

The Sun was beginning to set, and they did not know what would become of them in that deserted place. The King, who had more firmness than the Queen, his wife, told her that lamentations served no purpose, and that it was necessary to go forward in order to find some retreat. He took her under his arm and drew her into stony places where it was difficult to walk, especially for people who were not accustomed to it.

Having finally reached a ridge, they were agreeably surprised to see the beautiful avenues of Risette's castle. They entered therein with confidence, hoping that such a beautiful place could only lead them to some agreeable shelter.

The Queen, who loved flowers, and who could see that the terrain was covered with them, picked handfuls of them and put them in her bosom. The King, seeing her do that, said to her: "Why, Madame, what vulgar manners you have; if you want flowers, why not pick those that are on these fine trees, without taking those that one treads underfoot?"

With such and similar remarks they arrived within sight of the palace, by which they were wonderstruck with admiration, but when it was necessary to climb the crystal perron, the Queen did not want to set foot on it, imagining that it might break, and that she would fall into the river. The King, who had recognized its solidity, pulled her with all his strength, but he could not get her to budge. In the end, she wanted to take off her shoes, and it was necessary for Lucidan to become angry in order to prevent her from doing so. She therefore climbed up tremulously, and when she reached the last step, she was in such haste to enter that she hammered on the door with all her might; but as the knocker was made of the same material as the chimes of clocks, it made a din so terrible that she thought she would go deaf, as did the poor King of Caprare.

At that racket a doorman opened the door, cursing. "Who the Devil are the clumsy fools who are knocking like that? May all the devils pursue you."

"I beg your pardon," said Lucidan. "We did not think that it would have such an effect."

"Well," replied the doorman, "what do you want?"

"I'd like to speak to the master or the lady of the house," replied the King.

"And on whose behalf?" asked the doorman.

"On my own," said the Prince, proudly, weary of the doorman's abruptness. "I can see that you scarcely know people. Tell your master or your mistress that it's the King and Queen of Caprare."

The noise of the hammer and that of the doorman had obliged the Prince, who supping alone with the Princess, to send a page to discover what was happening. When he had informed him, Risette ran to her father and mother, whom she embraced, dissolving in tears. The Prince followed her; the surprise was great on the one part and the other, and some time passed without understanding, but in the end, everything was clarified, to the great contentment of Their Caprarian Majesties. A new supper was served.

The King and Queen were charmed by Princillon, who was already tall and very intelligent. After the meal, Prince Fortunate took the King and Queen, with the Princess, into his cabinet, where he told them everything concerning the story of the Princess and his own story, and the marvelous adventures of their marriage. Nothing could add to the astonishment of the couple; they could not weary of embracing their daughter, their son-in-law and heir grandson; then they told them the story of their misfortune, for which the Prince and Princess tried to console them.

They were conducted into a superb apartment, where they had the finest service. The next day, they were shown the beauties of the magnificent palace and the fine company that inhabited it. Fêtes were put on in order to divert them, and the Queen of Caprare had never seen such festivities. As she was a good housekeeper, she was afraid that her son-in-law might ruin himself in making so much expenditure.

The Prince told the Princess, his wife, that it was necessary to let Turbodine know of the arrival of her father, the King. They rang the golden bell, and the halcyon appeared shortly thereafter. After being instructed as to what to say to its mistress, it departed, and came back promptly to order the Prince, on the part of the fay, to go and reestablish the King, his father-in-law, in his Estates, and to that effect, told him that he would find a fleet equipped with everything that he would need; he was to leave Risette in the palace, where he would come back to find her when his expedition was over.

All of that was carried out punctually. Lucidan was chagrined by quitting his daughter, but the joy of seeing her so happy and such a great lady consoled him. He boarded the flagship of the fleet, which was one of the finest and most numerous, and they arrived in Caprare in a short time.

The usurper was expelled; Fortunate performed an infinity of fine deeds, and after having put Lucidan back on his throne, he returned to his beautiful Princess in order to savor all the delights of his enchanted abode.

Prince Fortunate had become a gambler, and the game he liked best of all was basset, the most detestable of all games, with would be capable of exhausting the treasures of all the fays in there world, especially when one is as unlucky as the Prince was. One day he put into it more money than he wanted to lose, but he played with such bad luck that he lost everything, and as much again.

He went to his casket in order to pay his debts, for he did not like to owe money—a rare quality in an unlucky gambler—and found in his casket what he needed, but he was in such a hurry and so occupied with his loss, that he did not think of leaving a gold coin, as he was accustomed to do.

He remembered at night the mistake that he had made, and was anxious about it, which caused him to get up earlier than usual. He ran to his cabinet, and opened his casket, but found nothing in it. His dolor was extreme; he woke Risette to tell her what had happened. She tried to console him, saying: "We don't lack anything in this palace; that money is almost useless to us, and was only given to us for our pleasures. In any case, if we want to have any, we only have to sell some precious stones, which we have in abundance."

"That isn't what worries me, Madame," he said. "I'm convinced that everything the fays do is not without mystery, and I fear that my disobedience might be punished."

The Princess got up and approached her dressing table. She no longer found the precious stones there that she had taken off the previous day. She thought that her maidservants might have put them away. She opened a cabinet that had been full of them, but she found nothing there. Fear gripped her, and she let herself fall into an armchair.

"Oh, Prince," she said, "we're doomed." As she said those words, she fainted. The Prince ran to her, but alas, what became of him when he saw the beautiful palace suddenly vanish, and he found himself with the Princess and Princillon on bare ground in an arid place!

Poor Risette was brought round from her faint by the Prince's cries. She thought she would die on finding herself in that state; one cannot imagine her laments and regrets, and those of the Prince. They called on Turbodine for help, but everything was deaf to their voices.

They spent the day and night in that fashion, without eating or drinking. At daybreak, Princillon perceived a loaf of bread nearby; he told his mother. The great need they had to eat obliged them to do so. As they finished that sad meal, mingled with tears and sighs, they saw Turbodine in her chariot. The sight of her covered them in confusion, but the good lady, who had punished them enough, did not want to heap them with all the reproaches that she should have made them.

"You have committed a grave error, Prince," she told him. "You have annihilated by your disobedience that which all the Art of Enchantment can never imitate, but it's necessary to console yourself and take other measures. Follow me."

As she said that she marched away, and the sad individuals followed her in a profound silence. They went in that fashion to the sea shore, where they found a ship of the utmost magnificence at anchor.

"Come on," said the fay, "let's board this ship; we'll find there the wherewithal to console us for our losses." She went aboard first, taking the hand of the Princess. The Prince and his son followed them. The fay embraced Risette, saying to her: "I have no reason to complain of you," but she added: "As for you, Prince, although I have always had the same affection for you, it's necessary that you go for some time without receiving any marks of it."

The Prince threw himself at her feet, and begged her pardon in terms so tender and so touching that she was obliged to forgive him.

The ship was as marvelous inside as it was outside; the cabins were superbly furnished. The Prince found a party of his servants there, and the Princess all her women, her clothes, her jewels and everything necessary to her, as well as to Princillon. Turbodine told her that they were going to Caprare.

They arrived there in a matter of hours and landed in the capital city. The Prince, the Princess and Princillon were superbly adorned. They were conducted to the palace by Turbodine, accompanied by an infinite number of the people, who gave marks of the joy they felt at the return of their Princess, whose death they had mourned.

The King and the Queen came to welcome them with infinite caresses, and expressed all their gratitude to the benevolent fay. They were all conducted to comfortable apartments, which the fay took care to render magnificent, and they disembarked so many riches that they did not know where to put them.

The fay took Lucidan into her cabinet with the Prince, his son-in-law, and told him that a fleet would arrive in his ports the following day destined to avenge himself on King Grimaut and to expel him from his country in his turn. The King told her that she was the mistress, that she had only to give her orders and they would be followed scrupulously.

The surprising story of Prince Fortunate and Princess Risette was already known throughout the kingdom of Caprare, but in order that no one would be unaware of all the circumstances, Turbodine had them printed, and in order to efface entirely the suspicion that Mirou was Princillon's father, she had him return from exile, and gave him the power of reason, while conserving his memory of everything that had happened, in such a way that he was an irreproachable witness to the virtue of the Princess. The fay gave him riches, and he cut a very fine figure at Lucidan's court for the rest of his life.

After Turbodine had done all those things, she embarked in the fleet with Prince Fortunate and his son Princillon, who was already fourteen years old, and who first bore arms against his grandfather's enemy.

In no time at all the realm of King Grimaut was put to fire and blood, and the fay's power, combined with the valor of her troops and those of the Prince and his son, soon reduced that country to the last extremity.

Grimaut was pursued by the fay all the way to his palace; in order to avoid her he fled all the way to the grain-lofts, where Queen Grimasse was also constrained to seek her salvation on the tiles, with the cats, but the skillful fay pursued them so closely that she caught up with them.

Grimaut had already passed through a skylight, and was pulling Grimasse up, who, having a heavy backside, had a great deal of difficulty climbing up to follow him. They were in that posture when Turbodine struck them with a yew wand, and they were changed into stone, without losing their form. Those two figures can still be seen today by travelers for more than ten leagues around. Having done that, she locked the grain-lofts, threw the keys into the sea and struck the locks with the same wand, putting them in a state in which they could never be opened.

King Grimaut had a son named Brillantin, who was fifteen years old, and a daughter name Fleurbelle, who was fourteen. There was nothing more beautiful than the young Prince and Princess, and the fay took them with her.

As soon as she had given the orders necessary to conserve her conquest, she returned to Caprare, where she was received in triumph, along with Fortunate and Princillon. She rendered an account to Lucidan of what she had done. Princillon did not quit young Fleurbelle; he loved her as much as his age permitted, and that amiable princess received his cares with pleasure.

That gave the fay joy, and she resolved with Fortunate and Risette to make a marriage; but she wanted the ceremony to be held in her realm. The time when her husband the King would cease to be a turbot was soon to expire; that is why she made preparations to return to the Ile of Rocks; and, after re-embarking on her magnificent fleet with Fortunate, Risette, Princillon, Brillantin and Fleurbelle, they soon arrived there.

She was received with joy by all her subjects. Risette and Fortunate were charmed to find the young Princess, their daughter, as beautiful as she was, but Risette was very surprised to see her governess with her. The fay told her that she had taken her out of the prison where Lucidan had incarcerated her, and that she had always been in her palace, where she had charged her with the education of the beautiful Princillette. The poor lady, who had learned of Risette's adventure, nearly died of joy on seeing her, and for her part, Risette felt no less pleasure.

Destiny, seconding the deigns of Turbodine, who was thinking of uniting Brillantin with Princillette, gave birth in those two young hearts to a reciprocal inclination.

Finally, the day so desired for the transformation of the King of Coquerico arrived; the passion that the beautiful fay, his wife, had conserved for him in spite of his infidelity seemed to have been augmented during the twenty years of his enchantment.

Nothing equaled the magnificence of the fêtes that the fay prepared to receive that dear Prince. She embellished her palace and her avenues with all the riches and all the beauties that her art could furnish. She appeared, dressed in a manner richer and more elegant than had ever been seen. Risette, Fortunate, Princillon, Fleurbelle, Princillette and Brillantin were adorned with the same magnificence, as well as all the lords and ladies of the Court, and even the people, who wanted to contribute to the grandeur of the fête.

The Queen emerged from her palace with that beautiful and numerous following, to the sound of a thousand instruments of war and peace. When they reached the sea shore, the fay approached it, and when she had struck the waves three times with her crystal wand, they opened immediately and formed a kind of vault, from the depths of which a man emerged of a majestic beauty, clad in the finest attire, who was recognized as the King of Coquerico. He was no longer very young, but he was no less good looking. The fay advanced to meet him and held out her arms to him.

"Come, dear Prince, she said to him, embracing him tenderly, "come and resume the place that is your due, in my heart and on my throne. Let us not talk about the past, and try to live happily from now."

The King returned her caresses, and did not amuse himself making protestations of fidelity, for I believe that he never had any desire to lack any. If all straying husbands were punished in that manner, there would not be so many.

The King gave his hand to the Queen and the entire people, delighted to see their King again, cried with all their might: "Long love King Turbot and Queen Turbodine." Prince Fortunate embraced his dear brother with a great deal of pleasure.

They arrived at the palace, where they found a marvelous repast, and that entire day was spent in different pleasures and in reciprocal caresses between all those amiable and illustrious persons, for they put off until another occasion the telling of their stories.

When evening came the spouses were put to bed with the same ceremonies as been observed at their first wedding. All the following days were as many different fêtes. The fay invited Mandarine, who was reconciled in good faith with Prince Fortunate, who still yielded in secret a few sighs at the loss of the charming Merline. The celebrations of the King's return were continued and augmented by the marriage of Princillon with Fleurbelle, and that of Brillantin with Princillette.

Some time after all these marriages, they received certain news of the death of Lucidan, which obliged Fortunate to quit the charming abode of the Isle of Rocks in order to go with his wife to take possession of the kingdom that belonged to him. They departed, therefore; Princillon and Fleurbelle accompanied them, in order to reign in the realm of King Grimaut. Brillantin and Princillette remained with Turbodine, who assured them of the succession of her realm, to which was joined that of Coquerico, along with the principality of Barbaux, where they reigned in the meantime.

Queen Turbodine gave the gift of Enchantment to Princillette, to whom surprising things happened, which will one day compose a most agreeable history.

Although all those realms were rather distant from one another, the Art of Enchantment procured them vehicles so convenient, which traveled so far in such a short time, that the Kings and the Queens saw one another frequently. They lived for a very long time, and very happily, as did their numerous posterity.

THE GOBLINS OF KERNOSY CASTLE

The Vicomtesse de Kernosy spent almost all of the year in her château, which she reckoned to be the most charming abode in all of Bretagne. It was a noble fief of which her ancestors had borne the name successively, where she had been raised herself since her earliest childhood, the advantageous situation of which offered something singular, agreeable to sight, in every direction. Her two nieces, both very lovable and young, remained in the place with her, but found it very sad to spend their best days in such a solitary dwelling, so distant from commerce with society, ten leagues from the nearest town and a quarter of a league from the village.

The castle is an ancient building, which nevertheless conserves an air of grandeur. First of all one sees iron doors, stout towers, profound ditches and partly-broken drawbridges, and then great galleries with no ornamentation, halls and specious rooms, the windows of which are no narrow that the daylight only enters imperfectly. Grass grows as high there in summer as in open country. In sum, the castle is the precise model of those to which it is said that spirits return.

That was also the common opinion of the region; marvelous things had been recounted therein for more than a hundred years, Mesdemoiselles de Kernosy knew, from their infancy, all the stories of the goblins of the castle, their governesses having told them a thousand times, but although they had almost always lived there, they had never seen or heard anything that could persuade them that there was any truth in the vulgar belief.

One evening, when the old Vicomtesse went to bed early, Mesdemoiselles de Kernosy retired to their room and sat next to the fire, not wanting to go to bed so soon.

"This is a fine time to be in this country," said Mademoiselle de Kernosy, on hearing the wind whistling in the windows. "In truth, I can't resist the mortal ennui that my aunt gives us."

"You're right, my sister," said Mademoiselle de Saint-Urbain, who was the younger of the two. "I'm in despair at being here." She smiled and added: "And my despair is augmented when I think that in Paris, people are going to balls at this very moment, while we're in this accursed castle, besieged by snow, without any pleasures."

The charming young woman was about to make a list of all the pleasures of Paris during the carnival, but Mademoiselle de Kernosy suddenly got up from her armchair, uttering a loud cry.

"What is it, my sister?" she said, astonished by her action.

"Look, look!" said Kernosy, fearfully.

Saint-Urbain looked, and saw a letter attached to a little silver chain descending in front of the fireplace, which was held at a rather elevated distance in order to prevent the paper catching fire.

"What," said Saint-Urbain, "it's a note that frightened you so much? I thought you were having frightful visions." She picked up the fire-tongs in order to capture the note. "Let's see right away," she continued, "what this signifies."

"What?" said Kernosy. ""You're going to take that piece of paper? You can't think so! Leave it alone, my sister, I beg you, and call someone."

"Let's call my aunt, then," said Saint-Urbain. "She'll be afraid of the spirit."

"Don't laugh," said Kernosy. "I'm terribly frightened."

"But of what?" said Saint-Urbain. "You can see that the spirit isn't here, since it's taking the trouble to write to us." As she finished speaking she took the paper with the tongs and opened it immediately, in spite of Kernosy, who was dying of fear.

"The spirit's writing is legible," said Saint-Urbain, looking at the note. "Let's see what it wants to tell us."

She read it, and found these words:

You are both too lovable always to remain alone in a place as solitary as this; one cannot have seen you and not have a heart sensible to your beauties and your ennuis; charge us with the care of your pleasures, and we will do our best to cheer you up. We will doubtless succeed, if tender and faithful hearts seem worthy of your attention.

The Goblins of the Castle.

"What is all this?" said Mademoiselle de Kernosy, who had had time to reassure herself somewhat.

"I don't know," Saint-Urbain replied, "but we're being promised pleasures and faithful lovers; my opinion is that we should accept the bargain."

Kernosy dared not take a step a step in her room, and Saint-Urbain, having looked into the fireplace, could no longer see the little chain; she said so to her sister..

"It's disappeared!" cried Kernosy. "Let's call someone."

At that moment, a candle-stub placed next to the note fell from its spike upon the paper, already very dry from having been suspended for some time in front of the fireplace; it caught alight easily, and was consumed rapidly.

That perfectly natural accident almost caused Kernosy to faint, and even Saint-Urbain lost all assurance; she called to their chambermaids, who slept in a tower nearby, and who came running. Saint-Urbain, very frightened, told them that her sister had just been taken ill; they attributed her fear to that faint.

Immediately, water was thrown in Mademoiselle de Kernosy's face, she was put to bed, and a short time later she felt much better; but she ordered her maids to remain in her room. Saint-Urbain slept beside her, in order to be more as-sured if they heard anything else.

"You did well," Kernosy whispered to her sister, "not to say anything to our women about the scare that we had; it would have been all over the place tomorrow, and people would think we were seeing things."

Saint-Urbain agreed that it was necessary not to talk about their adventure.

Finally, the daylight having reassured them, they went to sleep.

Neither of them woke up before mid-day, when the noise of a cart and horses was heard in the courtyard.

"What's that noise?" asked Kernosy.

"Perhaps it's pleasures that the goblin is sending us," Saint-Urban replied.

"Oh, my sister," said Kernosy, "I haven't yet recovered from my fright. Let's forget the goblin, if we can."

At that moment, one of the Vicomtesse's maidservants came in, and told them that a troupe of actors had just arrived; that they had brought a letter to Madame la Vicomtesse, which she had read, and that she had said afterwards that the actors could remain in the castle.

"What?" they said, getting up. "Our aunt wants them to stay? Some superior power must be mixed up in this."

Scarcely had they finished speaking than another noise became audible in the courtyard; they sent a servant to ask what it was, and she returned to say that it was a troupe of musicians who had just arrived.

Then Saint-Urbain said to her sister, taking her arm: "Let's go see what these people look like."

They went to the Vicomtesse's room. As soon as they came in, she said to them, with a cheerful expression they had never seen before: "Well, Mesdemoiselles, will you still complain about the ennui you have in being here? Here, it seems to me, are sufficient amusements for you." Looking at the fearful Kernosy, she said: "What's the matter with you? Now you're in a bad mood."

"I felt ill last night," said Kernosy, "but I believe it's nothing."

"Well, Aunt," said Saint-Urbain, "from what land are so many pleasures arriving?"

"You're too curious," replied the Vicomtesse, coldly. "Leave me alone, I have things to do. Go see the preparations that are being made for this evening."

"My aunt is assuredly the goblins' confidante," Saint-Urbain whispered to her sister. "You can see that she's keeping their secret."

They went into a great hall, and found workmen there occupied in setting up a theater and adjusting decorations, which appeared to them to be rather beautiful and elegant. From there they went to the chapel in order to say their prayers, and a short time later, they were summoned to dinner. As soon as they had left the table they returned to their room in order to take off their casual clothes and dress formally, in honor of the company.

In her pocket, Saint-Urbain found a note. She read it to Kernosy. This is what it contained:

You can see that we are keeping our word; we are seeking to divert you and we have found the secret of softening your aunt's insupportable humor. Mademoiselle de Kernosy's fainting fit has caused us much anxiety; have no fear, amour ought never to be frightening when one is young and beautiful.

"The goblins are very gallant," she said, as she finished reading the note, "but this one doesn't frighten me; it didn't come of its own accord, like the other; someone could have put it in my pocket while I was watching the painter who was fitting a decoration. Let's see what will become of this; but let's be careful that this note doesn't catch fire like the first, which frightened us so much. It's necessary to lock it away; perhaps we'll recognize the handwriting some day."

The two sisters spent the rest of the day on their attire, and their beauty, with that small assistance, was so surprising, that they found themselves worthy of going to shine at the most superb fêtes in the world.

Mademoiselle de Kernosy was blonde; she had a complexion of dazzling whiteness, an agreeable turn of visage, and large blue eyes, piercing all the way to the depths of the soul. A gracious smile revealed beautiful teeth, and even augmented the splendor of her mouth, whose lips had a color as vivid as coral; her neck and her hands further heightened all those advantages of nature. So many beauties could doubtless cause amour, but her advantageous stature, accompanied by a noble air, imposed so forcefully that one could not look at her without a sentiment of respect, and the evenness of her intelligence enabled an accuracy to be remarked in all her words that can only be acquired by practice in society and a perfect acquaintance with fine literature.

Young Saint-Urbain had a round face, a delicate complexion—but a little darker that her sister's—and black hair; her eyes were also dark, well spaced, and surprisingly vivacious. Her mouth, small and gracious, contained beautiful teeth as white as ivory and perfectly arranged; an air of ease, radiating from her entire person, did not detract from her noticeable majestic bearing, while dancing as well as walking. Although she was not as tall as Kernosy, her figure was so admirably proportioned that it would have been difficult to make a choice between the two sisters. Her manners, naturally engaging and cheerful, inspired joy in hearts as soon as she appeared. She had a prompt repartee full of wit; she was often able to animate a languishing conversation by means of some bold remark, abruptly advanced. At first one might have thought that she said it without reflection, but she always supported her discourse with solid reasons; nothing ever escaped her that was not good sense, which did not give pleasure, and was not worthy of her birth.

The two charming sisters had not yet emerged from their room when someone came to tell them that a man on horseback had just announced to Madame la Vicomtesse that three ladies of the neighborhood were about to arrive at the castle.

"So much the better," said Saint-Urbain. "I'll find the comedy more agreeable if there are plenty of spectators; do we know the names of these ladies?"

"They are," said one of their maidservants, "the Marquise de Briance, the Comtesse de Salgue and Baronne de Sugarde."

"That's very good company," said Mademoiselle de Kernosy, "but it seems to me that it would be even better if the Marquise de Briance's brothers were in the vicinity. They won't come back so soon; when one is in Paris, surrounded by pleasures, one rarely remembers the ladies one has left behind in the provinces."

"That's as may be," said Saint-Urbain, laughing. "Do you think that the Comte and Chevalier de Livry will find many ladies in the city more amiable than us? I remember that we didn't find a large number of them six months ago."

The Marquise's carriage came into the courtyard then, obliging the two sisters to go down to meet her. Madame la Vicomtesse got there first, decked out like a young woman; her dress, which she claimed to be amaranth brown, was a bright velvet the color of fire.

The ladies went up to her apartment, and were astonished to see a theater that was just was just being finished off in the great hall.

"A troupe of actors arrived this morning," said the Vicomtesse, "and I retained them to amuse my nieces during the carnival."

Her complaisance was praised, and the entire company went into the room.

The Vicomtesse was nearly sixty; she wanted to be beautiful, although she had not been even in her early youth. No woman ever had such a difficult humor. She was very rich, widowed five years before, but the design she had to marry again had not been executed, because, she said, she had not found anyone sufficiently able to love. She would have liked a hero like Amadis; Galaor appeared too fickle for her, Alexander did not love tenderly enough and Caesar had too many mistresses.[27] In sum, she was looking for an Amadis and, not having found any in Bretagne, she had made a voyage to Paris, from which, not having found any more, she had returned to her château to wait for fortune to throw up a knight worthy of being her lover. As she was rich, of great quality, and she possessed the most beautiful lands in the province, a quantity of the great seigneurs of the region crowded around her, but it is easy to judge how ungallant a person absolutely insistent on a hero would find provincials who talked about marriage right away.

Mesdemoiselles de Kernosy were submissive to that capricious individual. They had lost their mother in infancy; their father, when he died, had obliged them by his testament to remain under the guardianship of the Vicomtesse, his sister-in-law, and those amiable girls had been with her for four years.

The Vicomtesse was in no hurry to marry them off; she had refused all the parties that had presented themselves, although some of them were very advantageous; one did not have enough valor, another was poorly made, another was not of an appropriate age; in sum, none of them was to her taste. Meanwhile, she enjoyed placidly the considerable wealth of her two nieces.

That capricious woman loved to play the grand dame on her own stage; the manner in which she received company marked well enough that expense did not astonish her. During the conversation she ordered the preparation of a collation in which everything was the most exquisite for the season was served. Her orders were carried out so scrupulously that everything was ready for the play as soon as everyone got up from the table.

---

[27] Amadis de Gaul is the hero of a Spanish romance, an exaggerated imitation of French Medieval romances; Galaor is his equally heroic brother. Alexander the Great and Julius Caesar also figured in some of the more colourful French verse and prose romances.

All the ladies went into the hall; they found a well-lit little theater there; the stage set represented a magnificent chamber. All the persons of distinction—and all of the same sex—
took their places. The Vicomtesse's domestics and all the local
inhabitants, who had come running in response to the rumor of
the fête, composed an audience very easy to satisfy. Eight violins and four oboes played the overture, and the actors commenced the play which was called *L'Esprit follet*.[28]

It was performed well enough, and as it had a certain
rapport with their nocturnal adventure, the two sisters looked
at one another several times, but could not say anything, the
Marquise de Briance and the Comtesse de Salgue being placed
between them. At the end of the play, the orchestra played
excellent pieces from *Le Triomphe de l'amour*.[29]

They went into a neighboring room, where a magnificent
supper was served. The Vicomtesse had organized it; it was
the only thing that she understood well. The conversation was
lively. The Baronne and Saint-Urbain said that the day's
pleasures lacked a ball, and they were still sustaining their
thesis when a valet de chambre was perceived, who came to
speak to the Comtesse.

"Let's go, Mesdames," she said to them a moment later,
when the meal was over. "Let's pass on, if you please, into the
small gallery."

The company was equally surprised to find the chandeliers illuminated there, violins, oboes and a troupe of masks.
There were several there of very fine appearance, whom the
ladies did not believe that they had seen among the actors per-

---

[28] The five-act comedy *L'Esprit follet, ou La Dame invisible*
(1698) by Noël Lebreton Hauteroche. The title is a pleonasm,
as a follet is a kind of spirit, the word being frequently associ-
ated with the phenomenon known in English as a will-o'-the-
wisp, but it is also a pun relevant to the present story: *esprit*
has several other meanings, including wit or intelligence, and
follet also implies folly.

[29] A 1691 ballet by Jean-Baptiste Lully.

forming *L'Esprit follet.* One of them, dressed in the Greek style, came to take the hand of the Vicomtesse, who commenced the ball with a courante. As she finished it she said that she would succeed much better at the minuet and other less serious dances.

Kernosy and Saint-Urbain worked marvels; more lightness and accuracy had never been seen; their dances were accompanied by all the graces that Bretonnes know how to provide. The mask dressed in the Greek style hardly quit the Vicomtesse, to the great astonishment of her nieces. Meanwhile, a pretty mask approached Mademoiselle de Kernosy; his costume was black velvet, in the Spanish style; he had plumes the color of fire in his hat; his figure was beautiful; he had just danced, and the delicacy of his footwork, accompanied by a surprising lightness, had charmed everyone.

"The goblins of the castle," he said to Kernosy, "are very sorry to have frightened you; but you're so beautiful this evening that they can flatter themselves that your health is perfect."

Kernosy wanted to leave on hearing mention of goblins. The Spaniard stopped her. "Stay a moment, I beg you," he said. "I'll explain last night's adventure. He lifted his mask, and Kernosy, recognizing him as the Comte de Livry, the brother of the Marquise de Briance, was almost as surprised as if she had seen the goblin whose advent had caused her to lose consciousness.

That precipitate emotion was, however, very different from fear; she no longer had any thought of running away. "What! It's you, Comte?" she said to him. "What reason causes you to appear in this disguise, in a place to which you could come in the same fashion as Madame your sister?"

"I have too many things to say in response to the questions you're putting to me," the Comte replied, "to dare to do it here, and yet I'm dying of impatience to enlighten you. Do me the favor, when you leave here, of going to my sister's room." Seeing that Kernosy was profoundly thoughtful, he went on: "Will you do that, Mademoiselle? Then, I flatter myself that I might see you for a quarter of an hour without suspect witnesses. How many things I have to tell you!"

"The Marquise is too much my friend," replied Kernosy, blushing, "for me to refuse to go to be enlightened with her regarding everything that is happening here."

The Vicomtesse came to take the Spaniard to dance then, and interrupted the conversation. Kernosy had a strong desire to tell Saint-Urbain about her adventure, but she did not doubt that she was informed of it when she saw kneeling before her a little mask clad as Scaramouche, who was playing the guitar marvelously; his figure was slender and marvelously beautiful; a large quantity of black hair, naturally curly, easily allowed Kernosy to recognize him as the Chevalier de Livry; she left him the care of telling Saint-Urbain who the goblins of the castle were.

The ball did not finish until after midnight. Immediately, Madame de Kernosy conducted the Comtesse to her apartment, Saint-Urbain escorted the Baronne to hers, and Kernosy, who had been a friend of the Marquise for a long time, accompanied her as far as her room.

Saint-Urbain was too impatient to join the company that she knew to be in the Marquise's room to amuse herself with the Baronne; she made her a few compliments and came to catch up with them. Scarcely had she entered when the Comte and Chevalier de Livry, who had changed clothes rapidly, arrived.

The conversation was initially tumultuous; a thousand questions were asked without allowing time for responses; but finally, Kernosy having begged the Comte to enlighten her perfectly as to the design that had made them come incognito into a place where everyone was their friend, as there was no one suspect in the room, everyone having taken their places around the fire, the Comte commenced his story thus:

"It was a year ago that we had the honor of seeing you for the first time," he said, addressing Mademoiselle de Kernosy. "One remembers such a charming sight for a long time; you came to my sister's house with your aunt; my brother and I had just arrived from the army, and we had no other passion then but that of going to Paris in order to spend the time when we were away from our regiments. The pleasure of seeing you made us change our plans; we no longer thought about anything but staying in a locale where we had not thought, on arriving, that we could spend a week without dying of boredom. I will take the liberty of declaring that I was thinking about Mademoiselle de Kernosy, and I have no doubt that the Chevalier will also explain himself to Mademoiselle Saint-Urbain."

"That is not your narration, Monsieur le Comte," Saint-Urbain put in, smiling. "It's necessary that you leave something for the Chevalier to say, if the whim takes him also to tell us his adventures."

The Marquise laughed at Saint-Urbain's imagination, and, Kernosy having asked the Comte to continue, he went on:

"I shall not talk about Mademoiselle Saint-Urbain again, since she forbids me to do so. Mademoiselle de Kernosy received the marks of my respectful attachment with a coldness capable of chilling any other heart but mine; I continued to give her evidence of my respect and my tenderness, but she was only faintly touched by it. If Mademoiselle de Saint-Urbain will permit," he continued, laughing, "I will say that the Chevalier was either more fortunate or more amorous than me, for it's certain that he appeared more content."

"You're judging on feeble appearances," Saint-Urbain put in. "You're lucky that I can understand mockery."

"I intend to speak too," said the Chevalier, "and you'll see whether I'm able to make reflections in my turn."

"Shut up, Chevalier," said the Marquise. "I want to learn a thousand things from this story that I don't know yet."

"Indispensable affairs," the Comte continued, "recalled us to Court; we were obliged to depart, and I've never felt such sadness. Mesdemoiselles de Kernosy had returned home; their aunt had taken them away on the same day that I received the cruel letter that forced me to quit this locale. I flattered myself that I would at least have the satisfaction of saying adieu to Mademoiselle de Kernosy, but my sister told me that the Vicomtesse would not suffer people of our age rendering visits to her amiable nieces.

"Madame la Marquis will remember clearly the urgency with which I begged her to take me to Madame de Kernosy's abode, but she had a slight fever and she was inflexible to my pleas."

"I was ill," said the Marquise, "and, I want to confess, I feared that if you saw the amiable individuals again, your duty might be impeded by your amour."

"The Chevalier and I departed, therefore," the Comte went on, "and we did not say four words during the journey. I wrote to Mademoiselle de Kernosy before leaving and I left a valet de chambre to deliver my letter reliably. The Chevalier charged him with one on his behalf for Mademoiselle de Saint-Urbain. We awaited his return to Paris with impatience. Finally, he arrived, and assured us that he had delivered our letters, and that Mesdemoiselles de Kernosy had not wanted to reply to them.

"A few days later, that valet de chambre disappeared, and took one of our horses. That action made us doubt that he had delivered our letters faithfully; we were thinking about seeking clarification ourselves when all the colonels received orders to return to their regiments; it was necessary to obey; this province was too far away for it to be possible to pass through it on the way, and we had no time to ourselves. We departed, overwhelmed by chagrin, and I carried away in my heart the beautiful idea that Mademoiselle de Kernosy had left therein.

"I wrote to my sister begging her to find out, if she could what had become of our letters. She told me that she could not inform us, because Madame de Kernosy had gone to Paris and had taken her nieces with her. That contretemps, of leaving Paris precisely at the time when those charming persons were arriving there, augmented my dolor.

"On arriving at the army, we found Tadillac, who is my close relative, a gallant fellow with a very amiable face and a very cheerful humor; we saw one anther often, and we told him about our chagrins, letting him know the character of the Vicomtesse. He sought a means of approaching the château without alarming her, and after having thought hard, settled on the design of making himself loved.

"He is not rich, and the hope of Madame de Kernosy's wealth pleased him; he begged me seriously to aid him in that affair, and said that in recognition, he would facilitate my happiness. I told him that the Vicomtesse had not been able to resolve to marry again, because she had not found a hero, or a heart, to love her with sufficient delicacy.

"'Let me try,' said Baron de Tadillac. "I'll appear before her as the hero of a romance, and I'll have more delicacy than she can imagine." He added: "There's no great harm in pushing the thing to ridiculous lengths; it will only make it conform more to our amours."

That project amused us all through the campaign. The Baron was delighted by it, and I was veritably anxious because I was veritably amorous. The troops were put into winter quarters, and we finally departed to return to this region, with an incredible joy. We arrived at my sister's house ten days ago; we forbade our servants to talk about our arrival. I asked Madame la Marquise for news of you with an urgency that made her judge that my amour had not been weakened by absence.

"We conferred with the Baron to see how we might gain access to the castle. He went to Rennes in search of actors and musicians; he brought them diligently to my sister's house, and in the meantime, having bribed one of your domestics, it was easy for me, when the Baron returned, to commit the folly that frightened Mademoiselle de Kernosy so much.

"We made a little hole in the ceiling from above in order to pass the note and the little chain through. The Baron wrote the note, because no one knew his handwriting. He executed the enterprise very well, and I was in despair when I realized, because of the noise we heard, that Mademoiselle de Kernosy had been taken ill. I would have gone to beg her pardon for our folly immediately if I had not feared revealing myself to the maidservants we heard in the room, who did not go out again.

"We went to rejoin our men in a village two leagues away; we sent the actors forth this morning; one of them presented a letter to Madame de Kernosy. This is what it contained:

The Unknown Lover to the beautiful Vicomtesse de Kernosy

I saw you in Paris six months ago, Madame. What a sight! My heart cannot forget it; I followed you to all the spectacles, but, as respectful a lover as I am tender and faithful, I dared not declare my amour to you. My duty recalled me to the army; I pursued glory with pleasure, because I knew that you love it. Amour has called me back to you. I have therefore come, Madame, to try to render myself worthy of pleasing you by my cares and by my attachment; amour wants to be surrounded by games and pleasures; find it good that this troupe of actors amuses you: I shall render to you this evening.

"Madame de Kernosy," the Comte continued, "was charmed by that letter; she allowed the troupe of actors to remain in the castle; we arrived, disguised, with the musicians. An hour later, the Baron slipped a letter into Mademoiselle de Saint-Urbain's pocket while she was watching the completion of the theater.

"That is what the adventure was that gave you such anxiety; my sister has been kind enough to favor us with her presence, and that of the two ladies she brought with her, who know nothing of our designs. The Baron, dressed in the Greek style, paid court to Madame la Comtesse this evening; he said to me as he left, with his usual gravity: 'I can see that I can pass for a hero in Bretagne.' He did not want to explain himself further, but he ought to come here in order to inform us of the success of his amour.

"It seems to me that everything will favor our wishes if Mademoiselle de Kernosy and her amiable sister will permit us to hope that they will not be contrary to us, and if Madame la Vicomtesse de Kernosy can be brought to accord us the honor of her alliance."

Mademoiselle de Kernosy, who had always retained a tender memory of the Comte, replied to him very kindly. Saint-Urbain responded with the same honesty to the Chevalier, who spoke to her in a low voice, and whom she informed that neither she nor her sister had received their letters.

They were beginning to clarify that matter when the Baron came into the room, still dressed in the Greek style. He was well made, only nineteen years old; his face was very agreeable and he had a fine blond head

"What!" the Comte said to him, on seeing him still in his masque costume. "Are you continuing the ball?"

"No," said the Baron, "but I'll soon be continuing the campaign; another two conversations like the one I've just had, and the deal is done; but in recompense, if I'm losing my mind, the heart is gaining a good deal, for I have the most beautiful sentiments in the world. Madame de Kernosy assures me that she has never read any so delicate and so tender."

"But why," said the Chevalier, "are you still dressed like a fool? A good overcoat, in the present weather, would be much better than that old embroidery."

"Not so, if you please," said the Baron. "A lover dressed in the Greek style has far more charms in the eyes of the Vicomtesse than one merely dressed as a Frenchman; she even compared me right away to Alcibiades."

"You're too mad by half, Baron," said the Marquise, "but let's get on. Where are you up to?"

"I'm up to hope," the Baron replied. "I'm permitted to have a great deal of it, and I shall stay here to render myself worthy of that honor. It's necessary that these Messieurs"—he indicated the Comte and the Chevalier—"arrive here as if they were coming from the Marquis de Briance's residence. Having not found her at home, it will be perfectly plausible that they've come to search for her in a place where the company is so good."

The Baron's opinion was approved, and, the night already being well advanced, the Comte and the Chevalier judged it appropriate to depart in order to go and spend a few hours in the nearest village, in order to be able to return to the castle before the mid-day meal.

The two amiable sisters, after having wished the Marquise a good night, retired to their apartment. They did not go to sleep for a long time; the joy of finding two very pleasant men faithful to them furnished them with sufficient subject-matter for conversation.

Eventually, slumber reigned peacefully throughout the castle, except in Madame de Kernosy's room; she would have found it impossible to sleep, even if she had wanted to, after a conversation like the one that she had just had with her hero.

The ladies did not get up until the middle of the day. As for the Vicomtesse, she had got up quite early, and had made two or three drafts of tender letters before applying herself to the care of her attire. Her two amiable nieces awoke with the joy that makes one feel so well when one hopes to spend the day with someone that one loves.

Everyone was occupied with a different care. The Comtesse de Salgue had not been able to rest the charms of the young Baron de Tadillac, and the Marquise de Briance was sighing in secret for a young absent lover. In sum, Amour had resolved to triumph in that old castle, and not to leave hearts tranquil there.

At noon or thereabouts, the Comte and the Chevalier arrived in a post-chaise. First they asked for the Marquise de Briance; she presented them to the Vicomtesse, and told her everything that had been agreed between them. The aunt, followed by the two nieces, received them with joy, and begged them to remain, "in order to take part in the pleasures that hazard has sent," she said, smiling disgracefully.

The Baron, who had also been ordered by the Vicomtesse to behave as if he had just arrived, turned up almost at the same time, clad in a vulgar rustic costume and mounted on a horse that he had tethered a short distance from the castle. He had himself announced. The Vicomtesse assured the company that he had been a friend of hers for a long time. Kernosy and Saint-Urbain had great difficulty preventing themselves from laughing.

It was already late, the compliments having prolonged the conversation considerably; Saint-Urbain interrupted it to remind everyone that it was necessary to eat. The sight of the Baron had caused everything to be forgotten.

They went to table, and were there for a long time. The conversation was very lively; everyone was striving to please; amour was shining there in several different forms. The old Vicomtesse was charmed by the young Baron; he was saying seriously things capable of making the most melancholy men in the world giggle, and she could not get over her admiration. The Comtesse de Salgue was looking tenderly as Tadillac; the urgent attention that he was testifying for the aged Vicomtesse was causing her great anxiety. As she was unaware of his design, she feared that he might be in love with Kernosy or Saint-Urbain and might only be trying to dazzle the Vicomtesse in order to hide his passion more effectively.

Madame de Salgue was young and beautiful; her intelligence was agreeable. She had married an old provincial lord whose affairs retained him in Paris almost all the year round, without her being able to obtain permission to accompany him on that voyage. He was convinced that there was no gentleman in the province sufficiently lacking in respect for him to talk about amour to his wife; that liberty had, in fact, been taken, but the heart of the Comtesse, insensible until now, had finally reached the fatal moment. The Baron perceived that he did not displease her; he dared not speak to her in front of the old Vicomtesse, but his gaze made her understand that she was beginning to inspire him.

The Comte was more touched than he had been before for the beautiful Kernosy, and she appeared satisfied to see his sentiments. Saint-Urbain and the Chevalier were charmed by one another. Baronne de Sugarde, whom the Chevalier pleased greatly, perceived their intelligence, but she had a good enough opinion of herself to flatter herself that she could render him infidel; she was something of a coquette, and the Chevalier would doubtless have responded to all the tender things her eyes were saying to him if a very serious passion had not occupied all his heart for the moment.

As for the Marquise de Briance, she was only retained in that place by the interests of her brothers; sometimes, a tender memory cast her into a profound reverie, but her mild humor and the vivacity of her intelligence prevented anyone from perceiving that she was troubled. Her conversation was so agreeable that people sought out her company ardently, and no one was every bored while spending time with her. Her facial features were very regular; her forehead, her eyes, her mouth and teeth were admirable, and the composite whole formed a perfect beauty. She was very rich, a widow for three years, and all the considerable seigneurs of the province had sought to please her without being able to succeed.

Such was the amiable company that Amour had taken care to assemble at the Château de Kernosy. They were just finishing the meal when they heard a carriage arrive. Everyone was annoyed by that, for they did not want anyone else. Monsieur de Fatville, a councilor of the Parlement de Rennes, was announced.

"What a man!" said Mademoiselle de Kernosy. "He's going to make us sense the misfortune of not daring to tell people that we're not at home."

"Well," said Saint-Urbain, "He won't annoy us too much; in truth, he's a fop, but at least he'll provide the company with a laughing-stock."

Madame la Vicomtesse, who wanted to display her prudence before the Baron's eyes, issued a severe reprimand to Saint-Urbain for that pleasantry. She would have gone on for some time had the councilor not come in. He had a red coat braided with silver, a large sword hanging from a centurion worn over his coat, a hat embroidered with gold, with an old yellow plume, and a very long blond wing, so well-powdered that he was sprinkling it over his clothes and the surroundings.

As he came in he made ten or a dozen bows, all as profound as one another, and then approached the Vicomtesse. "You have a very good company here, Madame," he said, with a disconcerted air, apparently having no desire for his own to be augmented. The Vicomtesse responded with the usual compliments, which did him a good deal of honor.

"I've made my post-chaise, which has very good springs, hasten in order to arrive here soon," said Monsieur de Fatville, "for I was in a extreme impatience to see the incomparable Mademoiselle de Saint-Urbain." He approached her, and set about kissing her hand.

"I'm very much obliged to you," said Saint-Urbain, withdrawing it rapidly, "for having sacrificed the springs of your post-chaise for me."

"Oh, they're not spoiled," replied Fatville. "My lackeys have assured me of that." He looked at himself in a large mirror and continued: "I can't help expressing the joy I feel at being dressed cavalierly, so I only wear my black coat in the mornings."

"My word, that's prudent of you," said the Baron, "for that one suits you marvelously."

Fatville thanked the Baron with grandiose reverences; fortunately for the company, someone came to announce that the play would commence as soon as it pleased the ladies to give the word."

"You have comedy here, then?" said Fatville. "Personally, I saw it four times in Paris, but I don't like it, if I'm not at the very front."

"Hurrah for people of good taste," said Saint-Urbain. "You'll assuredly be at the very front, Monsieur de Fatville, you couldn't be better placed for you or for us."

They went into the hall; they found the chandeliers illuminated and the violins plated the overture. The Baron and the Chevalier planed Fatville on the stage; they even had the malice not to give him a chair, and he was stupid enough not to ask for one, because he had been assured that well bred people never sat down at spectacles.

They were playing *Andromaque* and *Monsieur de Pourceaugnac*.[30] The performance of the two plays and Monsieur de Fatville's countenance diverted the company equally. Weary from the journey, he was visibly having difficulty standing up. Even the Vicomtesse entered into the pleasantry at his expense, because she had noticed that the Baron had a taste for it. Fatville gazed at Mademoiselle de Saint-Urbain almost continuously, with gestures as insupportable as they were ridiculous.

A large supper followed the comedy; they were at table a long time, and after having drunk to everyone's health—a custom hardly ever lacking in the country—they also drank to their inclinations. Mademoiselle de Saint-Urbain commenced, taking a glass of very good grace; she informed all the messieurs that they were permitted to drink to theirs, after which they would have to improvise a couplet of a song to celebrate such interesting toasts.

"Gladly," said the Chevalier. "I'll give the example."

He demanded a drink and sung *impromptu* to a familiar air. The couplet was thought very pretty, and the old Vicomtesse, turning to the Baron with an expression she thought very tender, asked him whether he had any inclination worthy of being sung in such good company.

---

[30] *Andromaque* (1667) is a tragedy by Jean Racine; it had an enormous success and established the author's reputation. *Monsieur de Pourceaugnac* (1669) is a comedy-ballet by Moliere, with music by Lully. It was common practice at the time for theatrical programs to follow a tragedy with a comedy, for the sake of light relief.

"The Chevalier de Livry," replied the Baron, "makes verses so easily that it's necessary not to be astonished if he has forestalled me; I shall repair my fault. The Vicomtesse poured liqueur into his glass herself. A moment later he sang, turning in her direction, and she was charmed to be able to flatter herself that the lines were for her; but as he finished the couplet he gazed tenderly at the Comtesse de Salgue.

"It's my turn, then," said the Comte, laughing, "also to make verses; as I'm the last, I've had more time than the others; I've made two couplets."

"So much the better," said Mademoiselle de Kernosy; we'll have all the more pleasure in hearing you.

The Comte, who had a beautiful voice, sang two couplets:

The amour that shines in your eyes
Forces everyone to yield;
It is too soft, too and wise
For anything to shield.

Burning for your divine charms
And for your slenderness;
Reason has no arms
To condemn my tenderness.[31]

Saint-Urbain and the Chevalier sustained that the words were too serious to be sung at table. The Comte replied that his heart had dictated them, and that he could not joke about

---

[31] In the earlier stories in the present collection I have been content to translate the literal meaning of snatches of verse, ignoring the rhymes (which are harder to contrive in English than in French). There are several instances in the present story, however where the rhymes are of greater importance than the literal meaning, and I have therefore improvised in those instances, in order to reproduce a similar rhyme-scheme.

something as serious as his tenderness. The Vicomtesse approved that sentiment

"But Monsieur de Fatville loves me," said Saint-Urbain, apprehensive that her aunt might throw herself into a conversation on sentiments, "and he doesn't even have a verse for me."

"I was only taught to make Latin ones," said Fatville. "I won two prizes for them at school."

"Well then, make a drinking song in Latin," said Saint-Urbain, "And explain it to me in French."

Fatville opposed the objection that he did not know the tune to which the others had just sung.

"Make a madrigal, then," she said, presenting him with a notebook.

Fatville thought he would be dishonored if he did not make some lines; he did not try to do it in Latin, of which he only knew a few words, but took the notebook and went to shut himself in a cabinet, in order not to be interrupted.

Meanwhile, the whole company went into another room, to which the oboists were summoned; they listened to them for some time, and then they danced all the petty dances. At the end of two hours, Fatville appeared, notebook in hand. Everyone thought he had gone to sleep, but he assured them that he had spent the entire time making verses.

"It will doubtless be an elegy," said Saint-Urbain. "Let's see it."

She took the notebook, all the pages of which were full of scribbles from top to bottom, and so scratched out that not a single word was decipherable.

"Read it yourself," she said to Fatville, returning the notebook to him. "It's incomprehensible."

"It's a rough draft," replied the councilor. "If I'd had room to write, I'd have worked marvels, because I was beginning to get into the swing, but I'll finish it tomorrow."

"Read us the beginning," said the Vicomtesse. "I like madly tender verses."

Fatville obeyed immediately, and read, while sitting next to a side-table on which there was a lighted candle, two lines that he had completed:

Iris, more beautiful than the day
Can she love, yea or nay?

He recommenced the two lines four or five times.

"What!" said the Comte. "Isn't it finished?"

"No," said the councilor. "Isn't it enough, for the time I put into it? And then, I've made a plan for the continuation of the madrigal."

"Truly," said Saint-Urban, these two lines are worth more than an entire madrigal."

"Mademoiselle de Saint-Urbain knows everything," replied Fatville, laughing with a self-satisfied expression. "And Monsieur le Chevalier, who is also a poet, what does he say?"

"I find the beginning so beautiful," replied the Chevalier, "that I have a desire to finish it. Lend me your notebook for a moment."

"You'll see the rest of the project there," said Fatville, proudly. "Make use of it if you wish."

The Chevalier drew away from the company, who amused themselves making the councilor dance, just as badly as he versified. Some time later, the Chevalier returned. "Let's see, Monsieur de Fatville, whether I've followed your design well. Here's the finished madrigal."

Everyone gathered around him, and he read the following lines:

Iris, more beautiful than the day
Can she love, yea or nay?
Do the most ardent fires and tender sighs
Touch her heart with glad surprise?
That's a question I ask of Amour.
The god replies, I made her to please
As for love, that's another unease;

All I have that's bright, gracious and sweet
I want to pour out incessantly for her;
Nothing can resist without certain defeat.
With those words he left, his wings a-whirr.
And is that, little god, the news I'm due?
I know all that even better than you!

That madrigal won great applause, and Saint-Urbain was grateful to the Chevalier for having made use of Fatville's stupidity in order to make her that gallantry, which the Vicomtesse thought not bad, because she only took it as evidence of the Chevalier's wit.

"You see," said Fatville, who heard the madrigal praised, "I knew that the end of the project was amusing."

Everyone laughed at the councilor's impertinence, and as it was late, everyone retired.

The apartment that was given to Fatville was next to the Baron's. That proximity furnished another opportunity to play the goblin, in order that Fatville would not dare to emerge from his room and would not perceive that people assembled every night in the Marquise's apartment after the Vicomtesse had gone to bed.

The next day, the Baron went to pay court to the Vicomtesse before the ladies had emerged from their apartment. He talked about his amour while pacing back and forth with great strides, almost without looking at her. The good lady was charmed by everything he did; she even assured herself that he was walking with the best grace in the world. As soon as he had withdrawn, all the ladies came into the Vicomtesse's room to render her a visit, and they did not leave until two o'clock, for the mid-day meal.

Afterwards, some played chess, others ombre and others trictrac. Fatville lost sixty louis, and although he seemed annoyed, the Baron, who won, said pleasantly enough that if that continued he would end up taking him in amity. At six o'clock they went into the hall for the play. *Les Horaces* and *Le*

Médecin malgré lui were rather well performed.[32] Fatville, occupied with his loss, neglected to put himself on the stage.

After supper, they summoned an actor and an actress who had charming voices, and musicians who played the bass viol well. Mademoiselle de Kernosy had all the operas by Lully brought that he had in her room; they sang the most beautiful pieces from *Proserpine*; she accompanied them on the harpsichord. Saint-Urbain sang with the Comte, who had a very sonorous tone of voice, and those two amiable persons were in perfect accord. They began with the Elysian Fields; the Baron sang in the chorus, in order not to appear to the Vicomtesse to be a useless actor.

At an hour after midnight, everyone retired to their apartments, and the two sisters went to the Marquise's bedroom, where they found the Comte and the Chevalier waiting for them. They talked about the passion of the Vicomtesse for Baron de Tadillac; Kernosy doubted that it would produce the effects for which they hoped; Saint-Urbain, more inclined to believe that which gave her pleasure, was convinced that their plans would be successful. The Comte and the Chevalier de Livry were hopeful, and the Marquise de Briance continued to give them her advice.

They were all talking with a great deal of application when Tadillac entered, clad in a bizarre red and black costume like those employed to represent devils in operas. He had a terrible bonnet from which snakes of a sort dangled, and if he had put on his mask he would doubtless have frightened the company, which had not expected that. However, they knew the design he had to frighten Fatville.

"You're as unwise as you usually are," the Comte said to him. "Let's hear, then, what you're going to do"

---

[32] *Les Horaces* (1708) was a pantomime by Jean Balon based on Pierre Corneille's tragedy *Horace* (1640); it is presumably the tragedy that is actually being performed. *Le Médecin malgré lui* (1666) is a famous farce by Molière.

"It's necessary," said the Baron, "that Mademoiselle Saint-Urbain puts on a costume that will be brought to her, and then you have only to follow me."

"I'm almost afraid of those clothes," said Saint-Urbain. "However, in order to deter Fatville, there's nothing I wouldn't try."

The Baron's valet de chambre appeared at that moment, dressed in a costume even more frightful than his master's; he had brought another almost similar to his, for the actors had a great many of all kinds. Saint-Urbain put it on over her own clothes and took an extremely ugly red mask.

Lambert, the valet de chambre, led the company to his master's room without them encountering any domestic; all of them had been in bed for two hours. Tadillac had discovered a communicating door that opened into Fatville's room. He had regarded it immediately as a favorable opportunity to carry out the design he had projected; the door having been sealed a long time ago, the councilor's apartment, which was contiguous with Baron de Tadillac's, was entered by another way. The apartments of Messieurs de Livry and that of the Marquise were nearby; all of that composed a detached building where one could make a great deal of noise without being heard in the rest of the castle, because it was necessary to go along a fairly long terrace to enter the other building that formed a sort of symmetry with it.

When they arrived at the Baron's apartment they went in very quietly, and Lambert, who wanted to prove himself worthy of the confidence with which his master had honored him, asked the company to wait for a moment. He went up on his own to the large uninhabited rooms above the building's apartments, and with a machine that he had invented, he made a loud noise, which imitated fairly well that of thunder.

Fatville woke up and went to open his window. Lambert, who heard him, set fire several times to powder that he had ready. The night was very dark, and the flash of that fire surprised Fatville greatly; he shut the window more promptly than he had opened it, very astonished to see lightning and hear thunder in the middle of winter. He went in search of his bed, and was still groping when Lambert came to open the communicating door that he had taken care to unseal. He entered the councilor's room holding a lighted black wax candle.

That light, suddenly succeeding obscurity, dazzled Fatville so well that, at first, he could not make out the face of the person holding it. He perceived his bed, threw himself into it and hid under the covers. Lambert did not leave him in that situation for long; he went to pull the covers away and made three great bows; then he lit four candles he had brought and placed them in various places in the room.

Fatville, summoning up all his courage, cried, in a voice that fear rendered faint: "Baron! Help!"

"Alas," replied the Baron, who was watching through the partition wall with the ladies, "It's impossible for me to get out; the goblins have just come in here."

Meanwhile, Lambert, after having lit the candles, approached the bed, and Fatville tried even harder to hide under his bed-head. Lambert took advantage of that moment to introduce the Baron and Saint-Urbain. As soon as the door was closed again, all three of them approached the bed, prevented Fatville from hiding his head, and made profound bows.

Lambert took a tiny violin from his pocket, and played a minuet, to which the cheerful goblins danced very lightly. Fear persuaded Fatville that they were rising up all the way to the ceiling. When the nocturnal ball was over, the goblin extinguished the candles and went out, without him being able to tell where they went, so he believed that they were spirits, which had disappeared. They refrained from making any noise in the room next door.

Lambert played the violin, and the Baron cried: "Monsieur de Fatville, I'm dead! The goblins are dancing here like the damned!"

Fatville dared not reply, but, everyone having heard him move, they judged that he had not fainted. He was scarcely any better off, though.

The goblins resumed the route to their room, in order not to be surprised in their spirit functions. The Baron summoned people as soon as he was undressed and told them the story of the goblins as he wanted it to be believed.

Fatville, who had not had the confidence to get up, finally made the resolution to go and open the door when he heard people talking nearby. The pallor of his face and his fear, naively expressed, convinced the Vicomtesse's domestics even more of the apparition of the spirits; there was not one who did not believe that he had heard the noises. Others swore that they had seen something black moving along the terrace. In sum, fear had the effect that it usually produces on the minds of simple folk and servants.

The Vicomtesse, who was fearful, had no doubt that a cat, which had been shut in her bedroom by accident that night, and had broken a porcelain vase while leaping around, was a goblin that had appeared in that form. To confirm that thought, the Marquise narrated that she had heard a large dog walking all night long. The Comte affirmed that he had heard something like a horse galloping, and the Chevalier swore that he had seen three huge guinea-fowl. Mesdemoiselles de Kernosy simply said that they had heard a frightful noise. The Comtesse de Salgues and Baronne de Sugarde, who had not seen or heard anything, were no less frightened. When it was broad daylight, everyone went back to bed; no one dared remain alone in her room. The goblins, fatigued by their nocturnal functions, got up very late. All day long, there was no talk of anything but spirits.

The domestics told the story to the actors, who had a strong suspicion as to what might have happened, by virtue of the borrowing of their costumes, but they had been paid by the Baron and Messieurs de Livry not to say anything; they were not even obliged to have heard the goblins of the castle, because they had been lodged in the poultry-yard, where there was a rather comfortable small building.

Fatville ate very little at the mid-day meal; he could not get over his fear. He talked about the lightness of the spirits who had danced, and a most frightful fashion of laughing. There were no acrobatic feats that he did not think he had seen performed, so much does fear fascinate the eyes.

"But how were you able to see all that?" the Vicomtesse asked him, "Since you had no light?"

"Oh, Madame," replied Fatville, "they lit great fires around my room; then everything disappeared in an instant."

"Did they dance to songs?" asked the Baron, with a serious expression.

"Oh, no," replied Fatville. "They had instruments, and I don't know whether they didn't have trumpets."

"I wouldn't know either," said the Baron," if I'd seen them dance as you did."

"In truth," said the Comtesse de Salgue, "I believe you're both a little mad."

That dialogue did not prevent everyone from believing in the apparition of the spirits. Some even affirmed that there were a thousand examples of similar things in books. In that regard, various stories were told, which redoubled the fear of the Vicomtesse and the domestics. Finally, they left the table, and in order to dissipate the trouble that the goblins had caused, the Marquise de Briance asked whether there was going to be a play.

"There ought to be one every day," said the Baron, who was beginning to assume the air of a man established in the house. "I'll go in search of news."

He came back a moment later to tell the ladies that the actors were ready to begin. They went into the hall, where *Mitridate* and *La Coupe enchantée* were performed.[33] Fatville went to sleep, fatigued by the bad night he had spent. They played games after emerging from the play and did not take long after supper to retire to their apartments; but no one any

---

[33] *La Mort de Mitridate* (1637) is a tragedy by Gauthier de La Calprenède. *La Coupe enchantée* (1669) is a comedy by Jean de La Fontaine based on one of his fables in verse, which formed the basis of several other dramatic adaptations.

longer went about the house alone, the slightest gust of wind provoked terrible alarms.

Fatville could not bear to return to the room where he had suffered so much; he was given another, where two lackeys were set to sleep along with him. The Comtesse and the Baronne slept together, and the Baron de Tadillac, in front of everyone, ordered Lambert to come and sleep in his room.

The Vicomtesse made two of her chambermaids sleep to either side of her bed, put a valet and two lackeys a little further away and her coachman by the door. Monsieur Pierre, her almoner, was ordered to place his bed by the fireplace, for the good lady feared that the spirit might enter by that route. The almoner, who was extremely old and greatly inconvenienced, represented in vain to Madame la Comtesse that the great draught that was engulfed in that vast chimney would finally render incurable a rheumatism that he had had for ten years, but nothing could bend her will.

"Truly," he said, looking at his bed, "I've always recognized that Madame has little consideration for her foster-brother."

What words! The Vicomtesse had overheard him, even though Monsieur Pierre had pronounced them very quietly. She did not want to react to the gaffe at that moment, but as soon as the company had retired, Monsieur Pierre had a terrible remonstration, and anger occupied the mind of the Vicomtesse so well that fear could no longer find room there.

The Baron de Tadillac waited until everyone was in bed, and, without losing any time, accompanied by Lambert, he went to make a great deal of noise in the large unused grain-lofts that reigned over all the apartments in the castle; that confirmed the belief in spirits, and the following day, everyone told the story of what they had heard in so many different ways that the Baron understood that it was sufficient to intimidate by sound and leave fear the care of diversifying the apparitions.

He had many other exercises than that of playing the goblin; it was necessary to persuade the Vicomtesse that he loved her, and his heart bore him to please Madame de Salgue. For several days his gaze had explained the passion that he had for her well enough; finally, weary of that mute language, he wrote her a note, and having gone to the Vicomtesse's apartment, he found her still at her dressing-table, and complimented her on her beauty. As he began to press her to determine her in his favor, the Marquise de Briance, the Comtesse de Salgue and the Baronne de Sugarde came in, with Mesdemoiselles de Kernosy and Messieurs de Livry. Fatville arrived a moment later, and they went to table. The councilor's fear and the noise of the goblins were the subjects of conversation almost throughout the meal. Then they played a few hands of ombre, and at six o'clock there was the usual diversion. *Cinna* and *Le Grondeur* were very well performed.[34]

The Comte de Livry gave his hand to the Vicomtesse in order to pass into the hall, the Baron having asked him to do it, because he wanted to have a favorable opportunity to approach Madame de Salgue. Having presented his hand to her, he said, in a low voice: "Know, Madame, the thing most important to my fortune; this note will instruct you." He gave it to her suddenly, and quit her as soon as they had gone in; the Vicomtesse was already looking to see what he was doing, away from her.

The Comtesse de Salgue put the note in her pocket, and Tadillac had the pleasure of seeing that the haste to read it did not permit her to wait until everyone left the theater. Having got up during an intermission in order to say something to Saint-Urbain, instead of returning to her seat she went to a side-table that supported a girandole. She opened the Baron's note and read it with an attention with which he was very content.

---

[34] *Cinna, ou La Clémence d'Auguste* (1641) is a tragedy by Corneille. The comedy *Le Grondeur* (1693) is by Jean de Palaprat and David-Augustin de Brueys.

"What, Madame," said Mademoiselle de Saint-Urbain, "you take the time during a play to read your letters?"

"It's one that I received this morning," said the Comtesse, "and I had forgotten to open it."

The actors interrupted that conversation and the Baron, taking advantage of a fortunate doze on the part of the Vicomtesse, never ceased looking at Madame de Salgue; she perceived that, and the embarrassment that he remarked on her face caused him not to despair of his happiness.

They did not play for long after supper; everyone retired rather early; everyone had need of repose and wanted to repair the bad nights that the goblins had caused, The Baron did not fail to make noises, in order to prevent them from recovering from their fear too soon. The racket did not last long, because the goblin was as weary as everyone else.

The next day the weather was fine; the sun appeared brightly and the Vicomtesse went to seek diversion in the garden. Having letters of consequence to write, she went to her cabinet after the mid-day meal, and Tadillac took advantage of that time to talk to Madame de Salgue.

"Have you thought about me," he said to her in a low voice, "since I dared to write to you the sentiments that you inspire in me?"

"What do you suppose that I think in your regard?" replied Madame de Salgue, looking at him tenderly. "You've come here with a design regarding which I am not yet enlightened; I only know that I have no part n it. Amour might have brought you to this castle; Mesdemoiselles de Kernosy are amiable and beautiful; it even seems that it's Mademoiselle de Saint-Urbain who prefers you."

"What an error!" said the Baron. "Madame, believe in a heart that has never burned for anyone but you. Amour has only had a part in my affairs since I have had the honor of seeing you; I will tell you, whenever you please...."

He was about to continue when the Vicomtesse, opening the door of her cabinet, obliged them to separate and approach the rest of the company, who were taking pleasure in watching the Marquise, Kernosy and the Baronne playing ombre with all possible prudence.

The Vicomtesse was only in the room momentarily; she asked for a candle, and returned to seal her letters. The Baron drew closer to Madame de Salgue; she had remarked the promptitude with which he had just quit her.

"So," she said to him, as they drew apart from the company slightly, "it's the Vicomtesse with whom you're in love, then? I wouldn't have suspected it."

"You know very well, Madame," the Baron said, "that it's necessary not to judge by appearances; you have too much part in my destiny for me to delay any longer in enlightening you." He informed her of his project for a solid establishment and the involvement he had with the Vicomtesse.

Madame de Salgue thought that her lover was right; she desired almost as much as he did an event that would arrest him in a province where she was obliged to remain.

Someone came to inform the ladies that the actors were ready. "Go, Baron," Madame de Salgue said to him, smiling. "Go and inform the Vicomtesse yourself; I consider that she has an obligation to me to teach you your duty."

As she finished speaking the Vicomtesse emerged from her cabinet; the Baron gave her his hand all the way to the hall of the theater, where Fatville was already placed. The entire company had noticed that, fearing to remain alone in the Vicomtesse's room, he had gone out with the ladies, without even thinking of offering them his hand.

Bérénice and *La Foire de Bezons* were performed.[35] After the comedy, they played petty games, in which intelligence nevertheless shone; a few stories were told, made up on the spur of the moment. Saint-Urbain, who was beginning to get bored, when she finished her narrative, decided to let Fatville finish the romance that she had begun. That renewed the joy; never had a man said so many ridiculous things in order to

---

[35] *Bérénice* (1670) is a tragedy by Racine. *La Foire de Bezons* (1695) is a one-act comedy by Florent Carton de Dancourt.

avoid speaking. Finally, supper got Fatville out of difficulty, and the Vicomtesse was able to pardon Saint-Urbain for not having continued her romance, because she had resolved, in continuing it in her turn, to display before the Baron the most beautiful sentiments in the world.

Once again, they retired early; the goblins left the inhabitants of the castle in repose. Fatville was in conversation with the Comtesse de Salgue, who had gone to her room, no longer being afraid since she had learned from Tadillac about the ploy of the goblins. In a short time, the Comte and the Chevalier were with Kernosy and Saint-Urbain in the Marquise's room.

As soon as they had gone out, the two amiable sisters asked Madame de Briance to keep the promise she had made them to give them an orderly account of her adventures, about which they had only talked confusedly, representing to her that none of her friends could have a greater interest in everything regarding her.

Sighing, the Marquise told them that telling the story would renew her dolors; nevertheless, she contented their curiosity, and began thus.

Madame de Briance's Story

You know. Mesdemoiselles, that I am the daughter of the late Marquis de Livry, whose house is one of the most ancient and most considerable in the province. I lost my mother a few months after my birth; my father was deeply touched by that loss, having always loved her tenderly. She was only twenty-four; she was beautiful, and people who want to flatter me say that I resemble her. You said as much when you did me the honor of coming to my house last year, where you saw her portrait.

My father, who was only twenty-nine, touched by a veritable affliction, constantly refused all the propositions that were made to him to remarry. He loved my brothers and me with an inexpressible tenderness. We were only children; the Comte was only four, his brother three and I was only six months old. All three of us were brought up with infinite care.

As soon as we had reached an age to be able to learn, my father quit the château where he had usually resided since my mother's death and took us to Rennes, where he had a beautiful house. He brought a skilled tutor from Paris to educate my brothers—and, I may say, for me too, because my father wanted me to learn Latin, geography, fable and history at the same time as my brothers; he did not believe that ignorance ought to be the lot of women. He had found, by virtue of the example of my mother, that a cultivated mind, in which knowledge is placed without affectation and without banishing natural charms, has ever-renewed graces, more durable than beauty and even more amiable in the commerce of life.

My brothers succeeded perfectly in their studies, and had a taste for learning that gave me a great deal of facility. People talked about us all over the city; we were taken into the most celebrated company, and people had an admiration for us that might have contributed greatly to spoiling us. My father made great expense; he was rich, and my mother had inherited an opulent house, distinguished by the nobility of her family. In sum, we had reason to be content with our fortune.

I was fourteen years old when Monsieur le Marquis de Briance arrived in Rennes; he was a seigneur who, fatigued by the cares of war and the Court, came to seek repose in our province, where he had lands of vast extent producing a large income.

He settled in Rennes, rendered visits to the important people of the city, and came to my father's house, where he found the preparations for an assembly that was to take place in the evening.

Monsieur de Briance said very gracious things to us, with the politeness that one acquires at Court. My father invited him to stay and assured him that the company would be honored by his presence; he accepted the invitation joyfully.

The conversation was lively; young people were arriving continually, dressed for the ball. The Marquis de Briance looked at them all, and always found in me some remarkable singularities, which he praised. My father who loved me passionately, was delighted to hear the praise that he gave me incessantly. Although Monsieur de Briance was not of an age to be desired as a lover, most of the beauties of the assembly envied me his conquest; the approval of a man who had spent his life at court appeared to them to have greater weight than that of people of the province

Monsieur de Briance still had a good enough appearance, although he was nearly sixty; he was well made, extremely rich and of distinguished rank; as he was not married, there was no young demoiselle who did not want to see him attached to her. For myself, I did not pay any attention to the flattering praise he gave me, only regarding it as an effect of politeness.

An hour before supper, Monsieur de Briance's groom game to ask for him; he came back after having spoken to him in the antechamber. "I shall, Mademoiselle," he said, addressing me, "introduce you in a moment to one of the most handsome gentlemen in France, provided that Monsieur de Livry gives me permission."

"Those permissions," replied my father, smiling, "are sometimes dangerous to grant; you are the master and you can, Monsieur, bring here whomever you please."

"The person that I mentioned to Mademoiselle de Livry," said Monsieur de Briance, "is the Comte de Tourmeil; he is only seventeen years old, but never have more beautiful hopes been seen. I shall not tell you anything about his person, you can judge that for yourselves; as for his valor, which is always the first quality to desire in a man of condition, I can assure you that I have been surprised by the marks of courage and even of conduct that he had shown in the three campaigns he has made. He wanted absolutely to follow me into the army when he was only fourteen; I consented to it, and I've had reason to be satisfied; I love him as if he were my son."

"Has he the honor of being related to you, Monsieur?" I asked him, with an impulse of curiosity inspired by the portrait he had just made of the Comte de Tourmeil.

"No, Mademoiselle," Monsieur de Briance replied. "His father was my friend; he was wounded on an occasion when I was in command, and died of his wound a few days later. Never has anyone been as touched as I was by the loss of a friend. As he died, he recommended his son to me, whom he loved tenderly; I promised to give him all my cares and my amity, and I have kept my word exactly."

Someone came then to say that supper was served. Everyone went into the great hall and sat down at table. I confess to you that I did not hear the door open during the feast without an emotion that I had never felt before; I always thought that it was the Comte de Tourmeil, and I felt a fundamental sadness, in spite of the preparations for the ball, which I loved, when I saw that we were leaving the table without my having seen the person who was causing me so much anxiety arrive.

The place destined for the ball was a large drawing room; there were a large number of chandeliers and girandoles, the light of which was reflected by large mirrors framed in the wall-panels, rendering the illumination brighter and making it seem larger. The drawing room was painted white, with monograms and other ornaments in gold; the furniture was the color of fire braided in gold. Several persons of good taste complimented my father on the magnificence of that apartment.

We were twelve young demoiselles and as many young men, the foremost in the city, who were to dance. The others took their places in the seats in the second row. Monsieur de Briance, accustomed to find himself at the most celebrated assemblies, nevertheless assured us that he had not seen any more agreeable. My brother, the Comte de Livry, commenced the ball with an extremely beautiful young woman, the daughter of the first president of Rennes; both were admired by the entire company; she went to take the Chevalier, who, being rather scatterbrained, as you know, without thinking of doing the honors of the ball, came to take me as soon as the courante was over. I danced with him, and we received copious applause, which my father was charmed to her.

It was my turn to take someone; I feared not choosing well. I approached my father; he nominated Monsieur de Briance; I went to curtsy to him; he begged me to excuse him, in favor of his age, and said, introducing me to the Comte de Tourmeil, who had just come in: "Here is a young man who will acquit better than me the honor you wanted to do me."

My father ordered me to take him; he danced with a grace that is particular to him, and I believe that I did not dance as well as the first time, because I was only occupied in looking at him.

His figure was slim, and better formed than one ordinarily is at seventeen, his noble air and his beauty beyond all expression. He had a large quantity of black hair, naturally curly, which descended all the way to a magnificent sash that he was wearing over his blue velvet coat lined with gold brocade. Monsieur de Briance had summoned him to my father's house, where there was a ball and the assembly was celebrated and he had not failed to adorn himself.

Tourmeil appeared so different from all our young people, although some among them were very well made, that everyone hastened to see him. Monsieur de Briance was delighted by the applause that he was given. How much justice my heart found in that! The trouble I had felt in seeing him dance was greatly augmented when I saw everyone admiring him; although that disturbance caused me some pain, it was agreeable to me, and I did not know yet whence it came.

At the commencement of the ball, we were all arranged with the ladies on one side and the men on the other. Tourmeil by virtue of an impatience for which I was grateful to him, was the first to disrupt that order; he traversed the assembly with a charming grace and came to kneel before me. Monsieur de Briance was very glad that he had made that gallantry, and made the remark to my father, who was next to him. That action on Tourmeil's part gave the example to all our youth;

everyone followed their inclination. My brother, the Comte, was obliged not to quit the person with whom he had commenced the ball, and The Chevalier entered into conversation with a rather pretty girl who was beside me.

Tourmeil, content with what he had just done, looked at me tenderly, and his words were as touching as they were full of wit. We always danced together; he affected only to take me. Monsieur de Briance having told him once to take the demoiselle with whom my brother had started the ball, Tourmeil replied to him with a gracious smile: "I cannot obey you, Monsieur, because my heart orders me otherwise." After those words he came to bow to me. That response pleased Monsieur de Briance infinitely, but my father thought it excessive for a man of his age.

The ball finished rather late; I found, however, that it ended too soon. Tourmeil testified to me the chagrin he had in quitting me, but with such a natural expression that my heart was deeply touched by it. He asked me for permission to come and see me the following day. I was in an embarrassment that did not permit me to reply to him very precisely. Eventually, we separated; my brothers, who were charmed by Tourmeil, asked him, on quitting him, whether they might have the honor of being his friends. He responded as a man who knew the world.

I went to bed, but the tranquility of sleep, which until that day had not deserted me, was suddenly interrupted. The idea of Tourmeil returned to me incessantly; sometimes I admired his person, and shortly afterwards I was anxious at having shown little intelligence in the conversation we had had together. Several thoughts presented themselves in a crowd to my imagination. Finally, I went to sleep, but Amour was, I believe in intelligence with my dreams; he only represented Tourmeil's advantageous qualities to me.

I got up late; my brother the Chevalier told me that in the afternoon he was taking the Comte de Tourmeil to see the most beautiful ladies in the city, and that he would bring him back to the house afterwards. Amour had resolved to engage me so forcefully, that it was impossible for me ever to break his chains.

I encountered Tourmeil and my brothers at the home of a friend of my aunt, whom we had gone to visit. They were getting ready to leave, but as soon as I came in, Tourmeil turned to the Chevalier and said: "You won't reproach me any more now for the anxiety I've had in all the places we've been; find, I beg you, a pretext to remain here."

The Chevalier informed me of Tourmeil's design and said that he would not go, because he hoped that the daughter of the lady of the house might play the harpsichord in response to my plea, and he had not dared to ask that favor of her. Her mother ordered her to play; we listened to her with pleasure. When she had played for some time, I asked her for a piece of which I was very fond; it was a saraband, whose antiquity had not caused it to lose its beauties.

"I wish that there were new words to that saraband," I said to the Mademoiselle, "for it's the air that I find the most likeable."

"The Comte de Tourmeil could satisfy you in that regard," said my brother. "Monsieur de Briance has shown us some of his verses this afternoon, which are charming."

Tourmeil was pressed to make verses for the saraband; he defended himself honestly, but I finally intervened, saying: "And will I also be refused, Monsieur?"

"No, Mademoiselle," he said, "I will obey you even before you command." He took the notebook that I offered him, drew away slightly, and returned it to me shortly afterwards. We found these words therein:

Between Apollo and the god who can inspire,
Divine Iris, do not manifest qualms
When I tell you that I love your charms;
The charming god who lends me his lyre,
Is not the one who makes me tell you so.

Tourmeil sang the verse himself, and the Mademoiselle accompanied him on the harpsichord. The entire company avowed sincerely that no one could play the harpsichord better, nor sing with more accuracy.

I returned to my father's house with my aunt; Tourmeil asked my brothers not to make any more visits. He arrived as soon as me, and gave me his hand on descending from the carriage. We found Monsieur de Briance playing chess with my father. He told Tourmeil that he was delighted to see him in such good company.

My father's house was always full of all the men of distinction the city had; people often supped there, and before and after supper they played cards or chatted; thereafter, everyone did what gave them the most pleasure. There were a great many people that evening; I watched them playing for some time, and Tourmeil only paid attention to me. He spoke to me sometimes, but with a respect that pleased me greatly.

Monsieur de Briance looked at us, spoke quietly to my father, and then called to Tourmeil. "Monsieur le Comte," he said, "I shall have supper here, but it would abuse Monsieur de Livry's generosity if we were both to stay."

My father begged Tourmeil to stay, but Monsieur de Briance gave him a sign to the contrary. Never has anyone been struck so terribly by words than Tourmeil seemed to be by that order. Approaching me as if he were saying adieu to me for a long time, he said: "I have been ordered to leave you, Mademoiselle. That misfortune is too sensible for me to obey Monsieur de Briance's orders for a second time." He went out as he finished speaking, and I found myself extremely touched by his departure.

As I left the table I saw my brother the Chevalier reading a letter that had just been given to him. He let my father go back to his study and made me a sign to remain. "Here," he said to me, "is a note that I beg you to read." I unfolded it and I found these words:

What have I done to attract my misfortune? Of the large number of people who were in your home this evening, I am the only one who was not permitted to remain; nothing equals my despair; it is necessary to have the sentiments that you inspire in me to know perfectly what torment your absence provokes.

The note was not signed, but I saw clearly that it was from Tourmeil; I blushed on reading it and returned it to my brother. "How does it come about," I asked him, "that you are charged with this commission?"

"A reason even stronger than that of my amity," the Chevalier replied, "obliges me to enable you see his note and the letter he has written to me. Tourmeil begged me not to interpret as lack of courage the obedience that he rendered to Monsieur de Briance; he protested that after that final respect he would never obey him again, and he said precisely that he would wait in his room to make known to him the chagrin that he had caused."

My brother remarked my astonishment at reading that letter. "Tourmeil," he told me, "is going to commit a folly that will lose his fortune. Monsieur de Briance loves him as if he were his son; he even said that he has made him a considerable donation. It would be very cruel if a thing of such little consequence caused him a veritable misfortune."

"I would be in despair," I replied, moved by Tourmeil's misfortune.

My brother the Comte came to see what we were doing; we told him why we were anxious. He did not hesitate for a moment. "Go, my brother," he said to the Chevalier, "prevent Tourmeil from quarreling with Monsieur de Briance. In order that it will be easier for you to do it, it's necessary that my sister write a few words to him."

I was in some difficulty, but we had no time to deliberate, and an advice of people of fifteen and sixteen years of age cannot finish in a very prudent action. The Chevalier gave me his notebook, and told me that he would bring it back, so that my letter would not remain in Tourmeil's hands. I wrote, approximately, these words:

Can you think of quarreling with Monsieur de Briance? I dare to beg you to continue to render him what you owe him for the amity he has for you. Is not seeing me or ne evening such a great misfortune? And if you find that it is one, after having told me so, why complain of it?

The Chevalier took the notebook and ran to see Tourmeil. I went back into my father's room. He was finishing a game of chess with Monsieur de Briance. I was thinking about Tourmeil; it appeared to me that a man who wanted to renounce his fortune in order to see me for a few hours more must feel a very veritable passion. How dangerous those reflections were! I knew that it was necessary to defend my heart against amour, but I believed that I could surrender it to gratitude.

The game ended, and Monsieur de Briance approached me; he continued to give me praise, as he had the day before. I responded so poorly that I had no doubt that he would have a low opinion of my intelligence. I let him leave the house without worrying about what he might think. I waited for the Chevalier's return with impatience. He did not come back to my father's room; I found him waiting for me in mine.

"Well?" I said to him, with an emotion I could not hide. "Will Tourmeil be sage? Have you convinced him?"

"No," the Chevalier told me. "All my efforts were futile. But as soon as he saw what you had written in my notebook, he seemed as submissive to your orders as he had been untouched by my advice. He kissed your handwriting a hundred times; never has a man so amorous been seen."

That overly faithful story touched me deeply; I was occupied by it for the rest of the night. Tourmeil was amiable, and of a birth equal to mine. *Who can forbid me to hope*, I said to myself, *that I might one day be very happy by virtue of the penchant I have for Tourmeil?* I got up, and ornamented myself with more care than I had ever done; that design to please him made me know better than anything else the extent to which he occupied my mind. He came to my father's house early, encountered many ladies there, had nothing for them but politeness, and I applauded myself a thousand times for having rendered him sensible.

It was proposed that we go to see the actors whom the carnival had attracted to Rennes; my father consented to let me go with those ladies. My brothers were among the party, and Tourmeil, who was only seeking pretexts not to quit me, was also there. We found the worst actors who had ever appeared in the province; the play, although badly performed, did not seem to me to have lasted long enough. Tourmeil was sitting next to me; I could not be bored.

Although the spectacle was bad, there were nevertheless a lot of people there. When it finished, everyone hastened to leave; my brother the Chevalier gave his hand to a lady of our company and, as he tried to pass through the door, a provincial who had the same design shoved him abruptly. My brother put out his arm, for fear that the lady he was with might be jostled. That action prevented the provincial from going out. He became angry and said something brutal to my brother, whose only response was to slap him.

We were nearby and saw that action. Tourmeil and the Comte approached promptly, not doubting that the Chevalier and the man were about to fight. My brother had drawn his sword, but we were very astonished to see the provincial, without any continuation of the quarrel, extract himself from the crowd and go away coldly, as if nothing had happened.

We returned to the house, and stayed there. Monsieur de Briance arrived, and told us that the affair at the theater was already being related all over the city. We had warned my father, in order that he would not hear it elsewhere. He gave my brother a severe reprimand for his promptitude, but it was as a gallant man, for he always treated my brothers more like his friends than his children. He was not so indulgent with me, although he loved me dearly; he said that daughters were obliged to obey more exactly than men.

Shortly after supper, my brother the Chevalier, who wanted to go and see a person of whom he was amorous, left his room; I perceived it. The quarrel he had had that afternoon made me anxious; I thought it imprudent of him to go out alone in the streets to expose himself to the resentment of the offended provincial, whom, we had learned, was a local man of quality who had arrived in Rennes a few days before.

I followed the Chevalier and told him that I would warn my father that he wanted to go out, unless he consented to be accompanied by five or six of our servants.

"That would be a fine entourage," he said, laughing, "to go in search of good fortune." He tried to escape, but in the end, seeing that I was resolved to tell my father, he said: "Oh, well, since you don't want me to go out alone, tell Tourmeil to come with me and we'll take an escort."

"I went back to the room and begged Tourmeil to go with the Chevalier; he offered to do so generously. I had a strong desire to double the escort that I had proposed to my brother when I saw that Tourmeil was in the party.

The Comte was playing cards with my father and Monsieur de Briance, so I dared not speak to him. My brother and Tourmeil went out alone, and were not a hundred paces from the door when they were attacked by six well-armed men. They were fired upon, but the obscurity of the night saved them; a single shot attained Tourmeil and pierced the sleeve of his coat. My brother and he drew their swords and defended themselves, without being able to see what they were doing. The moon rose, and by that faint light the Chevalier recognized the provincial, who, standing a short distance away, was encouraging his servants to that fine action.

My brother wanted to go to him, but he was backed up against the wall and had three men facing him. Tourmeil had two, and put one of them out of action; the thrust intimidate the second, and caused him to retreat further. Tourmeil, seizing that opportunity, ran like a lion at the provincial, who, after having defended himself for some time, received a thrust through the body and fell to the ground. Tourmeil immediately ran to help my brother, who only had a slight wound in the arm, but his sword had broken; Tourmeil saved his life by scattering his three enemies.

One remained in the place, dangerously wounded; the other two put up no resistance, seeing their master unconscious and bathed in blood.

"He's dead," said one of the assassins; "Let's save ourselves." Before fleeing, however, he struck Tourmeil from behind.

Two of the Chevalier's friends, returning from supper, recognized him in passing; they told the lackey who was carrying a torch to turn toward my father's house, to which they took the two wounded men.

People were still playing cards there; I was anxious, and I had a secret presentiment of some misfortune. I ran as soon as I heard a noise in the courtyard; my brother and Tourmeil, covered in blood, were already there. At that sight I uttered a frightful scream; my father heard it and came running; the company followed him.

The Chevalier, perceiving his emotion, said: "It's nothing, Father. I'm not dangerously wounded, but think, I beg you, of having Tourmeil helped; he has just saved my life."

Tourmeil had lost a great deal of blood; he was laid down on a bed in the antechamber. Monsieur de Briance and my father were equally touched by that horrible spectacle. I was inconsolable; I wept with all the dolor that amity and amour can inspire.

"How fortunate one would be," Tourmeil said to me then, in a faint voice, "to give all one's blood in order to have some part of those precious tears!"

I only responded by redoubling my tears. My father and Monsieur de Briance had not heard what he had said to me; they were speaking to the surgeon who had just arrived. He found my brother's wound slight, but he seemed uncertain regarding Tourmeil's, and assured us that if he were transported it would augment the danger considerably.

My father, touched by Tourmeil's merit and generosity, begged Monsieur de Briance to permit him to remain in his house until he was cured. The people he had sent to the location of the combat came back to tell him that the provincial had been taken away, but that they had brought back one of the wounded men, who was still there; my father ordered that his wound be dressed and that he be cared for.

That unfortunate fellow was so surprised to be well treated in the house of a man whose son he had just tried to murder that the following day, he asked to make a deposition as to how the action had happened; his deposition subsequently served to terminate the affair in favor of Tourmeil and the Chevalier; it related that the attackers were four cavaliers from the company of a brother of the provincial, with one of his friends, whose name he did not know; that the provincial was not dead, and that his two companions, no longer seeing anyone, had come back and carried him away; that they had also promised to come back for him, and that he was very astonished to have been carried away by other people.

What dolors there were for me that night! Tourmeil, almost dying in our interests, was present incessantly to my mind; I repented of having engaged him to go out with my brother. *He has saved his life*, I said to myself, *but at the sacrifice of his own, and I am the cause of it*. Those reflexions, followed by many others, put me in an inconceivable agitation.

Finally, daylight appeared; I went to see my brother; I was told that he was resting, that he would not be in bed for long, and would get away with having his arm in a sling for a few days. I sent someone to obtain news of Tourmeil, and learned that he had a slight fever. I almost dared not ask what state he was in; I always feared that I might learn something fatal, and that apprehension did not cease for a week after he was wounded. When the fever quit him, the surgeons assured us that he was out of danger, and rendered a measure of tranquility to my mind.

Although my father incessantly devoted care to the recovery of Tourmeil and the Chevalier, he did not fail to seek information. There were abundant proofs to convict the provincial, who was pursued criminally. He dared not remain in the city; one of his relatives had him transported, wounded through he was, to his country house, where he remained hidden while the lawsuit was investigated.

I was in a pleasant enough situation. Tourmeil was recovering; I saw him almost every day; my brothers took me to his room and sometimes obliged me to stay there. Both of them were sensibly touched by the service he had rendered us, and spared no effort to testify a perfect gratitude to him. They told me that my father could not choose a more amiable husband for me and a better family than Tourmeil's. They even promised me that they would speak to my father about him together as soon as he had recovered his health. That was his most ardent wish, and the hope he had of marrying me contributed more than a little to his cure.

"It seems to me, Mesdemoiselles," said Madame de Briance, interrupting herself, "that it is too late to continue telling you my adventures now, but I promise to finish telling you the story tomorrow, if what I have just told you gives you the curiosity to know the rest."

Kernosy and Saint-Urbain testified to the Marquise how interested they were in everything she had just told them, and that they would have a great joy in learning the sequel. After having conversed for some time about what they had just heard, they took their leave of the Marquise and retired to their apartment.

The story that the Marquise had just narrated renewed the memory of a passion that had acquired profound roots in her heart; time had not effaced the image of Tourmeil that amour had imprinted so forcefully there; the efforts that she made during a part of the night to dissipate that sad memory were futile; finally, sleep suspended her difficulties.

The next day, the weather was as fine as it can be in winter; for several hours the sun dissipated a part of the chill of that rude season. Messieurs de Livry and the Baron de Tadillac went hunting in the morning, and returned to the castle in time for the mid-day meal with a quantity of game. The beauty of the day gave the ladies the desire for an excursion in a wood that surrounded the garden. Baron de Tadillac wanted to give them the diversion of a hunt; Messieurs de Livry had the same complaisance, and they asked the Vicomtesse to send someone to the castle in search of two running dogs that had served them in the morning.

It was a singular pleasure for the ladies to see those messieurs, who were all marvelous shots, not missing their mark. The Vicomtesse admired the Baron's skill and incessantly gave him praise. Saint-Urbain, always attentive to persecuting Fatville, asked him why he was not shooting; she persuaded him that he gave the impression of being skillful in that exercise. The councilor, swelled with pride by that praise, took a gamekeeper's rifle and set about firing, but he did it so poorly that his shot, missing the target at which he was aiming by a long way, wounded a beautiful black cow that was walking tranquilly a little further away.

The Vicomtesse was furiously angry with Fatville; the black cow was her favorite; she took her milk and had named her Isis in order to mark her merit. That accident disconcerted him; and, annoyed in his turns by all the stinging words that had been addressed to him, he began to lose his appetite for the commerce with the nobility of which he had thus far had a great deal of inclination, and went back to the castle angrily. The company followed him and they fund everything ready, when they returned, for the performance of *Pénélope* and *Le Florentin*.[36]

That little play spread so much joy in hearts that no one wanted to play cards after supper, following the custom of previous evenings. They searched for an amusement requiring less application, and did not take long to find one. The Baron proposed to hold a kind of lottery, with the promise that each person would carry out what was written on the ticket that they drew. They made seven of them and folded them up. The Marquise de Briance drew them.

The first was for the Vicomtesse; it said: *You will tell a secret to someone in the company.*

"My secret is ready," she said, looking at the Baron slyly.

The second ticket was for Mademoiselle de Kernosy. She found: *You will recite a madrigal.*

"I've got away cheaply," she said. "It's only a matter of having a little memory."

The Marquise gave the third to Saint-Urbain, It said: *You will tell a story.*

"What a ticket!" said Saint-Urbain. "In truth, you might have done without giving me that one, Madame; I'd have preferred anything rather than that."

"We're never content with what happens to us," replied the Marquise. "But let's see the Baron's ticket: *You will provide a fête for the ladies in three days.*"

After it was read, he cried, like a frightened man: "Oh, how scared I am of obeying it poorly!"

The Marquise then gave a ticket to the Comte de Livry. He found: *You will criticize the story that has been told.*

"Now I'm Mademoiselle de Saint-Urbain's inspector," said the Comte. "I warn her that I shall be very rigorous with her."

---

[36] *Pénélope, ou Le Retour de Ulysse* (1684) is a tragedy by Charles-Claud Genest. *Le Florentin* (1685) is a comedy in verse by La Fontaine.

The Chevalier opened his ticket, which was: *You will fill in the end-rhymes*.

The Comtesse de Salgue found in hers: *You will listen to the others*. "So much the better, she said, "I'm well content to be the audience."

Baronne de Sugarde then read the one that had fallen to her; it read: *You will provide the end-rhymes*.

"Let's see," said the Marquise, what fortune has saved for me; she opened her ticket and read: "*You will sing a song*."

"That won't be difficult," she said, "But here's Fatville's ticket." She presented it to him. "Here, Monsieur, see what your fate will be. He found there: *You will seek news of Isis*. Everyone laughed at that joke, which renewed the memory of his skill in shooting; he suspected that the ticket in question had been made expressly for him. In fact, the Marquise had put it aside, in concert with the Baron, and had drawn the others at random.

"Let's go," said the Baron, sitting down. "Let everyone execute what the tickets say. It's up to me to organize it, since I'm conducting the game. Madame de Vicomtesse will have the goodness to commence."

She stood up gravely, and told him in secret, with a mysterious air, that she found him worthy of esteem. The Baron made no reply, in order to be a faithful depository of the secret that had just been confided to him.

Mademoiselle de Kernosy was applauded by the entire company for her madrigal, which she recited from memory. Mademoiselle de Saint-Urbain postponed telling her story until after supper, following the order that the Baron prescribed for her just as she was about to commence, in order, he said, that the company would have an agreeable amusement all evening and that Monsieur le Comte would have more leisure to criticize it.

It was then the turn of the Baron to acquit what his ticket had ordered. He fixed the day of the fête that he was to give, taking a reasonable time, in order to succeed in it better, and continued to give orders.

"Now, Monsieur le Chevalier, it's a question of your end-rhymes."

"I can't fill them," said the Chevalier, "since Madame the Baronne hasn't given them to me; you know that her ticket commands that."

She asked for someone to help her make them. The Chevalier picked up the pen, everyone made a word, and these end-rhymes were given to him:

ambrosia
 turbulence
offence
rosier

fever
vermilion
billion
reaver

thread
dead
light

destine
bright
goblin

That's not easy to fill in," said the Chevalier, on reading them. "Mademoiselle de Saint-Urbain would have done well to refrain from placing the goblin therein; I can see that he's destined even to torment the castle's poets."

Jokes were made on that theme. Madame de Salgue did not get up, but said to the company: "I'm fulfilling my duty in listening to the others."

Madame de Briance did not let the thought of the goblin drop; she waxed lyrical about the malignity of the spirit and the firmness of Monsieur de Fatville, who had braved several

of them with an incredible intrepidity, without any accident
happening to him. A moment later, she sang the following
words to a new tune in order to acquit the duty that had been
prescribed for her:

> *Importunate reason, no longer afflict my heart*
> *With the fears and suspicions by which 'tis pursued.*
> *My shepherd has promised me an ardor apart;*
> *Let me yield to the hope of amour's sweet dart,*
> *And the gladness of my life rescued.*

That song pleased infinitely; it was repeated several
times, so that the entire company knew the tune as well as the
words. Only Monsieur de Fatville did not sing; he had no ear
for music. The Baron asked him for news of Isis.

"If we were in Rennes," he replied. "I would only have
good news to give you; I would have had her wound dressed
by the finest surgeon, and Madame la Vicomtesse would no
longer be annoyed."

Everyone laughed at that pleasantry.

The Chevalier de Livry said that he had filled in the end-
thymes. Curiosity immediately attracted the company to hear
them, and he read the following sonnet:

> *The most charming of those who live on ambrosia*
> *Brings to the fires of my heart a turbulence;*
> *Of rivals and the jealous, the importunate offence*
> *Incessantly, in loving you, makes life less rosier.*
>
> *I sense that next to you my sweet fever*
> *Makes me fearful, pale and then vermilion;*
> *Your eyes deliver me shocks by the billion,*
> *That would tame the most dangerous reaver.*
>
> *The Fates, of my days, will cut the thread*
> *I'll go with pleasure to the land of the dead*
> *Without you, amour makes me scorn the light.*

That god awaits you to know how to destine
My ultimate fate, whether dark or bright,
Or to roam the earth in the guise of a goblin.

That sonnet was well received, although it had been delivered *impromptu* and had been composed in the same fashion.

"It only remains to criticize Mademoiselle de Saint-
Urbain's story," said the Comte, "although it requires the order of a lottery ticket to make it formal."

Saint-Urbain's turn having come to perform, she said
that, not having wanted to surprise anyone with fabulous adventures, they would be more content with a story taken from
Athenaeus,[37] a Greek author, of which there is a French tradition. Immediately after that prologue of sorts, she commenced
her narration.

The Story of Zariade

Histaspe, who commanded in Media, had two sons,[38]
whom the people called the children of Venus and Adonis,

---

[37] Athenaeus of Naucratis remains famous as the author of
Deipnosophistae [Dinner-Table Philosophers], which could be
reckoned a model for such "conversation pieces" as the present work; Book XIII includes a brief version of the story of
Otadis, daughter of Omartes, and Zariadres, the latter names
slightly altered by Saint-Urbain.

[38] Histaspe—the French translation of Athenaeus has
Hispaspe—appears to refer to Hystaspes, a Persian satrap of
the sixth century B.C., who did, in fact, have two famous sons,
the elder of whom was the emperor Darius the Great and the
younger Artabanus. The present story is, of course, entirely
fanciful.

because they had a divine air, were perfectly well made and their beauty attracted everyone's eyes.

The elder, whose name was Zariade, had given laws in his earliest youth to the entire country that extends from the Caspian Sea to the banks of the Tanais. One day, that Prince, fatigued while hunting, lay down under a clump of trees near a spring, the murmur of which cast him into a profound slumber and procured him a repose that was seemingly tranquil, but which bore many troubles into his heart.

In the dream he saw a young woman, magnificently dressed, lying on a bed of grass in the middle of a delightful garden. In her hand she was holding a little portrait that a god crowned with poppies had just presented to her.

"How handsome he is!" she exclaimed, gazing at the portrait—which was that of Zariade—attentively. He thought he could hear her speaking, and the voice of the young woman, who charmed him by the splendor of her beauty, made such an impression on her mind that nothing could ever efface the idea that he had conceived of her.

"What divinity!" he said, when he awoke. "Has Amour come to show her to me? Is it possible that it is only a vain idea? No, undoubtedly, that god has formed it in order to triumph over all hearts."

Zariade was no longer occupied with anything but the dream; his heart had been penetrated by it, and he was in despair at not being able to determine whether that beauty might only be a vain idea, of which the world had no original. He knew how to paint better than any man of his time, and, no longer able to live apart from that divine object, he made a portrait of the lovely individual, whose features amour had engraved so forcefully in his memory. He put it in his cabinet, and those who were introduced there admired it as a masterpiece of nature and art.

The Prince, believing that it might diminish his anxieties, related his adventure to his confidants and the grandees of his Court that he cherished the most. They sympathized with his amour, but that was a feeble remedy.

A foreign Prince who arrived in the Court, asked for permission to make reverence to him. Zariade received him in his cabinet; after the compliments usual in such an encounter, the great number of inestimable curiosities assembled in that place became the subject of the conversation. The foreign Prince, surprised to see the portrait, which Zariade had put in the midst of several pictures by the most famous painters of antiquity, paused for a long time to consider it, and in the astonishment into which the excellent piece had thrown him, he let slip the words: "Such a perfect resemblance has never been seen."

Those words immediately fixed Zariade's attention. Amour, joy and curiosity agitated him simultaneously. Having recovered slightly from his initial transport, however, which had caused him such an unexpected pleasure, he asked what fortunate clime had seen that divine person born.

"Her name is Otadis," replied the foreign Prince. "I have seen her a thousand times in the court of her father Omarte. He reigns over the provinces that are beyond the Tanais."

"What!" exclaimed Zariade. "It's the Princess Otadis, of whom I have heard mention as the most beautiful woman in Asia? My destiny is too fortunate."

The stranger who had announced such agreeable news was heaped with honors and presents. He was made the confidence of the dream and the passion to which it had given birth for the beautiful Otadis. The foreigner accepted the proposition that was made to him to accompany the ambassadors that Zariade wanted to send to Omarte's Court, and departed with them diligently, in order to reach that Court as soon as possible. When they arrived there, they asked for the beautiful Otadis in marriage for their Prince.

Omarte knew what Zariade's power was; he had heard mention of his virtues and his graces, but he did not want the Princess, his daughter, to be distanced from him. She was the heir to his Estates, and, having no male child, his intention was that she take for her husband a prince of her blood.

Otadis had not been able to resolve to make a choice so contrary to the sentiment that she contained in her heart; Amour had wounded her with the same arrow with which he had inflamed the handsome Zariade; the god of dreams had represented the Prince to her with the charms that seduced hearts, and the Princess, faithful to that beautiful idea, scorned all those who were presented to her as husbands. Nothing was comparable to the object with which her imagination was filled; she could not love others; he was not a work of nature, the gods had formed him.

However, the foreign Prince whom Zariade had charged with seeing Otadis on his behalf asked for an audience, which was granted to him. While prostrating himself before the Princess, he said that Zariade, son of Histaspe, sovereign of Media, the most handsome of all men, assured her of his profound respects; that he had sent him to inform her of the ardent desire that he had to possesses her since the gods had enable him to see her supernatural beauty, alone capable of rendering him happy, in a dream.

The conformity of their destiny began to interest Otadis in Zariade, but how astonished she was when the foreigner, presenting her with the portrait of the Prince, showed her that he was the same one that Amour and slumber had presented to her, and the idea of whom they represented to her continually. What was then her dolor because her father wanted to send the ambassadors away without granting the request that they had made. Her passion obliged her to make that confidence to the generous foreigner who appeared to be so zealous on Zariade's behalf.

A short time afterwards the ambassadors had their audience of dismissal; he returned with them, taking their master the sad news of Omarte's refusal; but he calmed the anger that the Prince allowed to carry him away by a faithful relation, which he gave him in private, of everything that the beautiful Otadis had said in his favor and the veritable sentiments of her heart, the secret of which she had revealed to him.

Zariade, transported by amour, raised troops and conducted them diligently to the banks of the Tanais, in the hope of either forcing Omarte by his valor to grant him the Princess, his daughter, or rendering himself his master, at whatever cost. He had several bridges of boats constructed over the river, in order for his army to pass over it more easily, and in the meantime sent the foreigner to Omarte's Court, where he was to see Otadis secretly, and instruct her of everything that was in preparation for the success of that enterprise.

The indefatigable Prince went incessantly to the banks of the Tanais in order to encourage the laborers. Having to employ himself one day to maintain good order among them, in order to prevent a delay that might have prevented their work from being promptly concluded, he saw a good-looking man arrive in a small boat. It was his favorite, the foreign Prince.

"Well?" he said, embracing him. "Has the divine Otadis approved the design that my amour has formed for her?"

"Yes, Sire," replied the foreigner. "The adorable Otadis will be yours if your heart regulates her destiny, but there is no longer time to hide from you that her marriage is to be celebrated in three days, and you would make the conquest of all Asia thereafter in vain. Omarte is absolute; Otadis dare not resist his orders. After a superb feast, she will receive a golden cup from her father's hand, as is the custom of this land, and she will present it to the fortunate mortal who has been chosen to be her husband."

"Let us go, then, to receive that precious cup," cried the handsome Zariade, transported by amour and anger. "Let us go and disturb that cruel wedding, or die at Otadis' feet."

From then on, no longer consulting anything but his despair, suddenly abandoning his army, he departed secretly, only accompanied by the foreign Prince and a small number of men. After having traversed the Tanais on one of the bridges that had just been completed, he threw himself into a small chariot harnessed to eight horses of such prodigious speed that in three days he arrived in Omarte's Court, where he put on garments similar to those worn in that country, for fear of being noticed.

Having entered the palace, he penetrated into the hall of the feast, where he saw Otadis, who was already holding the golden cup, which Omarte had just given to her. The chagrin of being so close to the moment that would decide his destiny caused her to shed a few tears, which further augmented her beauty. She left the festival hall, only accompanied by her maidservants, in order to go, in accordance with custom, to pray in the next room.

Zariade followed her, entered that chamber adroitly and approached the Princess. "Here I am," he said, "ready to deliver you from tyranny."

Otadis would have taken him for a god coming to her aid if she had not recognized him, but his features were too well engraved in her heart. She gave him the golden cup that determined the choice of her husband, and, consenting to his abducting her, they both ran away by way of a staircase where few people might encounter them. From there, traversing the palace gardens, they reached the door where the chariot of the fortunate Zariade was waiting for them with the escort and the foreigner, his favorite.

As soon as they had mounted it, they made such prodigious diligence that they were on the banks of the Tanais before Omarte, afflicted by the abduction of his daughter, was able to discover who it was that had undertaken such a temeritous enterprise.

They passed over the river on the previously mentioned bridge of boats. Without losing any time, Zariade took the Princess to his camp, where their marriage was celebrated with all imaginable magnificence. That union filled the entire army with joy. Otadis made great largesse, and Zariade was at the peak of happiness, by virtue of the possession of a Princess as virtuous as she was beautiful.

The two spouses sent ambassadors to Omarte to ask his pardon and to ask him to give his consent to their union. He knew how worthy Zariade was of the Princess, so he signed the peace, which brought the felicity of the two young spouses to its culmination.

It was thus that Mademoiselle Saint-Urbain ended her story. The Comte de Livry, far from criticizing it, as his ticket had ordered him to do, praised it. The Marquise de Briance and the Chevalier de Livry said that the story was extremely embellished by ornaments that had been added to it very appropriately; that an ancient author they had read reported it too succinctly, and that it was more agreeable to ornament the narration of an implausible story with a few embellishments than to report it simply, with exactitude, and to render it flaccid by too much fidelity.

Madame la Vicomtesse, refined, as usual, criticized Otadis for allowing herself to be abducted by her lover and having married him without her father's consent. Saint-Urbain replied that it was not permissible to alter the facts, and that in those days, amour pardoned everything, but at present, people were more sage.

"You could have done whatever you want," said the Vicomtesse, "if you had mingled enchantment with it; it would have amused me more, for I confess that those sorts of fictions please me greatly."

"If I had known your taste, Madame," said Saint-Urbain, "I would have served you in accordance with it."

"It isn't too late," said the Comte de Livry, "to give that satisfaction to Madame la Vicomtesse, and if she will permit it, I will tell her a tale of enchantment shortly."

The Vicomtesse seemed delighted; all the ladies showed the same enthusiasm, and Fatville asked whether it was a true story; if not, he would go to bed.

He was assured that he could go to bed in all security.

As soon as he had gone, Madame la Vicomtesse called for silence, and the Comte de Livry commenced as follows.

Bearskin

There was once a King and a Queen who had only one daughter, the only one of several children they had had that they had been able to conserve. The Princess compensated them by the beauty and charms of her person for the dolorous loss of so many young princes. She was called Noble-Thorn. The infinite cares that were taken in her education succeeded marvelously and at twelve years of age she was as knowledgeable as her masters. Her intelligence and her rare beauty were the cause that her hand was sought by all the marriageable Princes that the Kings of those days had.

The King and the Queen, who adored her, dreaded losing her and were in no hurry to grant the urgent wishes of the Princes, her lovers. Noble-Thorn, content with her lot, was afraid herself of a marriage that would distance her from the King and the Queen, whom she loved tenderly.

The rumor of the beauty of Noble-Thorn was carried all the way to the Court of a King of Ogres, whose name was Rhinoceros. That Prince, powerful in lands and riches, had no doubt that the Princess would be given to him as soon as he had requested her, and he dispatched his ambassadors to the King, Noble-Thorn's father. They arrived at his Court and requested an audience, under the pretext of renewing an old treaty of alliance that had once been made between the two crowns.

People were diverted at first in seeing such extraordinary individuals; the young Princess herself laughed wholeheartedly. Nevertheless, the King ordered that they be received with such magnificence. On the day of the audience the entire Court strove to appear superb, but the joy soon turned to sadness when it became known that King Rhinoceros was asking for Princess Noble-Thorn.

The King, who was listening to the ambassador attentively, was so surprised by the proposal that he remained mute. The ambassador, fearing a refusal, hastened to continue speaking, assuring the King that if he did not grant his daughter to

Rhinoceros, he would come in person at the head of a hundred million ogres to ravage the kingdom and eat the entire royal family.

The King, who knew the fashion in which ogres act, had no doubt that the effect would soon follow the ambassador's threat. He asked for a few days grace, in order to prepare his daughter to receive the honor that Rhinoceros was doing her, and terminated the audience abruptly.

The good father, mortally afflicted by not daring to refuse his daughter, retired to his cabinet and summoned her. The Princess flew there, and when she learned the sad fate for which she was destined, she uttered dolorous cries, and threw herself at her father's feet, imploring him to order her death rather than such a marriage.

The King took her in his arms, wept with her, and told her about the threat that the ambassador had made.

"If you refuse, my daughter," he added, "we will all die, and you would have the horror of seeing us devoured by the cruel Rhinoceros."

The Princess, as frightened by that image as by her frightful marriage, consented to give her hand, wanting to sacrifice herself in order to save the King, the Queen, and the entire kingdom; she went herself to reassure the Queen, her mother, who was in a deplorable state. Noble-Thorn, resolved to do anything for persons so dear, consoled her mother by means of everything plausible that she could imagine, and with a confidence that rendered her even more admirable, she watched the preparations for her marriage and marched to the altar, where the ambassador was waiting for her, with a modesty that drew cries and sobs from everyone.

She departed with the same firmness, and only took with her one young woman, whom she loved very much and who was very attached to her; her name was Coriande.

As it was many leagues from that realm to that of the ogres, the Princess had time to open her heart to Coriande and allow her to see the excess of her dolor. Coriande, moved by the Princess's misfortunes, shared her pain, unable to give her any other consolation, and swore to her that she would never abandon her. Noble-Thorn, sensible to the rare and tender amity that the young woman was showing, felt her pain less as soon as it was shared.

Coriande had not dared to tell the Princess that she had gone to find the f\ay Azerole, Princess Noble-Thorn's godmother, in order to tell her about the frightful destiny that awaited her, and that she had found the fay so angry that no one had consulted her about the affair that she had even told Coriande that she would never involve herself in the affairs of Noble-Thorn.

Coriande did not think it appropriate to augment her mistress's chagrin by telling her that, but she was occupied by it, and secretly deplored the fate of the Princess, thus abandoned by her godmother. The length and the fatigue of the journey did not diminish Noble-Thorn's beauty at all; the ogre on seeing her, was so surprised by it that he uttered a cry that made the isle on whose he had established his abode tremble.

The Princess fainted with fear in Coriande's arms, and Rhinoceros, who was in the form of the animal whose name he bore that day, put her on his back, with Coriande, and ran to his palace, where he imprisoned both of them. Then he resumed his natural form, which was scarcely less frightful, and helped Noble-Thorn with urgency.

When the Princess opened her eyes and found herself in the monster's hairy arms, she could not find the strength to hold back her cries and tears. The ogre, who did not think that anyone could find him disagreeable, asked Coriande what was the matter with her, and whether she thought that such a little crybaby could please. Coriande, fearful of the ogre's wrath, replied that it was nothing, and that the Princess was subject to the vapors.

Noble-Thorn had closed her eyes in order to spare herself the horror of seeing her hideous husband, and the ogre, who thought that she had fainted again, felt a slight surge of humanity. He went out, and ordered Coriande to look after her; Coriande assured him that she only needed to rest.

The ogre left the Princess, and went out to hunt bear, his favorite diversion. He counted on catching two or three for Noble-Thorn's supper.

As soon as he had gone, the Princess threw her arms around Coriande's neck, weeping. The poor young woman, moved by her mistress's dolor, racked her brains, and, seeing several bear skins that the ogre had amassed in order to clothe himself in winter—for he was very miserly—she advised the Princess to hide herself under one of them. Noble-Thorn consented to that, after assuring Coriande of the difficulty she had in leaving her alone, exposed to the ogre's fury.

Coriande therefore chose the most beautiful of the skins, and set about sewing the Princess inside it. But what a marvel! Scarcely had the skin touched Noble-Thorn that it applied itself of its own accord to the Princess, and she appeared as the most beautiful she-bear in the world.

Coriande attributed that unexpected aid to the fay Azerole; she said as much to the Princess, who was convinced of it herself, for, in her metamorphosis, she had conserved the understanding of speech and all her intelligence.

Coriande opened the doors and let out the she-bear, who was impatient to go. Coriande had no doubt that the fay was guiding her, as she had contrived the metamorphosis. As soon as she could no longer see her dear mistress, she abandoned herself to regrets, but after an hour she heard the ogre coming back and pretended to be profoundly asleep.

"Where is Noble-Thorn?" cried Rhinoceros, in a thunderous voice.

Coriande acted as if she were waking up, and rubbed her eyes, as if she had no idea where the Princess was.

"What!" said the ogre. "She's gone out? That's impossible, for I have the key to my door."

"Yes, yes," said Coriande, pretending to believe that the ogre was putting on an act, "it's you who have eaten her, and you'll be severely punished for it; she was the daughter of a great King; she was the most beautiful person in the world;

she wasn't made to marry an ogre; you'll see what will happen to you."

The ogre, bewildered by that accusation and the cries with which Coriande accompanied her reproaches, swore that he had not eaten the Princess, and became so angry that Coriande's feigned dolor was changed into a very real anger, for the ogre threatened to eat her if she did not shut up.

She did, in fact, shut up, and pretended to search for the Princess, which appeased the fury of Rhinoceros somewhat. He even searched with her for a week; but Azerole had ordered matters well. She had guided the she-bear invisibly, and the unfortunate Princess had found an abandoned boat on the shore, into which she had climbed. But as can be imagined, without the aid of the fay she would have perished a thousand times, for once the Princess was in the boat, she sensed it drawing away from the shore.

Frightened, in spite of her woes, by the present danger, but not seeing any remedy for it, she lay down and went to sleep.

When she woke up she found herself on the edge of a meadow so pleasant and so abundantly dotted with flowers that the sight of it cheered her up. The she-bear, who felt the boat stop, leapt into the meadow, and thanked the gods and the fays for having brought her to such a beautiful place without any accident.

Her first concern, once that duty had been fulfilled, was to search for the wherewithal to live, for she had a great appetite. She advanced across the meadow and went into a beautiful forest, in which there was a hollow rock carved in the form of a cavern, and right next to it a pretty spring that ran into the meadow, and large oak trees laden with acorns.

The she-bear, who was not accustomed to that nourishment, was scornful of it at first, but when her hunger became more pressing she tried to eat some of them. She found them very good. Then, having slaked her thirst at the spring, she resolved to retire into the cavern by day, in order to avoid evil encounters, and only to emerge at night. Another reason also determined her to do that; while she was drinking at the spring she had seen her reflection in its water; her horrible ursine form had frightened her; it would not have taken much to make her regret her own, even though she would have been obliged to become the companion of Rhinoceros.

That reflection consoled her, however, and made her desire to accept her situation and her ugliness with more tranquility. As she had a great deal of intelligence and reason, she understood that ugliness is not such a great misfortune when beauty can only cause difficulties. The she-bear moralized in that fashion in her cavern; she drew veritable wisdom from it, and began to be content with her lot.

That country was governed by a young king who still had his mother; no one was as handsome, as charming and as filled with good qualities as that Prince. He was adored by his subjects, respected by his neighbors and greatly feared by his enemies; just, clement and magnanimous, moderate in his victories and great in adversity, he had all the virtues. The only complaint made against him was that he was indifferent to beauties; but he feared himself, because he knew that he had a very sensitive soul and he had had been told by his mother the Queen that a King must know how to reign over himself before reigning over others. His face was as perfect as his soul, so all the women of his Court burned with the desire to inflame him. His name was Zelindor, and his homeland the realm of Felicity.

If the beautiful she-bear had known the name of that realm she would not have been so astonished to find herself so content with her condition, for it was one of the privileges of that cherished land for people to be happy there.

Zelindor, being young and gallant, gave or received fêtes every day; he often went hunting, because that image of war pleased his magnanimous soul.

The she-bear had already being living in that region for three months when Zelindor came to hunt in her forest. Contrary to her custom, the she-bear had emerged from her cavern by day in order to take a walk along the sea shore. She was returning home slowly, respiring the air perfumed by the flowers with which the meadow was doted, when she perceived the entire hunting party in front of her. She forgot the danger that a she-bear is running on such an occasion, and stopped in order to watch to pass by.

All those accompanying the King recoiled in fear at the sight of that terrible beast. The brave young King was the only one who advanced, sword in hand, in order to pierce her.

The she-bear, seeing him approach, humiliated herself at his feet and lowered her head in order to await the thrust. Zelindor, touched by that action, struck the she-bear lightly with the blade of his sword, without doing her any harm. Then she got up and began flattering him by means of the mimes she thought mot agreeable, kissing the King's hand and licking it.

The King, even more surprised by the beast's caresses, forbade those who had approached to fire at her; he even detached a beautiful sash that was passed over his shoulder and circled his waist, and put it around the she-bear's neck; she allowed him to do it. He conducted her thus, personally, all the way to the palace, and ordered that she be put in a little garden of flowers adjacent to his cabinet. The she-bear understood very well everything that was said to her, but she could no longer pronounce a word, and that discovery cost her tears.

As soon as she was in the garden the young king came to see her and gave her something to eat with his own hand. Her heart, which had not changed along with her form, was moved when she considered the beauty of the young King. *What a difference there is*, she said to herself, *between the frightful Rhinoceros and this handsome Prince!* But, by turning the same reflection on herself, she immediately added: *What a horror my face is! What use is it to me to find him so handsome?* The desperate she-bear shed even more tears at that moment than she had shed on perceiving that she was mute.

She quit what the King had brought her and went to lie down on the beautiful grass that bordered a magnificent pool in the garden. Zelindor, who could see that she was sad, came to sit next to her, and said the most touching things to her. The poor she-bear found her despair redoubled by that and fell backwards, almost dead. The King, touched by her condition, gathered water in his hand, sprinkled his she-bear's muzzle with it, and did his best to help her. The she-bear opened her eyes, which she had bathed with tears, and, her two forepaws taking the King's hands, she shook them respectfully, and seemed to be thanking him.

"But you're charming," said the young Zelindor. "Why, my good she-bear, you seem to understand me!"

The she-bear nodded her head affirmatively.

The King, transported by the joy of discovering her reason, embraced her. The she-bear defended herself modestly and recoiled.

"What!" said the prince. "You flee my caresses, my she-bear? Oh, that's pleasant. What do you want, then? Don't you like me?"

At those words, in order to hide her disturbance, the she-bear prostrated herself on the grass at Zelindor's feet; then, getting up immediately, she broke a branch from one of the orange trees that ornamented the perimeter of the pool, and presented it to the King.

That prince, more charmed than ever by his she-bear, ordered that she receive great care, and lodged her in a beautiful grotto of rocks surrounded by statutes, where there was a bed of grass to which she could retire at night. He came to see her every day, talked about her to everyone, and was mad about her.

The she-bear made sad reflections when she was alone. The handsome Zelindor had rendered her amorous, but what means did she have of pleasing him in such a hideous form? She could not sleep or eat. She spent her days scratching the most beautiful verses in the world on the trees of the garden with her claws; jealousy was added to her amour. She was mortally melancholy, except when the King came to see her.

Another anxiety came to her: perhaps the King was married. She was herself, in a way, to Rhinoceros, whom she found even more horrible since she had seen the charming Zelindor.

One evening in the moonlight, retracing all her misfortunes on the edge of the pool, to which she often came because the young King always walked there, she shed so many tears that the water was troubled by them. A large carp, which was not asleep, appeared on the surface.

"Ursine beauty," she said to the Princess, "don't be so afflicted; the fay Azerole is protecting you, and will render you as happy as you are beautiful." Then, leaping lightly on to the grass, the carp appeared as a beautiful lady, tall and majestic, and magnificently dressed.

The she-bear threw herself at her feet. "Have courage, my daughter," said the fay Azerole. "I've tested your patience long enough; the recompense will come. You are not married to the ogre Rhinoceros, and you will marry the handsome Zelindor. Keep the secret for some time yet; every night you will quit your bearskin, but it's necessary that you put it on again during the day."

Then the fay disappeared, and, as midnight chimed, the bearskin quit the Princess. How many thanks she rendered in her heart to her kind godmother! How much pleasure and joy she felt! She spent the night picking flowers; she made garlands and wreaths of them, which she attached to the door of her lover's cabinet.

The time that had been prescribed to her without a limit gave her impatience, but in order not to prolong it further by her fault, although it cost her a good deal, she put on the bearskin again at daybreak. She wrote charming things, sometimes about her jealousy, sometimes about her tenderness; her heart furnished her with entirely new thoughts and expressions that delighted the King, for he read them.

He had permitted people to come to see the she-bear; the crowd displeased her. When one has a grand passion, only solitude is agreeable. She wrote that to the young King; the verses that expressed the sentiment were so tender and so delicate that he was charmed by them and had the garden closed; no one but him entered it.

For his part, the young prince, reflecting on the intelligence that he found in the she-bear, dared not admit to himself that a invincible penchant attracted him toward her; he rejected that thought, and only wanted to find himself capable of humanity and compassion. However, he no longer liked hunting; he found no amusement anywhere, and only had pleasure on seeing his she-bear. He talked to her about a hundred things; she scratched, in the sand or on tablets that he gave her, opinions, advice and maxims full of sagacity.

"But you're not a she-bear," he said to her one day. "In the name of the gods, tell me who you are. Are you going to refuse the confession much longer? You love me, I can't doubt it; my happiness even depends on believing it, but save my glory by preventing me from responding to the amour of a she-bear. Admit to me who you are, I implore you, by the very amour that you know so well."

The moment was pressing; the she-bear had a great deal of difficulty resisting, but the fear of losing her lover made her choose to annoy him; she only replied by means of leaps and capers, which made Zelindor sigh bitterly. He went away, his heart in revolt against himself in finding himself capable of such a ridiculous passion.

In despair at having been able to imagine that the she-bear might be a reasonable person, Zelindor resolved to rid himself of that monstrous passion, and, recommending that great care be taken of the she-bear, he decided to travel. He wanted to depart without seeing her, and, only taking two of his favorites with him, he mounted a horse and drew away from the palace.

He was scarcely in the forest where he had encountered the she-bear when, retracing that adventure, he ordered his favorites to go away and leave him alone. The young courtiers were extremely attached to him and afflicted to see that his humor had been so changed for some time. They obeyed him, and drew apart a little way.

The young King dismounted from his horse and, lying down at the foot of a tree, he deplored his singular destiny and fell into a profound reverie, from which he was extracted by the tree against which he was leaning, which trembled violently and opened up to allow the emergence of a lady of rare beauty, so brilliant with precious stones that the King was dazzled by her.

The prince stood up precipitately and bowed profoundly to the fay—for he had no doubt that that is what she was.

"Let time act, Zelindor," she said to him. "Do you believe that a King who protects us can ever be unhappy? Return to your palace; run to save from her despair the one whom too much delicacy has caused you to abandon."

The fay disappeared after those words; the King, fortified by an oracle that his heart did not want to doubt, remounted his horse precipitately and returned to his apartment as rapidly as possible.

He went into the garden immediately, and, not seeing the beautiful she-bear there, he ran to search for her in her grotto.

The unhappy Princess had learned of the King departure from those who were caring for her while they were conversing with one another. She had not seen him for three days; that catastrophic news overwhelmed her; she fell unconscious on her bed of grass, and it was in that disastrous state that the King found her. With what haste he approached her! She was as cold as ice; her heart had almost no movement. The King uttered piercing cries and bathed her with his tears, calling her by the most tender names.

The sound of his voice penetrated all the way to her soul, and retained it just as it was about to fly away. She opened her eyes and extended her paws to embrace her lover, believing that she was about to die, but the tenderness of the King and the forgiveness for which he was asking recalled her to life. He implored her to forget his curiosity, and swore to her that he adored her. That confession filled the poor she-bear with joy; they spent a delightful day, and although only the King spoke, the she-bear nevertheless did not weary of hearing him and of responding to him in her fashion.

She showed the young King what she had written during his absence; he was enchanted by it. In fact, such a fortunate mixture of intelligence and the natural, or reason and passion, had never been seen; in sum, it resembled the famous *Lettres d'une Péruvienne*, a masterpiece of sentiment that the public still admires.[39]

Zelindor only stopped reading to throw himself at the feet of his tender mistress and to kiss her paws.

Insensibly, the hours went by; the lovers had never measured them accurately, endless in absence and too rapid in pleasure. Midnight chimed and the bearskin fell away, leaving the divine Noble-Thorn exposed. She had a magnificent robe, and her beautiful hair for coiffure.

"What a prodigy!" cried the King. "What! It's you that I was fleeing, you that I feared to love?"

The ashamed Princess made no response; her modesty embellished her further. She was also fearful that the fay Azerole might reproach her for having forgotten herself sufficiently to allow the secret to be penetrated by her lover. She was still in that anxiety when the fay appeared.

"Fortunate lovers," she exclaimed, "enjoy the fruit of your troubles from tomorrow on; that is enough of torments." To the Princess, she said: "You, my daughter, give your hand to your lover in recompense for his tenderness; and you, handsome Zelindor, go to prepare everything in your Court to marry this Princess. Have no fear, after your union, of any metamorphosis; but it is necessary for Noble-Thorn to submit to that law for another twenty-four hours. Go, let her sleep; she needs repose; I will take care to render her worthy of you."

---

[39] This reference must have been introduced into the Garnier reprint by its editor, as the work in question, an epistolary novel by Françoise de Graffigny, was not published until 1747.

The young King left, leaving the fay and the Princess together. He was transported by a joy so vivid that instead of going to bed he woke up the entire palace, assembled the council and said that he wanted to get married the following day, that it was necessary to prepare his throne and illuminate the entire castle, especially the gallery. He also ordered all the ladies to dress magnificently. From there he went to see his mother, the Queen, in order to invite her to his wedding.

The Queen, who had just learned that her son had made everyone wake up, seeing him excessively animated and talking with a gaiety that he had lost a long time ago, feared that some accident had happened to him. What he said to her, however, was so precise, so coherent and so sensible that, apart from the precipitate marriage, she found him as she had always seen him; she only wondered who the person was that he had chosen.

"You'll be charmed by her, Madame," the young King replied. "I can't tell you any more than that."

Zelindor occupied himself until daylight having an apartment furnished for the divine Princess. That care, which was fulfilled in accordance which his own idea, appeared to him to be most agreeable; nothing was so elegant and so well-wrought.

The ladies of the palace, awakened by the news and not hearing the name of the person that the King as marrying, all flattered themselves privately that they might be object of his choice, so they did not neglect anything in their adornment. They believed that they could not devote enough time to it, although it was not until the evening of the day that it was necessary for them to be in the gallery; more than one had a heart touched by the young King.

The hour arrived; the palace was superbly illuminated; the Queen and the ladies went into the gallery, which was shining with so many lights that they would have put the broadest daylight to shame. Young Zelindor, even more charming and adorned with all that art could add to his noble figure, finally appeared and paraded his gaze over that host of beauties.

"In truth, Mesdames," he said to them, "I would have a sensible regret of not having made a choice among you of a beauty worthy of the throne if the one who is about to appear did not justify me."

With those words, sitting down on his throne, he ordered that his she-bear be fetched.

Everyone looked at him, unable to conceive what the King could be doing. People whispered: "Is the King going to marry her?"

The she-bear appeared; she was conducted by two princes of the blood, each of whom was holding an end of the King's sash, which as around her neck. As she approached, the young King descended from his throne and touched the head of the she-bear lightly with his scepter.

"Appear, beautiful Princess," he said to her, "and come and efface, by means of your charms, the insult I am making to so many beauties."

Scarcely had those words been pronounced than the bearskin fell away, and the admirable Noble-Thorn, appearing in all her splendor, eclipsed all those who had pretended thus far to beauty.

The fay Azerole became visible at that moment; she had adorned the Princess herself, so you can imagine that nothing was lacking in her attire. Zelindor threw himself at Noble-Thorn's feet; she raised him up tenderly and gave him her beautiful hand.

The wedding was celebrated with a royal magnificence, and the two spouses, charmed by one another, lived in a union and a tenderness that would have made the vulgar boors who believe that marriage is the tomb of amour die of shame.

Zelindor had from Queen Noble-Thorn, in less than two years, two sons as charming as one another.

While that had been happening to Noble-Thorn, Rhinoceros had not ceased searching for her and tormenting poor Coriande, whom he accused of having favored the Princess's escape. When he came back from his excursions very weary, he beat her so badly as to leave her for dead, but Coriande was so attached to her mistress that she much preferred suffering all the ogre's fury to learning that the monster had found her.

He searched so far and wide, however, that he finally discovered that the Princess was in the realm of Felicity and that she had married its sovereign. That news caused him so much rage that he would have devoured Coriande if he had not thought that it would be too much pleasure for her to die so quickly. He told her that he knew where Noble-Thorn was, and swore, by the most frightful blasphemies, that he was going to avenge himself. He took Coriande and, attaching her to the sails of a windmill, he told her that she would spin like that until he returned, when he would eat her with her mistress, after roasting them over a slow fire.

He did not know that the good Azerole was also protecting Coriande. Knowing her attachment for Noble-Thorn, she had fascinated the eyes of the ogre, who, when he believed that he was beating Coriande, was only beating a sack of oats, the same one that he attached to the windmill.

He finally departed, wearing his seven-league boots, and soon arrived in the kingdom of Felicity. He was informed of the happiness that the Queen was enjoying, and he felt his fury enraged by it. He contained himself, however, and having taken lodgings in one of the outlying districts of the capital, he disguised himself as a seller of distaffs, having only that means of entering the palace, where the Queen might have recognized him. He therefore decided to wander the surrounding streets, shouting at the top of his voice: "Golden distaffs and silver spindles for sale!"

The nurses and governesses of the little princes were at the windows, and that merchandise pleased them greatly. They had the merchant climb up to their chamber. Although they were surprised by his frightful face, they had even more desire for the distaffs, and bargained for them.

"I am," he told them, "more curious than pressed for money. I know that my distaffs and spindles are worth kingdoms, but I'll give you all six of them if you'll let me spend a single night in the little princes' room. I have ambition, and I'll be greatly considered in my homeland if I can boast of having had that honor. See if you like them; at that price, my distaffs and spindles are yours."

"The nurses and the governesses, astonished by the merchant's stupidity, impelled by the desire to have treasures so cheaply, and seeing no inconvenience in it, agreed to that request and told him to come back in the evening, that he would have a good bed in the little princes' room. He seemed delighted, left his distaffs, came back in the evening, and went to bed, as he had requested.

As soon as he was sure that the nurses were profoundly asleep, he got up quietly, went into the Queen's bedroom, which he knew to be close to that of her children, took from the sheath that was attached to the princess's bed-head a knife that she always wore in her belt, pitilessly cut the throats of the two young princes, and then came back quietly to replace the knife in its sheath; then he ran away, as quickly as possible.

As soon as the nurses and governesses woke up they were astonished no longer to find the merchant of distaffs there. Remembering that he had told them that he was in a hurry to return to his homeland, they imagined that he had doubtless left early in the morning. But what was their dolor and astonishment when, approaching the cradles of the young princes, they saw the beautiful children with their throats cut, drowned in their own blood. They uttered frightful screams; the entire palace came running, including the King and Queen. What a spectacle for them! The King's despair, the Queen's mortal dolor and the dolorous cries of the entire Court rendered the catastrophic moment even more horrible.

No one knew whom to accuse of such an enormous crime; the governesses and nurses took great care not to reveal their frightful secret, and it was necessary to carry the Queen away, who had fainted in her husband's arms.

The author of the tragic adventure was sought in vain; everything that the King could publish was futile, the most excessive rewards had no effect. Rhinoceros alone knew his secret, and was certain that it would not be revealed.

The ogre had hidden in another quarter of the city, and having got rid of his merchant's costume he had donned that of an astrologer. He waited placidly for the curiosity and dolor of the King to bring him to his dwelling, which did, in fact, happen. So many people had said before the monarch that there was a marvelous man who unveiled the past and the future clearly, and so many examples were cited, that Zelindor wanted to try the famous diviner; he went to see him in person and interrogated him regarding the frightful murder of his children.

The astrologer, delighted to be able to perpetrate a horrible wicked deed, told the young King gravely that the guilty party was in his palace. He shivered at those words. The pretended astrologer went on, and assured him that if he summoned all the women who were contained there, and visited personally the knives that they wore in the sheaths at their belts, he would infallibly discover the murderess, whose knife would still be blood-stained.

The astonished King followed the monster's advice as soon as he returned to the palace and found no sign of what he was seeking. He therefore returned to the astrologer and told him that the searches had been in vain.

"You haven't searched everyone," said that infamous individual, feigning great anger at the fact that his science seemed to be doubted.

"What!" replied the King. "You want me to search the Queen, my mother, and the Queen, my wife?"

"Of course," said the terrible Rhinoceros, "and I advise you not to fail in that."

Zelindor had no faith in what the astrologer had said and returned home very sad. The Queen, his wife, came to met him with open arms; he paled as he approached that princess, as soon as he perceived the sheath at her side. He took it, opened it, and drew out the knife still stained with blood.

"Oh, perfidious woman!" he cried. With those words, he fell unconscious into the arms of those who were with him.

The Queen, very frightened, asked what the matter was, and what was wrong with her husband, the King. She was informed.

"What horror! What a lie!" cried the innocent Noble-Thorn. "Me, cut the throats of my dear children!" She could not say any more, and fell as if dead on to a sofa.

The King, who saw her in that sad state when he opened his eyes, immediately turned them away and ordered that she be taken away to the tower, which was done immediately, and she was only left with two women to serve her. Her trial was conducted on the basis of the deceptive appearances, and she was sentenced to be burned alive.

The poor Princess, scarcely recovered from her faint, finding herself in a frightful place and her two maidservants in tears, asked them whether it was possible that the King, her husband, could even suspect her of murdering her children. She was told that he could, and that furthermore, her condemnation had already been pronounced.

"O Heaven!" cried the unfortunate Queen. "Of what am I guilty, to merit such torture? What! Zelindor has accused and condemned me without hearing me? I have lost his tenderness; I have nothing more to do but die."

The King, for his part, pierced by a mortal blow, could not resolve to see Noble-Thorn die, no matter how guilty she might be, and, seeing that the pyre had been built and that the Queen was about to be attached to it, had the doors of the palace opened and descended into the public square just at the moment when the innocent Queen emerge from her tower with a constancy as assured as it was modest.

"Stop!" he cried. His voice was too faint and too tremulous; it was scarcely audible, and the Queen mounted the pyre.

The barbaric Rhinoceros, disguised for the third time, was in the square among the people, in order to feast his cruel eyes on the torture of the unfortunate Noble-Thorn. He animated the people with his discourse, and recounted, with horrible details, how the Queen had cut the throats of her children.

Suddenly—O prodigy!—a thick cloud departed from the Orient and came to descend upon the pyre, which it inundated with a rain of orange-blossom. Then it opened up and allowed the sight of the fay Azerole, seated on a ruby chariot, with the father and mother of the young Queen, the two little princes sitting at their feet on magnificent cushions, and the faithful Coriande holding their tethers.

"Credulous and yet excusable King," said the fay, "see to what an excessive tenderness for your children was about to expose you. Noble-Thorn was about to perish and render you inconsolable forever." Touching the frightful Rhinoceros with the tip of her wand, she added: "It is him that it is necessary to punish. It is him who believed the crime consummated, and who accused the Queen malevolently."

The ogre remained immobile by virtue of the subtle power of the wand. The fay put the beautiful Noble-Thorn in her chariot, and related her entire history. The charmed people, who always change in accordance with the different impressions that affect them, did not wait for the fay to finish speaking. They seized Rhinoceros and threw him into the pyre, which, already being alight, consumed the wicked ogre in a moment.

Zelindor, in tears, implored the fay to obtain his forgiveness from the beautiful Queen. Noble-Thorn threw her arms around her husband and embraced him tenderly. Such a touching scene caused everyone to shout: "Long live King Zelindor and Queen Noble-Thorn!"

The two spouses implored the fay to enter their palace, along with the King and Queen she had brought. The illustrious company was received there with unparalleled acclamations; the trumpets never ceased to sound and the drums to beat for an entire week. Young Noble-Thorn introduced her husband to the King and Queen, her mother and father, who thanked him very kindly for loving their daughter so much. The fay endowed them with all sorts of happiness, and they lived happily for a multitude of years.

The Comte de Livry having stopped talking, everyone praised his memory. Madame la Vicomtesse outbid all the others again and praised his complaisance.

"I assure you, Madame," he said to her, "that I reproach myself strongly for the length of that tale, but I had scarcely remembered it than I thought of adding things to it that are not in the original."

The Vicomtesse replied that apparently, the original was not as good, and that she preferred his manner of telling it.

They talked for some time about the characters in the story, and as it was time to allow Madame la Vicomtesse to retire, everyone wishes her a good night, and everyone withdrew, very content with what they had just heard.

The two charming sisters conducted Madame de Briance to her apartment, and stayed there, as they usually did. The Comte and Chevalier de Livry arrived there, as did Baron de Tadillac. Saint Urbain asked him whether he had seen Madame de Salgue; he played the discreet lover and assured her that he only spoke to her in public; that his greatest passion was that of soon seeing Madame la Vicomtesse absolutely declared in his favor; that she had sworn him an eternal tenderness, but that he was not in a humor to remain for entire years sighing and lamenting.

Madame de Briance said that the Vicomtesse wanted to spin out the perfect amour, and maintain it; that it was necessary for everyone to think of their own affair, and that they should assemble the following evening in order to voice their opinion, and find an expedient that would assure them of a fortunate success. Messieurs de Livry had no other interest; the Baron was also intent on nothing but a happy ending; all three of them approved of that sentiment, and Madame de Briance dismissed them.

Kernosy and Saint-Urbain having remained alone with her, begged her insistently to tell them the rest of her adventures; and, not being able to dispense with it honestly, she had the complaisance to continue her story thus,

Madame de Briance's Story Continued

You doubtless remember, Mesdemoiselles, that my brother had recovered from his wound, and that Tourmeil was beginning to get better. His greatest pain was then the apprehension that the return of his health would soon put him in a state to quit my father's house and deprive him of the joy of seeing me every day—for that was the way he put it.

He was not yet out of bed when Monsieur de Briance received letters informing him that his presence was necessary in Paris for the judgment of a very important lawsuit, which his adversaries were pressing hotly during his absence, with the design of prevailing therein. Monsieur de Briance, knowing that that was their intention, made all the preparations for his departure and came to give the news to Tourmeil. Passing from there into my father's apartment, they remained there for a long time, shut in together, and only emerged when my brothers appeared; he approached them and took his leave of them, begging them to continue their cares for the invalid he was leaving in their home, whose wound, which was getting better every day, gave hope for a prompt recovery.

The next day, my father, who was with my brother the Chevalier in his cabinet, received a letter from Monsieur Briance. Someone came to ask for him and he left abruptly, after having put the letter in a desk that was not locked. My brother having brought it to me immediately, we ran together to Tourmeil's room, not doubting that we would discover the subject of their conference, which we had a great desire to know. This is what it contained:

I am departing with a veritable chagrin at quitting you, Monsieur, but I hope to rejoin you in a month or two; I shall await the time with impatience, since, in accordance with the word of honor that you have done me the honor of giving me, I can count on concluding the affair that you have decided, which I desire extremely. You will talk to Mademoiselle de Livry about it when you judge it appropriate; I believe that she will not find it disadvantageous. Continue, I beg you, Monsieur, all your kindness for Tourmeil

Le Marquis de Briance

What was our joy on reading that letter! My father and Monsieur de Briance appeared to us to be in accord regarding our happiness; I delivered my heart entirely to the penchant I had for Tourmeil, who, for his part, was in transports of joy that are indescribable. I regarded him as a husband chosen by my father and my inclination. My brothers were charmed by that alliance, which they had desired so much, and they went incontinently to replace the letter in my father's desk, in order that he did not perceive the petty theft.

Tourmeil, being finally reestablished in perfect health, went to thank my father and then returned to Monsieur de Briance's house. We were very surprised to see such a disastrous separation; we had not expected that blow; on the contrary, we had hoped that the occasion would lead my father to declare in our favor. What confirmed the suspicion we had that he might have changed his mind was a letter from Monsieur de Briance that Tourmeil had just received, in which he instructed him to go immediately to join him in Paris, because his affairs obliged him to spend the winter there.

Tourmeil, far from obeying, spent the carnival very agreeably in the city of Rennes, where his merit had attracted the affection of honest people to him. There was no fête to which he was not invited, and he was received there in a manner to make him understand that if he offered his prayers somewhere, they would be favorably received; but only finding himself in assemblies where I was present, he always remained faithful to me, and more disposed to lose his fortune than to renounce our amour.

He pretended not to have received Monsieur de Briance's letter, in order not to be obliged to respond to it; finally, unable to defer writing to him any longer, he told him, in order to have a pretext to remain with me longer, that his wound was not yet completely healed.

Whenever his affairs obliged him to spend a day without seeing me, he wrote me letters or sent me verses of his making, full of wit and fire; that did not seem surprising to me, for I sensed very well that amour had dictated them.

My father found himself obliged by politeness to allow me to spent a few days in the home a lady who was of one of my friends, who had a beautiful house near Rennes. However briefly that absence would last, I felt it keenly, and Tourmeil was inconsolable. I had expressly forbidden him to come there, because I feared that my father might be annoyed by seeing him introduce himself into a company to which he had not been invited.

The day after our arrival, while traversing the hall, I encountered a young peasant who presented me with a basket of flowers, very beautiful for the season; it was Tourmeil's valet de chambre. I did not have time to let him know the joy that his master's continual attention gave me. The lady in whose home we were appeared; he perceived her and withdrew promptly, for he had orders not to make himself known. I made my decision, not doubting that he had been seen coming in. "I believe, Madame," I said, "that I ought to thank you for these gallantries that I am receiving in your home; see what one of your servants has just given me."

"I have none," she said, "who are capable of such a pretty gesture; but I wish I had thought of ordering it." She looked at the basket attentively, and, on lifting up a bouquet that was in the middle of it, she found a note there. I was slightly nonplussed, but, only seeing verses that were not even written in Tourmeil's handwriting, I was reassured. Here they are.

The most savage climes and the saddest retreats
Lose on seeing you what they have of the odious.
To render charming all the places where you are,
Is the least effect of the power of your eyes.
The fields, on seeing you appear,
Seem to have taken on new colors;
The brilliant Queen of flowers
Has less right than you to give birth to them.
The gods of this rural abode,
In the depths of woods content their felicity
By an eternal liberty,
Against the god who is the master of the gods,
Will no longer be in surety,
Perhaps they will encounter you.

The lady of the house told that story to the entire company; I still pretended to believe that it was from her that the verses and flowers I have received had come. My father believed it too, because I had made no mystery of it.

The next day, as we were at table, we heard the best oboists there were in Rennes. They were asked who had sent them; they replied that a man had come to fetch them on the part of the lady whose house we were in, and had paid them very generously in order to make them depart with more diligence. I recognized Tourmeil in that new gallantry, which was once again put to the count of my father's friend, for the oboists still sustained that it was on her part that someone had come to fetch them. In fact, they had been deceived themselves.

"Never," she said, laughing, "has it cost me so little to do the honors of my house."

Finally, we returned to Rennes; we arrived there late, and I was about to go to bed when I heard violins and oboes under my windows. The concert was composed of the best musicians in the town; they played various pieces of opera and Spanish follies, which I loved dearly. Shortly afterwards, a beautiful voice sang several couplets to the same tune, accompanied by a theorbo. Here are the first two, which I still remember:

I am going to see the adorable Silvie again,
Her sweet charms embellish all places;
Alone she makes the joy of my life;
May I find it again in her eyes!

Upon her complexion, brilliant youth
Makes it dangerous attractions bloom;
The powerful god who charms and wounds us
Has given her his power and his arrows.

The symphony resumed at each couplet, and I have never heard anything so lovely; what charms could better enchant my heart? My brothers understood very well who the author of that gallantry was. My father resolved then to inform me of his designs and to declare them to everyone, in order to deter those who might have some penchant for me.

The day after our return to Rennes, Tourmeil came to the house as early as decency would permit. He saw me again with a satisfaction that one only knows when one is in love. I asked him how he had occupied the two days that he had spent apart from me; his response was that he had only left his room once, being unable to dispense with going in the evening to a house where I ought not to suspect that he had any design to divert himself, since one ordinarily only encountered subaltern officers there, who, in spite of their insipid and inappropriate discourse, listened preferably to witty people who had good things to say, and that the depraved taste in question had excited him to make verses on the rhymes made famous by the honor they had in serving the most famous princess in the world. I took the paper on which he had written them. It contained:

One does not find spirit here in any bust,
The coldest speeches are filled with ice,

And one makes ennui here of such rude spice
That they might one day kill the most robust.

Vainly, reason, by her presence august
Would like common sense to traces lessons;
All that she says would pass for essence.
A law has been made only to speak just.

One sees irises there drunk on mad pride,
All coarse soldiers have a welcome supplied,
And against their sweet talk no dyke is raised.

There plumes stir all wayward hearts,
In sum, by the gifts of Amour are amazed,
Fools, like ourselves, fall prey to his darts.

Here, all ennuis appear in their turn,
Causing me chagrin and languor extreme;
But if I saw the one of whom I dream,
I would rather be here than return
To the very abode of the gods.

My brothers and I recognized there the character of all those for whom the verses had been made. Tourmeil was amusing himself with us, but our joy was too great to last for long. A man of our province, considerable by his nobility and his great wealth, had asked for me for his eldest son. He was a tall fellow of nineteen, neither well nor badly made, and who, having never seen anything, fell into inconceivable puerilities.

Than new lover gave Tourmeil some anxiety. He was sure of my heart, but I could not dispose of myself. He finally determined to have my father explain. My brothers were entirely with him, and disapproved overtly of the proposed marriage with the provincial. They treated him with extreme coldness and I said disagreeable things to him, but the young man, devoid of education, did not feel them, and was not annoyed by anything.

One evening when my father was not supping at home, my brothers retained Tourmeil; our provincial, who was not invited, stayed anyway. After having been angry for some time, we decided to make fun of him. Tourmeil intoxicated him with praise throughout the meal. Eventually, we were warned that my father would soon return; we did not want him to find Tourmeil at the house; I begged him to leave, and my new lover said, on seeing him go: "I'm sorry that Monsieur de Tourmeil is leaving; the fellow cheers me up enormously. If he comes to my house to pass four or five months, we'll amuse ourselves agreeably."

"In that case," said the Chevalier, speaking to me in a whisper, "I advise you not to oppose this marriage."

I could not reply to that folly, for my father came in, and we obsessed him so much that was impossible for the provincial to do speak except to take his leave of the company.

The frequent requests that we made of my father for the conclusion of my marriage with that young man were the cause of my brothers and I finally making the resolution to speak to him about the design that Tourmeil had to enter into our alliance. My elder brother, the Comte de Livry, took charge of the affair. He chose his time so well that he had the leisure to speak to my father in private and represent to him that, apart from all the advantage that would be found in that alliance, he believed that we had an indispensable obligation to do something in Tourmeil's favor, and that such a consent would only be a feeble recompense for the great service that he had rendered our family.

"I perceived some time age the design on Tourmeil's part that you are declaring to me on his behalf," my father replied. "I esteem him infinitely, but he isn't rich; it's necessary that he elevate his house, Monsieur de Briance wants him to marry a young woman whose wealth is so considerable that it will reestablish his affairs; I believe it unnecessary to tell you that it is to his advantage; you can see that as well as me, and it is no less advantageous for your sister to marry Monsieur de Briance, who is returning imminently to terminate that affair.

She will have difficulty finding a better party; I hope that she will obey with a good grace, for my word has been given, and I warn you that I shall keep it."

That little speech, pronounced with a tone of parental firmness, disconcerted my brother and threw him into such great consternation that he could not give me the sad news without my perceiving the dolor by which he was penetrated. Tourmeil was in despair, and I was immoderately afflicted; our passion was redoubled by that obstacle to our happiness. It was necessary, however to hide my tears; my brothers took my interests to the point of attracting my father's anger.

Tourmeil no longer dared appear, and I only saw him occasionally; my brothers introduced him themselves in secret, but the entire time of our meetings was spent shedding tears. Finally, my father told me his resolution on that subject. I did not neglect anything to bend his will, but it was futile, and I fell into such dejection that, fever having gripped me, and I was near death for a week. Some time afterwards my brothers, finding a little amendment, decided, with the design of bringing some relief to my malady, to introduce Tourmeil into my room one evening; in fact, the pleasure I had in seeing him contributed not a little to the reestablishment of my health, and the welcome I gave him consoled him for his misfortune.

It appeared surprising to me that my father, who loved his children so tenderly, could resolve to render me unhappy, but I owe the justice to his memory that he thought that I would forget Tourmeil easily when I no longer saw him, and he wanted to give me a rank above the other ladies of the province by making me marry Monsieur de Briance.

It was an affair settled between them, and the letter we had interpreted in accordance with our inclination had no other objective than that marriage. My father declared it as soon as the contract was signed; he received everyone's compliments. Everyone thought me very fortunate, because the public was not informed of the trouble of our family, which would doubtless have made known the dolor I felt, and one can say in praise of Tourmeil that, in spite of his despair, he never let a single word escape that could mark his passion. The profound respect that he had always had for me closed his mouth; satisfied by my tenderness, he only attributed our woes to ill fortune.

Finally, Monsieur de Briance came to see me. I shall remember that day all my life, so cruel for my repose. I had summoned my courage in order to obey with good grace, but Amour did not want that. I made little response to everything that Monsieur de Briance said to me as a gallant man. I was depressed by my illness and even more so by my dolor, but, unfortunately, I appeared so beautiful in that languid state that he almost no longer quit me. I dissolved in tears as soon as he had withdrawn

Tourmeil, who could no longer master himself, only regarding Monsieur de Briance as an odious rival, was absolutely determined to fight him. My brothers, seeing that their efforts to prevent him were futile took charge of a letter he wrote to me asking to see me one last time. I consented to it. They were so moved by our conversation and so touched by our dolor that they judged it appropriate to separate us.

They were preparing to take Tourmeil away, when the apprehension I was in that he might doom himself caused me to catch him by the arm and represent to him that his design to fight Monsieur de Briance would be no less fatal to me than to him, since that combat would cause a scandal capable of staining my reputation, and that he would no longer be able to be tranquil with us, nor think of ever seeing me again in his life, whatever advantage he might obtain over his enemy.

Those words calmed his fury and made such a strong impression on his mind that he protested in quitting me that his obedience and submission to my orders should convince me more than ever of the sincerity of his passion. After many tears were shed, my brothers took him away, and I remained in an inexpressible affliction.

Having left me, Tourmeil wrote a letter to Monsieur de Briance to say that the rich heiress about whom he had spoken to him did not suit him, and that he wanted to travel for a few years before thinking about his establishment.

At first Monsieur de Briance was touched by Tourmeil's departure, but a few cares that he had noticed on his part for me, soon consoled him for his absence, and in the impatience he had to marry me he gave me no repose until the day of our marriage.

I was adorned; I allowed myself to be dressed as others wished, to be conducted to the church with the same docility and brought back to my father's house, where I spent the day receiving the compliments of all the people of distinction that were then in the town

The next day, Monsieur de Briance took me to his home; nothing could be added to the magnificence of his house and that of his carriage. He gave me jewelry of considerable value, and heaped me with all the presents that give pleasure to a young person; but that was not capable of touching my heart; I had lost the only wealth that rendered it sensible. However, I lived with so much complaisance for Monsieur de Briance that he was very content with his destiny and his love for me seemed to be augmented every day.

Tourmeil, having felt so keenly that to would be impossible for him to support such a catastrophic blow, had returned to Paris, to the home of one of his uncles, who was his guardian and who loved him tenderly; he made him understand that, having fought a duel over a rather slight quarrel, it was necessary for him to leave France until the affair was settled.

The uncle, who had heard from Monsieur de Briance about the combat of his nephew and my brother, believed easily in that second adventure, and immediately gave him money. As soon as Tourmeil had it, he took the road to Lyon, in order to go to Venice. That was, however, after having written to my brothers and bidding me adieu, assuring me of his immortal passion, and wishing me a repose that I have never enjoyed since his departure.

My brothers hesitated for a long time as to whether they should show me that last mark of Tourmeil's amour, but the

Chevalier finally brought me the fatal letter, and I read it a thousand times; it renewed all my dolor and I was so cruelly afflicted that the Chevalier repented of having given it to me. I found there that Tourmeil instructed the Chevalier not to make any response, because he would change his name and embark with the troops that the Venetians were sending to Morea, where he would seek the end of a life rendered so unhappy, which he would sacrifice to me without regret.

I hid my dolor very carefully. The languor I was in was augmented by the violence that I did myself. The physicians having prescribed taking country air, Monsieur de Briance took me to one of his domains, the solitude of which seemed more appropriate to my sadness that the frequent visits of high society. Content with our marriage, he spent almost every day hunting and procuring for me, by his urgent cares, the pleasures that he thought capable of being agreeable to me.

My brothers, who were on the point of going to Paris to commence entering into the service, came to see me at the beginning of spring. They had been in that great and famous city for about six months when my father, having become overheated in pursuit of a deer, caught a pleurisy that took away from us within seven days a heart very zealous for his children and the best father there ever was. Monsieur de Briance felt that loss as keenly as I did; that misfortune caused us to return to Rennes; my brothers also went there, and, having shared the finest succession in the province with Monsieur de Briance, who gave them marks of his amity by an unparalleled disinterest, they returned to Paris, the pleasures of which had taken away their taste for those of other cities; since then, having obtained approval for the two regiments they had bought, they have always remained in the service, only coming to this region once a year, where the honor that they had of seeing you gave them so much impatience to return.

I had been married to Monsieur de Briance for almost two years when he was attacked by a violent fever that put him in danger as soon as the third day. I found myself sincerely afflicted; he perceived it, and on the last day of his malady, having asked me to send everyone away, he took my hand and said to me: "Madame, I would die with the regret of having caused your woes if I had not always had reason to believe that your virtue had enabled you to surmount the penchant you had for Tourmeil. His departure, which preceded my marriage by a few days, made me realize the dolor that he felt; but I believed that it was only the transport of a young man that time would appease. It is just that I repair that harm; I am instituting him as my heir, and if he returns, as I hope he will, I beg you, Madame, to receive him as a husband worthy of you. I wish with all my heart that he will fill my place."

I remained so nonplussed and touched by that discourse that I did not have the strength to respond to it. My tears redoubled; a weakness on Monsieur de Briance's part followed; I called for help, and a few hours later he died, testifying until the last moment a perfect knowledge and a heroic courage.

His death disconcerted me; I renounced commerce with society and I left Rennes, where we were then, to live in reclusion in the country, where I have always remained since, and without the pleas of my brothers and their interests, which are very dear to me, I would not have abandoned the solitude in which I have always lived since the death of Monsieur de Briance, in which I am retained by the cruel anxieties I feel regarding the absence of Tourmeil. I will confess to you that I have sought information about him with a great deal of care, but as he quit his name when embarking among the Venetian troops, it has been impossible for me to discover what has become of him.

Kernosy and Saint-Urbain told Madame de Briance that she ought not to give up hope, that she was too ingenious to give herself pain, and that Tourmeil, by his prudence, might have escaped the dangers that his despair had made him seek so far away. The two amiable sisters, after having done what they could to maintain her in that thought, finished their conversation by thanking the Marquise for the story that she had been kind enough to tell them, and retired.

The following day, the actors having taken their leave of the company, departed with many regrets, to go immediately to Rennes, following an order, they said, that they had received from people they could not dispense with obeying.

A few hours after their departure, a man of good enough appearance was seen to arrive in the courtyard of the castle on horseback, followed by two valets. Madame la Vicomtesse, having been informed of his arrival, went to receive him very obligingly. She took him to her cabinet, where they remained in conference for more than two hours. Baron de Tadillac, astonished by that long audience, said in jest, on the subject of the man, that he would believe him to be his rival if he had not remarked, on seeing him pass by, that he was not to the taste of Madame de Vicomtesse, who did not want an aged lover.

Eventually, the Vicomtesse came to find the company, and Fatville, when he entered the hall for the mid-day meal, ran to embrace the unknown man, who was one no longer, because he called him "uncle."

She told her nieces not to engage in the games when they left the table, because she had to talk to them in private. That good aunt, having showed them both into her cabinet, after a long and tedious speech, in order to prove to them that they both had infinite obligations to her, told Mademoiselle de Saint-Urbain, as a sequel to those pretended obligations, that she had just signed the articles of a very advantageous marriage for her with Fatville's brother, who was very rich, a little less impolite than him, and had acquired a more sociable humor by virtue of the acquaintance of honest men that he had seen in the army during several years of service,

A thunderbolt could not have astonished Mademoiselle de Saint-Urbain as much as that news, so unexpected and so contrary to her inclination. She did not hide the dolor that she felt in consequence. Mademoiselle de Kernosy appeared as afflicted as her sister; all that only served to attract to them a long lecture on the blind obedience that well brought-up young ladies owe to their parents, from which Saint-Urbain had no desire to profit.

Finally, the aunt, believing that a diversion was necessary from the tears, left her nieces in the cabinet and came to inform the company of the news of Mademoiselle de Saint-Urbain's marriage. Fortunately, the Chevalier de Livry was not present; his disturbance would have revealed the interest that he had in the matter.

The Comte de Livry left the room promptly in order to warn his brother about the news and to take measures with him capable of reflecting the misfortune by which he was threatened. On the other hand, the Marquise de Briance, having the interests of her brother to protect and knowing from experience what the desolation could be of a young woman about to lose the person she loves, went to find Saint-Urbain, who was dissolved in tears. She represented to her that the marriage that had just been proposed was far from being concluded, that a thousand pretexts could be found for deferring it, and even for breaking it, and that, after all, the Vicomtesse not being her mother, she could, in extremity, refuse to obey her and not sacrifice herself to her caprices.

Kernosy approved that opinion; Saint-Urbain, always disposed to seize an agreeable hope, believed that she glimpsed that she was not entirely unfortunate, and thought it very appropriate to gain time adroitly. She wiped away her tears and became determined, following the sentiment of her sister, supported by Madame de Briance, to receive Fatville's uncle with an apparent civility, in order not to anger the Vicomtesse, who, seeing her return in a tranquil humor, did not doubt for a moment that it was an effect of her moralizing, and applauded herself more than once for having had the intelligence to convince her niece

Fatville's uncle appeared at that moment, and paid his compliments to Saint-Urbain, whose gave him very little response, and Fatville added to the present subject everything inappropriate that he had heard said on similar occasions. Madame de Salgue, having perceived that the marriage was not to Saint-Urbain's liking, only spoke to her about it in order to commiserate with her. Baronne de Sugarde, convinced that the Chevalier had no hope of marrying her, and that after such an event she could more easily appropriate that lover by her charms, cunningly dissimulated the joy that she felt in the depths of her heart and refrained from testifying to Saint-Urbain any sentiments other than those that her friends displayed.

The Chevalier, who had just returned with his brother, had a great deal of difficulty constraining himself, in order to hide the chagrin that he felt in seeing Saint-Urbain in a kind of indifference regarding the fatal news, and on learning the confirmation from the very mouth of the Vicomtesse, who informed the company at that moment that Fatville's brother would arrive that evening

Then, transported by amour and despair, without taking the time to examine anything, he ran to the stables to take a horse, and, in order to get away from the castle with more diligence, he pushed it at top speed along the road to Rennes, by which his odious rival ought to arrive.

Day was beginning to decline when the noise of several horses extracted the Chevalier from his reverie. He perceived in the distance a man on horseback enveloped in a large red cloak, followed by three persons also on horseback, and, not doubting that it was his rival, he ran with sword in hand to attack the one who appeared to be the master.

"Let's see," he said, as he approached him, in a tone of voice that anger rendered unrecognizable, "if you're more worthy than me of the wealth that you're seeking to steal from me."

The man, who was prejudiced by a chagrin as pressing as that of the Chevalier, promptly threw off his cloak and drew his sword.

They were fighting with an equal advantage when the men of the stranger's retinue came forward in order to separate them; but he ordered them to withdraw.

The sound of that voice suspended the anger by which the Chevalier de animated. First he caused his horse to recoil for a few paces, and, lowering the point of his word, he cried:

"What! I've just attacked a life that I would defend a thousand times at the price of my own!"

The stranger, who was Tourmeil, surprised to hear the voice of the Chevalier de Livry, which he distinguished very well, remained motionless, not knowing what to think of such an adventure. Finally, the two friends, having recovered from their astonishment, both feeling their hearts moved, approached one another and embraced with all the joy that a veritable amity can cause.

The Chevalier wanted to tell his friend in a few words the design that had brought him to that place. Tourmeil interrupted him immediately in order to talk to him about Madame de Brinmece. At that moment, curiosity drove them both to ask several questions at the same time, and no conversation was ever less coherent or more interesting; they lost their way therein.

A man on horseback who was traveling at a great gallop stopped in order to ask them whether it was very far from where they were to the Château de Kernosy, and testified to them that he was in a great hurry to get there. The Chevalier, curious to know the motive for that haste, told him that they were going there, and that he could accompany them.

The man was the valet de chambre of Fatville's elder brother, and a great talker. He was delighted to have found something to talk about; that pleasure, relenting his desire to continue his journey, caused him to tell them at length the story of the accident that had constrained his master to stop in a village two leagues from Rennes, where a wound was being dressed that he had received when falling from his horse. He had sent the valet to take the news to his brother, his uncle and Madame la Vicomtesse.

Tourmeil, hearing all that, said in private to the Chevalier de Livry that Amour was not favoring the intentions of his rival and that the delay would give them time to break a marriage that did not seem to have any appearance of fortunate success. Then they continued on their way without speaking to one another. The Chevalier was occupied with the present state of his destiny, and Tourmeil was sensing the transports of joy that were augmented as he drew closer to the place where Madame de Briance was. It was not that the apprehension of not finding her in the same sentiments in which he had left her did not cause him any anxiety, but nothing can outweigh in an amorous heart the pleasure of seeing the person one loves.

When they arrived at the castle, Tourmeil asked the Chevalier not to make him known to the company before he had learned how Madame de Briance wanted him to handle Madame la Vicomtesse.

There was no talk there of anything but the Chevalier de Livry; everyone was anxious about his absence. Kernosy, Saint-Urbain and Madame de Briance, fearing that some misfortune might have overtaken him had asked the Comte de Livry and Baron de Tadillac to go and look for him on the road to Rennes, but night was already somewhat advanced when they mounted up and they had gone astray; after several futile detours, they arrived back at the castle at the same time as the Chevalier, who took Tourmeil up to his room. He would have liked to go up secretly, but that was not possible. He gave an order that a fire should be lighted promptly and that his friend should be provided with all necessary refreshments and allowed to rest until he could join the company. Then he had the valet de chambre of Fatville's brother introduced, who made his compliments to Madame la Vicomtesse on the part of his master and gave her the news of his injury.

The presence of the Chevalier reassured all the beautiful ladies who were interested in him; only the Fatvilles and the Vicomtesse were solely attentive to the valet de chambre's speech. After several questions put to him about the details of his master's fall, they both decided to leave the next day in order to have him transported to Rennes.

Meanwhile, Saint-Urbain and the Marquise questioned the Chevalier about his abrupt departure. The shame of having made that futile excursion prevented them from discovering its true motive; he said to them in a low voice: "I will tell you the reason that made me mount a horse with so much diligence this evening, and I am sure that Madame de Briance will be grateful to me."

The Vicomtesse, having rejoined the company, asked the Chevalier where he had been. The Baron, who saw that the question embarrassed the Chevalier, as well as the Comte de Livry, who had also just arrived, replied to her: "It's a small secret that regards me, Madame, of which I shall have the honor of rendering you an account one of these days." By that means he got them out of difficulty.

That same evening, Fatville and his uncle, before going to their apartment, took their leave of the company for a few days. Everyone having retired, Kernosy and Saint-Urbain went to the Marquise's room, where they were to discuss the means of breaking the marriage that the accident to Fatville's brother had retarded. Her prudence made them hope that the result of the meeting would not be unfruitful, and that the ascendancy that the Baron had over the mind of the Vicomtesse seemed to assure them that everything would succeed as they wished.

The Comte and the Chevalier were already there, in a joy that the two amiable sisters did not think appropriate to the urgent state of affairs in question.

"What favorable hope," asked Saint-Urbain as they came in, "inspires the joy that is spread all over your faces? May we be permitted to share it?"

Madame de Briance spoke in reply, saying: "After the unexpected happiness that Heaven has sent me today, anything can be expected of fortune. Tourmeil has returned, and has returned with the same sentiments that he had had on his departure. The Chevalier has been on the Rennes road this evening; he found a man whom he had sent him, in order to discover whether my presence would be agreeable to him."

Kernosy and Saint-Urbain had so much interest in everything regarding Madame de Briance that they forgot their own interests momentarily and no longer spoke about anything except Tourmeil. The impetus they gave to the joy that penetrated them and their manner of congratulating the Marquise represented perfectly the pleasure that agreeable news made them feel in the depths of their soul.

Then the Chevalier, seeing everyone of the same mind, said: "I see that no one will be annoyed if I bring the man that Tourmeil has sent me here." He went out, after having told Saint-Urbain in a few words that the Vicomtesse's project had put him in despair, and returned immediately to the room with Tourmeil, whose neglected appearance, like that of a man arriving from a long voyage, did not prevent him charming, by his good looks, all those who did not know him yet.

Madame de Briance struck by a sight so dear and so unexpected, uttered a loud cry and remained motionless on her chair. Tourmeil, surprised to see her in that state, threw himself to his knees at her feet and kissed her hands, without having the strength to pronounce a word. There was then no one in the assembly who was not instructed of his passion; the Chevalier had warned them before coming in. Kernosy and Saint-Urbain did not believe him to be a person sent on Tourmeil's behalf; they recognized immediately, by his majestic bearing, that it was him.

The Comte de Livry, utterly joyful in recovering the best of his friends, ran to embrace him, and, judging that Madame de Briance and her lover were far too occupied with their happiness to be able to talk about anything else, he proposed to the two sisters and the Chevalier to go into a nearby cabinet, where they would take, with Baron de Tadillac, who had just arrived, certain measures to determine the Vicomtesse to marry him.

The Chevalier gave his advice on that subject tranquilly, having his mind in repose regarding Saint-Urbain, who had promised him never to obey her aunt when she proposed a marriage contrary to the choice of her heart. The Comte was no less satisfied by the conversation that he had with Mademoiselle de Kernosy, and the Baron promised to make every effort with the Vicomtesse in order to break the marriage that she had proposed to Fatville's brother and procure them all the accomplishment of their desires. To recompense him for his good will, the two amiable sisters, seeing him impatient to know where Tourmeil was, told him that he would find him in Madame de Briance's room. Immediately, he went to render him a visit. His compliments did not last long, but his heart was on his lips. Afterwards, he came with them to rejoin the company, who gave further marks of the joy that everyone felt.

They made him party to the result of the assembly and the embarrassment they had in finding an assiduous man who would have the intelligence to pretend that he was a courier and to say to the Baron, on giving him a letter on behalf of his guardian, to make a response the same day, because he was obliged to return diligently. Tourmeil offered them one of his gentlemen, capable of succeeding in any enterprise whatsoever, and, having told them where he had left him, with his other domestics, the Baron went there early the next morning in order to instruct him as to everything he had to do.

Meanwhile, the Marquise, who did not want to introduce Tourmeil to the Vicomtesse yet, nor divulge his return without having removed all the obstacles that might be able to suspend the execution of the late Monsieur de Briance's testament, by which Tourmeil was instituted his universal heir, asked the Baron, whose genius put him above such difficulties, to imagine a means of allowing him to remain in the castle unknown for a few days.

"That's a settled affair," he said, "if you think it good that Monsieur de Tourmeil represent the master in the troupe of our rustic actors."

"What appearance is there that that can be done?" replied Saint-Urbain. "It would be necessary for them to be here."

The Baron, having replied that they were not far away, put off informing them of his plan until tomorrow, and Tourmeil promised that he would play the role well enough to deceive Madame la Vicomtesse, and persuade her that he really was a rustic actor. The conversation ended there, and, the night already being well advanced, everyone retired.

The Chevalier de Livry took the Comte de Tourmeil to his room. The latter was too preoccupied to deliver himself entirely to slumber; the pleasure of being near Madame de Briance and finding her still faithful filled his mind so forcefully that he lost the night's repose. The Marquise, agitated by the charming trouble that the pleasure of seeing again someone that one loves, did not spent the night with any greater tranquility.

In the morning the Baron came to inform Tourmeil and the Chevalier that, in order to satisfy the lottery ticket that order him to regale the ladies with a fête, he had retained the actors and musicians, who were awaiting his orders in a village three leagues from the castle; that he had faked their departure in order surprise the Vicomtesse by their return, because she only found extraordinary things to her liking. In order that Tourmeil was dispensed from playing any role, he had asked him to assume the quality of the troupe's director.

"That's not all," he continued, looking at the Chevalier de Livry. "Let's think about the denouement of our adventures. Help me, please, both of you, to enable our pretended courier to arrive here, bringing me the letter on the part of my guardian that I mentioned to you. I'll give you the model of it: it will propose an advantageous marriage to me, and give me a positive order to depart diligently. I shall complain of the rigors of fortune, I shall communicate my letter to the Vicomtesse, and that is precisely what will make up her mind."

"But if she consents to your departure," said the Chevalier, "what will we do?"

"It will be necessary to leave, of course," replied the Baron. "I can see that you don't have much faith in my charms. I'll find new expedients, if necessary; let's take a chance on what I've resolved. I hope that Monsieur le Comte de Tourmeil will have kindness to make a legible copy of the draft I'll give him shortly. Madame la Vicomtesse doesn't know his handwriting; being a kind of prisoner here, he'll have time to succeed, and even to add to the letter, of which you dread the outcome so much, anything that he judges more appropriate to render it very urgent."

The Chevalier took that opportunity to inform Tourmeil of the various interests that had assembled everyone in the castle, and made him understand that the jealousy that he had conceived against the Baron was only founded on improbable reports that had been given to him in Rennes regarding the passion of his pretended rival for Madame de Briance. Tourmeil, touched by the Chevalier's discourse, full of amity, admitted to him that he had had let himself be taken in too easily, and that he had thought he was fighting against the baron when he was attacked in a wood on the Rennes road, but that the favorable welcome of Madame de Briance had entirely disabused him of his credulity, so he begged him not to mention that admission to anyone.

The Baron came to find them again then and read the letter, the fabulous invention of which gave them a great deal of pleasure. Then he put it in Tourmeil's hands, in order that, when it was transcribed, it could be given to the gentleman who was to pass for a courier. Then, not wanting to waste any of the time that he had been given to arrange a fête for the ladies, he told the Chevalier that, having conceived the design to combine the diversion of the comedy with a kind of opera, he could only address himself to him, who had a great facility in making verses, in order to have some dialogue for one or two scenes; that he would like the piece very rapidly, in order to have the most skillful musicians in his retinue to put it to music. The Chevalier replied that the anxieties by which his mind was agitated would prevent him from undertaking that work, but that Tourmeil would succeed in its better than any other.

"If it is more convenient," said Tourmeil, "I can justly be preferred, but for any other reason the choice ought to fall on you."

The Baron, impatient with these compliments, said to them: "I can see that this is going to pass in politeness; I need a diversion for the accomplishment of the fête I have to give, and if you annoy me, I'll propose that you make the music."

Finally, the Chevalier and Tourmeil agreed to give the Baron the verses he desired. He went away, his mind content, in order to pay court to the Vicomtesse, who had just got up.

Madame de Briance came to her brother's room, where she had the pleasure of seeing Tourmeil, and, not being able to dispense with rendering a visit to Madame la Vicomtesse, she went into her apartment shortly before the mid-day meal, accompanied by the Chevalier, who offered to give her his hand after being informed by his valet as to whether he had taken care to execute he orders given to him that morning in order that Tourmeil would have everything he needed during the day and that his meal would be served punctually.

As Tourmeil had promised to work on the verses that the Baron had requested of him, they stayed longer with Madame la Vicomtesse. Madame de Briance, in order to defray the expenses of the conversation, said that she had a tale of enchantment to relate. The Vicomtesse, who had a marked taste for works of that sort, was delighted that Madame de Briance wanted to lend herself to that sort of amusement; she even begged her not to defer the pleasure. Madame de Briance, informed by the Chevalier de Livry that Tourmeil had one that he had written, which was in his casket, sent him to fetch it. The Chevalier brought it immediately and, seeing that everyone was disposed to listen to Madame de Briance, he left in order to go and keep Tourmeil company.

The Marquise, oblige to deprive herself of the pleasure of seeing her lover, made one out of at least reading his work. She commenced thus.

Starlet

A King and a Queen, the rulers of a very beautiful kingdom, reigned over virtuous and very valiant subjects. It was a great good fortune for them that the latter quality was found in their people, for they were obliged to sustain a continual war against a King who, for sufficiently plausible reasons, claimed a tribute from his neighbor. That King was named King Warlike, a name that suited him marvelously. He came every year with arms in hand to demand from King Peaceful the execution of certain very ancient treaties made by necessity. Peaceful always refused to submit to them, as much because they were onerous as because he had never been engaged in them.

Peaceful had a very well made son who was young, charming, and full of intelligence and valor—perfect, in sum, if he had not known amour. But almost as soon as he had emerged from childhood, that fatal passion had taken possession of his heart so firmly, and mastered it to such an extent that his glory was obscured by it. Uniquely filled by the object of his amour, he allowed his father's realm to be ravaged with impunity; insensible to the desolation of his country and the murmurs of his people, he was only occupied with his mistress.

Peaceful, justly irritated by the Prince's conduct, threatened with being forced out of his capital and abandoning his subjects, who, in their despair, might recognize King Warlike in order to conserve their lives and their property, so poorly defended by their legitimate sovereign, resolved to talk to his son seriously.

Ismir—that was the name of the young Prince—came to see the King when he got up.

"My dear son," the worthy old man said to him, "you have seen the valor with which my subjects have defended our heritage, while you were not if an age to share their perils in battle. They hoped that you would not belie for long the blood from which you emerge, and that one day you might surpass the glory of your ancestors. However, since you are in a state to second their efforts and avenge our insults, how is it, my son, that you disdain to take command of my armies?

"Do you not know that a Prince ought to set an example? The world has its eyes upon you; you must account for your actions to posterity; what opinion do you want it to have of your virtues? I have grown old in labors; I have sustained the glory of this empire; now, enfeebled by the years, almost deprived of sight, I cannot aid my people to repel the violence of an aggressor who is making war on us unjustly; counsel and experience are the only resources they can still find in me. I have counted on your arm; will you disappoint my hopes, my dear son?

"Will you let me descend into the tomb with the dolor of seeing the crown that awaits you stolen from you? No, you will not make me blush; be worthy of me, of the illustrious blood that flows in your veins. Run to the defense of your faithful subjects, who will soon receive your laws."

"My father," the Prince replied, tranquilly, "it is not a lack of courage that makes me regard with indifference the peril by which your kingdom is menaced. Nor will it be the hope of reigning that will make me undertake its defense, and I only see with a violent dolor the moment that will crown me by virtue of a legitimate succession. None of those motives can touch my heart. But you are rendering me unhappy by refusing me permission to marry the beautiful Starlet; that is the only possession to which I aspire; my mother treats her like a vile slave because the secret of her birth has not been revealed to you; my pleas have been unable to soften her, nor to efface that odious title, with which I beg you not to wither her. Grant my wish and I will become a hero."

"What!" said the old King, emotionally. "A slave appears to you to be preferable to the salvation of the State, to the respect you owe our father? What am I saying?—to that which you owe yourself! You would dishonor your life by an alliance so shameful, when the daughters of the greatest Kings ardently desire to see you choose between them? A slave, a girl without a name, without relatives, captured in a city abandoned in the terror of our armies, only conserved by the compassion of my general, whom the Queen your mother took out of pity—you want me, unworthy son, to give you to that wretch? That she become my daughter? And that, to satisfy your extravagant desire, I cover myself with ignominy and allow a slave to sit on my throne? Do not presume so; and if any sentiments still remain to you, blush at the weakness of such a proposal."

"That slave of whom you are so scornful, my father," said Ismir, slightly agitated, "is greater in her irons than the most elevated princesses; her virtue, her courage and her sentiments render her worthy of the most august throne. Why would I become the husband of a princess intoxicated by her rank, capricious and devoid of attachment to me? Starlet, it is true, has not known either parents or a high alliance, but are you not a great enough King to take the place of all that? I have no need of vain titles; amour alone can render me happy. Goodness and beauty have forged by bonds; Starlet's virtue has rendered them immortal, and I would rather abandon the crown than renounce...."

"That's enough, my son," said King Peaceful, interrupting. "You will know my will tomorrow."

The Prince saluted his father respectfully and withdrew, very anxious about the consequences of that conversation.

The King went to the Queen's apartment, and related to her, in the bitterness of his heart, what had just passed between his son and him. That princess, naturally proud and ill-tempered, easily obtained from her husband the King that he would leave the matter to her, and assured him that he would soon be avenged. The King was so angry with his son that he gave the Queen limitless power to reduce the Prince to obedience, without even asking about the means that she would employ.

Starlet was the first to feel the Queen's fury; she was arrested and cruel soldiers put her in irons.

"Why are you putting me in chains?" she said to them, with an amiable mildness and tone of voice capable of softening rocks. "If it is by order of the King or the Queen, only tell me and I'll obey; but they are mistaken if they think, by such rigorous treatment, that I can be constrained to renounce the charming Ismir. I can never marry him, but I will always love him."

Without deigning to respond, the barbarians took her away violently and took her to an old tower, where only people accused of the greatest crimes were usually imprisoned, and, having thrown her in that frightful prison, they closed the doors carefully and withdrew secretly.

The beautiful and unfortunate Starlet recognized the Queen by those features of her vengeance. Her soul was not moved by those cruelties, but it was a great chagrin to her not to see again the person for whom she had sacrificed her life; occupying herself with him was a kind of relief for her, and no movement of anger against her persecutors escaped her. Tightly bound, and lying on the bare ground, she remained thus until the evening. Then an old slave brought her something to eat and untied her, without opening her mouth.

Starlet thanked her affectionately, without complaining about anyone, and the slave withdrew. A hard and small camp bed was the only furniture that Starlet was offered to rest her body, so delicate and bruised by the irons in which she had been enchained. She threw herself upon it, shedding tears that the memory of her lover extracted from her, and spent the cruelest of nights, but she was suffering for her lover, and that thought alone animated her suffering further.

She was brought food at the usual times, but she did not touch it. A beautiful she-cat as white as snow, leaping over the roofs every evening, came in through the window of the wretched cell and ate Starlet's supper. She slept there at night, stretched out beside the beautiful slave, and warmed her; that was not a mediocre service, for it was frightfully cold. The hours, which seemed mere moments when she was with Ismir, became long years now.

Meanwhile, the rumor spread that the beautiful Starlet was missing. No one was unaware either of the Prince's love for the charming slave or the repugnance that the King and Queen had for her; thus, people were easily persuaded either that Starlet had fled or that the Queen had had her killed. No one dared mention it to the Prince; he did not even suspect what had happened, because. since his conversation with the

King he had not dared present himself to the Queen, his mother, with whose violent character he was familiar. It was, however, only in the Queen's apartment that he saw Starlet; she was so sage that she had never received him elsewhere, and he preferred to deprive himself of the pleasure of seeing her for a few days than expose the charming your woman to the wrath that the Queen must have against him. He also feared that Starlet, using the empire that she had over his heart, might force him herself to yield to the desires of the King, his father, and he would have suffered death rather than renounce her and leave her under the tyrannical power of the Queen.

As it was not possible for him to remain ignorant of the disappearance of his beautiful Starlet for long, however, an intimate confidant of the Prince finally risked announcing that bad news to him.

Who could describe the dolor and despair of Ismir? He made a hundred resolutions, and only settled on that of killing himself; his confidant was only able to deflect him from that by representing to him that if Starlet was still alive, as he had reason to believe, the King and Queen would condemn the innocent beauty to death, regarding her as the unique cause of that of the Prince, and that it was necessary to conserve himself for her sake and wait. The unfortunate Ismir yielded to that wise advice, but he resolved to shut himself in his cabinet and not emerge until the beautiful Starlet was returned to him.

King Peaceful. having learned of his son's excessive dolor and his fatal resolution, was informed at the same time that King Warlike, having won various advantages and forced all the passes, was about to arrive at the gates of his capital. He ran to his son's apartment.

"To what shame, my son, is a foolish amour going to deliver you?" the afflicted father said to him. "You are abandoning, in a cowardly fashion, your homeland, your father and your crown. See, Ismir, the extremity to which I am reduced; appease my cruel dolor and my despair; enjoy the cruel pleasure of seeing my old age and the illustrious blood of your ancestors wither away. King Warlike, at the head of a formidable army, is already under our walls and threatening to scale them. My leaderless troops, ready to abandon us, are about give you the frightful spectacle of seeing me delivered as prey to the fury of an irritated enemy. If the interest and conservation of your father cannot touch you, if you are resolved to let me perish, to let me expire, I consent to it, but in the name of the gods, my dear son, save an unfortunate and faithful people, and yourself!"

He stopped at those words; dolor stifled his voice, and he fell upon a seat, tearing his white hair.

Ismir, moved to the depths of his soul by the cruel situation in which he saw his father, took the hands of the sad old man, squeezed them tenderly in his own, and fell to his knees. "My father," he cried, "deign to pardon me. Live, if you want me to live; add to that, to complete the favor, that Starlet will be returned to me after I have vanquished our enemies; I will fight them; conserve your crown; Starlet alone will be my felicity; tell me that she is still alive."

The old King, delighted to find his son worthy of him, embraced him, shedding tears of joy. He assured him by the most sacred oaths that no one had taken the life of Starlet, and that he would see her on his return.

Convinced by those oaths, already enjoying in hope the joy of seeing his dear Starlet, the tender Ismir kissed the King's hands, which he washed with his tears. He was brought magnificent armor, glittering with gold, rubies and diamonds; his father wanted to arm him personally, and gave him a superb charger. Ismir, more beautiful than the daylight, impatient for battle, embraced his father's knees once more; filled with joy and ardor, he mounted the horse proudly, went straight to the gates of the city, which he had opened immediately, and charged the enemy.

The joy of soon seeing Starlet threw him into a sweet reverie that was almost fatal to him; he suddenly forgot that he was in the presence of enemies, and only recovered himself when he was completely surrounded and in the greatest danger of losing his life or his liberty.

The advance guard, who had seen a cavalier of such fine appearance coming forward, mistook him at first for one of King Peaceful's principal officers, whom the King might have sent to make a few proposals, but having remarked that he was still advancing, without deigning to respond to the questions that were asked of him, they surrounded him. Ismir then emerged from his profound reverie and realized the peril to which he had imprudently exposed himself. Far from being frightened by it, however, promptly drawing his sword, he fell like an eagle upon those who were closest to him.

He felled twelve of them in a moment, and made room for himself. The others, irritated and ardent to avenge their companions, then attacked him from all sides, but the terrible Ismir soon made them repent of their temerity, cutting the arms off some, running others through, and sending heads flying. He tipped over, killed or put them all to flight. Meanwhile, his troops, whom the prodigious speed of his charger had prevented from joining him, finally arrived, and took such good advantage of the terror that the incomparable Ismir had sown in the enemy army and the disorder that he had imported there, hurled themselves courageously against troops astonished by such an abrupt an unexpected attack, and made all of them give way. In vain King Warlike made great efforts to rally his fleeing troops. Ismir remarked him and there was a terrible combat between them, in which each of them displayed his valor and strength. King Warlike, finally defeated, saw that he was in his enemy's power, and the dissipation of his army was completed.

Thus that glorious day finished. Ismir returned to his camp, where joy reigned all night long, and sent news of his victory to King Peaceful. He treated his illustrious prisoner generously, had him served in the same fashion as himself, and, having put him on a richly harnessed horse at daybreak, he took him to his father, the King.

Peaceful received him with inconceivable transports of joy and ordered celebrations that were to last several days.

Ismir, still occupied with his amour, awaited the recompense that he had been promised; his father did not mention it and he dared not remind him of it that day, but he went to him the next morning to demand Starlet.

"What are you daring to day, Ismir?" replied the King, in a firm and absolute tone. "Do not hope that an unworthy complaisance will ever make me consent to something that would tarnish the glory with which you have just covered yourself. Choose a princess worthy of you; do not talk to me again about something that has already irritated me too many times; you will force me to make a violent decision."

Thus promises are executed when the fear of peril has dissipated.

Utterly determined as Ismir naturally was, he trembled at those thunderous words, not for himself but for Starlet. He did not say a word in reply, and, dissimulating his anger, he went out, went to find the prisoner King and, approaching him with great emotion, made him tremble with terror.

"Have no fear, Sire," he said to him, in a tremulous and altered voice. "I am going to set you free; I can do that, I am your vanquisher, so receive my hand; but on one condition, which is that as soon as you have arrived in your country you will promptly reassemble your army and come to take possession of this kingdom, from which honesty and good faith have been banished. I will aid you to make the conquest of it myself."

King Warlike, astonished by such a strange proposal, stared at Ismir, whose physiognomy was completely changed, and, after having thought for a moment, he replied: "Prince, liberty is so valuable that I would accept it with great gratitude even if you had not added to it a present as considerable as the one that you have just made me; but, precious as it is, I could never accept it if it were necessary to betray my virtue and despoil my liberator of a possession that I would conserve for him at the expense of my life. No, I will not tarnish my glory thus."

O virtue, how powerful your example is! Ismir, recalling all his own, and touched by such a generous refusal, dissolved in tears. Then he recounted his dolors to the King and the reasons he had for complaining of his father. King Warlike listened to him attentively, commiserated with him, and promised him a refuge in his estates if he had need of one.

Ismir, still resolved to liberate his prisoner, came at nightfall to open the doors of his prison personally, accompanied him on horseback until he was out of the city, and returned secretly to the palace.

King Peaceful, having learned the next day of his enemy's escape, did not doubt that his son was the author of it. The Queen, even more angry, forced her husband to have Ismir arrested immediately, and he was imprisoned in the bottom of a tower at the extremity of the gardens, where a numerous guard was placed on him. He was unmoved by that, glad to be alone and to be able to think continually about his amour.

Meanwhile, young Starlet, still a prisoner, only felt the deprivation of her liberty because she could no longer see her lover. The public celebrations, the noise of which reached her, had caused her to suspect that he had won the victory, and the aged jailer confirmed that for her, which consoled her a little for what she was suffering because of her separation from Ismir.

One night, when she was at the window of her cell, bathed by beautiful moonlight, in one of those moments when the silence of nature entire seems to give more force to ideas, Starlet's heated imagination retraced all her misfortunes for her in colors so vivid that her eyes, accustomed to tears, shed them in even greater abundance, and her cheeks and her bosom were entirely covered by them.

Her cat, her unique and faithful companion, was sitting on the windowsill beside her, and looking attentively at the unhappy Starlet, who did not perceive it. The charming cat began to sigh in her turn, and she wiped away her mistress's tears with her paw. Starlet could not help caressing her.

"Alas, my dear Blanchette," she said to her, "you alone in all the world sympathize with my woes. Ismir himself, occupied with his glory, is perhaps no longer thinking about me."

"I shall try to relieve them, beautiful Starlet," replied the cat, "and to begin with, I can inform you that your lover is not ingrate, and is suffering as much as you are in the tower in which his father has imprisoned him."

Many people, no doubt, will be surprised that Starlet did not faint on hearing a cat speak, but apart from the fact that she was saying very interesting things, since she was talking about her lover, Starlet was very well-equipped intellectually by the reading of tales of enchantment, of which the fine minds of that land made their unique study. However, it is necessary not to dissimulate the truth; she was a little surprised. Far from being frightened, though, she took the cat in her arms and came to sit down on her meager bed in order to listen more at her ease to what she had to say to her.

"What, my little Blanchette, you're interested in my troubles?" said Starlet, giving the pretty animal a thousand kisses.

"Yes, charming Starlet," the cat replied, "as you shall see." Then, leaping to the floor, she suddenly became a great and tall lady, clad in ermine, with strings of diamonds in festoons over her skirt, and coiffed with delightful hair.

As soon as Starlet saw that sudden metamorphosis, she threw herself at the fay's feet.

"Get up, beautiful Starlet," the fay said to her, embracing her. "I am Herminette, and I usually reside in this tower, in order to help the unfortunates who are sometimes imprisoned here as unjustly as you have been. But as I presided over your birth, and you are the daughter of the King of Fortunate Arabia,[40] I also have a more particular concern for you. Not being

---

[40] Arabia Felix, the name used by early geographers to designate the southern section of the Arabian peninsula, was intended to mean "fertile Arabia," but the adjective can also

able to force the Destiny that is pursuing you, I wanted at last to console you, because of the goodness of your heart, which I have recognized in the care that you have given me in the form that I had borrowed. I have judged you worthy of my help and my favors, the effects of which you shall see.

Starlet was so transported by what she heard, and so delighted to learn that her birth equaled that of her lover, that she had no thought of interrupting the fay Herminette. But as she had told her that Ismir was in prison, she dared to ask her about that matter, and whether she might deign protect him too. The fay satisfied her curiosity regarding the detention of the prince, and added that she could not do anything for him as yet.

"However, my dear child," she added, "I will immediately give you the means of seeing him and consoling him. In the meantime, take this little box I am giving you, and remember only to open it in the moment of your greatest peril. I will always protect you, if you do not reveal that secret to your lover. I will enable you to get out of the tower; that is all that I can do for you for the moment."

With those words, the fay struck the walls of the cell with her wand; the stones fell, gently, and, arranging themselves with admirable artistry, immediately formed a broad and comfortable stairway, on to which Starlet stepped. Then the fay embraced her again and made her promise that she would not tell her lover by whom she had been liberated.

Delightedly, Starlet went down the marvelous stairway and found herself in an immense plain faced by one side of the tower. Turning round thereafter, she saw the stones that had formed the stairway rise up again of their own accord and resume their original position, as if skillful workmen had carried out the operation.

She drew away, and went straight to the tower where the Prince was imprisoned. That tower, situated in a corner of the

---

mean fortunate, and it was thus translated into French as *Arabie heureuse* [Fortunate Arabia].

park, was surrounded by guards, except on the side facing the plain, because there was only one window there, very narrow and solidly barred. A sentinel was stationed, day and night, on the platform of the tower.

Starlet shivered as she drew closer to Ismir's prison, and, favored by the clouds, approached the little window without being perceived. The Moon, then disengaged from the clouds, lent her enough light to perceive her dear Ismir. He was lying on a rush mat, pale, disfigured and almost motionless; but the eyes of a lover cannot be deceived.

"Ismir! My dear Ismir!" she called, softly. "Here is your Starlet, whom amour is bringing back to you. Come closer, dear Prince, come and assure her that you still love her. If only it were possible for me to reach you!"

That cherished voice, which went all the way to Ismir's heart, stirred all his senses. He stood up, unsteadily, and found enough strength to approach the window, where the charming Starlet was holding out her arms to him.

"Sovereign of my days, delights of my soul!" exclaimed the amorous Prince, kissing Starlet's hands a thousand times. "Is it you that I see?" He did not have the strength to say any more; joy and dolor gripped him so forcefully that he thought he might faint, and if the beautiful Princess had not retained him, he would have fallen. The tears that he shed in abundance, and with which he bathed Starlet's hands, relieved him slightly.

His lover was scarcely in a better state. Finally, after a long silence, more eloquent than the best organized speeches, they began to talk about their common misfortune, asking one another a hundred questions, repeating the same things a thousand times, and swearing an eternal ardor to one another.

Starlet did not tell her lover how she had escaped from the tower in which the Queen had imprisoned her, but she had the pleasure of telling him that she had been born a Princess. It mattered so little to Ismir that Starlet lacked that title, although he was unsurprised by it, that he did not even ask how she knew. He only talked about means of rejoining her soon. Not doubting that the King would set him free as soon as he learned of Startlet's escape, he advised her to leave that deadly place promptly, imploring her to hide her beauty as much as possible, fearing that his death would be inevitable if he learned that someone else loved her and was fortunate enough to please her.

"My heart is yours forever, dear Prince," Starlet replied tenderly. "Be convinced of my constancy; I would choose death rather than be unfaithful to you."

The reassured Prince begged Starlet to let him know promptly the refuge that she had chosen, addressing the letter to Mirtis, his confidant, a young nobleman who was extremely devoted to him. He indicated the hamlet on the far side of the plain as a place where she might be able to wait for him for a few days. They were making their plans in this fashion when a large white cat, passing close to Starlet at a run, cried to her: "Save yourself, my daughter; the King's men-at-arms are searching for you in order to kill you."

Fear seized the two lovers. The surprised Starlet could not see any other means of avoiding the troop than wrapping herself in her cloak and hiding in a thick bush that had grown at the foot of the tower.

She was just in time, for Peaceful, informed that Starlet was no longer in her cell, had immediately made men-at-arms and musketeers mount up in order to go in her pursuit. His design was to have her burned alive; but those troops, who passed very close to Starlet, did not see her, and rode away in all directions.

As soon as they had gone, the poor Princess trembling with fear, went back to the window where Ismir was almost dead with fear, so much was he in dread for her. Starlet cut off a lock of her beautiful blonde hair and gave it to the Prince as a pledge of her amour.

Fear give her wings, and she ran toward the hamlet with so much agility that the grass barely bent under her feet; they were bare, and her legs, like columns of ivory, effaced the whiteness of lilies and daisies. The Princess was so troubled, however, that she went astray, and at sunrise, finding herself on the edge of a vast forest, she plunged into it.

After walking for an hour, she arrived on a beautiful expanse of grass irrigated by a rustic spring, shaded by oaks as old as time, of a prodigious height. Overwhelmed by lassitude, Starlet sat down there. Recalling all her woes, comparing the short time during which she had enjoyed the happiness of seeing her lover again with the immensity of that which might pass before she saw him again, she shed so many tears that the ground was soaked by them. Slumber, of which she no longer knew the sweetness, came to close her eyes, and she fell asleep profoundly.

That forest was the one inhabited for several centuries by the yellow centaurs; it was the shelter they had chosen after the unfortunate fight they had had against the Lapiths at the wedding of Pirithous. A few of them, who were hunting, chanced to pass close to Starlet. The novelty of such an object, and her ravishing beauty, caused them to stop, and many others soon joined them. The Princess, when she opened her eyes, was gripped by an extreme fear in finding herself alone in a wood in the midst of such a troop, but when she saw the centaurs admiring her and saying to one another hat she was doubtless a fay or some divinity, the fear soon dissipated.

Since humans are conspiring to kill me, she said to herself, *and the only one from whom I can request aid is unable to give it to me, let's see whether this species of creature is perhaps less barbaric. In any case, I would be making vain efforts to run away, and it's necessary for me to request protection.*

After those brief reflections, the Princess looked up at the centaurs modestly. "My friends," she said to them, "you see before you an unfortunate young woman who is fleeing the fury of a powerful King; grant me shelter among you. I only have gratitude to offer you in exchange, and my amity, if you care to receive it."

The centaurs, who were not expert in compliments, but were frank and sincere, replied to her that they would be delighted if she wanted to stay with them, and that they would protect her with pleasure. Then one of them told her to climb up on his back; the others helped her, and the troop drew away. They took Starlet to a vast cavern where several centauresses lodged, to whom they handed her over in order that they might look after her.

The centauresses welcomed Starlet joyfully and hastened to serve her. Every day they procured her new diversions, such as hunting, fishing and jousting, which the strong centaurs did with one another. Starlet awarded the prizes; it was either a flower or a crown of oak-leaves; they received it from her hand with more satisfaction than an empire would have given them.

They loved her and respected her, and were sincerely afflicted because she was always sad and solitary; one day, they asked her the reason for that profound sadness. Starlet had too much confidence in them to refuse them the story of her misfortunes; they were touched by them, and the Princess took advantage of that obliging disposition.

"Since you have so much good will for me," she added, "it's necessary that one of you go to the court and invite Ismir to come and hunt a white hind with silver feet, which has taken refuge in this forest. He will understand immediately what that signifies."

She could not continue, and shed a torrent of tears. The centaurs, coarse but benevolent and sensible, swore not only to carry out her commission but also to ravage the kingdom of her persecutor and even put him to death, if she wished. "Heaven forbid," cried the Princess, "that I ask such a vengeance of your amity. Ismir's father will always be respected by Starlet, and I would defend his life at the expense of my own."

The centaurs, who had naturally simple and just hearts, found in such a generous sentiment new motives to respect Starlet. One of them was chosen to go to King Peaceful's Court; his intelligence and common sense made Starlet hope that he would succeed in his negotiation.

Meanwhile, aided by the centaurs, she built a small habitation, to which she often retired in order to shed the tears that the memory of her lover caused her. The forest was so dense and full of centaurs that no one dared approach it. According to an old tradition spread throughout the land, they devoured humans, so the general terror ensured the particular security of the Princess; she lived there in a profound peace, only troubled by the anxiety of her amour.

The delegated centaur soon arrived in the capital; he learned that Ismir, released from the tower, had fallen into a melancholy so somber that the physicians despaired of curing him; that the King, very afflicted by his condition, invented new diversions every day to dissipate his son's sadness, but the Prince took no part in them, did not want to see anyone, and almost always remained behind closed doors.

The centaur easily divined the cause of Ismir's malady, and as he did not want to take chances with his secret, he made the decision to go boldly into the King's gardens, hoping to draw Ismir there.

The sight of such an extraordinary creature did not fail to create a great stir at the Court and to spread alarm there. The centaur merely strolled gravely, and saluted the people who appeared at the windows. There was talk at first of killing him, but, apart from the fact that it might not have been easy, it was feared that other centaurs might come to avenge him, so the project was abandoned.

He appeared every day at the same time, nourished himself on fruits, and lay down on a carpet of grass in the depths of the park.

A few members of the Court, more courageous than the others, risked approaching him, and even walking with him; that boldness was taken for a sublime effort of intrepidity, for, since the centaur had taken possession of the garden, hardly anyone appeared in it. People approached him more closely then; he was offered milk and fruits; he drank and ate, thanking those who presented such things with a good grace.

That familiarity seemed charming; people came in crowds, and the company became so numerous that the centaur was sometimes overwhelmed by it. People talked to him and asked him many questions, and as his responses were ambiguous, they did not fail to say that he was prodigiously intelligent. Those who understood him the least praised him the most; stupid people remembered his remarks, and those who were even more stupid wrote them down; from that came a great many books, which people made a semblance of understanding, and also the fashion of expressing oneself that has since been called persiflage, which no academy has yet managed to define.

Those stupidities amused the good centaur, but he became bored eventually with having become so fashionable but not seeing Ismir. His reputation was established, as happens to many people as a result of what ought to have made them lose it; only he was astonished by that, he did not know that there are centuries of dementia when fools set fashions, just as there are some when reason and common sense preside, when they repose or fall into childishness.

There was so much talk of the marvelous centaur, and so much of what he had said was repeated, that all of it reached the ears of the solitary Ismir. He did not pay any great attention to it at first, but, tormented by the few people he permitted to see him, he went down into the gardens one day. The crowd that surrounded the centaur drew away slightly out of respect, crying: "Make way, make way for the Prince.

The centaur would have recognized Ismir even without those cries, so vivid was the description that Starlet had made of him. If the Prince found the yellow centaur admirable in his species, the centaur was no less impressed by the graces and majestic appearance of Ismir.

"Sire," he said, inclining, "I've desired for a long time to be your friend, and I beg you to grant me a favor." The Prince made a sign that people should draw away further, and responded benevolently to the centaur, who, in order not to expose Starlet's secret too much, proposed to Ismir that he come to their forest to hunt the hind with the silver feet.

The Prince, by virtue of the force of the passion that enlightens the mind so clearly, immediately deciphered the symbol, and was astonished that his charming Starlet had not been devoured by the centaurs, among whom he understood that she had retired. He stared at the handsome centaur in order to penetrate him all the way to the soul, and, seeing him tranquil and assured, he promised to go as soon as the following day, at dawn, to hunt in the yellow forest, if he would care to guide him there.

"That is my plan, Sire," replied the centaur, "but come alone, and leave to our inhabitants the care of guarding you; you will find that you have no better friends.

Ismir made the centaur a thousand amities, and spent the rest of the day with him informing himself of the mores, laws and customs of the giant creature. Ismir, charmed by the envoy, did not want to quit him, supped with him and lay down with him in the grass. The centaur, delighted with those marks of confidence and finding himself alone with Ismir, finally revealed to him the entire secret of his embassy and talked to him a great deal about Starlet.

Ismir thought he might die of joy, and did not know how to express his gratitude to the centaur. He did not sleep at all that night; daybreak took too long for his liking, and as soon as it appeared he woke the good centaur, who was profoundly asleep, for he was not in love.

The Prince had magnificent arms brought for him and the centaur, and he climbed up on his back; they drew away immediately. On the way, Ismir promised him that as soon as the King had pardoned him for his marriage to Starlet, he would send an embassy to cement a durable peace with the republic of centaurs, and would have a thousand of them for his guard. The conversation often reverted to the Princess, and they eventually arrived within sight of the yellow forest, the approach to which caused Ismir a violent emotion. They penetrated into the dense forest with incredible difficulty, without the Prince wanting to rest, and finally arrived at Starlet's little habitation.

She was there, and as soon as he tender lovers perceived one another, they ran toward one another, embraced one another tightly, and delivered themselves to all the pleasures of being reunited. Their tenderness interested the centaurs and centauresses to the point that tears came to their eyes.

Starlet, perceiving that Ismir had been wounded by the powerful thorns that bristled on the edge of the forest, obliged him to lie down on a bed of grass in her little redoubt, gave him something to eat, and, with her white and delicate hands applied herbs to his wounds, the virtue of which the centauresses had taught her. She would not suffer that anyone should share those tender cares with her.

Ismir was soon cured; amour often cures the worst maladies. The Prince was happy with his mistress among the good centaurs; however, Starlet did not want to receive his pledge of faith, nor give him hers, without the consent of those to whom she owed the light of day; with that, their felicity would be perfect. Ismir, seeing the Princess determined on that project, proposed that they embark. Starlet consented to that, convinced that the fay would direct their course.

They announced their departure to the centaurs, who were truly afflicted by it, and escorted Ismir and Starlet as far as the sea. When they departed they left in that wild place a memory of their charms and virtues that tradition still keeps there.

They did not remain on the shore for long, and soon perceived the prettiest ship in the world at anchor; they approached and saw with an extreme surprise that it was made of cedar and rose-wood; the rigging was composed of garlands of flowers and the sails of golden gauze, on which the figures of large cats were embroidered. A hundred white Angora cats served as sailors. Starlet understood easily that the marvelous ship was a new benefit of the fay Herminette; she invited the young Prince to board it, and they embarked to the mewling of the cats, which made a desperate noise as a sign of rejoicing.

The two young lovers had no reason to repent of their confidence; the vessel was filled, not only with everything necessary to life but also magnificent and elegant garments of all colors and for all seasons. Having taken to the sea, the ship sailed by virtue of a very favorable wind, and the white cats maneuvered it marvelously. In calm weather they played admirable concerts on excellent instruments, and the Princess, for her amusement, learned from them how to play the guitar.

Ismir, delighted to see the Princess without witnesses and at all hours, never ceased to talk to her about his amour; she always thought she was hearing it for the first time and swore a eternal tenderness to him in her turn; only the night separated them, and they had as much impatience to see the next day as if they had experienced the rigors of a long absence.

It was very difficult to keep a secret with so much amour. Ismir always found that Starlet suppressed certain circumstances in the story of her imprisonment. He complained of it so tenderly that Starlet could not help admitting to him that Herminette had revealed the secret of her birth to her, and finally revealed to him what the fay had sternly instructed her to keep hidden. She applauded herself for having made that confidence to her lover, but she was soon in difficulties because of it. The sea became agitated, and the sky was covered by dense clouds, from which horrible lightning flashes and frightful thunder departed.

Starlet perceived clearly that it was a vengeance on the part of the fay; she tried to soften her and implored her only to strike her, since she alone was culpable; and, disdaining to make use of the box that Herminette had given her, which might have saved her from such a great peril but might not have preserved her lover, she ran to throw herself into his arms, at least to have the pleasure of expiring with him. In vain, Ismir pressed her to open the box. "Since it can only save me," she replied, "I find it useless."

Scarcely had she finished those words than a thunderbolt fell on the ship with a horrible din and precipitated them into the abysms of the sea. The two lovers, holding one anther tightly, and reappearing on the surface, were driven at the whim of the waves. A wave separated them; the obscurity of the night and the agitation of the waves prevented them from rejoining one another, and they were cast up separately in different countries.

Ismir had fainted from dolor; he was floating on the sea; fishermen perceived him, jumped into the water, and brought him to their habitation.

The country where the Prince had been cast up was called the Isle of Repose; one never heard the slightest noise there, people always spoke in whispers and only walked on tiptoe. There were never any quarrels, and rarely wars; when it was absolutely necessary to sustain one, only ladies fought, at a distance, by throwing lady-apples. The men did not get mixed up in it; they slept until noon, spun, made knots, took the children for walks and put on rouge and beauty spots.

Those men helped Ismir so delicately that he soon opened his eyes. When he saw himself surrounded, and did not see Starlet, he uttered cries had frightened the fishermen; they blocked their ears and made signs to him to speak quietly. Then he began to tell them in a low voice the reason for his despair, and those good folk wept warm tears—but their wives, who returned from hunting and came in, on seeing their men in tears, ordered them to leave. Ismir explained the cause of that compassion to them, and they consoled him with a courage that contained a little harshness.

Ismir spent the night in the hut and the following day he gave a great many precious stones to those masterly women in gratitude for the care he had been given; they paid scant attention to them and gave them to their husbands.

The Prince went out and after having traversed a vast plain he arrived at a city made entirely of rock crystal, shining like the sun. He went into it in the hope of finding his dear Starlet there, and went through several quarters almost without encountering anyone. He reached a superb palace made of the most beautiful crystal in the world and went into the courtyard in order to rest.

Sitting on a bench, he ran his eyes over the superb edifice. Then he went around it several times, astonished not to see any doors there. The people of the country did not care for them; they made too much noise. When they came home, silken ladders were thrown down to them, by means of which they entered through the windows; they came out the same way. They had no staircases either; they made it too easy for people to come to see them; they did not like importunate, tedious and always pointless visits.

The palace was the dwelling of the King of the country; his ministers, who were occupied with the important care of teaching the young princesses to walk, having perceived Ismir, and judging by his magnificent garments that he was some foreign ambassador, promptly returned the princesses to their cradles, sent down a large blue velvet sack suspended by silk cords and made signs to the Prince to climb into it. Ismir understood their signals and was immediately hoisted up into a rich apartment.

He advanced toward a four-poster bed, the curtains of which were very rich, and lifted up by purple and gold ribbons. Twenty cassolettes of the most exquisite perfumes were burning around the bed, where the monarch, lying full length, was listening attentively to his chancellor, who was reading him *Bluebeard*.

Ismir, astonished to see a man of admirable plumpness, sustained by the brightest and shiniest colors, with a crown on his head, could not doubt that it was the King.

"Sire," he said, after having saluted in a rather cavalier fashion, "are you ill?"

"No, my child," he replied, in a whisper. "I'm very well, but I'm reposing a little while the Queen is at war."

"What!" said Ismir, sharply. "Have you no shame, to behave thus? You let your wife go to war while you repose? In truth, that's unpardonable."

"My son," replied the King, "Such are our immemorial laws and customs. If you wish, my chancellor will read them to you; for myself, I can't be bothered to learn them."

Ismir, transported by a double anger at seeing so much laxity, picked up a strong lance—the only one in the realm, of which no use was ever made—and gave a hundred blows to the effeminate King, shook his blankets rudely, and threw them out of the window.

He was about to treat the chancellor and the ministers in the same way, but they started to weep, in company with their dear master, and begged Ismir to calm his anger. As he was naturally good, he was easily moved to pity, but nevertheless said to the King: "Sire, if you do not promise me to abolish your ridiculous customs and to go to war yourself, like other Kings, I shall overturn your beautiful crystal palace. Furthermore, I want to accompany you, and right away; if not, I shall thrash you, your chancellor and all your beastly ministers."

One can imagine the terrible fright. The poor King swore, sobbing, to do whatever Ismir wanted, for he feared a redoubling of the blows of the terrible lance, which the Prince was brandishing in a very martial fashion.

The King had the Queen's arms brought out and put them in his sack, with Ismir, to whom he gave the finest horse in his stables. The King mounted another and they set forth immediately for the army.

The Queen, at the head of a large squadron of ladies, was disputing valiantly the crossing of a small river, on the other side of which the enemy were in battle order. Lady-apples were flying from all directions, and anyone who had the slightest bruise retired from the combat.

Ismir watched that beautiful conflict for a moment, and burst out laughing. "Sire," he said to the King of the Isle of Repose, "would you like me to get rid of all those people for you?"

"Very gladly, my dear friend," he replied.

Immediately, Ismir released the bridle of his horse, traversed the Queen's squadron, and, like a torrent descending a mountain, crossed the river and arrived on the other bank.

The enemies, who had not expected such great temerity and had thought at first that Ismir was a young lady, so handsome was he, were soon undeceived when he aimed the point of his lance, and struck, killed, felled and overturned everything. The Queen was terrified, because Ismir's horse had animated all the others so well that they too crossed the river, in spite of their riders.

The King, perceiving that Ismir was going to go on until the end, killing without quarter, ran to him and took the bridle of his horse.

"But in good faith, you can't think so!" he said to him. "Stop! Des one kill people thus, without mercy? It will be terrible if you teach them to kill too and they come to treat us in the same fashion. We only want to make them flee. Look, there's no longer anyone left except those you've killed or wounded."

Ismir shrugged his shoulders, but stopped nevertheless, seeing that everyone had fled, and, while conversing, took the King, the Queen and the army back to the crystal palace.

The Prince, who had acquired so much glory, was no more vain in consequence; in passing the troops in review he examined all the ladies in the army curiously, hoping that Starlet might be among them. The chagrin of having made that search in vain caused him to sigh bitterly and he became sad, in spite of everything the King—who was the most immoderate chatterbox in his entre realm—said to him, in a low voice.

Instead of going back into the palace, Ismir resolved to search for Starlet in every country, and on all the seas. He went to take his leave of the King and the Queen. The King protested that he could not bear him to leave so soon, and made him so many pleas that he climbed back into the ridiculous sack and was hoisted back up to the apartments.

Prince Ismir, who only yielded to those importunities with repugnance, was in a very bad mood, and asked the King why he did not have any staircases in his house.

"My predecessors never had any," he replied.

"A fine reason," Ismir retorted, brusquely, "for maintaining a custom so stupid and so inconvenient."

The King, over whom Ismir had acquired a great deal of ascendancy, promised to have one constructed if he would draw the design for him. Touched by so much deference, Ismir believed that he ought not to leave people so docile in ignorance, and consented all the more willingly to remain with them for a year, because he hoped to receive news of his dear Starlet there rather than elsewhere. He found some relief in not being in the place where his amour had been born, and where it had made such great progress.

During his sojourn on the Isle of Repose he had brought about a prodigious change in the mores of the effeminate inhabitants; he had accustomed their ears to noises, given them some knowledge of architecture, sculpture and the useful arts and had even undertaken to form them for war. He succeeded in disciplining them and they performed exercises and military maneuvers well enough, but he had not been able to give them firmness of soul, valor and audacity.

Three different armies made sudden descents on the coasts; Ismir, delighted to encounter such a good opportunity to put his lessons into practice, assembled the various corps of troops and wanted to lead them against the enemy, but those shadow soldiers could not sustain the sight of them, and their terror was such that Ismir found himself abandoned immediately. He performed prodigies of valor, at least to save the King. That unfortunate prince and Ismir were captured and the city sacked; while the enemies were completing the ruination and pillaging the riches, they had Ismir taken to one of their boats.

The Prince, who had lost almost all his blood, was unconscious. He remained in that condition for a long time, and when he opened his eyes he was astonished to find himself alone and the boat adrift. He found himself as strong as before, not sensing any wound, and the marvelous boat enabled him to arrive in two days at a port that he recognized immediately; it was that of the capital of his realm.

A few people who were walking about in full mourning recognized Ismir immediately, helped him out of the boat,

and, shedding tears, prostrated themselves at his feet and started shouting: "Long live the King!"

Those acclamations made the Prince shiver, and he soon
learned that the King, his father, and the Queen, his mother,
had died almost at the same time, of the chagrin of having lost
him.

Exhausted by hunger and fatigue, Ismir forgot his needs
in order to deliver himself to his regrets; his entrails were
stirred; he wept bitterly for his father and his mother, and
wanted to be taken to their tomb right away. It was only after
having satisfied his piety that he put on his royal garb and received the homages of the nobles and the respects of the people.

Starlet was not the last of his thoughts, and the very next
day he also sent a celebrated ambassador to the yellow forest,
in order to make the centaurs party to his succession and to
ask for a thousand of them for his guard. They received those
marks of amity with much gratitude and sent those whom the
King had requested; they were commanded by one of the most
considerable in the forest, who brought the new King a pigeon
and a dove. The pigeon had the talent of finding lost things.
As soon as Ismir as informed of that, he commanded it to go
in search of Starlet, and, thinking that he could not take too
many steps in order to assure himself of success, he also ordered a great admiral to set to sea with a fleet of a thousand
vessels.

The dove never abandoned the King, and ordinarily
perched on his shoulder; the centaur commander assured the
King that she would be useful when the time came to recognize Starlet.

Several days having passed, Ismir's subjects, who saw
that he was forever plunged in sadness, solitary, and often
shutting himself away with the captain of his guards, resolved
to propose to him that he should give them a Queen in order to
assure his house of the succession of the throne. The most
considerable came to find him, and begged him on the part of
his people to render to their prayers, in order that there would

be princes of the blood. At that proposal, Ismir felt his heart constricted, and the tender amour that he conserved for Starlet caused his tears to flow.

"I do not want to refuse my people the recompense they expect for their attachment to me," he replied, "but I implore you, my friends, to give me time to make further searches for the beautiful Starlet, who, as you know, I love so tenderly. My amour for her has only increased; she merited that, and even if she were not the daughter of the powerful King of Fortunate Arabia, her virtues alone would render her worthy of the throne. If, in a year, I am given the certainty that she is no more, you can choose for me yourselves a Princess to your liking; before then, do not mention it to me again if you do not want to afflict me, which I do not believe that you do."

The delegates, having humbly prostrated themselves, faces to the ground, replied that nothing was more reasonable than what the King proposed. Further vessels were equipped and put to sea with an incredible diligence on order to go and search for Starlet again in all the parts of the world. As soon as they arrived in some port, or on the smallest beach, someone cried: "Whoever can give us news of the beautiful Princess Starlet will be recompensed with a beautiful province, which our King will give, with a hundred thousand gold coins and a fine horse."

That magnificent promise tickled all ears, but Etoilette was not found. The admiral would have wearied of so many futile journeys if he had loved Ismir less, but, not being able to resolve himself to returning without having news of the Princess, he kept on sailing

Let us see, however, what had become of her.

The waves had carried Starlet to a shore very close to a beautiful city; she was rescued by the King of the country, who was strolling along the sea shore. That prince was so moved by the youth and charms of Starlet that a generous compassion made him order that the beautiful stranger be transported to his palace, and that as much care should be taken of her as if she were his own daughter. He had had a daughter once. but she had been lost for a long time, and, no longer hoping to see her again, he resolved to adopt the one that fortune had conducted to his coasts.

She was, therefore, served and dressed as a princess and adored by the entire Court. The Queen made her a thousand amities, and the King's son even more than the Queen. Starlet received their caresses with all imaginable gratitude, but she shed tears continually; fêtes, hunts, tourneys and everything else that the King could imagine to dissipate her dolor, did not diminish it.

The Queen, who loved the beautiful young woman veritably, begged her one day to tell her the cause of her sadness; only the royal prince was present at the conversation. Starlet made no difficulty about recounting her misfortunes to them; she only suppressed the secret so much recommended by Herminette. Experience instructs better than all lessons; she feared being punished by the fay for a second time.

Starlet depicted her amour for Ismir so naively that she touched the good Queen and the young Prince, but when she revealed that she was the daughter of the King of Fortunate Arabia and that she had been captured when the city was sacked, the Queen threw her arms around her neck, took her in her arms and called her "dear daughter" a thousand times. The young Prince, delighted to recover such a lovable sister, immediately went to make the King party to such a fortunate discovery.

While the Queen and the Princess were delivering themselves to joy and their hearts were overflowing, the good King arrived. Starlet wanted to throw herself at his feet, but he hugged her tenderly in his arms and there was nothing but embraces, kisses, clarifications, and a confusion of infinitely touching words and things.

The joy became general and was communicated to the entire Court; cannons were fired, violins were played, pigeons, sweetmeats and preserves were eaten, and the most exquisite wines were drunk until people ran out of breath. Rockets, petards, marionettes and the people made a furious racket. Everyone wanted to see the Princess at the same time, and everyone brought presents, jewels, diamonds, fabrics, little dogs, sheep, monkeys and parrots. Starlet received everything with a good will and gratitude that enchanted everyone, and no one returned without having taken coffee with milk or redcurrant syrup.

The tumult finally diminished and the Princess resumed thinking about her dear Ismir; the uncertainty of his fate poisoned all her pleasures; she sighed, she relieved herself with tears, and lamented not being able to share with the Prince the happiness that had arrived for her.

In order to complete her difficulties the King her father accorded her to the powerful Emperor of the Deserts, in order to cement and render more durable a peace that he had just concluded with that redoubtable neighbor. The Princess thought she would die of dolor at such afflicting news; she threw herself at the knees of the King, her father and represented to him that, having pledged her faith to Prince Ismir, she absolutely could not belong to another.

The King treated her as a visionary, in spite of her tears and her arguments, and ordered her to make ready to receive the Emperor of the Deserts for a husband. She came a hundred times to throw herself into the arms of the Queen and implore her aid; that good mother shared her dolor and tried to console her, but she could not imagine any remedy; it was necessary to obey.

The Princess had such a violent chagrin in consequence that she refused all nourishment; she did not sleep at all. The preparations for her marriage still went forward, and the fatal moment drew nearer. One night, when she was afflicted even more than usual, she remembered the little box of the fay Herminette, and the present danger appeared to her to be more considerable than those she had run at sea. She resolved to make use of it this time, and opened it.

A dark vapor emerged from it and enveloped Starlet. A quarter of an hour later, the cloud having dissipated, she found herself on a ship of mother-of-pearl, in a chamber ornamented with mirrors and hung with silver brocade. She perceived, by the movement of the vessel, that it was at sea. A beautiful rock crystal chandelier illuminated the chamber.

The Princess, recovered somewhat from her astonishment, got up from the sofa on which she was lying and found herself facing a great mirror She saw with alarm that she had become an Ethiopian woman, clad in the Moorish style, in silver and rose-colored gauze, with a guitar slung over her shoulder, sustained by a string of diamonds, white and rose-colored, and a belt and brodequins garnished in the same way.

That magnificence did not console her for the loss of the most beautiful complexion in the world.

"Barbaric Herminette!" she cried, dolorously. "If you have conserved my lover, would he still love me under this frightful appearance? Take away my life, if you have condemned me to see him change."

She did not leave it at that, and ran on to the deck, determined to hurl herself into the waves. As she climbed up, a powerful hand retained her; she turned round, and saw the fay.

"Feeble Starlet," Herminette said to her. "The loss of your beauty is making you seek death, as if that advantage were the only one that could render you happy."

"Alas," replied the afflicted Princess, shedding a torrent of tears, "I only cherished it for Ismir, and Ismir will no longer love me." Sobs stifled her voice.

"But if destiny had attached the life of your lover to the loss of your beauty," said the fay, "which would you choose: that he died, and you recovered your face, or that he lived and you remained an Ethiopian?"

"That he lives," replied Starlet, swiftly, "but that I die, if I cease to please him."

"You shall both live," replied the charming Herminette, embracing the Princess, "and you shall live happy and content. So much confidence and such a perfect love merit that I protect you."

As she finished speaking, she disappeared, and Starlet no longer worried about her color. The little ship drifted fortunately, and eventually entered the port of Ismir's kingdom.

The beautiful Ethiopian leapt ashore lightly, and, turning her guitar around, which she played divinely, traversed the city, directing her steps toward the royal palace.

Ismir was descending its stairway at that very moment, in order to go and walk along the sea shore, as he did every day, and to see whether his admiral, of whom he had had no news, was arriving.

Starlet recognized the Prince immediately, and, seeing the crown on his head and a mantle of black gauze, did not doubt that he had become the King. She was only astonished to see a dove on his shoulder. She advanced tremulously and made him a very elegant and very delicate compliment.

The young King, delighted by the intelligence and grace of the Ethiopian, was convinced by the magnificence of her adornment that she was an important person. It is necessary to say everything: a secret presentiment, which only true lovers know, inspired curiosity in him; he therefore approached her urgently and asked her what brought her to his Court.

Starlet, penetrated by such a vivid joy at seeing her lover, thought she would die of dolor at not being recognized; but the joy prevailed, and above all the confidence she had in the promises of the fay. Without replying to the King, she tuned her guitar and sang these words, which she evidently made up as she went along:

I have come from a distant country
To put an end to your regrets.
Starlet, white as snow,
For you, for a perfect love
Refused a mighty king
Who made her a gift of his heart.
But that King, handsome, it's said,
Would never be worth for her
Ismir the dark-eyed and blond;

And she would rather be killed,
The genteel white virgin.
Than see herself infidel;
That is the whole of my song.

Ismir was delighted by the song. "Lovely black woman," he said to the Ethiopian, "do you know my dear Starlet, then, since you assure me that she is still alive?"

Scarcely had he spoken those words than the pigeon arrived in a flurry of wings and came to perch on the head of the Princess. The dove agitated its wings. The fay Herminette also appeared suddenly, and, touching the Ethiopian with her golden wand, she spared her the trouble of answering, for she then became once again the faithful, divine and ravishing Starlet.

Ismir nearly died of joy and astonishment. He precipitated himself at the feet of his mistress, who lifted him up immediately in order to put him at those of the fay.

"Always love one another thus, my children," she said, embracing them. "I have come expressly to crown such beautiful fires."

Ismir was beside himself. Starlet no longer knew herself; the sole sentiment that she was able to distinguish in such a confusion of thoughts was the gratitude that she wanted to express to the fay. The King gave them his hand and took them to his apartment. The surprise was redoubled there, for they found the King, the Queen and the Prince of Fortunate Arabia there, whom Herminette had transported instantly, by means of the powerful charms to which all Nature is submissive. With the best will in the world, they accorded the beautiful Starlet to the constant Ismir; the wedding was only delayed until the following day.

Ismir, having finally become Starlet's husband, was as happy a husband as he had been a faithful lover, and they always lived in the bosom of pleasures and the most perfect contentment.

Having finished her reading. Madame de Briance received the compliments of the entire company.

"In truth, Madame," said the Vicomtesse, "I don't remember having passed such an agreeable day in my life, and the tale that you have just had the kindness to read to us is a charming work. I cannot conceive how one would not amuse oneself making them perpetually when one has the talent to imagine them in that fashion."

The Marquise de Briance replied to the Vicomtesse's polite remarks with others, and everyone recalled what they had found most remarkable in that little work.

The Chevalier, who had gone to keep Tourmeil company, had passed his time no less pleasantly with that friend. After Tourmeil had finished the two scenes of the opera that Baron de Tadillac had requested of him, the Chevalier de Livry summoned him to keep the promise he had given him to tell him what had happened to him since their separation.

Tourmeil said that he was about to acquit that promise, and that he would even make the confidence of certain details that one can only reveal to a perfect friend. He commenced thus:

The Comte de Tourmeil's Story

I departed with the despair inspired in me by the loss of the pleasant hopes of my felicity, which I had believed to be certain, and I made the journey from Rennes to Paris without being conscious of it; I was beside myself. The thought that Mademoiselle de Livry was going to become the wife of Monsieur de Briance put me in despair. That cruel idea, faithful in tormenting me, presented itself incessantly to my mind in all the forms that could render it more catastrophic to me. Often, I dissolved in tears, and my courage could not stop them.

Having arriving in Paris I went to stay with one of my uncles. I told him, briefly, the story that you know. I do not know whether he allowed himself to be convinced; my mind was so confused that I said very little to him that was plausible; his amity for me was, I believe, what caused him to add faith to my words. He gave me some money and promised to enable me to obtain more in Venice. Finally, after having written to you and to Madame de Briance, I left Paris, guided by my anxieties alone, which did not permit me to stop in any place in the world; without being pressed, I made extraordinary haste.

My uncle had written to Venice in order that the money he had promised me would be given to me there; it was a considerable sum; and, believing that he was giving me agreeable news, he told me of the marriage of Monsieur de Briance and Mademoiselle de Livry. The certainty of my rival's happiness threw me into a mortal languor. I was ill for almost a month, and I was beginning to recover when I learned that the Republic's troops were soon to embark.

A gentleman who had been with my father and had been attached to me since my childhood, seeing that I was not in a state to take care of my equipage, offered to extract me from the anxiety of not being ready soon enough by rendering me that service. As soon as he had finished, without waiting for my strength to be entirely reestablished, I presented myself to the general at the moment when he was giving his orders for the embarkation of troops. I told him that I was a Spaniard, that my name was Don Fernand, that, having had a disagreement following a battle, I had absented myself in order to conclude my affair. The facility with which I spoke Spanish assisted in deceiving him. He received me with a generosity that touched me; he even offered to employ me, for which I thanked him, and I served in the quality of a volunteer.

The army went into action almost as soon as we landed; there were a few occasions when I gave evidence of the little attachment I then had to life. My despair was called valor and attracted the esteem and amity of our generals. Fortune, which reserved me the price of the torments that it made me suffer, conserved my life, the end of which I regarded as the sole good to which I could aspire.

One day, when I went for a walk in the environs of the camp, only accompanied by the gentleman that I mentioned, who was then my squire and to whom I had told of my woes, I was lamenting as we crossed a beautiful plain when we heard a tumultuous noise, mingled with a few women's screams. We saw soldiers appear a few moments later dragging two prisoners. We ran to save those two unfortunates from a destiny more cruel than their captivity.

The soldiers, to whom I was fortunately known, withdrew on my order with sufficient respect, and a little money that I gave them finished resolving them to yield their slaves, overwhelmed by the distress into which their disgrace had cast them. The magnificence of their garments caused me to judge that they were persons to whom respect was owed, and a few Italian words that they spoke rather confusedly, turning their eyes in the direction from which they had been brought, informed me that they did not believe that they were yet in safety.

I tried to reassure them; I offered them everything that depended on me, and asked them where they wanted to be taken. After some thanks that they made me in haste, the one who had spoken first said: "Save us from a cruel man who believes that the slavery in which he retains us ought to extent as far as our hearts."

I confess to you that if I had been in a state to become amorous, I would doubtless have done so for one of those lovely slaves, whose beauty, youth and dolor were so touching that my insensibility on that occasion is doubtless the proof of my passion, the strongest that I have ever given to Madame de Briance.

("That being," said the Chevalier, smiling, "one of the details of which you have not made her the confidence."

"True," said Tourmeil, "but is it not sufficient for me to have remained faithful? Why seek to make a merit out of having done my duty?")

I conducted the beautiful slaves to our camp, which was not very far away (Tourmeil continued). Having ceded my tent to them and having charged my squire with serving them as well as the place where we were might permit, I went to see the general. Having returned to one of my tents, I began to write.

"What?" sad my squire, who was always trying to extract me from my chagrin. "Is it possible that you aren't going to ask me for news of our beautiful slaves? Don't you want to go and see them?"

"I'll see them tomorrow," I replied to him. "My own misfortunes occupy me so much that it's unnecessary to be astonished that I'm less sensible to those of others."

"Are you in the same sentiments for those beautiful individuals," he asked me, "as Alexander for his prisoners?"

"You want to flatter me with great comparisons," I replied, "but I assure you that I do not fear, like Alexander, falling in love with my prisoners; I can expose myself to the power of their charms; let's go see them."

He went with me, and I found the two beautiful slaves lying negligently on a bed in their tent. The one whose beauty was the more perfect appeared to be the more afflicted. I tried to console her with the assurance of her liberty and that of facilitating their return to the place to which they wanted to be conducted.

"You are too generous, Don Fernand," said the one who appeared to a few years older—they had been informed of my name—"in rendering liberty to your slaves. If any price more worthy than our perfect gratitude were capable of flattering a man such as you appear to be, we would offer you a ransom that would doubtless be able to touch a soul less noble than yours.

"We are Greek, born in Argostoly, capital of Cephalonia; we were brought up on that island. Our parents held a considerable rank there, by virtue of their wealth and their birth. My sister's name is Fatime and mine is Praxile. We lost my mother while we were still in infancy and were destined by my father to marry two of our close relatives. The celebrations that preceded those unfortunate weddings cost us our precious liberty. A few days before the one chosen for our marriage we went for an excursion at sea in a small boat that was rather ornate but had no defense. Soliman, an old corsair who roamed that sea, hid from our view by favor of a rock, with the design of surprising us more easily, and as soon as he was in the open sea, having abducted us without meeting very much resistance, set sail diligently, leaving the small number of those who had accompanied us in our little boat.

"I shall not talk to you about our dolor, generous Don Fernand; it is easy to imagine, if imagination can go so far when one has not experienced that misfortune. We were served with a great deal of care and more respect than we had expected of that barbarian. Soliman took us to his homeland, and it was only after our arrival that he appeared to be in love with Fatime. That passion redoubled our dolors.

"Finally, after three months of slavery, still agitated by our misfortunes and the fatal dread that Soliman, weary of Fatime's rigors, would be driven to some violent action, as he had threatened quite often, we bribed one of our guards with the gems that remained to us. He facilitated our escape during the night, gave us horses, and ran away himself from Soliman's fury. When we encountered your soldiers, who took us prisoner, we were on our way to the nearest city to asked for a refuge against the cruelty of Soliman; but Heaven, in response to our woes, seems to have wearied of being contrary to us, since, in encountering Don Fernand, we have found a protector generous enough to give is hope that we might see our homeland again."

"Yes, Madame," I replied, touched by the story I had been told, "you shall see your homeland again, I promise you, and I shall keep my word."

She made me sincere thanks and heaped me with compliments. However, the beautiful Fatime had not ceased to shed tears; her beautiful languid eyes, which sometimes turned toward me, would doubtless have set another heart than mine ablaze.

("Those beautiful eyes," said the Chevalier de Livry, "have been removed from the story you told my sister.

"The more beautiful Fatime was," said Tourmeil, "the more the sacrifice is worthy of Madame de Briance.")

Praxile (Tourmeil continued), astonished to see Fatime testifying such an intense dolor at a time when the hope of liberty ought to be consoling her, said to her: "What, my sister, you're afflicted more deeply when Heaven is favorable to us than when it seemed to have abandoned us?"

"It's not without reason," I said. "The beautiful Fatime is regretting the absence of the fortunate lover who was to be her husband."

"Oh, Don Fernand," she said to me, raising her eyes, "don't add to my woes the injustice you are doing me."

She blushed after having pronounced those words, and Praxile told me that the indifference that had always reigned in Fatime's heart had made her take offense even at the suspicion of a passion.

I quit them, after reiterating all the offers of service that I had made them.

In the following days the rumor of my adventure and of their beauty having spread through the camp, the most considerable men of our army asked to see them. The first time I took them there, one of our general officers, who was one of my intimate friends, was smitten with a violent passion for the beautiful Greek, but, having perceived it, she begged me insistently not to bring him to their tent again.

That plea embarrassed me; I wanted to make use of some pretext to conduct my friend to the feet of the beautiful Fatime again, but all my artifices were futile. The beautiful Greeks pretended to be ill and constantly refused entry to their tent to all those who presented themselves. I alone had the privilege of seeing them when I made the request.

Fatime seemed plunged in a profound sadness; she sighed, and, if I dare say it, sometimes looked at me tenderly. My squire, who was always trying to make me forget the passion I had for Madame de Briance, called my attention to all the actions of the beautiful young woman.

One day, the two sisters having one into my tent when I was not there, found a notebook that I had left there. Fatime opened it at a place that was filled with French verses written in my hand, and, not being able to understand them, she asked my squire to explain them. He, not foreseeing the consequences, translated them into Italian. It is necessary, for the continuation of my story, that I recite them to you.

Yield, feeble reason, yield to my sadness;
In spite of your vain counsel, I want to dwell there incessantly;
What possession can soften the excess of my woe?
I have lost the object that I adore,
Too charming memory of my faithful ardor,
Alas, you still please me.
Even in irritating my dolor.
No, I cannot pretend to banish you from my soul;
Redouble my amour, augment my languor,
Rather than to reason, I surrender my heart to you,
You defend it better than a new flame.

("Those lines appear to me to be good," said the Chevalier. "There is reason to believe that dolor inspires better things than joy."

"If that is so," said Tourmeil, "I would rather be the most detestable poet in the world that think henceforth of lamenting my misfortunes. But let us get back to my story.")

My squire had noticed that Fatime blushed during the translation of those lines. That same evening, as he went past their tent, he heard the beautiful Greeks talking about me. He ran promptly to tell me that he had just learned a secret on which the repose of my heart might depend.

I thought that he was about to tell me something regarding Madame de Briance; that thought made me go outside with him. He led me precipitately to the same place where he had overheard them talking, and having lent and ear, he drew me closer, saying to me in a whisper: "Listen."

It was Fatime who was speaking; she was saying to her sister: "Yes, Praxile, I found less to lament when I was in Soliman's power; death could deliver me from his injustices; I would at least have had the relief of dying tranquilly; but the sight of Don Fernand has taken away from me forever the tranquility of which I had always made my happiness and my glory."

"I don't know what to say to you," said Praxile, "to console you for a misfortune that irritated Heaven is adding to our misfortunes. You have resisted with all your might the involuntary penchant that you feel for Don Fernand; he is unaware of your sentiments; you have done your duty; nothing more remains but to flee diligently from a place where your glory does not appear to me to be secure."

"My glory," said Fatime, proudly, "is secure no matter where I might be; but here my heart cannot resist, and it is the sight of the redoubtable Don Fernand that I want to flee. The verses that his squire read to us confirmed for me what his sadness had already made me suspect: he is in love, and his amour, utterly unfortunate as it appears to be, occupies him nevertheless with a passion that would be the happiness of his life." She sighed and exclaimed: "Unfortunate Fatime, what god has caused you to feel his wrath, by inspiring in you such tender sentiments, which you must hide?"

After having heard those last words I drew away, and I said to my squire: "What relationship does that conversation have with the repose with which you flattered me just now?"

"What?" he replied, quite astonished. "Can the passion that the charming Fatime has for you not perhaps make you forget...?"

"No," I replied, interrupting him. "No, nothing will ever efface from my heart the tender and unfortunate love that I have for Madame de Briance; what I have learned only adds to my woes that of knowing that I'm an ingrate."

I continued my way to my tent then, and whenever I had occasion to see the two beautiful Greeks thereafter, I never said anything to Fatime that could make her suspect that I had heard what she said to her sister. I even tried one day to talk to her about the merit of my friend, who was burning for her with a passion as tender as it was unfortunate, but Fatime, looking at me with an air that impressed me with respect, said: "Don Fernand, since you have rendered me liberty, cease to treat me as a slave."

Finally, after a month's sojourn in our camp, the beautiful Greeks begged me to keep the promise I had made them and to have them conducted to the port of Zante, where they had learned that a few merchant vessels set sail for Greece at that time every year.

"Until today," said Paxile, "when we thought that we ought to set forth to see our homeland again, we have preferred, generous Don Fernand, to be in your company than any other place in the world, and nothing would cause us a more sensible chagrin than not being able to mark to you, as we are obliged to do, our great gratitude."

The lovely Fatime added very little to her sister's thanks, occupying herself urgently with the preparations for their departure. The one appeared desolate, the other could not prevent herself from letting the joy she was experiencing in the depths of her heart burst forth. I confess to you that, in a happier state, I might perhaps have been less faithful, but, accustomed not to think about anything but my own misfortunes, my heart did not sympathize with Fatime's.

I therefore had a cart prepared for the beautiful Greeks; two slave girls that I had given them to serve them were destined to accompany them in their voyage, and I left them one of my men, named Desfontaines, whose fidelity was known to me, to accompany them until their embarkation.

My desolate friend begged me insistently to retain them for a little longer, in the hope that he might touch Fatime's heart, but I resisted all his pleas.

Finally, the day destined for the departure of the two beautiful Greeks having arrived, I went to their tent early in the morning. I found them about to mount their cart; my squire was giving his hand to Praxile. I gave mine to Fatime, whom I led to her vehicle without saying a single word to her. She sat down next to her sister and I mounted a horse in order to escort them personally a few leagues from the camp.

When we had arrived at the place where I was to quit them, having stopped the cart in order to bid them adieu, they got down under a clump of trees not far from the road. It was there that Fatime's constancy abandoned her. At that fatal moment, a few tears that she could not retain flowed from her beautiful eyes. I was veritably touched; I approached, and seeing me nonplussed, she looked at me tenderly and said: "What, Don Fernand, are you interested in our departure, then?"

"One cannot quit the beautiful Fatime," I said, "without sensing a sharp dolor; and" I added, sighing, "regretting that it did not please Heaven that my heart had been free to form prayers worthy of her."

"Oh, Don Fernand," she said, withdrawing abruptly, "let me go; what idea have you just added to all the woes of my life" She returned to her cart as quickly as possible. Praxile, who was amusing herself talking to my squire, followed her immediately. Having said a few words to them, I let them go and resumed the road to our camp.

It was because of that blow that I felt my heart afflicted by the most severe shocks of human weakness; I cannot hide from you, Chevalier, that the tears, the beauty and the tenderness of Fatime made me wish for the power to cure myself of a passion whose frequent ideas caused me insupportable transports in the particular. I was leading the saddest and languid life in the world. I appeared quite otherwise to the eyes of those I had the honor of frequenting, but nevertheless, I never let any opportunity escape, however perilous it might be, to expose myself to the evident danger of losing it.

A few weeks went by without my having any news of Desfontaines, to whom I had confided the conduct of the beautiful Greeks. My order had been only to escort them to the place of their embarkation, but the desire to travel that the man had always possessed had led him to depart with them without my consent. Finally, I received a letter from him that he had written to me before putting to sea; it begged my pardon and informed me that Praxile appeared perfectly content to return to her homeland, but that Fatime was in a languor that gave rise to the dread that the fatigues of the sea might expose her to the danger of losing her life, even though the journey was short.

Two months after his departure, Desfontaines came to rejoin me with the army.

"Well," I said to him, "did our beautiful Greeks arrive in their homeland safely?"

"They arrived there safely," he replied, "but the beautiful Fatime did not enjoy that pleasure for long; she died a few days after having seen her family."

What was my emotion at that news! You cannot conceive it, Chevalier; I cannot conceive it myself. My man, having perceived that, fell silent, and I said to him, overwhelmed by dolor: "Tell me, then, if you please, what accident terminated the life of the unfortunate Fatime."

"Our voyage had been fortunate," he said. "We embarked with a joy only troubled by Fatime's poor health. The father of the beautiful young women having been informed of our arrival, he came to receive them in the port, accompanied by two young men, magnificently dressed and very good looking, who testified a joy as perfect as his. Praxile embraced her father with an indescribable satisfaction, and Fatime, at the sight of him, appeared to forget her languor. They introduced me to their father; I was heaped with presents and treated as Don Fernand might have been himself.

"A few days after our arrival, everything was prepared for the marriages of the two young Greeks, who were to wed the two young men I had seen come to welcome them when they emerged from the ship, but that celebration was troubled by a violent fever that seized the beautiful Fatime; she languished for a few days; finally, she expired, testifying an infinite courage and no regret of life.

"Never has dolor appeared in as many forms as it did then. The father of the beautiful girl, the sister and the lover destined to be her husband were all in despair, and I was as afflicted as them. After having satisfied the desire I had to see that beautiful land, I testified to Praxile the design I had to rejoin you; she charged me with this box, and ordered me to present it to you on her behalf."

Desfontaines gave me the box; I found two letters in it, one from Praxile and the other from the father of the beautiful Greeks; they were full of marks of their gratitude for me and their dolor for the loss of Fatime. Afterwards, I opened a little packet that was in the same box; it contained portraits of the beautiful Greeks, enriched with diamonds of considerable value. I sighed at the sight of the portrait of the unfortunate Fatime and I charged the captain of a vessel that was due to depart for Argostoly with everything I could find of the most curious, in order to send to Praxile and her father, with a letter to express how much I shared their just dolor.

I learned, on the return of that captain, who brought me a letter from Praxile, that she had married the relative destined for her, and that she would have been very happy if the loss of Fatime had not troubled her felicity.

That tragic loss redoubled my chagrins; I reproached myself for having contributed, by my ferocity, to Fatime's unhappiness, and when opportunities to signal myself became less frequent in the army, where there was some kind of respite, my anxieties came in a host to overwhelm my mind. Sometimes it was Madame de Briance who occupied it, sometimes it was the death of Fatime. Finally, no longer being able to live in repose in Morea, I returned to Venice at the beginning of winter, with several of my fellow volunteers, who went to spend the carnival there.

As soon as I had arrived in the city, my squire went to see the banker from whom I had once received money. He found several letters there for me, which the man had kept, not knowing by what route he could enable them to reach me, for I had not informed him of my embarkation with the Republic's troops.

I opened my letters and the first being, by chance, the one that had arrived last, I found therein the only news that could resolve me to return to my homeland: that of the death of Monsieur de Briance. My uncle informed me of it, and also of the details of his testament, which was in my favor. I regretted him as the best of my friends; his death effaced from my memory all the misfortunes that he had caused me.

The ardent desire I had to see Madame de Briance again made me depart promptly. I wrote to my uncle that in a short while I would come to find him in Paris, but that I did not want them to stop in any other place.

I finally arrived in Rennes, and that was where I learned that you and Monsieur le Comte de Livry were at Madame de Briance's home. That news would have given me an extreme joy if I had not learned at the same time that Baron de Tadillac was there with you, that he had remained there for a few days unknown, and that he had then come to Rennes to seek a troupe of actors, and finally, that you were all at the Château de Kernosy.

I did not doubt then that Tadillac was in love with Madame de Briance, and I accused her of an infidelity that I had so little merited; I also complained of your forgetfulness, but having reflected, I said to myself: *They do not know what has become if me; perhaps Madame de Briance believes that I am no longer in the world.* A moment later, I went on: *Let us go and heap her with reproaches, and see whether the unknown rival is more worthy than me of a possession that has cost me so much.*

I left Rennes; I left almost all my men in a village a few leagues from here. I had a mind and heart so full of my chagrin and my jealousy, that I mistook your voice at first, and I took you for the rival of whom I had me in search. A few words that you said in engaging in combat with me aided me to realize my mistake. I had praised fortune for the opportunity that it had given me to fight my rival; it required nothing less than the joy of finding a friend like you to suspend my anger.

"I'm obliged to you," said the Chevalier, then, "for the complaisance you have had for me in telling me what I had so great a desire to know. I am convinced of your goodness by the story that you have just told of your adventures, but I regret the beautiful Fatime. It is an effect of your prudence not to have spoken about her to my sister; in her place, I would have had furious suspicions of your fidelity."

"I gave her the portrait yesterday," said Tourmeil, "without mentioning the beautiful Greek's passion; I only said that I got it from a merchant of Cephalonia; I made a pleasure of sacrificing the portrait to Madame de Briance without wounding the memory of Fatime."

The Chevalier found that conduct on Tourmeil's part very judicious, and, not wanting to leave him alone, he remained in conversation with him for the rest of the day; then he returned to the ladies, who were delighted that Fatville and his uncle, by departing that morning, had liberated them from two very tedious provincials.

Madame de Briance, perceiving her brother, suspected strongly that her lover had been left alone; she invented a pretext that gave the entire company an occasion to retire earlier than usually. The chosen few went, as usual, to her apartment. Tourmeil, having also gone there, had the pleasure of learning from the mouth of his mistress that she had the same sentiments with which he had left her when he quit her.

The following day, the weather being fine, Monsieur de Livry and the Baron, on leaving the table, proposed an excursion. The Vicomtesse, always complaisant regarding diversions in which the Baron had some part, went down into the garden without wasting any time and had the ladies climb into her carriage in order that they might have the pleasure of going, without being fatigued, to a wood where the paths were very spacious. The Baron went up to the coachman's seat, preferring that occupation to that of conversation. Madame la Vicomtesse took account of that gallantry, and admired at length the good grace of the new Phaeton, who did not suffer the cruel fate of the first, for he guided the horses and the vehicle safely to the place he had premeditated.

First he drew away from the castle, and then engaged in several lateral lanes where he would have had difficulty turning round if he had had any design to do so. The second carriage, which was driven by the Chevalier de Livry, followed the traces of the one in front. When darkness fell, the Baron, pretending to be searching for the road, drew away further still; the Vicomtesse's valets had been bribed in order not to indicate the veritable one.

Madame la Vicomtesse commenced to be alarmed; the other ladies, seeing that they were well accompanied and in a familiar region, were not anxious. The Baron and the Chevalier continued advancing; finally, they perceived a bright light. At first, everyone was of the opinion that they should go to that place in search to a guide who could, with the aid of a few torches, conduct the carriages without going astray as far as the Château de Kernosy. The Baron had stopped while awaiting the decision of that opinion. The confused noise of the words that various people were proffering at the same time was preventing him, he said, from hearing the opinion of Madame la Vicomtesse.

She imposed silence, in order to tell him that it was necessary to keep going toward the light that was visible in the distance. He obeyed immediately and continued his route until he had emerged from a beautiful avenue, whereupon a square building was fully revealed, the windows of which, all illuminated, composed by their symmetry a sight as agreeable as it was surprising. When they were within range of the building, they heard the sound of a number of instruments being tuned, and the voices of several persons who seemed to be occupied with the functions with which each of them was charged.

Madame la Vicomtesse deliberated for rather a long time as to whether she should make herself known, and Mademoiselle de Saint-Urbain, seeing that she was having difficulty making up her mind, said: "Why not? This adventure does not appear perilous; I hope that we will get out of it without any problem."

The Baron descended from his seat and said: "I'll go and enquire" he said, "as to where we are."

The two carriages having stopped, someone opened the door without waiting for anyone to knock. When they were in the courtyard, four men dressed as savages came to greet Madame a Vicomtesse and, having perceived her at the lead of several ladies who had already dismounted, two of them went ahead of her and the others placed themselves at the sides of the troop following her, and all four escorted the company as far as the entrance to a large drawing room ornamented by a quantity of chandeliers, the light of which caused a new day to succeed the one that had just ended.

Two savages who were waiting in the room, having approached armchairs to a large fire, withdrew, after having bowed profoundly.

It was about a quarter of an hour after they had entered when a young child appeared, dressed in the Roman style and asked whether it would be agreeable if the Seigneur of the Brilliant House came to offer his services. The Vicomtesse, charmed by that proposal, asked the pretended dwarf to assure the master of the house that it would be an extreme pleasure to see him.

When the child had gone, the Baron said that he was jealous of that unknown Prince, who seemed to be disputing with him the honor of Madame la Vicomtesse's company. Then the Seigneur of the Brilliant House appeared, preceded by four men in Roman garb, who were carrying torches. He was wearing a robe the color of fire, in the Armenian style, lined with marten fur, a magnificent sash over a long jacket of golden cloth, and kind of small cap on his head covered with plumes, white and the color of fire. In his hand he was holding, gracefully, a gilded wand.

It was Tourmeil, who, in order to give the Baron pleasure, was representing a character in the little fête, and who, being obliged to appear in a bizarre costume before Madame de Briance, had not wanted to neglect anything. There was only Baronne de Sugarde who had been left in ignorance of the verity of the little adventure, in order to have the pleasure of her astonishment. She was charmed by the Seigneur of the Brilliant House, and forgot for some time the liking that had always been remarked on her part for the Chevalier de Livry.

"Fortune has conducted you into my empire, Madame," said the Seigneur of the Brilliant House to the Vicomtesse. "I have already rendered thanks to her, and I am flattered that this great day must be the one on which great enchanter has predicted a supreme happiness for me, by virtue of the arrival of a lady whose great qualities render her amiable, and whose charming humor leads one to prefer her person to the great wealth she possesses. I shall refrain from raising my thoughts as far as you, Madame; I know," he continued, indicating the Baron, "that destiny has reserved you for this faithful chevalier. He is worthy of you by his amour and his merit; I shall not trouble a union that will be so beautiful."

The ample terms that Madame la Vicomtesse employed in her response to this obliging discourse would have rendered it too long and perhaps tedious, if the savages had not come to interrupt the flow of her speech by bringing a table that was magnificently laid.

The Seigneur of the Brilliant House did the honors of his house; everyone sat down at table; he sat next to Madame de Briance and talked to her in a familiar fashion. That made Madame de Sugarde desolate; she could not bear the thought that the seigneur, whoever he might be, appeared to be more touched by the charms of another woman than her own. The Vicomtesse complimented Madame de Briance on her conquest, and said to the Seigneur of the Brilliant House that it was doubtless by that beauty that the enchanter's prediction would be accomplished. He replied gravely that he, too, was beginning to believe so.

Oboes played during the meal; the savages served at table. As soon as it was finished, the Seigneur of the Brilliant House conducted the company into a room separated by a small vestibule from the one in which they had just had supper, still holding Madame de Briance's hand—because, he said, he did not want to oppose the orders of destiny by exposing himself too closely to the charms of the Vicomtesse.

She placed herself first in an armchair that had been prepared or her facing a well-designed little theater; the ladies took their places in the second row, and, the musicians having placed themselves in the third, the actors appeared as soon as the symphony had ceased. They performed *Le Bourgeois Gentilhomme* with all its delights, and attracted the applause that they merited.[41]

"Those are our actors from Rennes," said the Vicomtesse, recognizing them.

"That's true," replied the Seigneur of the Brilliant House. "I knew that they had had the honor of pleasing you, Madame, and with a stroke of my wand I transported them here in order to amuse you."

Madame la Vicomtesse understood, by that response, that everything that was happening was a gallantry on the part of the Baron, and, for fear that he might think that she had been taken in to begin with, she said, raising her voice: "Whoever the master of this house might be, I am very obliged to him for having made all these agreeable enchantments for me, which must surely have cost him more difficulties and cares than he would like us to believe."

Baronne de Sugarde, having also recognized the actors, judged that it was Tadillac who was giving the fête, but the Seigneur of the Brilliant House still embarrassed her; he had

---

[41] *Le Bourgeois gentilhommme* is a 1670 comedy ballet by Molière.

so much intelligence, and a manner so polished, that she could not mistake him for a country actor, nor for a provincial.

The seigneur who was the cause of that jealousy, accomplished in all fashions, got up as soon as the play had finished, made a great reverence to Madame la Vicomtesse and commenced the ball with her. The ladies, fearing that Monsieur de Livry and the Baron de Tourmeil might be fatigued by too much dancing, each begged in her turn those of the actors who were distinguished in that exercise. The men did the same with the actresses; the company, by that means, having become more numerous, the ball went on much longer, and the pleasure was no less agreeable for it.

They had already been occupied in that diversion for two hours when they saw four savages come in suddenly, each carrying two torches. Immediately, the seigneur of the house presented his hand to Madame la Vicomtesse and conducted her into the hall where they had eaten supper; the entire company followed, as well as the actors. Refreshments were served, which the exercise of dancing rendered most agreeable. Some took chocolate, others coffee, and others liqueurs, of which there was a profusion; in sum, everyone found something satisfactory, in accordance with their taste, for ices and marmalades were not lacking either.

Having done that, they returned to the ballroom, but the company was astonished to see the theater illuminated again, with a stage set that represented a wood so naturally that it would not have taken much to make them believe that it was the one from which they had gone astray in coming from Kernosy Castle to the Brilliant House. The symphony was heard; as soon as it had finished, the following words were sung, which Tourmeil had composed, and in which he had not forgotten Madame de Briance, knowing full well that she would be present at the little opera—which only had two scenes, as Tadillac had wanted.

(If, in a few places, one finds that they lack accuracy, it is less the fault of the author than the person who is recounting these events, for having only heard the words once, it is very difficult to remember them exactly.)[42]

Scene I
Tircis, Philemon

PHILEMON
When Amour, in these tranquil places,
Wants to assemble the sweetest pleasures,
Why, Tircis, do you trouble them
With sighs and futile cares?

TIRCIS
I am seeking in vain in this remote wood
A sweet repose that returns me to myself;
Alas, I there any tranquility for me?
Pitiless Amour has resolved that I love.
I have fled to flee myself from his barbaric laws;
But he has made my shepherdess so lovely
That as soon as he offers her once to our gaze
She can only be avoided by going away.

PHILEMON
In favor of a lover so tender and so faithful
Launch, Amour, launch your arrows,
Pierce the heart of that beauty
Since she already has your attractions,
In favor, etc.

---

[42] This odd insertion implies that "the person who is recounting these events" is one of the dramatis personae, although the narrative voice of the frame narrative has previously seemed to be objective, omniscient and situated outside the narrative. Perhaps it merely reflects the fact that the actual author, Murat. identifies particularly strongly with one of her characters; if so, Mademoiselle de Saint-Urbain is surely the likeliest candidate.

498

TIRCIS
Pierce the heart of that beauty.

PHILEMON
In favor of a lover so render and so faithful,

TIRCIS & PHILEMON
Launch, Amour, launch your arrows.

TIRCIS
The ingrate is coming into this forest.

PHILEMON
I do not want to trouble amorous secrets.

Scene II
Tircis, Silvie

SILVIE
I have come to seek in this solitude
To lament the evils of the amorous empire.
Might I not calm my sad anxiety here...?
Oh! I find you here [aside] *May my fate be happy!*

TIRCIS
Cease, cease to flee an unhappy lover.
Why do you unleash your unjust anger
Against such a perfect ardor?
Some god who is contrary to me
Amour, tender Amour answers for my heart.
I swear to your attractions an immortal ardor;
I will always burn with a flame so bright;
And if I dare to betray such tender oaths
May the most redoubtable of the gods,
The god who makes the happiness of lovers,
Never be favorable to me.

SILVIE
I would like to believe your oaths;
They have disarmed my anger;
A young and vain shepherdess
Is applauding herself for causing your torments,
But my amour assures me at every moment
That I merit a sincere heart
I want to believe your oaths;
They have disarmed my anger.

BOTH TOGETHER
Let us redouble our vivid ardors
Let us banish the sad alarms;
So that all Amour has of charms
Will reigns forever in our hearts

SILVIE
In vain I thought I could break my chain;
It is my destiny to sigh for you.
I shall no longer oppose the penchant that draws me;
Far from lamenting my pain,
I shall always lament unjust anger.

THE GOBLINS
Which makes me prefer the furies of hatred
To the pleasure of such a charming and sweet amour
Etc.

TIRCIS
Nightingales of this peaceful place
Forget, if possible, your most tender amours,
To sing the beauty that has rendered me sensible,
Employ the beautiful days.
Remember the songs I shall teach you;
They alone will always please.
Never will my faithful and tender heart

Make you sing of further amours;
Philomele, come to hear me.
Amour, who alone makes the joy of my life,
Of a fortunate mortal, make the gods jealous.
Their glorious destiny gives me no envy;
To be loved by the beautiful Silvie
Is a destiny a hundred times sweeter

DUO
Let us redouble, etc.

The author of those words and the person who had set them to music had reason to be content with the applause of the company. They left the room in order to go into the drawing room, where they conversed for a long time, while warming themselves, about the beauties of that little opera.

Day was beginning to break, and the Seigneur of the Brilliant House, who had not discontinued doing the honors of his abode, and for whom the fatigue of having being awake all night had opened the morning appetite, judged that the entire assembly must be in the same need.

He ordered that the table be set, and although the repast was as magnificent as the supper, the pleasures of the table were not those that occupied them most; everyone appeared delighted to be next to their inclinations. Messieurs de Livry were alongside Mesdemoiselles de Kernosy; the Baron was paying his court to Madame la Vicomtesse; the Comte de Tourmeil, indifferent to all the delicious dishes that were in front of him, was only thinking about talking to Madame de Briance; on the other hand, Madame de Salgue congratulated herself on seeing that Tadillac was only rendering homages to Madame la Vicomtesse. Only the Baronne, devoured by her jealousy, could not suffer that someone other than her had been able to win, by her charms, the heart of the seigneur of the house.

The company was so replete with joy that they would have reached the hour of noon insensibly while at table if

Madame la Vicomtesse's domestics had not come to inform her that the carriages were ready.

The broad daylight, having dissipated the enchantments of the previous night, allowed the realization that the house where they were belonged to a gentleman neighbor of Madame la Vicomtesse who, three or four years before, had made it into a large detached house in the modern style. The gentleman only came to it in the summer. His absence had facilitated the Baron's means of bribing the concierge and making him consent, in return for an honest recompense, to the fête being celebrated there, the invention of which pleased the ladies to much that they lavished a thousand praises upon it.

From then on, Madame la Vicomtesse could no longer live without the Baron; she was enchanted by his noble and magnificent manners, and the Seigneur of the Brilliant House, with all his advantageous qualities, had not diminished the passion that the lady in question felt for Tadillac. There is no reason to be astonished by that, for the Seigneur of the Brilliant house had left her in the error she had made in sincerely believing that he was the master of the troupe of actors.

They did not arrive at Kernosy Castle until noon. The Vicomtesse's servants were not distressed by her absence; Saint-Urbain had been careful to warn them that they would not be returning until the morning. They told the Baron as he came in that a courier had arrived in order to deliver a letter to his own hand, and who seemed to want to speak to him very urgently.

The Baron acted as if that news came as a great surprise to him, because it was given to him in the presence of the Vicomtesse, who took note of what was said to him and ordered him to come and inform her when she woke up of the news that the courier had brought him, because she was going to obtain a few hours of repose, in order to recover from the fatigues of the night. Before going into her room she advised him to go and get some sleep as well, and to tell her servants that they should not fail to send the courier up when he came to ask for him.

The ladies, following the example of Madame la Vicomtesse, went to bed. Messieurs de Livry and the Comte de Tourmeil—who had arrived with the actors, whose chief he appeared to be—spent the rest of the day together in various diversions. The Baron de Tadillac could not join them because the pretended courier came back just as they were about to go into their apartment. The domestics sent him up, in accordance with the order they had received, and Tadillac retained him for a long time thereafter, in order that no one would suspect the supposition of the man in question.

The Baron went to the Vicomtesse's room as soon as she had woken up. His sad expression made her shiver; she wanted to know the reason for the dejection that appeared on his face, but for all response, she only heard profound sighs. Finally, the Baron told her that he was very unhappy, that he was being snatched away from her company

"Eh! Why?" said the Vicomtesse, quite astonished.

"Look, Madame, if you please, at the letter I have received," said the Baron. It was the letter that Tourmeil had written.

Having read it, she tried to console him with a discourse that came straight from the heart.

"Your uncle is very pressing," she said. "I see that he is offering you a considerable party and that he is instructing you to go, without losing a moment, to keep the promise that he has made on your behalf. But you might find a fortune as considerable elsewhere. I...."

As she was about to continue, Madame de Sugarde came in; the Baron was obliged to withdraw, and was not found at the play that evening.

Madame la Vicomtesse spent her time there making reflections on Tadillac's absence; finally, fearing that he had made his decision and that he would obey his guardian, she left on her own, and went to lie down on a small bed that was in her cabinet. Her anxiety did not abate and her mind did not become tranquil until the arrival of the Baron, whom she had summoned.

"You are going to see," she said, as soon as he had come in, "the extent to which I am touched by a veritable merit. I cannot suffer that a man like you should seek elsewhere a fortune that it depends on me to render as agreeable as the one offered to you on the part of your uncle. I declare that I consent to marry you, and that nothing henceforth will be able to separate us if you love me as much as I flatter myself that you do."

The Baron interrupted her by throwing himself at her knees, and said a quantity of things that the Vicomtesse took for an excess of his passion.

Saint-Urbain came in at that moment to say that supper had been served They went out of the Vicomtesse's cabinet together; the Baron gave her his hand to go down, and went into the hall still holding it, with a cheerfulness that was a good augury for the two lovely sisters and their lovers.

The evening was not protracted; everyone separated when they left the table, because the diversions of the previous night had caused an indispensable necessity to take repose. After having paid his court to Madame la Vicomtesse, whom he had just conducted to her apartment, the Baron went to Madame de Briance's apartment, where he found the Comte de Tourmeil, Messieurs de Livry and Mesdemoiselles de Kernosy. He rendered them an account of the success of his letter; he was congratulated on it, and he received the compliments with such good grace that it was evident that he was content. That was not without reason; he knew that in marrying Madame la Vicomtesse, as he had always desired, he was assuring his fortune and his happiness.

"Your wishes are accomplished," the Chevalier said to him. "What will become of us now? Nothing flatters our hopes yet."

"You're very prompt," the Baron replied. "I've scarcely had a moment to thank Madame la Vicomtesse; tomorrow I shall work for you. I hope that Monsieur le Comte de Livry will be content, and that Mademoiselle de Saint-Urbain will never be the wife of Monsieur de Fatville. I even dare to flatter myself that if the opportunity presents itself to make Monsieur de Tourmeil known to Madame la Vicomtesse, she will be delighted to learn of his passion for Madame de Briance and that she will make use of all her credit to advance their marriage."

The following day, the Baron, who sincerely desired to contribute to the happiness of his two cousins, went in the morning to render a visit to Madame la Vicomtesse, in order to talk to her in private. He proposed to her the alliance of Messieurs de Livry for her two nieces. The Vicomtesse accepted the proposition of giving Kernosy to the Comte de Livry; "But," she said to the Baron, "since I have accorded you a part of what you request, give me the pleasure of speaking to Saint-Urbain and disposing her to obey me. I have reasons that oblige me to want absolutely her marriage with Monsieur de Fatville; if I could dispense myself from it, I would do so in order to please you. Go, then to announce to her that the Messieurs de Fatville and their uncle will arrive here today."

The commission that the Baron had just received, against his expectation, embarrassed him. He did not think it appropriate to reveal to the Chevalier the verity of the fact, nor to desolate Saint-Urbain by telling her of her aunt's intention; he only told her that Messieurs de Fatville would be arriving that evening. That amiable person, extremely afflicted to hear such terrible news, pretended to be ill and went to bed, in order not to be obliged to appear. Madame de Briance kept her company. Kernosy did not want to quit her, but Madame la Vicomtesse insisted absolutely that she come to do the honors of the house.

The councilor Fatville and his uncle arrived in the evening; shortly thereafter, Fatville's brother came in a litter, because he was not yet sufficiently recovered from his fall to ride a horse, and he entered the theater hall, where everyone was. The Vicomtesse received him agreeably and told him immediately that as soon as the play was finished she would introduce him to her niece, who had been taken ill.

The Chevalier de Livry sensed movements of anger at the sight of his rival, and his prudence would not have been able to retain them if it had not been seconded by that of his brother and the advice that Tourmeil had given him.

After the play, the Vicomtesse took Fatville and the company into Saint-Urbain's bedroom. That unexpected visit embarrassed the niece greatly. But whatever her embarrassment was, the one remarked on the face of Fatville's elder brother was far greater; he could not put two words together and never ceased looking at Tourmeil, whom he found in the room. Madame de Briance, who was beside him, told the Vicomtesse that she had sent for him in order to learn a few pieces from their little opera. That discourse augmented Fatville's suspicion; he looked at him even more fixedly. Tourmeil not wanting to be known, left immediately, but the provincial did not appear to be any more tranquil in consequence.

The Vicomtesse, who could not understand the cause of that mental agitation on either side, took Messieurs de Fatville away and left Saint-Urbain at liberty with Madame de Briance.

Following their exit, they discussed the reasons for the emotion that had appeared on the provincial's face at the sight of Tourmeil, and, finding nothing plausible, they concluded that he added to many other faults that of being unreasonably jealous.

Meanwhile, the Chevalier was in despair; he did not find Saint-Urbain resolute enough to disobey her aunt.

"Oh, my brother," he said to Tourmeil—for he often called him by that name—"how unhappy I am! How I envy your destiny. You are tenderly loved, nothing opposes your hopes."

"You are loved as well," replied Tourmeil, "and when one is loved, it is to offend Amour to complain with so much violence. You do not love if you do not hope. Hope is inseparable from amour, and at the same time that one believes that one loves without that flattering aid, one would die of dolor if hope were not hidden in the depths of the heart that believes that it is lost."

Tourmeil tried in vain to console the Chevalier; it required a great effort to resolve him to return to the Vicomtesse's room; he finally went there, and gazed when he went in at his rival with a terrible jealousy, of which he would not have been the master if he had not sensed his friend by his side, who did not want to abandon him on this occasion.

Less prejudiced that the Chevalier, Tourmeil considered the provincial with more attention than he had done in Saint-Urbain's bedroom, and after hearing him speak several times, he said to the Chevalier: "Its him; yes, it's him."

The Chevalier demanded an explanation of those words.

"Let's go out," said Tourmeil, lowering his voice. "I'll raise your hopes again."

The Vicomtesse then proposed to Messieurs de Fatville to sign the articles that their uncle had drawn up after supper. Kernosy, afflicted by that proposition, left the room in order to go and warn her sister of her aunt's design

Meanwhile, Tourmeil having told the Chevalier the secret that ought to contribute to rendering him happy, sent someone to ask the Baron to come and find him.

The Vicomtesse, who observed a great stir in the company, fearing that Saint-Urbain, little disposed to follow her will, might be thinking of escaping in order to go to a convent or to one of her relatives, gave secret orders for the doors of the castle to be locked. They brought her the keys with less discretion, however; a harebrained valet gave them to her in front of Messieurs de Fatville.

The presence of Tourmeil and the Chevalier de Livry, the murmur that was spreading through the castle and the sight of the keys that had just been brought, all seemed to announce to the elder Fatville the impossibility of his marriage. The apprehension of some misfortune troubled his mind so strongly that, throwing himself at the feet of the Vicomtesse, he said to her: "Oh, Madame, do you want to doom me? I have been recognized, I have no doubt of it. Monsieur de Tourmeil and the Chevalier de Livry are here; make my peace with them; I accept all the conditions they want to impose on me."

"What is the matter?" said the Vicomtesse, surprised by the provincial's words and action. "What quarrel do you have with the Chevalier de Livry? Where have you seen the Chevalier de Tourmeil of whom you speak?"

"Oh, my nephew," cried Fatville's uncle, "you are dooming yourself with your fear; without that, Madame la Vicomtesse would know absolutely nothing about the unfortunate adventure that happened to you."

"Yes," said the Chevalier, coming in, "Madame knows nothing about it; but I shall inform her of it. Fatville, whom you see, Madame," he continued, "is the accomplice of the assassination in Rennes that followed the quarrel I had had with a provincial gentlemen; I was wounded and Monsieur de Tourmeil, the dearest of my friends, nearly lost his life in generously defending mine. It was by the hand of this coward that Tourmeil was struck from behind. We did not know his name, because the assassin who was caught did not know it himself, he only deposed that the man who had wounded Tourmeil was a friend of the provincial with whom I had quarreled."

Fatville's uncle, who had intelligence, judging accurately by the confusion that his nephew was in that he was in no state to respond, gave the Chevalier de Livry all the reasons that an honest man can give for defending a bad cause and for trying settle the affair amicably.

"This," Fatville the councilor said then, "is doubtless what the accursed goblins had come to predict. This stupidity would not have fallen to earth and would have been deflected, if we had not been too occupied elsewhere."

The Vicomtesse, who prided herself on her grandeur of soul, seemed indignant at the bad action of Fatville, and yet, out of consideration for his uncle, she begged the Chevalier to pardon the unfortunate gentleman.

The Chevalier, who was veritably generous, accorded the Vicomtesse all that she asked of him with a good grace.

"But I cannot enjoy the mercy that Monsieur le Chevalier de Livry is willing to grant me," said the frightened Fatville, "if Monsieur de Tourmeil is not as generous as him."

The Chevalier, who saw that there was no longer any means of hiding the Comte de Tourmeil from the Vicomtesse, asked her to pass into his cabinet. The Baron followed them there. They explained to her briefly the various interests that had obliged Tourmeil to disguise his veritable condition for a few days.

The Vicomtesse forgave the mystery, in favor of the air of romance that she found in the adventure, and the Baron, fining her in a good humor, said to her: "There is no appearance that you would have given Saint-Urbain to Fatville without having pressing reasons. I approve of the fact that the Chevalier has pardoned that perfidious individual, since you have asked him to do so, but Madame, can you not make more useful service of the pardon that Tourmeil will doubtless also grant in response to your pleas?"

The Vicomtesse found that Baron de Tadillac was right; she saw herself in the obligation of some gratitude to the Chevalier, who had just granted her plea for Fatville's pardon with such good grace, and as she did not admit to her romance the scant care that heroines have for their interests, her resolution was, following Tadillac's advice, to profit from the opportunity to the extent of the twenty thousand livres that she owed Monsieur de Fatville. After all, Fatville was only too happy to get out of the affair so cheaply. He had given his word to Madame la Vicomtesse that he would write off that debt before marrying Mademoiselle her niece, and his uncle had even offered a sum as considerable, in proposing the accommodation with Messieurs de Tourmeil and the Chevalier de Livry.

The resolution made, the Chevalier went out, and the Baron remained alone with the Vicomtesse; not wanting to allow the good will in which he saw her to cool, he proposed to her, without further ceremony, to give Mademoiselle de Saint-Urbain to the Chevalier de Livry, who had a good deal of wealth, merit and birth, and to whom she already belonged, having accorded Mademoiselle de Kernosy to his brother.

"My eyes are finally open," said the Vicomtesse, then. "Your two cousins are in love here; but since, by their means, I have found the same advantage that I found in giving my niece to Monsieur de Fatville, and furthermore, that I can easily judge that you desire the alliance in question, I accept with pleasure."

The consent of the Vicomtesse charmed the Baron; he begged her to ensure, that very evening, the happiness of so many amiable persons and his own, by permitting her to declare the fortune that she reserved for him.

The Vicomtesse, moved by the Baron's speech, summoned Madame de Briance and Messieurs de Livry, in order to inform them that she accepted the proposition that the Baron had made on their behalf. No more perfect joy ever succeeded a more frightful sadness.

The fortunate lovers ran to announce their good fortune to Mesdemoiselles de Kernosy. Madame de Briance was delighted to see her brothers even more perfectly united with her by that alliance, and the Fatvilles were satisfied by the generosity of their enemies. Madame de Salgue, exempt from jealousy and touched by the amour and charms of the Baron, was the first to testify to the Vicomtesse the joy she had at their marriage. Baronne de Sugarde alone was discontented; she had no more hope of the Chevalier de Livry. That reflection could only cause her chagrin, but the time was not appropriate to allow her sentiments to appear.

The night passed without it being possible for the god of sleep to reign for a moment over a population was devoted to joy; the agreeable disturbance that fortunate amour bears into hearts agitates them as much as the most cruel sadness. Everyone instead of going to bed, employed themselves vigorously in terminating the Fatville affair before the night was over. Tourmeil pardoned him on conditions advantageous to the Vicomtesse, but in his own regard, he only knew the pleasure of according a generous pardon to his enemy, as the Chevalier de Livry had done.

As soon as it was daylight, the Fatvilles left the castle, and the lovers, satisfied with their destiny, thought of nothing but choosing the day of their marriage; it was only postponed by three days; even so, they found the time too long for the liking of their impatience. Magnificence reigned therein less than joy and amour. The Comte de Livry married Mademoiselle de Kernosy; the Chevalier, Mademoiselle de Saint-Urbain; and the Baronne de Tadillac, Madame la Vicomtesse.

Tourmeil was not so fortunate, only marrying Madame de Briance a few months after her friends, family reasons having delayed their marriage. He sighed and complained dolorously of being alone on a day destined to felicity.

"You have a fortune to which you are giving no reflection," the Baron said to him on the day of their wedding. "You are, you say, the most unfortunate of lovers? I am sure that you are today the most amorous."

Tourmeil did not much care for that species of consolation, but Amour only delayed his happiness in order to render it even more perfect; he married Madame de Briance and was veritably happy with her. It even seemed that their marriage rendered their amour more ardent and more tender.

They spent a few more months together at Kernosy Castle; after that time, Tourmeil and Messieurs de Livry took their beautiful wives away. The Baron might perhaps have suffered ennui in remaining alone with his own, if the neighborhood of the charming Madame de Salgue had not compensated him for it.

THE FAY PRINCESS

There once reigned in the empire of the fays a princess celebrated for her great knowledge. She was born with a heart naturally borne to tenderness, but she loved liberty even more. She knew the value of it so well that it was with all the difficulty in the world that she decided to marry. She only determined to do it in order to ensure the happiness of her people; she also wanted her marriage to be made secretly. Those sorts of engagements have always have an air of gallantry, and gallantry was one of the things to which the princess in question was infinitely sensible.

She chose for a husband one of the neighboring kings, who, by virtue of an inconstancy common in the time of the fays, quit her some time after his marriage in order to return to his estates. The Queen, whom he left pregnant, gave birth very fortunately to a girl, whom the fay named Princess. That title belonged to her, since she was to succeed her mother, the Queen. Nothing had yet been seen in that land of marvels as perfect as that lovely princess. Her beauty surpassed all ideas; it is therefore impossible to describe. The fays who presided over her birth found nothing to add to the graces with which Nature had ornamented her.

When she had reached the age of twelve years, she was given, to the contentment of the entire empire of the fays, the keys to the powder of youth. That was a confidence, and even a dignity, that was never accorded to anyone but the heir presumptive to the throne. The Queen had given her as a governess the fay Menodie. The knowledge of that illustrious person was almost equal to that of the Queen. She was ordinary known as the Fay of the Serpent; I have never known why. I do know from a reliable source that she had been charged with looking after the seals of the kingdom, before the education of the princess was confided to her, and that she acquitted that important commission perfectly, fulfilling that first responsibility worthily.

The efforts of the Queen to hide the dolor that the inconstancy of the King caused her were futile; she suffered impatiently from his absence and few days passed without her writing a long letter to him. But she pressed him in vain to come to the Court; his passion for the Queen was extinct; perhaps he even had a new one in his heart. At any rate, the pretexts succeeded one another and were renewed, and his letters always promised his return, and sometimes calmed the Queen's anxieties for a few moments.

One day, when she was due to receive ambassadors that her husband the King had sent her, all the fays were ordered to go to the palace and to display the magnificence of the Court. She wanted to appear with new charms herself in the hope of making them talk about her eulogistically to the King. It is a species of coquetry that is not uncommon. To achieve that effect, she wanted to make use of the powder of youth and to repair what dolor had been able to efface of her natural beauty, but there was none in the treasury. The fay Princess, to whom it that important deposit had been confided, as I said, had given it to all those who asked for it. Her generosity was the cause of all her misfortunes.

If that accident had thrown the Queen into a terrible anger I would not have been at all surprised, but it put her in a sullen mood, which is incontrovertibly a thousand times more difficult to sustain, as anyone who has suffered from it will agree. She expelled the princess from her presence; she took away the keys that she had confided to her, and suspended her lessons in enchantment, a profound science into the unknown mysteries of which he had begin to receive initiation. As discontented amour is always unjust, she also threatened to imprison her for ten years in a tower if her father the King did not return to the Court within six months.

Those threats overwhelmed the fay Princess with dolor. She shut herself in her cabinet and did not want to appear at the audience that the Queen gave to the ambassadors. It is true that she was in too great an affliction, and everyone knows that in such situations one does not want to appear in public. Her absence on such a famous occasion astonished the entire Court, and the most considerable persons, having been informed of the reasons for the quarrel, came in a crowd to offer the young fay their services; for it has always been seen and always will be, that courtiers or people given to intrigue offer to be useful to discontented princes.

The lovely Princess thanked them for the attachment that they expressed, but begged them to suspend their urgency, and asked them for the rest of the day in order to decide what course of action she ought to adopt. The fay Menodie interrupted that conversation. She had just left the Queen, having tried in vain to soften her. When all the courtiers had withdrawn, she mingled her tears with those of the princess, who confided her fears to her, told her the story of the Queen's threats, and confessed to her that the idea of prison had something so frightening for her that she was resolved to travel the world rather than submit to such a punishment.

The governess, being worthy—as they almost all are— loved the princess with a tenderness that caused her to share her woes. The last conversation she had had with the Queen determined them to depart immediately; she arranged in three pearls everything that was necessary for the voyage, and when the package was made they mounted two canaries, which flew away with great rapidity.

The Queen only learned of their departure when they were already out of her realm. She repented of having pushed her anger so far; she was all the more mortified because it was no longer possible for her to make the princess come back against her will, but she enchanted her so that she could only be seen at twenty paces, hoping that the tedium of always being alone would engage her to return.

Meanwhile, the voyage of the fay Princess continued without obstacles; she drew away diligently, and when she was quite certain of having covered a distance so considerable that I dare not number the leagues, she wanted to take a moment's repose in a place that appeared agreeable to her; it was undoubtedly in a delightful valley irrigated by a charming stream.

Menodie opened one of the pearls then. A tent of crimson fabric embroidered in gold emerged from it, with a bed, sofas and everything that might be necessary for their comfort. Then the fay opened the second pearl, in which there was a table set with the most delicate dishes; the princess supped just like anyone else, and when she was in bed the murmur of the stream lulled her to sleep agreeably.

Without knowing it, she had arrived in the kingdom of the most gallant and amiable prince there was in the whole inhabited world. His name was Zelindor. In order to be happy he only lacked being in love, for it was not possible that he was not loved. His face and his mind were infinitely agreeable. His courage had rendered him redoubtable to his enemies at the age of twenty, he had won battles on emerging from childhood; and by his mildness and his sagacity he rendered his people happy, so they loved him passionately.

The ardor of pursuing a deer had distanced him from his retinue. At first he did not recognize the place where he had gone astray, and, seeking to rediscover, if not the hunt, at least his path, he arrived on the edge of the stream where the young fay was asleep. He was dazzled by her beauty.

After having recovered from his initial astonishment he wanted to go into the tent in order to wait for the beautiful person to wake up and to offer to conduct her to his Court, or wherever she wanted to go. With that design, he crossed the stream, but he was very surprise no longer to see what had caused him so much admiration. He turned back, and as soon as he had retreated to the original distance he perceived the fay Princess awake, and looking at him with the same attention that he had paid to her.

The noise he had made in crossing the stream had awakened that rare beauty. She was unaware of the charm that her mother had attached to her person. It was, therefore, with reason that she had been surprised to see the prince approach as close to her has he had done, and then go back over the stream without having afforded her the slightest politeness.

The prince's gaze convinced her that he repented of his impoliteness. He advanced toward her again, but, that second step having been no more fortunate than the first, the princess disappearing again, the prince experienced an astonishment impossible to describe. He remained immobile for a few moments. His eyes searched for the lovely stranger, but no longer saw her. He crossed the stream again, overwhelmed by sadness, and drew away forever from a place so fatal to his liberty, which had represented to him something all the more dolorous for having been so agreeable.

For her part, the fay was offended by the scornful treatment that she had received. She experienced an anger stronger than it should normally have been against a man who was unknown to her. Her first impulse was to open the third pearl, which served as a cage for the two canaries and abandon a place where Amour had just given her the most illustrious captive that he could submit to her. Menodie had folded up the baggage carefully; they both took their pretty mounts again, and night surprised them in a forest far away from the place where Prince Zelindor had encountered them.

But there are sentiments against which flight is futile. That adventure had cast the young fay into a profound sadness. She had forgotten the disgrace that had made her abandon her mother's Court; she was no longer occupied with anything but the unknown man. She could not only remember all the features of his charming face, but also the softness of his gaze. Afterwards, reflecting on the singularity of the way he had treated her, she made every effort to hate him; she even thought occasionally that she had succeeded in detesting him.

The fay Menodie, who recognized the cause of her disturbance immediately, resolved to employ her knowledge to protect her from all the imprudence that great youth combined with violent passion might provoke. She constructed a tower with the three pearls that I mentioned, after having taken out of them, as you can imagine, everything necessary that they continued. One was employed to form the walls; the other two provided the new building with a ceiling and a floor. When it was ready, Menodie and the princess withdrew into it, and the latter spent the night on a sofa, incessantly occupied with the cruel thoughts by which she was agitated.

The dawn appeared before she had obtained a single moment of repose. With a stroke of her wand she opened the tower, with the design of walking in the forest on her own, hoping that a change of scene would also change her thoughts. It is a mechanical movement of which one cannot be cured; futile as we know the remedy to be, is there anyone who does not make use of it?

Scarcely had the young fay taken a few paces than the sound of a hunting party struck her ears. She ran immediately to shut herself in the tower, resolved never to have any commerce whatsoever with men. By virtue of finding one of them too likeable, she detested all the others. Such sentimental abuses are, alas, all too frequent.

In a moment, the tower was surrounded by hunters, who gazed in a profound silence at the marvel offered to their gaze. The beauty of the fay was as surprising as the singularity of her palace. Beauty, when it is extreme, naturally inspires respect in men; in consequence of that respect, these remained sufficiently distant from the young fay not to experience the charm that rendered her invisible. They did not doubt that she was a goddess, and that idea led them easily to adoration. Several ran to alert their king, who was not very far away, to the marvel they had encountered.

The entire multitude was as if enchanted, so rhapsodic with admiration were its members. In the meantime, the princess had sunk into a profound reverie, and perhaps she would not have perceived what was happening if the fay Menodie had not raised the tower a considerable distance from the ground with a stroke of her wand, which only allowed the charms of her celestial beauty to be seen very imperfectly.

Insensible to the admiration she inspired, the princess was forming the design to leave that location when she heard the sound of hunting horns again and saw twenty better made hunters advancing toward her. They formed an agreeable rustic dance, the figure of which imitated the one consecrated to sacrifices. Those hunters were followed by fifty more; the later presented her with flowers and fruits that they had been able to collect momentarily. A young prince, whose physiognomy was very agreeable, advanced to the foot of the tower and begged the new goddess to receive his presents.

The young fay, who had appeared until then hardly to be sensible to everything that had just happened, became so to the triumph of her beauty. Her benevolent humor made her desire to give marks of her gratitude, and the fay Menodie, who was not unaware of any of the movements of her heart, had her advance to the crenellations of the tower, and her first glance changed all the fruits that were presented to her into gold, and all the flowers into precious stones. After that metamorphosis, the tower rose so very high into the air that it was soon lost to sight.

Menodie, who knew the reason for the princesses' anxiety, thought, with reason, that she would travel the entire world before rediscovering the repose that she had lost. She talked to her first, therefore, about the stranger with whom she was occupied.

"I can't believe," she said to her, "that your beauty didn't have the same effect on him that it usually has on all those who see you; it's necessary, believe me, to return to the same place where we perceived him, and if he turns out to be culpable, I promise to avenge you for the chagrin he has caused you."

The fay Princess trembled at the mere thought that anyone might threaten her lovable stranger; the sick feeling proved to her that he had become dearer to her than her own life. She feared that Menodie might allow herself to get carried away by her sentiment, but the proposition she made to see him again filled her with joy.

"I'd like that very much," she replied. "We'll solve the mystery. There's certainly some circumstance of which we're unaware, and I can't resolve to believe him culpable. When the heart is insensible, the eyes cannot express a tenderness as intense as the one I remarked in him. Perhaps my mother the Queen is punishing me for my departure in a cruel fashion, and she's the cause of the pain I feel."

The princess was accusing her mother in order to excuse her lover. Those sorts of accusations, unjust as they may be, are, alas, very pardonable because they are quite natural. Menodie found that idea plausible, and having posed the tower on the summit of a mountain she spent the night in study, trying to discover what the fay queen had wrought against her daughter.

Her labor did not go to waste; the truth was revealed to her and the enchantment demonstrated. It was not possible for her to destroy it, but she tried at least to moderate its effect. Her books also told her that the unknown man was named Zelindor, that he was the sovereign of a great kingdom, and that he felt for the fay Princess all that the most tender amour can inspire.

That conformity of sentiments persuaded the fay Menodie that their amour was a decree of Destiny. The prince was worthy of the princess, and she could not fail to be happy in marrying a great king who experienced a violent passion for her. She therefore resolved to serve their amour—but an almost insurmountable difficulty traversed her project: Prince Zelindor was promised to the only daughter of the sovereign of the Deadly Isle.

The latter was a cruel giant of surprising strength, against whom Zelindor had just sustained an exceedingly bloody war, which had only been terminated by that marriage. The prince had only consented to it with difficulty, and uniquely out of deference for his subjects, who, seeing the intrepidity with which he confronted the greatest perils, had feared that he might succumb therein, and had, in a way, constrained him to make that engagement.

The princess, his fiancée, did not resemble her giant father at all. She had none of his bad qualities. Fortunately, she took after her mother, who had been a beautiful princess that the giant had once abducted. The giant's daughter was awaited in Zelindor's estates; all the preparations to receive her had been made, and the giant was to accompany her himself and be present at her coronation.

Menodie imparted all her discoveries to the fay Princess. The embarrassments and dangers did not present themselves to her mind immediately; she only thought about Zelindor's amour. What joy did she not feel on learning that she was adored by that charming prince, the first sight of whom had made such a deep impression on her heart. She embraced Menodie a thousand times, asking for her help, for the prince and for her.

"Amour will serve you better than I can," the fay told her. "Zelindor is going to be exposed to great dangers; he will have need of our aid; let's not waste any time; let's depart, go to find him, and tell him that you've judged him worthy of our protection and our tenderness; he has merit, since he is only in danger in relation to you."

The fay and Menodie arrived at Zelindor's palace in a few hours. They descended in the gardens. Menodie assumed the form of a little old woman; her costume was antique, but so laden with jewels that the guards and courtiers allowed her to reach the prince's chamber without the slightest obstacle. It is very true that wealth and adornment have prerogatives of which men will never be able to deprive them. Zelindor invited the fay to enter his cabinet, telling her very politely that he would give her an audience momentarily.

It was easy for Menodie to overhear the final orders that Zelindor gave to the ambassadors that he was sending to the giant of the Deadly Isle to retract his word and break his engagement to marry the princess his daughter. His courtiers opposed that resolution; they threw themselves at his feet, trying to make him change his mind, but their leas were futile. The prince did not know any other misfortune than that of being separated from the beauty he adored; his amour was all the more intense because he dared not flatter himself with the happiness of seeing her again.

He had not confided the adventure that had happened to him to anyone, so he was surprised on entering his cabinet when Menodie told him that she had not only come to give him news of the person who had made him break his word to the giant but also to offer him her services in the war that his refusal was about to draw upon him

The prince was transported with joy to hear mention of the beautiful stranger. "What!" he said. "Is it possible that I will be permitted to see that charming person again?"

"She is in your palace," the fay replied, "but by a cruel fatality, you will not be able to see her unless you are a certain distance away from her. That misfortune, great as it might appear to you, is not the only one that you will experience. I warn you that there are many other difficulties that you will have to overcome if you persevere in your sentiments."

"Let us go and commence my victories by the conquest of the heart of the one I adore," cried the prince. "My courage and the hope of being loved will easily enable me to overcome my other enemies."

"I will take you there and abridge the route for you," the fay said to him; and, taking him by the arm, she lifted him up and sustained him in the air all the way to the place where the young fay was waiting."

Zelindor paid hardly any attention to that surprising manner of travel. The hope of seeing the princess again had spread a joy mingled with trouble in his soul, which left no room within him for other thoughts. Menodie made him stop at the distance that the fay had fixed. He found the princess leaning against a pomegranate tree, so beautiful and so charming that he wanted to run to her in order to throw himself at her knees.

"Stop!" cried the fay Menodie. "You'll cease to see what you love."

That cruel threat rendered him motionless. The desire to please her lover had further augmented the natural charms of the princess; an agreeable serenity, mingled with a pure joy, was spread over her face and caused her satisfaction to burst forth. There was nothing affected about her adornment; she was only clad in a simple gauze; the fashion in which that attire was worn made its ornament; it is, however, true that the color had not been chosen indifferently. Her hair was only attached with flowers. After having devoted the first moments to mutual admiration, the gazes of the two lovers became so tender that, in spite of all the eloquence of the eyes, they wanted to be able to speak to one another.

Menodie, who knew that the princess was fulfilling an inevitable destiny, wanted to spare her all the troubles that it was in her power to enable her to avoid. She gave birth with that design to an arbor of jasmines and honeysuckle, long enough to enclose the two lovers at the distance the fay queen had ordered. She touched the arbor with her wand, so that everything the prince and the young fay needed to say to one another, although in a low voice, would be very distinctly audible at the other extremity of the arbor.

That amiable assistance was well received, as one can imagine, for lovers do not like to talk loudly; independently of the fact it is sage to behave in that manner, in order to prevent the indifferent from hearing many things that are often very insipid and yet delightful for those who pronounce them, it seems to me that the words *I love you, I adore you, I will love you as long as I live* and a thousand similar things cannot be shouted at the top of the voice, as it would have been necessary for Zelindor and the princess to have done. At any rate, that idea of the worthy governess gave rise to a singularity that is remarked in several buildings. Our two lovers were so satisfied with their conversation that the princess obtained from Menodie that it proved to be possible for people sometimes to imitate such a favorable prodigy, and it is said, I am not sure on what foundation, that Italy was the first country where the usage of that amiable echo was known.

The fay Princess told her lover her rank and birth; she gave him the detail of what had obliged her to quit the Court of the Queen, her mother; she added, with elegance and an infinite tenderness, that she owed the greatest of benefits to that misfortune, and that she would regard it henceforth as the source of all her pleasures. She confessed to him the penchant she had had for him since the first moment that she saw him. Finally, she recounted to him everything that had passed through her heart when she had thought that he had nothing but indifference for her. He swore a hundred times to love her forever and to overcome by means of their constancy everything that opposed their union.

They spent several days in that happy state. The prince only appeared in his palace momentarily. He had abandoned the care of his empire, and was no longer occupied with anything but his amour, when the fay Menodie came to say to him: "Prince, it is necessary to deprive yourself for some time of a conversation so full of charms. The giant of the Deadly Isle will enter your kingdom today; tomorrow he will attack your troops; his victory is certain if you do not fight at their head."

The capital of the kingdom was three hundred leagues from the frontier, but the fay Menodie could cover a longer distance than that in an hour when she desired to do so. She begged the prince not to worry and assured him that she would transport him to the frontier at the moment when it was necessary to organize his troops for battle.

All the knowledge that experience and wisdom can give cannot persuade the heart of anything. The princess should certainly have been more convinced than anyone else of the power of fays, but the peril to which Zelindor was about to expose himself for her penetrated her nevertheless with dolor. She did not believe that it would be possible for her to live for a moment without him, and whatever Menodie could say to console her, she was bathed by tears. Their adieux were so touching that Zelindor was ready a thousand times to sacrifice his kingdom and the care of his glory for her. The princess was obliged to order him to quit her.

Menodie had constructed a ship of peacock plumes for Zelindor's voyage; the sails were gauze and the masts branches of tuberoses. Two young children with butterfly wings were charged with the care of steering it. The prince embarked on the pretty vessel at first light, but nevertheless arrived before the sun rose.

The ship approached the ground between the two armies, and that was where the prince disembarked. The giant could therefore not be unaware of his arrival. He was distressed to lose the advantage he had hoped to obtain from his absence, and his troops, frightened by that new prodigy, fell into consternation, which was further augmented by the cries of joy uttered by Zelindor's army and by the sight of a brilliant cloud that contained the princess and Menodie.

The prince, transported by amour and joy, drew nearer to the charming princess, but he then lost sight of her. It is still a great deal to be able to hear the person that one loves. "I cannot," she said to him, "go any longer without following you; I have brought you arms with which to combat the giant, and I will be present at your combat."

Is there any valor that so much generosity and the presence of the person one adores cannot inspire?

The arms that the princess had brought with so much care were a buckler made of a single diamond and an enchanted sword, with which the prince armed himself immediately, and he marched in that state toward the giant. At the moment of his embarkation, before even being armed by the princess's favors, he had sent a challenge, in order spare by means of a single combat the blood of his subjects. Zelindor needed all his valor and all his intrepidity to measure himself against a mortal such as the giant, His grandeur scarcely allowed the sight of the deformity of his face; his entire body was covered with steel armor a foot thick.

Without his enchanted sword, and even more so without the presence of the princess, Zelindor would probably have succumbed against such an adversary. The combat was furious, the buckler parried mortal blows; finally the prince delivered one successfully to a weak spot in his enemy's armor. At the same moment the giant caught fire, and burned entirely in less than a quarter of an hour. Zelindor immediately ordered that he be helped, but it was impossible to obey him.

On any other occasion the prince would not have been satisfied by a victory that cost so little; it was a sacrifice that his vanity had made to his amour. He had raised his eyes toward the brilliant cloud and was seeking the gaze of the fay Princess in order to thank her when an elephant covered in golden scales appeared in the air; it was borne by six violet wings that covered an enormous area. It picked up the prince with its trunk, placed him on its back, rose up into the air with incredible rapidity and was soon lost to sight.

The cries of dolor and general astonishment of the entre army are indescribable. Those troops, so proud a moment before of the valor and success of their king, were no longer thinking about taking advantage of the victory.

The fay Princess, a witness to the misfortune that had just occurred, which was common to her and her lover, fell unconscious in Menodie's arms. The sage fay transported her as rapidly as possible to a small uninhabited island, and after having brought her to her senses, she tried to console her by making her glimpse a glimmer of hope.

"I have no doubt," she said "that the abduction of Zelindor is a consequence of the hatred of your mother, the Queen; she cannot be without indignation that we have overcome the effects of her unjust anger, or knowing you to be happy with a prince so worthy of your tenderness, but I shall employ all my knowledge to vanquish her once again."

"Alas," cried the young fay, "in what circumstances I am losing you, my dear Zelindor! When my lover had no more perils to fear, at the moment of vanquishing the most formidable of all giants, we hoped to be acquitted forever; the excess of my tenderness has cost you your liberty, and perhaps your life."

Those words were punctuated by a thousand sobs; every moment added something to her despair. A hundred times she would have thrown herself into the sea if the fay Menodie had not prevented her from doing so.

"You lover is alive," she said. "Why push your despair so far? If you will promise me to calm down, and if you can wait for my return, I will go to search for the prince in all directions, and I flatter myself that I shall find him."

Impatient to see that design executed, only the hope of its success being able to attach her to life, the princess promised Menodie everything she cared to demand.

The sage fay, fearing that the Queen might profit from her absence to abduct her daughter, decided to enclose the island within charms so powerful that it would be impossible for any being whatsoever to visit it without her consent. She built a little house of cedar and aloe-wood, which she surrounded with a grove of myrtles and orange trees, irrigated by a little steam of water brighter than crystal, which snaked around the feet of the trees, bordered by grass and flowers. It was in that place that the princess and Menodie embraced a thousand times, shedding further tears, and that Menodie mounted her chariot drawn by winged serpents in order to go in search of Zelindor.

When the fay Princess found herself alone, abandoned to the sadness of amour—for it must be agreed that the chagrins of that passion are painful—she abandoned herself to all that melancholy can have of blackness. She did not come out of her room for a month, but impatience mingled with her other woes, and at the end of that time she decided to walk occasionally in the wood adjacent to her habitation and on the sea shore. She often spent her nights without closing her beautiful eyes, lying on the grass, occupied in lamenting her misfortunes.

Her dolor was only too just; Prince Zelindor was even more unfortunate than she imagined. The Queen—for it was indeed her whose ill-humor had wanted satisfaction—after having had him carried away, had him taken to a sheer rock in the middle of the sea. The elephant deposited him in that frightful solitude and disappeared. The prince then found himself surrounded by monsters, which seemed to want to devour him at every moment.

He had had the misfortune of dropping the enchanted sword with which he had fought the giant; the surprise of his abduction had caused it to slip from his hand; he had only conserved the diamond buckler. His courage did not abandon him in such great peril; although he had no weapon, he advanced with the intrepidity that was so natural to him.

The buckler had the virtue of preventing the monsters from approaching him; without that aid, nothing in nature could have preserved him from their fury. Sometimes, he struck them with his buckler, and then they metamorphosed into a liquid that immediately produced new monsters, often more terrible than the ones that had preceded them.

Zelidor sent his days in that difficult exercise; when night fell, lassitude obliged him to retire into a cavern, where, lying on the ground, he abandoned himself to the most cruel reflections. He had no doubt that death would soon put an end to all his misfortunes; he awaited it without dread; the loss of his mistress occupied him more than that of his life.

In the middle of one obscure night he saw a great light appear, by the favor of which he perceived a woman of extraordinary grandeur. Her gaze had something terrible about it. She threw herself upon him, and, snatching away his diamond buckler, she threatened to augment the misfortunes by which he was overwhelmed even further.

"I am the Queen of the Fays," she said to him. "You can never escape from my power, and I am going to subject you to a vengeance so cruel that posterity will be frightened by it. But if you will consent never to see the fay Princess again; if, for the surety of your word, you will marry the daughter of the giant of the Deadly Isle in two hours, I will transport you to your estates, I will take you to that princess and I will heap you will all sorts of benefits."

"I can see very well," the prince replied, "that you are the mistress of my destiny, but you cannot do anything to me more cruel than separate me forever from the presence of the beautiful fay that I adore. I would rather lose my life than spend it without seeing her."

"You will repent of your constancy," the Queen of the Fays said to him then. She touched him with her wand and disappeared, and the prince found himself alone in a delightful garden. At the moment when dawn began to appear, the rays of light revealed to him all the ornaments with which it was embellished; nature and art seemed to have made every effort to augment its magnificence.

Zelindor walked sadly along a pathway terminated by a basin of white marble filled with transparent water. An enameled golden balustrade surrounded the basin. He approached it and tried to staunch, with the aid of his hand, the ardent thirst that was consuming him, but he was astonished to see in the middle of the basin the portrait of the fay Princess in the statue of Venus that was the ornament of the superb water feature. The statue was in white marble; the Graces and Pleasures were variously occupied in paying their court to her.

The Prince remained so transported with amour by that sight that it suspended for a few moments the memory of his misfortunes. So many surprising things had happened to him successively in a very short span of time that he no longer knew what to think about his own destiny, when the fay Menodie appeared in the air and dropped a ring at his feet. He saw it fall, in fact, but at the moment when the amiable prince bent down to pick it up, he was transformed into a flowering thorn-bush.

Menodie witnessed that metamorphosis, but she could not prevent it. The Queen, naturally more powerful than her everywhere else, was even more so in her own palace. The prince's misfortune had anticipated by a moment the gift of the ring that might have protected him from it.

She did not abandon herself to futile regrets; she immediately made the decision to go to find the fay Princess, resolved to neglect nothing to persuade her to return to the Court. It appeared to her, with reason, that only the pardon of the Queen of the Fays and the return of her amity for her daughter were capable of putting an end to Zelindor's enchantment and misfortune.

In an instant she had traveled the distance that separated the Queen's palace from the desert island to which the princess had retired. Their first embraces were mingled with tears. One would weep for less. The good fay had returned alone, and the hope of lovers is often unjust for those who employ themselves in serving them. Menodie thought that it was prudent to hide the truth from her, so she told her that she had been unable to discover the place where Zelindor inhabited, but that she could assure her, on her word as a fay, that he was still breathing. She added that it must be the case, since she had searched for him fruitlessly all over the world, that the Queen had imprisoned him in her palace; that she knew full well that that was a place where it was impossible for her to visit, and that she could not give her any other advice than that of returning to the Court, where, according to all appearances, she might obtain news of him.

The confidence that the young fay had in Menodie caused her to recover some hope. The mere idea of learning the destiny of her lover determined her to expose herself to the wrath of her mother, the Queen, and to all the ill-treatment that her temper might suggest to her. She therefore set forth. Menodie accompanied her as far as the frontier of the fay queen's estates. Their separation was tender. A governess who takes the side of a lover against that of a mother does not ordinarily fall out with her pupil.

As soon as Princess appeared, everyone ran to her and followed her to the palace in a crowd. She presented herself to the Queen, bathed in tears and in a paralysis that prevented her from saying a single word. The severity with which she was received made her tremble a thousand times for her lover's life; at the end of the audience, however, the Queen expressed to her more good will than she had hoped. Ill-humor and anger had stifled her sentiments, but they were not extinct, and in the depths of her heart, the Queen loved the princess.

The unfortunate Princess received the compliments of the entire Court, and experienced great tedium in receiving them. When she was able to obtain a moment of solitude, she was charmed by it, and as often as possible she went to walk alone in the palace gardens. She sometimes lay down on the grass, and in order to protect herself from the sun she placed herself close to a flowering thorn-bush, which pleased her more than all the other trees in the garden. Who is the physicist who can account for the instincts with which amour is filled?

Zelindor, therefore, saw the princess, for his present enchantment had destroyed the first, and it was with great pleasure on his part that he sometimes held her between his branches. Except for speech and form, he had lost nothing of his original estate. With what sensibility he saw his dear princess go a hundred times, personally, to fetch water to sprinkle on her favorite flowering thorn-bush.

One day, she was surprised by her mother while she was occupied in that charitable care. At that moment the fay queen sensed her hatred of the prince redoubled, and, addressing the fay Princess, she said: "Go and pick a branch from that flowering thorn-bush for me."

The princess trembled at those words, but, accusing herself of a weakness that she could not find reasonable, she carried out the order. Blood immediately ran from the branch that she had broken, and, the fay queen having rendered the use of speech to Zelindor at that moment, he uttered a great scream, and said: "What! It is you, my Princess, who is giving me death?"

It is impossible to describe what the fay Princess felt at that frightful moment. She let herself fall to the ground beside the bush, and, mingling her tears with the blood of the unfortunate prince, she would have died of dolor if the most unexpected help had not arrived. A thousand voices—for the courtiers were always crowded around—cried in the garden: "Here comes the King!"

The fay queen, who believed herself to be no longer loved, was sensible to that news. A moment of his presence returned all the tenderness of his wife, and in the first embrace he asked her for mercy for the princess, their daughter, and for Zelindor.

That mercy was immediately granted. Zelindor recovered his natural form; but as the loss of his blood had reduced him to the last extremity, the Queen spread over him a liquid that not only healed his wound but returned all his strength and charms to him.

"You are the cause of all these misfortunes," she said to the King. "Your inconstancy has given me such a great aversion for all men that I wanted to punish Zelindor for the love my daughter has for him; but you have resumed all your rights over my heart, and I consent to render them happy, since they have procured me the pleasure of seeing you again. I know that it is the amity you have for our daughter that has brought you back to me."

The King wanted to hide from her that the fay Menodie had come to beg him to help the young princess and the prince, her lover; but, seeing that she was not unaware of any circumstance of what had happened, he assured her in the most tender terms that his amity for his daughter was only the first principle, and that it would be the pledge of the amour that he had for her. He embraced Prince Zelindor and the fay Princess a thousand times.

They took the path to the palace, and several days were spent in fêtes there, to celebrate the marriage of the fortunate lovers, whose passion appeared to have been further augmented since the certainty they had of their happiness. At the same time, the marriage was declared of the King and the Queen.

Some time after their wedding, our lovers went to reign together in Zelindor's kingdom, where the people, who had remained faithful, received them with the demonstrations of joy that are so justly attached to the love that one has for good kings.